A SENSITIVE POINT

Cori presented her back and squared her shoulders. "You rattle me. I never feel safe when you're underfoot. It's like walking through a field of land mines."

He felt her tremble beneath his light caress. Cori had a sensitive point just beneath her ear—her right ear, to be exact. Jake stroked that vulnerable spot again and received the same response. His lips followed, whispering their way down to the collar of her flannel robe.

"I think you had better leave," Cori whispered. Her hands gripped the back of the chair for support. Thunderation, if he didn't stop what he was doing she would melt all over him!

"I think I had better stay . . ." he murmured as his hands stole around her waist, pulling her against him, letting her feel his desire for her.

Cori's legs were about to fold up like an accordion. Valiantly, she battled to ignore the warm flood of pleasure his kisses and caresses evoked. Her heart hammered against her ribs, and an unfamiliar fire began to burn in the core of her being.

"I'm not . . ." She faltered and tried again. "I'm not what you think, Jacob, and I . . ."

"What do I think?" he queried as his greedy kisses flooded back up her neck to the vulnerable spot beneath her ear.

She not only heard his husky question, but she felt it vibrating across her flesh, starting more disturbing fires. "I'm . . . not . . . experienced with men. I wouldn't know how to please you . . ."

"Let me be the judge of that, sweet witch."

PASSIONATE NIGHTS FROM ZEBRA BOOKS

ANGEL'S CARESS   (2675, $4.50)
by Deanna James
Ellie Crain was a young, inexperienced and beautiful Southern belle. Cash Gillard was the battle-weary Yankee corporal who turned her into a woman filled with hungry passion. He planned to love and leave her; she vowed to keep him forever with her *Angel's Caress*.

COMMANCHE BRIDE   (2549, $3.95)
by Emma Merritt
Beautiful Dr. Zoe Randolph headed to Mexico to halt a cholera epidemic. She never dreamed her caravan would be attacked by a band of savages. Later, she refused to believe that she could love and desire her captor, the handsome half-breed Matt Chandler. Captor and slave find unending love and tender passion in the rugged Commanche hills.

CAPTIVE ANGEL   (2524, $4.50)
by Deanna James
When handsome Hunter Gillard left the routine existence of his South Carolina plantation for endless adventures on the high seas, beautiful and indulged Caroline Gillard learned to manage her home and business affairs in her husband's sudden absence. Caroline resolved not to crumble and vowed to make Hunter beg to be taken back. He was determined to make her once again his unquestioning and forgiving wife.

SWEET, WILD LOVE   (2834, $3.95)
by Emma Merritt
Chicago lawyer Eleanor Hunt was determined to earn the respect of the Kansas cowboys who openly leered at her as she was working to try a cattle-rustling case. The worse offender was Bradley Smith—even though he worked for Eleanor's father! She was determined not to mistake passion for love; he was determined to break through her icy exterior and possess the passion woman who lurked beneath her.

Available wherever paperbacks are sold, or order direct from the Publisher. Send cover price plus 50¢ per copy for mailing and handling to Zebra Books, Dept. 3118, 475 Park Avenue South, New York, N.Y. 10016. Residents of New York, New Jersey and Pennsylvania must include sales tax. DO NOT SEND CASH.

Mississippi Mistress
GINA ROBINS

ZEBRA BOOKS
KENSINGTON PUBLISHING CORP.

ZEBRA BOOKS

are published by

Kensington Publishing Corp.
475 Park Avenue South
New York, NY 10016

First printing: September, 1990

Printed in the United States of America

This book is dedicated to
My husband Ed, for his assistance
and support. And to our
children, Christie, Jill, and Kurt,
with much love . . .

Chapter 1

St. Louis, Missouri
March 31, 1856

"Jacob! Jacob Wolf!"

Jake swiveled his head around. Quickly he scanned the milling crowd on the wharf, searching for the face that belonged to the familiar voice. A warm smile settled on Jake's rugged features when Dal Blaylock pulled off the plug hat that sat atop his sandy blond head and waved it like a flag. Being taller than average height, standing six feet four inches in his bare feet, Jacob Wolf never had difficulty staring across the throng of people that congested the waterfront. Since his childhood friend was only two inches shorter than Jake, they both towered over crowds.

While Dal elbowed his way through the maze of roustabouts and passengers who hovered around the six steamboats that nuzzled against the docks, Jake squeezed through the wall of humanity like a salmon swimming upstream.

"What are you doing in St. Louis?" Jake questioned, extending his hand to his longtime friend.

"I've been indulging my appetite for racing horses and

women," he responded with a teasing grin.

Dal unclasped Jake's hand as a pint-sized roustabout scurried between them to load cargo on one of the steamers. Dal's golden brown eyes traveled over Jacob's muscular physique, noting the deep tan he had acquired the past year, surveying the frontiersman's garb that hugged his powerful frame. Although Jake was only a year older (fourteen months, to be exact) than Dal, he looked as if he had aged considerably in the year they had been apart.

"Life on the Missouri must have been hell," Dal remarked, gesturing toward the lines of experience that were carved into Jake's bronzed face.

"Hell and then some," Jake assured him. His keen green eyes flooded over Dal's immaculate attire. "It looks as though life has been treating you kindly."

"I can't complain," Dal chuckled.

Jake suddenly envied Dal's clean, wholesome appearance. The past year had taken its toll on Jacob—long, harrowing hours of catastrophe following on the heels of disaster. The banks of the Missouri had been no place for the faint of heart, that was for sure. Jake had always thrived on challenges, and the past year had tested his abilities to their very limits.

"I'll buy you a drink and you can tell me all about life in the wilds," Dal offered.

With a compliant nod of his raven head, Jake pushed his way through the crowd toward the nearby tavern. Once they were seated and had guzzled their first tankard of ale, Dal unleashed his barrage of questions. Jake held up a callused hand to call a halt to the rapid-fire inquisition.

"I did succeed in using the two snagboats to clear the jams of timber that clogged the Missouri," he informed his inquisitive friend. "We can now extend our steamboat service upriver. But I nearly got myself killed

8

three times in the process of bringing civilization to the back country. One thunderstorm and devastating tornado ripped the upper works off the boat, and we had to design a new roof for the pilothouse from buffalo hide." Jake eased back in his chair and smiled, remembering. "The storm also took the tops off the smokestacks, and we had to improvise with dried animal skins."

An amused chortle tumbled from Dal's lips and his tawny eyes twinkled wryly. "Wasn't it you who said you were anticipating the challenges of the mighty Missouri? Weren't you complaining about being tired of the mundane life on the Mississippi and the boredom of aristocracy?" he ribbed Jake.

Jake expelled a volcanic snort. "Okay, Dal, so I've had to eat crow. But God help me when I have to confess to my grandmother that I've seen enough adventure for one lifetime. That persnickety old crone told me it was time to settle down and behave like a Southern gentleman instead of tromping off to clear the Missouri for passage. But I refused to listen."

Dal snickered at the scowl that puckered Jake's craggy features. "So now that you have had your last fling in the wilderness, are you planning to ease into the sedate life of the gentry, take a docile wife and live in the manner expected of a man of your wealth and position?"

Somehow Dal doubted a restless, dynamic man like Jacob Wolf would ever be content portraying a sophisticated gentleman who catered to a properly bred lady. Since childhood, Jake had always been a cut above the grade, a soul who possessed an adventurous spirit. He had craved excitement and challenges. The lines and crow's feet on Jake's handsome face lent testimony to his vast and varied experience. Jake had seen and done far more than most men, and he thrilled to challenges that demanded keen skills and quick wits.

To Dal's way of thinking, what Jacob Wolf hadn't done

didn't need doing. There wasn't a more capable, versatile man anywhere. Jacob Wolf could outshoot, outfox and outfight any man in any given situation. He had experience and a cool, calculating aura of authority that made most folks back off when they foolishly dared to cross him.

"I'm sure Augusta will be delighted to hear you have decided to heed her advice and relinquish your wild and unruly ways," Dal teased, shaking off his pensive musings. "I can just hear her saying 'I told you so.'"

Jake grunted in response to the remark and stared contemplatively at his half-empty mug of ale. He glanced back through the window of time, reflecting on the last time he had seen his grandmother . . .

As if it were only yesterday, Jake could visualize Augusta Breeze stamping into the parlor of her plantation home in Natchez, pounding her cane on the floor as she approached him.

Augusta Breeze dressed in traditional black and she looked to be a frail gray-haired dowager of seventy-four who was on her last leg. She was anything but! The dowager had the heart of a lioness and a temper hot as a forest fire. She was blunt and opinionated and insolent at times. Augusta never requested when she could demand. She never employed tact when plainspokeness served her just as well. Augusta delighted in throwing her weight around and spinning her sticky theories on life like a black widow spider. For the most part, Jake allowed his grandmother to rant and rave because she enjoyed spouting like a geyser. He humored her and indulged her because, feisty and outspoken though she was, he loved her dearly.

"What is all this nonsense I've heard about your traipsing off to expand the family's business?" Augusta had spumed on day while Jacob sat casually on the sofa, sipping brandy.

"Cousin Layton already tattled to you, it seems," Jake had smirked into her annoyed frown.

"Of course, Layton tattled," Augusta snapped brusquely. "That boy has been a snitch since he was three feet tall! Now he's three feet wide and barely five feet tall and he's still running to tattle to me!"

"Gram, there is profit to make on the Missouri," Jake declared switching the topic from his foppish cousin to the matter at hand. "There is a demand for supplies and we can provide the transportation. With the snagboats I've designed, we can clear the river and ship necessities to the trappers and traders all the way to the mouth of the Missouri."

"Poppycock!" Augusta raged, rapping her cane against the floor. (She had done that so many times the past twenty years that it was a wonder the boards didn't collapse beneath her.) "You aren't fooling me one tittle with your talk of humanitarianism and profit." Her hazel eyes flashed behind her wire-rimmed spectacles. "You are simply restless for another adventure. It's bad enough that I can't keep you off the river and on your own plantation to pursue a normal life. We *own* the blessed steamboat company, and yet you insist upon acting as the captain, pilot, and only God knows what else! I swear you'll never learn your place!"

Augusta sucked in a deep breath and glared at her swarthy grandson. "First I couldn't keep you off our steamers. Then you felt the insane urge to traipse off to Texas to help those settlers battle Mexico. And worse, you convinced Dal Blaylock to accompany you to a territory that was overrun with wild Indians, Comancheros, outlaws, and I don't know what all! Dal's grandmother held a personal grudge against me for years because you dragged her baby boy off to fight a battle that

11

was neither of your concerns!"

"We both survived and the Texicans were freed from Santa Anna's rule," Jake parried calmly. He stared at the bundle of brittle bones and feisty spirit, wondering again if Augusta's family had married her off to Frederick Breeze only as a bizarre joke and a play on names. Her name described her personality. His grandmother was a human hurricane at times, and the name Augusta Breeze suited her perfectly.

The dowager wagged a bony finger in her grandson's face. "You would have remained in rowdy Texas if I hadn't begged and pleaded for you to return to assume control of the company," she reminded him tartly.

Begged and pleaded? Augusta? Jake grinned. This aging harridan had hired five local toughs to track him down in Texas and haul him home. Augusta had never begged in all her life!

"And now, only a few years later, the adventure bug has bitten you again. Sailing up and down the Mississippi like driftwood no longer satisfies your restless spirit." Her wrinkled face froze in a determined frown. "You aren't going anywhere and that's that! You are going to find yourself a woman you care about, one who cares about you. You're going to settle down and raise babies and you're going to manage our three steamboats from the shore, from Wolfhaven to be specific! If you don't, you're going to wake up one of these days to find you've grown old and the only women who'll have you are the gold diggers who care only about your money."

"I was born under a wandering star," Jake insisted with a charismatic grin.

The smile didn't melt Augusta's disgruntled frown. Jake hadn't really thought it would.

"Balderdash! Mark my words, young man. One of these days you're going to be sorry you didn't listen to me. You'll tire of this vagabond life. By then you'll be

12

used up and worn out, just like I am. And who'll console you and keep you company in your dotage?" Her hazel eyes drilled into him. "No one, I tell you! You'll be wishing for what you can't have. You'll be alone and miserable and too old to trounce off to another of your madcap adventures to only God knows where!"

Used up and worn out? Augusta? Jake laughed to himself. Oh, that he would still be as full of vim and vigor as Augusta if he was fortunate enough to live so long.

"I'll settle down when I'm damned good and ready, Gram." Jake flashed her a stern glance.

Augusta knew that look all too well. As valiantly as she tried, she had never been able to convince Jake to do her bidding. He had too much of his grandmother in him—stubborn to the core and headstrong to the hilt. They had always been like two stags locking horns, each refusing to budge an inch. They both retreated occasionally to regroup but they never admitted defeat.

Recognizing a skirmish lost, Augusta switched battle tactics. She brandished her intricately carved cane at her favorite grandson—the one who could also infuriate her to the extreme.

"You just wait and see if the day doesn't come when you wish you had a loving wife to come home to, a family to call your own. One of these days, what I've been trying to tell you is going to soak into that spongy brain of yours and you'll wish you'd listened to me. You'll grow tired of your battles against nature and wild savages and ever-changing rivers. And all those prospective brides will have been snatched up by men with more sense!"

"Your choices in a spouse left a lot to be desired," Jake smirked, knowing he would get Augusta's goat. Sure enough, he did.

Her back stiffened like a ramrod. "There wasn't anything wrong with my selections," she protested hotly. "Each one was well-mannered, formally educated, and a

13

suitable match. They all worshiped the ground you walked on. But you are infuriatingly particular and impossible to please. Isn't there one woman on this continent whom you could ever hope to love?"

"Find me one just like you, Gram," Jake challenged with a playful wink. "Then we'll talk marriage." He knew the unexpected compliment would set the old girl back on her heels.

Hazel eyes widened behind the wire-rimmed glasses perched on the bridge of her nose. "You would have a quarrelsome shrew who badgers you at every turn, who argues with you for the mere sport of it, who defies your authority every chance she gets?" she croaked in disbelief.

Jake unfolded his long lean frame and swaggered across the room to drop a parting kiss on Augusta's flushed cheek. "A quarrelsome shrew with your spunk would prevent me from being bored to death if I ever do decide to settle down," he insisted. "When I find a female who can match you stride for stride, I'll marry her."

Her eyes lifted to her grandson and a strange, unexplainable expression was mirrored there. "What I want, more than anything, Jacob, is for you to find a woman you can love, one who loves you in return. I wish you could enjoy what I . . ." She clamped her mouth shut, shrugged off the sentimentality that had crept over her, and then waved him away. "Off with you, then," she grumbled resentfully. "I can see I'm wasting my breath. And if you don't write to me at least once a month, I'll hold it over you for the rest of your lonely, miserable life!"

After that last confrontation with Augusta, Jake had ambled out the door to begin his task of untangling the treacherous Missouri. And during the months that followed, Jake hadn't run across a single woman who

14

could measure up to the high-spirited dowager. Hell's fire, he hadn't met a female who could hold a candle to his grandmother in all his thirty-one years of hard living and extensive travels! After the good Lord made Augusta He had broken the mold. The properly bred ladies Jake had known were doll-like puppets who walked and talked as they had been taught to do. They said what they thought a man wanted to hear—all rehearsed praises and idle chatter that bored Jake to tears. Women were carbon copies of one another. When a man met one of them he had met them all.

After a year on the Missouri, Jake found Augusta's prediction coming back to haunt him. As difficult as it was for him to admit, he was growing tired of his wild wandering ways, weary of daily battles. And yet, there was still this strange restlessness deep down in his soul. Something was still missing in his life, even when he swore he had seen and done it all . . .

"Jacob? Do you have these mental lapses often?" Dal smirked, tugging at the fringed sleeve of his friend's jacket.

Jake had been so immersed in thought for the past few minutes that he hadn't responded to Dal's questions.

"I guess I'm going to get married and command the steamboat company from the shore while I take an active part in running Wolfhaven," Jake said out of the blue.

Dal's mouth dropped open and he gaped at his rugged-looking friend. "Good Lord, I must be hallucinating. I thought I heard you say you were getting married!" he croaked like a bullfrog.

"I am," Jake affirmed.

"Married to whom?" Dal chirped.

Jake's broad shoulders lifted and dropped in a careless shrug. "What difference does it make? One woman is as

15

good as another if she has the proper credentials. They're all alike, after all. They want to entrap a man for benefits they can receive. Wealth attracts females. This time I'm going to let myself get caught."

Dal choked on his ale. While Jake whacked him between the shoulder blades to restore his breath, Dal struggled to compose himself. "I still can't believe my ears," he wheezed.

"There is nothing wrong with your hearing," Jake insisted. "I've sown enough wild oats and I've seen enough of the world. It's time for a change, for better or for worse. As soon as I find a female who is not unpleasant to the eye, one whom I think I can tolerate having underfoot for a few hours a day, I'll marry her. Gram can delight in saying she told me so and it will add another ten years to her life." Determined green eyes swung to Dal. "And you will be my best man."

Dal still couldn't believe they were having this conversation! He'd also had a difficult time selecting a wife to meet his expectations, but Jacob's standards had always been even higher. The fact was, Dal considered Jake to be a confirmed bachelor—too much man to be contained by one woman. Jake's appetite, desire for variety, and reputation with women was second to none. He had bedded more than his fair share of females, finding not a single one who intrigued him for more than a few weeks at a time. There had been no courtships to speak of, no emotional involvements, only brief, casual affairs.

And now this man of varied tastes was going to randomly select a wife who mildly appealed to him, whom he could accept as if she were a new stick of furniture in his home? Inconceivable!

"Don't look at me like that," Jake snorted defensively. "I can name dozens of people who married for convenience and position—my own father for one and my grandfather for another. My mother was heir to a fortune and Papa had one of his own, one that could be doubled by wedding a Breeze to a Wolf. Gram was given in marriage to promote what her family referred to as a decent bloodline. What I'm suggesting is hardly revolutionary, Dal."

"And do you intend to remain faithful to the future Mrs. Wolf?" he smirked before taking another gulp of ale.

Again, Jacob shrugged in that characteristic manner of his. "If she pleases me, perhaps, and if she doesn't, perhaps not. I will cross that bridge when I come to it."

Owl-eyed, Dal watched Jake down a half a mug of ale in one swallow and unfold himself from the chair. Dal still couldn't believe the complacency that had overcome this giant of a man. Jake Wolf, a man of tremendous vitality, was going on a wife hunt? He was going to douse his hopes of finding the woman of his dreams and settle for a female with whom he could be no more than *compatible?* That didn't sound like the Jake he knew!

"I think you're making a grave mistake," Dal declared as he followed in his friend's wake.

"Obviously, you share my belief that there is no woman to match you," Jake shot back. "If there were, you would have married her by now. It seems we share a common flaw, my friend. Too particular, perhaps?" He flashed Dal a teasing grin that caused smile lines to sink into his bronzed features. "Maybe it's time we both quit living on dreams of what we want and settle for what we can find in a female."

As much as Dal hated to admit it, the comment struck home. "Maybe you're right," Dale mumbled. "I can't spend my life breeding racehorses and traveling hither and yon to acquire the finest horse flesh here and in Europe. Perhaps if I get myself a few children to dote over I can instill my love of racing in them. Skirt-chasing

17

sure as hell hasn't gotten me anywhere except in trouble a time or two."

"And I'll let my children enjoy the challenges that lured me far and wide in my youth," Jake announced with firm conviction. "Now all we have to do is find ourselves tolerable wives to bear our children so we can fuss over them."

"A double wedding!" Dal chuckled as they ambled across the wharf. "My grandmother will be delighted. She has harassed me on the subject for months. I swear she has been taking lessons from Augusta. Your grandmother probably put mine up to it, thinking if I would marry you would too."

"It wouldn't surprise me one bit," Jake smirked.

Chapter 2

Jacob pulled up short when he ventured into the Breeze ticket office on the waterfront. The branch office hadn't changed all that much in the year Jake had been away. But he was shocked to see Terrance Sykes, the captain of one of the Breeze Steamboat Company's sleek ships, selling tickets!

A welcoming smile pursed Terrance's lips when he recognized Jake in his frontiersman garb.

"What the blazes are you doing behind the ticket window?" Jake croaked in disbelief.

The smile faded from Terrance's weatherbeaten features. "Your dear cousin demoted me while you were away," he announced, his tone indicating his bitterness. "Layton seems to think that because you left him in command of the fleet that he is now the reigning king of Breeze enterprises. You may also be surprised to learn that your cousin has acquired another ship during your absence."

Two thick black brows jackknifed. "If he purchased another ship, he would have been interviewing a new captain, not demoting the best one we had!"

"That's logical," Terrance muttered acrimoniously. "Layton Breeze doesn't know the meaning of the word."

19

Realizing he had slandered a member of Jacob's family, Terrance apologized. "Forgive me for speaking against your cousin. He's your flesh and blood, but he and I never have gotten on very well. He saw his chance to dismiss me and so he did."

"On what possible grounds?" Jake wanted to know.

"Layton insists I'm getting too old to captain one of the ships and that I would serve the company better as a ticket agent."

"Too old at forty-three?" Jake hooted in astonishment.

His sharp glance swung to Dal, silently accusing him of withholding information. But in Dal's defense, Jake realized they had been much too busy discussing prospective wives to get around to talking about the changes Layton had made in Jake's absence.

Dal smiled sheepishly. "I intended to tell you. But you threw me off balance with your wedding plans."

Jake wheeled back around to scowl at Terrance. "This is ridiculous. I'll not have my best captain behind a desk. You have more experience on the Mississippi than anyone."

"Besides yourself," Terrance stipulated.

"But it was you who taught me everything I know," Jake growled. "Layton overstepped his bounds." Snapping green eyes circled the crowded office. "Where is my pesky cousin? I intend to have a word with him."

"One word?" Dal snickered, watching the anger rise in this mountain of a man like lava in a volcano. "Layton will be fortunate if you don't chew off both his ears."

"You'll find His Majesty strutting his stuff on his new steamer," Terrance informed the fuming Jacob Wolf. He gestured through the window to single out the magnificent steamboat that surpassed all the other vessels that lined the dock. "The *Mississippi Belle* is headed home to Natchez in two hours. On board you will find His Royal Highness, catering to the group of prospective investors

20

he's gathered around him. He has visions of increasing the number of ships in your line, thereby driving out all competition so he can take control of the river."

Jake peered out the window to survey the majestic, three-hundred-thirty-foot floating palace. The gigantic white ship that was trimmed in blue reminded Jake of a wedding cake, with its crown of a pilothouse setting above the hurricane deck. The huge black smokestacks that towered on either side of the pilothouse were flared at the top, reminiscent of plumes on a crown. The paddle boxes that covered the side wheel were decorated with the portrait of a young woman who cradled a bouquet of red roses.

The designer of the grand vessel, Jake decided, had a penchant for elegance. The ship was ornate and teeming with intricately carved railings. Judging from the size of the monstrous ship, Jake estimated the steamer held at least forty staterooms, all of which probably resembled bridal suites, if the glamorous exterior was anything to go by.

Jake wasn't far from wrong. The interior cabins were paneled in walnut and polished to a shine. The floors were covered with costly carpets and huge French mirrors hung on the walls of the main saloon. The ship was filled with velvet upholstered chairs, marble-topped tables, crystal chandeliers, and masterful oil paintings.

"It seems I've left my cousin in charge too long," Jake muttered as his gaze flooded over the vessel, estimating its staggering cost.

"About thirteen months too long," Terrance snorted. "The position of power went straight to Layton's head. Luckily, it was empty to begin with or it would have burst wide open."

Thoughts of frustration and outrage sloshed in Jake's mind as he barreled toward the door, moving bodies out of his way in his haste to confront his cousin.

Determined though Jacob was, the indignant squeal of a woman and the muted growl of a man's voice cut through his mind. Jake screeched to a halt to scan the crowd. When he did, Dal slammed into him because Terrance had backended Dal.

A tussle was in progress between Kyle Benson and Cori Pierce. Kyle had made outrageous demands on the sassy brunette and she had punctuated her rejection with a well-aimed blow of her parasol. Kyle growled furiously as pain gripped his midsection. With a sneer curling his thin lips, Kyle lunged at Cori, intent on punishing her for jabbing him with her makeshift sword.

That was Kyle's second mistake. Cori Pierce was five feet three inches and one hundred and ten pounds of unleashed fury. She wielded her bright yellow parasol as if it were a rapier, stabbing Kyle in the shoulder. But still the angry man pounced, his fingers biting into her forearm.

Now, there were some folks who simply stood aside to observe battles that broke out on the wharf. It was a common occurrence, but it didn't usually involve a man and a woman. Most knock-down drag-outs involved roustabouts and keelboatmen who boasted their abilities with their fists and were forced to prove their talents. They were a rough and tumble breed of men, whose favorite hobbies consisted of drinking, whoring, and fighting.

Although some individuals refused to get involved, Jacob Wolf had never been one of life's bystanders. He was a man of action. When he saw the brown-haired rake assault the shapely brunette, Jake leaped to her defense.

It didn't matter that the lady in question was managing quite well by herself. Jake suspected she was soon to be out-muscled. When he saw the lady's nemesis raise his arm as if he meant to backhand her into submission, Jake reacted to instinct. Considering the size of the ring the

22

offender wore on his right hand, Jake expected the jewelry would leave a noticeable scar on the woman's outraged face.

Before that happened, Jake launched himself toward the man, who was cursing a blue streak. Jake swung Kyle around the instant before he struck Cori. Kyle automatically ducked when he spied the doubled fist coming his way. The punishing blow Jake had aimed at Kyle's curled lips glanced off the side of his head, striking Cori Pierce just below the left eye. It was most fortunate for her that Jake's swinging fist had lost its full impact when it grazed Kyle. Jacob packed one helluva wallop. If Cori had been hit squarely with that meaty fist, she would have been out cold for days, years maybe. As it was, she felt as if her head had exploded.

In horror, Jake watched the young beauty wilt to the deck like a fragile violet scorched by the blistering desert sun. He was so shocked by what he'd accidentally done that he was momentarily paralyzed. While he stood there, stunned to the bone, Kyle delivered a sharp punch to his challenger's midsection. The answering blow jolted Jake back into action. Reflexively, he poised himself to attack. And attack he did!

This time Kyle Benson received the full impact of Jacob Wolf's punch. The beefy fist caught Kyle in the jaw, causing him to spin around like a top. With a furious snarl, Kyle staggered and tripped over Cori's unconscious body. Cursing vehemently, Kyle gathered his legs beneath him and leaped over the limp body that lay on the wharf like a misplaced doormat. But Jake met him head-on with another steely fist.

"Do you think we should jump in and help Jake?" Terrance questioned Dal, who was calmly watching the fracas and glancing at the battered face of the brunette who lay amidst the shuffling feet.

"Why should we?" Dal questioned. "There's only one

23

challenger. Jake can handle three at a time without breathing hard. We would only get in his way. But I think it might be wise to drag the lady out of the boxing ring before she gets trampled."

Reassured of what Terrance already knew in his heart to be true, he followed Dal to retrieve the unconscious lady. Gleefully, Terrance watched Jake pummel Kyle Benson with his fists. Terrance disliked the arrogant Kyle Benson. The only thing better than giving that cocky scoundrel what he deserved was watching Jacob Wolf knock the rascal silly.

Kyle's floundering blows seemed to have no effect on Jacob, except to annoy him. When Kyle kicked Jake in the groin, it infuriated him. As scrappy and dirty a fighter as Kyle was, he was no match for Jake. With a roar, Jake clenched his fists in the back of Kyle's jacket and the seat of his breeches, hoisting him up like a feedsack. In long hurried strides, Jake charged toward the edge of the dock and hurled his opponent into the river.

Meanwhile, Cori roused from her stupor, her head thumping like a bass drum. Blurry-eyed, she watched Dal and Terrance pull her to her feet. Her gaze shifted to the burly giant who was growling like a grizzly bear as he hurtled Kyle through the air.

Cori probably should have been grateful that Jake intervened. But the pulsating pain in her cheek dulled her good sense and left her rudely unappreciative of her knight in shining armor. She had been furious with Kyle Benson for voicing lurid demands and she was outraged with the big gorilla who had knocked her flat. Kyle was paying his penance, but the oversized baboon had yet to receive his due for socking her in the jaw.

Wiggling free from the supporting arms that held her upright, Cori snatched up her parasol and stamped toward Jake.

"That will teach you to strike a lady," Jake snarled just

before Kyle did a belly-buster in the river. "If I ever see you . . . ouch!"

The jab of Cori's parasol provoked Jake to pivot to face the fuming brunette. Flashing ebony eyes fastened on him, selecting another vulnerable spot to strike. The red welt on Cori's cheek tightened as she glared flaming arrows at Jacob.

"A lot you know about treating a lady like a lady, you big baboon!" she hissed, whacking him soundly in the chest with her improvised weapon. "I was doing just fine by myself, thank you very much! If I had wanted assistance I would have signaled for it. All you did was make matters worse."

To Jake's utter amazement, the sassy firebrand yanked up her lemon-yellow skirts and stuffed her dainty foot in his crotch.

"Argh!" Jake howled as he stumbled backward.

With a splash, Jake landed atop Kyle, who was floundering toward solid ground. He never made it. Both men went under and resurfaced a few seconds later to see the saucy hellion grinning in smug satisfaction. With a theatrical flounce, Cori wheeled around and brushed off her hands. Flinging both men another mocking glance, one that caused Kyle to curse a blue streak, Cori lifted her skirts to continue on her way.

Before Cori sailed off like a flying carpet, Terrance grabbed her arm to detain her. "Miss Cori Lee Pierce, I think I should introduce you to your employer."

Her gloating grin evaporated and her doelike eyes fell to the face that was plastered with wet raven hair.

"Layton Breeze was only the interim commander of the Breeze fleet of steam boats. This is Jacob Wolf, the rightful and very competent manager of the company." Terrance went on to say. His attention swung to Kyle's pulverized face. "And Jacob Wolf, I have the delightful pleasure of introducing you to the captain of the

25

Mississippi Belle. Kyle Benson meet *your* employer as well."

"*Former* captain," Jake gritted out. "You're fired, Benson."

While Dal extended himself to offer Jake a helping hand, Kyle sputtered in outrage. "You can't fire me. Layton Breeze hired me."

"The hell I can't," Jake sneered as he steadied himself on the dock and shook like a duck emerging from a pond. The thick fringe of buckskin rustled around him, flinging water everywhere. "Terrance, pack your gear. You have just been reinstated as captain. The *Mississippi Belle* is now under your command."

Cori was so flustered by the news and the blow to her cheek that she swayed back against Terrance. Frantic thoughts whirled in her dazed mind as she assessed the swarthy giant in dripping wet buckhide. She had assumed the ruggedly-dressed oaf to be some backwoodsman who never bypassed a good fight when one came his way. This handsome rogue certainly looked the part of a frontiersman. He bore no resemblance whatsoever to Layton Breeze. Layton reminded Cori of Humpty Dumpty, who had no neck to speak of. Layton also possessed an egg-shaped head and a rotund body supported by tree-stump legs. Layton flaunted his wealth and his position while Jacob Wolf concealed it beneath his rough-edged garments and his rowdy manner.

No matter what Jacob's intentions for intervening in her row with Kyle, an apology wouldn't form on Cori's lips to save her life! She had good reason to despise the family who owned and operated Breeze Steamboat Company, and she had taken a job on the steamer to exact her secret revenge. But she vowed fiercely that this swarthy lion of a man would never learn her intentions. In fact, nothing would make her happier than to see Kyle, Layton, and Jacob roasting in hell!

26

"I hope you are all right, my dear," Dal murmured with customary Blaylock charm. His golden-brown eyes drifted over Cori's voluptuous figure, liking everything he saw, eager to see even more. "Jake had no intention of harming you, I assure you. And I hope you bear no grudge against me because I've been keeping company with him."

Cori glanced past the attractive blond gentleman, who reassuringly squeezed her hand, to find a pair of garnet green eyes boring down on her. Jacob Wolf looked dangerous to her. His brawny appearance was intimidating in itself. The lines that bracketed his lips not only indicated his displeasure with the entire situation but also his annoyance with her for shoving him in the river.

For a moment, Cori granted herself the luxury of surveying Jacob Wolf, despite the fact that she considered him to be one of her declared enemies. He was a member of the all-powerful Breeze family, and that was the first strike against him. The second strike was that his mere presence rattled her. The third strike, of course, was the fact that he'd struck her.

And yet, despising Jake on general principle as she did, Cori couldn't ignore the emotional impact caused by his muscular physique and his strong, commanding features. There was something about this masculine specimen that caught a woman's eye and held it steadfast. His damp clothes clung to him like a second skin, exposing the bulging muscles of his arms and thighs. His lean waist and flat belly were accentuated by the tight garb, leaving a woman to speculate on things that never should have crossed her mind! The stubble of beard on his face drew attention to the deep cleft in his chin, the craggy bronzed features, and the green eyes that were flecked with gold.

Jake's speculative stare caused Cori to tilt a proud chin and rein in her outrageous thoughts. Skully had taught Cori to keep her emotions in cold storage. But the incident with Kyle Benson had provoked her outburst of temper. Now, learning that his incredible hunk of masculinity was Jacob Wolf rattled her. Watching him scrutinize her like a physician probing a cadaver rankled her to no end.

Why, one would have thought she was standing there stark-bone naked the way Jake was staring through her! That rake! He should have been on his knees, begging forgiveness for knocking the stuffing out of her. But was he? No, he was not! Thunderation, Jacob Wolf was staring at her as if she were a meal he was about to devour. How dare he!

"It is a pleasure to meet you, Mr. Wolf," Cori snapped, her tone indicating it was nothing of the kind.

Flinging her nose in the air, she set her yellow plumed hat on her head at a jaunty angle. With a toss of her dark curls she marched toward the gangplank. She rested her parasol against her shoulder like a soldier cradling a rifle. Her very stance and her stern expression dared anyone to approach while she was in a snit.

Cori muttered under her breath as she sailed off. She had to notify Skully of Jacob Wolf's arrival. Blast it, Jacob was bound to complicate matters if he boarded the *Belle*. And damnation, the man looked like trouble from the tip of his raven black head to the toes of his scuffed boots.

A frown plowed Jake's brow as he monitored Cori's retreat. "Appreciative little snip, isn't she?" he smirked, distracted by the graceful sway of her hips in the lemon yellow satin gown.

When Kyle clamped his hand on the dock to pull himself out of the river, Jake growled down at him and then shoved the anchoring hand backward, forcing his adversary to find another place to come ashore.

"Feisty is nearer the mark when describing Cori Pierce," Terrance chuckled. "Layton hired her to

28

entertain aboard this new floating palace of his. Although Cori has a voice like a siren and plays the harpsichord like an angel, she is a high-spirited sprite. She is usually quite skillful at warding off men's advances." Terrance's gaze drifted downstream, where Kyle was struggling onto the wharf without assistance. "No doubt the good captain tried to . . ."

"*Ex*-captain," Jake grunted in correction.

"*Ex*-captain," Terrance amended with a gloating smile. "Kyle was undoubtedly using the power of his position to have his way with Cori. He chases her constantly. Apparently he got impatient and abandoned his attempt to charm her into submission. While it is true that men flock to her like kittens trailing fresh milk, she doesn't seem all that interested. She is notoriously fickle and refuses to spend too much time with any one beau."

"She's the one," Jacob announced.

His eyes followed Cori across the deck of the *Mississippi Belle* before she vanished on the shadowed stairway. The vision of the fiery imp clobbering Kyle with her parasol put an amused smile on Jake's lips. Damn, that spitfire fought like a wolverine. She was no shrinking Southern violet, that was for sure. She had the temperament of a tiger, the tongue of a cobra, and the courage of a lion. Now here was a woman who was Augusta Breeze's match!

"I beg your pardon?" Terrance frowned bemusedly at Jake's abrupt declaration.

"You took the words right out of my mouth," Dal declared. Jake's eyes weren't the only ones that trailed the curvy brunette until she disappeared from view. "She has all the necessary qualifications—stunning good looks, poise, and plenty of spunk."

One black brow climbed to a teasing angle. "The last time we pursued the same female I had to forfeit because of my extended trip up the Missouri. But this time, my friend, you will find a relentless rival in pursuit of the fair damsel's hand," Jake said with perfect assurance.

"Her hand?" Terrance crowed. "What the devil are you two babbling about? Both of you would be lucky to steal a kiss from Cori Lee Pierce! Haven't you been listening to me? If she had wanted a husband she could have the pick of the crop, believe you me. You know what kind of passengers inhabit the hurricane deck of luxurious steamers: well-to-do planters, land speculators, wealthy businessmen. Cori has been floating up and down the river for eight months, singing her way into the hearts of bachelors and married men alike. She has befuddled and miffed all of them. One moment she is a teasing flirt and the next instant she is cold as ice. She is an intriguing paradox, to be sure, but . . ."

"I love a challenge," Jake remarked, undaunted by the discouraging news.

"No more than I," Dal piped up.

"It's going to be difficult to plan a double wedding with only one bride between us," Jake snorted. "I saw her first."

"But according to the proverbial adage, all's fair in love and war," Dal taunted as he straightened his cuff and struck a sophisticated pose.

Jake muttered under his breath. While he looked like a drowned rat, Dal appeared the epitome of dashing good looks and polished manners. His blond features boasted a clean-shaven face and a suave smile that had melted the hearts of many a fair lady. Damn . . .

"I'm not looking for love, only a wife," Jake reminded him sharply. "*I* pick Cori. *You* back off!"

"You're both wasting your time," Terrance warned.

"Go fetch your belongings, Sykes," Jake ordered. "You have a ship to command."

Clicking his heels together, Terrance presented Jake with a snappy salute. "Aye, sir, I'll return within the hour. But I still say this challenge for Cori Lee Pierce is a

30

waste of time and energy. She won't have either of you. She is sure to recognize dedicated bachelors when she sees them."

"Ten dollars says you're wrong," Dal dared to wager.

"Twenty dollars says she'll be my bride and you'll be attending my wedding in Natchez," Jake proclaimed with absolute certainty.

Terrance studied both men's determined stares. He almost sympathized with the attractive brunette who had unknowingly become the prize of Dal and Jake's contest. "Well, I guess we'll just have to wait and see if Cori wishes to become an heiress to steamboats or racing stables filled with prize thoroughbreds, won't we?" He ambled on his way. "My money is still on the lady."

Jake stared at the huge steamboat that rocked with the lapping water. His astute gaze caught a glimpse of yellow satin and a dark, curly head. With renewed interest, he watched Cori sweep across the hurricane deck and closet herself in one of the rooms situated beneath the pilothouse.

"You're determined to make a game of this, aren't you, Blaylock?" Jake murmured absently.

"A game?" Dal's gaze had also uplifted to the door behind which Cori had disappeared. "Not at all. I happen to appreciate the lady's fiery spirit as much as you do. Why should I settle for a docile, dull wife for our double wedding? I have as much to offer the lady as you do. And I have no need to remind you that our tastes in women have often left us pursuing the same female. No, my friend," Dal continued. "I'm playing for keeps."

"But if Cori consents to become my bride, you will not interfere?" Jake wanted to know as he squarely faced Dal.

"Will you, if the situation is reversed?" Dal questioned the question.

Jake shrugged. Dal hated those enigmatic shrugs. They told him nothing.

"Very well," Dal sighed. "We'll set our wedding date for May twenty-third. That will give the loser ample time to find himself a suitable bride."

"Are you sure you've given yourself enough time?" Jake snickered before he pivoted on his heels and swaggered away.

"I'm not the one who'll be making a frantic search for a wife," Dal snorted. "After all, you're the one who declared one female was as good as another. Find yourself someone else."

Jake strode away without a backward glance. Cori Lee Pierce would be his wife and Augusta would cease her lectures on settling down to manage the steamboat company from Wolfhaven. Cori had all the necessary credentials and she went far beyond Jake's expectations. He could see a lot of his grandmother in the curvaceous brunette.

In his brief encounter with Cori, Jake had learned a great deal about her. She was appealing to the eye. That was a delightful bonus. She wasn't afraid to stand up for herself. Jake appreciated a woman with backbone. She didn't cower when faced with the prospect of being fired from her position after she had shoved her employer in the river. That took a helluva lot of nerve. And that single characteristic confirmed Jake's belief that Cori would more than suffice as a wife.

Cori Lee Pierce was a bit of a hellion, just like Jake was. He was attracted to her physically, so he would have no problem with joining his bride in bed to produce heirs. Why, they might even fall in love as the years progressed. If he was *capable* of falling in love, Jake amended. It certainly hadn't happened yet. In thirty-one years, Jake hadn't even found himself remotely close to taking that emotional plunge. Properly bred women were one-dimensional creatures who held little lure for him except in bed. If he was lucky, Cori might be the exception to the

32

rule and he might actually enjoy spending time with her instead of merely tolerating the presence of his wife in his home.

Getting a little ahead of yourself, aren't you, Wolf? Jacob chuckled at himself. He had yet to return to the lady's good graces and here he was speculating on whether he could ever love her. And his courtship was going to be hampered by competition. Dal Blaylock was a worthy rival, after all. Dal was tactful and debonair. Jake was blunt and to the point, like Augusta. Dal was blond, wealthy, and charming. Jake was dark, extremely rich, and . . .

Well, he could be equally charming if he put his mind to it, Jake encouraged himself. But if he lost Cori to Dal, he would be a good sport and select a tolerable wife. After all, his goal was to satisfy Augusta and beget himself children to dote over in the years to come.

In actuality, he probably would have been better off to adopt three or four orphans, Jake decided as he strode into the pastry shop on the wharf. Children, after all, were the important issue here, not the wife . . .

Even while he lectured himself on his priorities, Jake found Cori's big brown eyes flashing before him, flashing in that delicately carved face that was marred by a welt the exact size of his fist . . .

Jake groaned miserably. His hurried courtship, amid fierce competition, would be complicated from the onset. Hell's fire, how was he going to overcome the obstacle of slugging Cori on the cheek . . . ?

"May I help you, sir?" the proprietor of the pastry shop inquired, dragging Jake from his contemplative deliberations.

"A box of bonbons, if you please," he requested and then sighed heavily, thinking once again of the bruise on Cori's cheek. "On second thought, better make that two boxes . . .

33

Chapter 3

"What in heaven's name happened to your eye?" Cori's companion asked with a concerned gasp.

Disgruntled, Cori tossed her parasol aside. "I ran into a brick wall by the name of Jacob Wolf," she muttered.

A dismayed groan rang through the air. "*The* Jacob Wolf?"

"None other. I can endure the black eye I'll probably have," Cori grumbled. "But I pray to God that man doesn't wind up aboard this ship for the journey to Natchez. He's no Layton Breeze, I can tell you that!"

Her companion's shoulders slumped. "Jacob Wolf's presence could cause us serious problems."

"I'm aware of that," Cori replied as she dipped a cloth in the basin and then collapsed in the chair to nurse her swollen cheek. "Dealing with this black eye during musical performances isn't going to help, either. Thunderation! Things have been going splendidly until now."

"What are we going to do?" Came the bleak question.

"Exactly what we've been doing, only we'll have to be more cautious if Wolf shows up."

"Did you tell Skully?"

Cori nodded affirmatively. "I also told Skully that I

34

may have jeopardized my job after I shoved Jacob in the river."

"What? Why?"

Cori waved her companion to silence. "Just fetch me another cold cloth," she requested. "And then help me out of this gown. It is tainted with the foul aroma of Kyle Benson, who lost his position as captain, by the way."

"He's been harassing you again?"

"We came to blows on the wharf," Cori announced before cursing the vision of Kyle's puckered face that rose above her.

"I thought you said Wolf struck you."

"It's a long story. I'll explain later. At the moment, this headache is splitting my skull—"

The firm rap at the door sent Cori's companion diving for cover beneath the double-width bed. With an inspecting glance, Cori tugged the bedspread into place and approached the door. To her dismay, the now dry, cleansed to a shine, and dashingly handsome Jacob Wolf stood before her, garbed in the fancy trappings of a gentleman. He bore gifts of bonbons, fruit, and flowers. Cori slammed the door shut so quickly that the flower blossoms were snapped from their stems. Petals fluttered to her feet.

Jacob stared at the decapitated flowers he had hurriedly thrust at Cori. Since irreparable damage had been done to the bouquet, he tossed the stems over the railing and shifted the fruit basket to his right hand while clutching the two boxes of bonbons in the other. He had heard the drone of voices behind the door when he approached. It was obvious the lady had company and it had damned well better not be that ornery Dal Blaylock, if the man knew what was good for him! It would be just like that charming rake to scuttle to Cori's room to shower her with sympathy and ply her with flattery before Jake arrived.

35

"I brought peace offerings," Jacob declared to the closed door. "May I come in? I would like to apologize for hitting you. It was an accident and I deeply regret that your lovely face got in the way of my fist."

"Apology accepted. Go away."

Jacob frowned at the door. "My bonbons are melting."

"I have an atrocious headache," Cori countered.

"I'm truly sorry about that."

"You already said that."

A deflated sigh escaped Jake's lips. "Please, Miss Pierce. I beg only a few minutes of your time," he said in his most persuasive voice. "I want to present you with gifts and ask you to marry me."

That got Cori's attention. The door swung open and Cori stared at the giant of a man in stunned amazement. "You want me to marry a woman beater?" she sniffed sarcastically. While her left hand held the cloth to her throbbing cheek, she reached out with her right hand to accept the basket of fruit. "All is forgiven. Good-bye, Mr. Wolf."

Cori tried to shut the portal but, quick as a wink, Jacob wedged his foot inside, preventing her from slamming the door in his face a second time. Without invitation he barged inside, expecting to find Dal lounging in the chair. But the room was empty.

A perplexed frown furrowed his dark brows as he surveyed the luxurious cabin that boasted a double bed, lacy curtains on the window, tapestries, and plush carpet. Jacob had yet to confront his cousin and inquire about the purchase of this stunning palace, but it was indeed a magnificent vessel. Cori's cabin was as grand as Jake's.

"Do you talk to yourself often?" Jake questioned, still puzzled by the lack of a third body in the room. He could have sworn he heard voices.

Cori tensed, but Skully had trained her exceptionally well. She had become adept at hiding her emotions

36

behind carefully blank stares. "I never talk to myself," she insisted. "It is a sign of emotional imbalance."

Jacob's glittering green eyes riveted on her, quiet and watchful. "I heard voices."

Cori presented her back. "I was rehearsing the lyrics to one of the songs I planned to sing this evening, provided I overcome this hellacious headache." She gave the lie without batting an eye. "I suppose I'll take the bonbons, too," she added purposely changing the subject.

"What about the marriage?" Jacob questioned point blank. Although he could feel another presence in the room, he abandoned the subject and cut straight to the heart of the matter, as was his custom. Jake always spoke his mind, just like his grandmother.

Cori raised a delicately arched brow. "Are you going to fire me for pushing you in the river?"

"No," Jacob assured her. "Are you going to marry me?"

"No," Cori replied, miffed by this mountain of a man who had invaded her privacy and put her in such a state. True, swarthy sexual appeal oozed from Jacob Wolf's pores. And true, he was wealthy beyond her imagination. And yes, he was devastating in his frontiersman's garb as well as his black velvet jacket and breeches. But no, she would not marry the enemy! That was not her idea of revenge . . .

"Why won't you marry me?" Jacob wanted to know.

"I don't know you, for starters," Cori burst out in frustration.

This sinewy giant rattled her. In her twenty years of existence she had never run across anyone like him. He didn't mince words and she was at a loss as to how to deal with his straightforward manner. Skully had taught her to counter smooth lines of flattery that were meant to crumble her defenses. But Jacob was not only blunt and to the point, he was also crazy! How did a female deal with

37

a male maniac? Why would he propose marriage to a woman he'd only met? With his rugged good looks and wealth he could snap his fingers and a bevy of women would rush forward, each eager to acquire the position of his wife.

"We will have time to get to know each other before our wedding on May twenty-third," Jake assured her as his betraying gaze flooded over the gaping gown Cori had been in the process of removing when he arrived.

Her brown eyes widened incredulously. "We may not even like each other! And here you are, setting a wedding date."

Jacob found himself up against a stone wall. Having never decided to marry until now, and having no practice at proposing, he had obviously handled this situation horribly. But damn it, he had Dal Blaylock to consider. The man was an expert in wooing women.

"I like you well enough," Jake said pleasantly.

Cori stared helplessly at him. She had been proposed to on numerous occasions, but never *ever* had a man asked for her hand after he punched her in the eye! Was that why he had proposed? Out of guilt? Thunderation, he had really gone overboard to make amends!

"The answer is no, Mr. Wolf, although I am flattered by the offer." Astounded was nearer the mark.

"Then would you consent to have dinner with me?" he asked in desperation.

"I think not."

"What if your job is at stake?" he threatened, half jesting, half serious.

Ebony eyes blinked in bewilderment. "Are you always this impulsive and impetuous, Mr. Wolf?"

"Actually, no," he confessed, staring at the luscious curve of her lips. She had the most kissable mouth ever to be carved into a feminine face. His gaze dipped to survey the creamy swells of her breasts, which rose and fell above the décolletage of her gown. "I have decided I want children to enrich my life, and to beget children a man needs a wife."

"How many?"

"How many?" Jacob parroted, frowning. "Only one wife."

"No, children," Cori corrected. "How many children do you want?" Thunderation, why was she ever bothering to ask? Curiosity, she supposed.

"Three, maybe four," Jacob replied as he continued to assess the curvaceous brunette. My, but Cori was gorgeous, black eye and all.

"When?" Cori queried, staring at the mountain of a man who filled her chamber to overflowing.

"When?" Jacob blinked. "Well, I'm told it's rather difficult to acquire babies in less than nine months."

Cori felt a flustered blush stain her cheeks. Jacob Wolf had her so rattled that she kept leaping from one topic of conversation to another in mid thought. "I was . . . a . . . referring to the hour at which you wish to dine, Mr. Wolf."

"Jacob," he corrected and then grinned at her becoming blush. "Six o'clock . . . for dinner, that is . . . not for making babies." Another peal of laughter clamored across the room when Cori blushed up to her eyebrows. "We can wait until we know each other a few hours before we start our family."

Impulsively, Jacob stepped closer, peering down at Cori from his towering height. Without preamble, he swept her off her feet and kissed her full on the lips, lips that were frozen in embarrassed astonishment.

Cori, of course, had been the recipient of dozens of kisses, bestowed on her by various and sundry men. She had endured timid pecks, slobbery and ravenous embraces, most of which did more to repulse than excite. But Jacob Wolf's kiss was in direct contrast to the way he looked and behaved. He was a huge, forceful, plain-spoken man, but he kissed Cori with a tenderness that

39

knocked her sideways. He didn't squeeze the stuffing out of her or ravish her. He held her to him as if she were a fragile China doll. He took no more than Cori was willing to offer and yet she didn't even give a thought to resisting him. Her betraying body seemed to crave the feel of his brawny arms engulfing her, the feel of his sensuous lips courting hers with gentle expertise. It was as if she were drawing some hidden emotion from this dynamic man, something sweet and magical and utterly intriguing. And at the same time, he was drawing forbidden feelings from her.

As if they possessed a mind of their own, her arms encircled his neck and her eyes fluttered shut to enjoy the sensual pleasures he so easily aroused in her.

Jacob had expected to be mildly aroused by this spitfire's kiss. But the jolt he received sent shock waves undulating through every nerve and muscle. He had only meant to appease his male curiosity. But the first kiss demanded a second. This time Jake kissed her hungrily, as if he had been starved for this long-awaited treat.

Hell's fire, it had only been twenty-four hours since he'd been with a woman. One would have thought it was months the way his body responded to the feel of her breasts meshed to his chest, her hips molded familiarly to his thighs.

His hand slid over her derriere as his mouth twisted and slanted, tasting the sweet nectar of a kiss that was far more intoxicating than a bottle of wine. A tormented groan rumbled in his chest as his senses reeled.

What the sweet loving hell did he think he was doing? He had bombarded Cori with gifts, proposed marriage, and now he was kissing her as if they were already lovers! She probably thought he was a lunatic, and with just cause, Jake was sorry to say.

That frustrated thought prompted Jake to set Cori abruptly to her feet. When her knees folded up beneath her, Jacob slipped a supporting arm around her waist to steady her.

"Should I apologize for that as well?" he queried, his voice nowhere near apologetic. It rumbled with disturbed passion.

"Most definitely," Cori squeaked, her tone two octaves higher than normal. "You are much too forward, Mr. . . . Jacob."

"I'm sorry. I'll come for you at six," he bleated as he pried himself away from temptation and aimed himself at the door.

"Is there going to be any more kissing?" she choked out.

He paused to lean against the partially opened door. Willfully, he gathered his composure and flashed her a teasing grin that made his eyes twinkle. "Would you like some more kissing?"

Her chin shot up. "Absolutely not," she declared indignantly.

"You found my kisses repulsive?"

"No, but . . ." Cori slammed her mouth shut like a drawer before she divulged the fact that he had kissed her blind and stupid and she had enjoyed every minute of it.

Jake studied her for a long pensive moment. "If those kisses were any indication, Cori," he had the nerve to say, "we might wind up with a houseful of children." He bowed slightly before he exited the same way he came in—like a misdirected cyclone.

Cori sat down before she fell down. It was her horrendous headache that provoked such unexplainable reactions, she assured herself. Jacob Wolf defied everything Skully had told her about men. Jake had rattled her, that was all. She would be able to handle Jacob much better with a table between them . . .

A face, one that sported a mischievous grin, emerged from under the bed. "I see what you mean about Jacob Wolf."

Cori blanched. When Jacob was kissing the breath out

41

of her she had completely forgotten there was a body stashed under the bed. Her cheeks blossomed with color. "How am I supposed to handle a man like that?" she wailed in exasperation, cursing her traitorous body for the lingering aftereffects of his devastating embrace.

Her companion chuckled at the wild blush on Cori's enchanting features. "Maybe you should marry him."

"Marry the enemy?" Cori squawked, horrified. "You're as crazy as he is. Stop being ridiculous!"

"We could have what we want and no one would be the wiser."

"That isn't the way we planned it," Cori loudly protested.

"Plans can change."

"Not these plans," she spouted, and then groaned at the pain that crashed through her skull.

Outside the door, Jacob Wolf was frowning in confusion. He had heard the quiet murmurings of an unrecognizable voice and Cori's blaring objections. There was someone else in that room, Jake was sure of it. Although he hadn't been able to decipher the words of the whispering voice, Cori's heated declarations rang in his ears as he ambled away.

Marry the enemy? That isn't what we had planned? Who the hell was in there? And what the devil was going on?

Curiosity was killing Jacob Wolf as he strode off to confront his cousin. He hadn't anticipated his extraordinary response to that voluptuous brunette. She had caused an upheaval of fierce emotions in him. The taste of her kiss clung to his lips and the feel of her supple body was imprinted on his, making him crave more than what they had shared in a moment of madness.

Hell's fire! No wonder men chased after that feisty firebrand. She devastated a man's emotions, not to mention the dramatic effect she had on his anatomy . . .

Jacob's thoughts trailed off when he walked into another argument in progress, the second one that day.

Terrance Sykes had arrived in the pilothouse to inform Layton of the change in personnel and Layton was in a full-blown snit.

"For your information, Mr. Sykes," Layton sneered sarcastically. "My cousin is blazing his way up the Missouri, just as he has been doing for the past year. And even if he has returned, which I very much doubt, I will not have you replacing the very capable Kyle Benson. My cousin is not in command of this new steamer. I am. And you can take your gear and stuff it up your—"

"Careful, cousin Layton," Jacob warned as he veered into the pilothouse.

Jake's scrutinizing gaze wandered over his cousin, who hadn't changed one whit since they'd last met, except that he'd put on a few more unnecessary pounds. Layton still looked like a whiskey barrel, and his features still hung on his face like a wrinkled raisin. The fact that he always dressed in white did make him look a lot like Humpty Dumpty. Layton fussed over his expensive tailor-made apparel, and finding a stain on his garments always put him in a frenzy. Even as a child, Layton abhorred getting dirty and refused to join in any games that might soil his clothes.

Layton wheeled to see Jacob glaring down at him. "Jacob, I'm glad to see you again," he declared with a pretentious smile.

"Of course you are," Jake scoffed. One look at Layton indicated that he was visibly distressed to see that Jake had returned.

"Stow your gear in one of the cabins in the texas," Jake directed Terrance, despite what Layton had said earlier. "I want a private word with my cousin."

When Terrance strolled out, Jake's stony gaze bore down on the skittish Layton Breeze. "I fired Kyle Benson after he exhibited conduct unbecoming a ship's captain, and he will remain fired," he announced in a tone that anticipated no argument.

43

Layton puffed up with so much indignation that he nearly popped the buttons of his white satin vest. "Now see here, Jacob, I purchased this steamer and—"

"With corporate money," Jake interjected before Layton could build up a full head of steam. "That makes it partially mine. Now that I'm back, *I'm* making the decisions."

Layton had always detested Jake's domineering attitude, his capabilities. He was everything Layton wasn't. "If you think I won't inform Gram of your bullying attitude, you're mistaken."

"Always the tattletale," Jake chuckled. "You know Gram put me in charge of the company. It's time you stepped down from your throne, Layton. Your crown is beginning to dent your brain."

Layton's stubby arms waved in expansive gestures. "When I gather my investors, this steamer will be all mine! I'm starting my own company!"

Jake stared through the glass room at the muddy river, unconcerned with Layton's tirade. "Fine, but until that time, the steamer is mine to command." A frown settled over Jake's bronzed features when Calvin Thompson stumbled into the room, reeking of whiskey. "What the hell are you doing here?"

Layton's pudgy chin went up. "He's my pilot."

Jake's arm shot toward the door through which Calvin had just stepped. "You're fired, Thompson. Get off my ship!" His voice boomed like a cannon.

Thompson did as he was told and Layton sputtered in outrage. "Damn you, Jacob. You can't waltz in here and fire all my personnel. I'm part owner of—"

"The hell I can't!" Jacob snorted, his temper rising a quick ten degrees. "Thompson is a lush. And when he's sober, he's an idiot. It's a wonder he hasn't run this ship aground already!"

"This isn't the end of it," Layton spewed, his face flushing the color of raw liver. "I intend to tell Gram how you bullied me about. It was my business dealings that acquired this vessel during your absence and I . . ."

Jacob took only one ominous step toward his fuming cousin. But that one step, and the foreboding sneer that curled Jake's lips, was enough to make Layton turn tail and skedaddle out the door.

When he was alone, Jacob heaved a weary sigh. He had spent a year working day and night, only to return to a fiasco of Layton's making. Jake was suddenly thankful he was considering going ashore to enjoy the peaceful life at the plantation. The estate was self-sufficient since he had put it under the care of a loyal and very seasoned overseer. Wolfhaven ran like a well-tuned engine, unlike this floating palace that had been in Layton's charge . . .

"I saw your cousin scampering to his quarters," Terrance remarked as he ambled into the pilothouse. "I assume that means you have regained control of the company."

"Darn right," Jacob grunted as he eased a hip onto the tall-legged chair that set behind the wheel.

"Now if only you can solve the mysterious robberies that have plagued the *Mississippi Belle* the past few months," Terrance sighed.

Jake jerked up his head to peer curiously at Terrance, who leaned negligently against the doorjamb. Hell's fire, it sounded like this vessel was a jinx. Layton had put a fire-breathing captain in command of it and a firewater-drinking pilot behind the wheel. Robberies too? Damn.

"They have been most peculiar thefts from what I've been told," Terrance went on to say. "Several of Layton's prospective investors have become the victims of robberies. The thieves, who bear different descriptions, seem to vanish from the ship by either diving into the river or sneaking ashore when the steamer pulls in to gather cordwood. Layton has been losing his would-be investors right and left."

Jacob mulled over the comments while he absently

45

traced the spokes of the wheel. His gaze drifted past the two huge smokestacks set on each side of the glass pilothouse. "What are the descriptions of these river pirates?"

Terrance shrugged his shoulder. "They seem to come in all sizes and shapes—short ones, tall ones, round ones, and thin ones. Layton swears there is a nest of them that sneak on and off at each port and vanish in the commotion of wooding up and loading cargo. But they are a shrewd bunch and Layton hasn't come remotely close to capturing them."

Although Jacob had intended to pursue the disconcerting subject, his thoughts jammed when he spied Dal Blaylock strolling on the promenade with Cori Pierce on his arm. It was jealousy that stabbed at him like a dull-bladed knife. It was the frustration of seeing a flirtatious smile on that shapely brunette's lips. Cori had eyed Jake with wary consternation since the instant he barged into her room. And even though they both had gotten carried away with their explosive kisses, Cori had retreated behind a wall of self-reserve the instant he let her go. But now she had emerged from her self-imposed shell and Dal was on the receiving end of some very suggestive glances. Jake began to see what Terrance meant about that female changing moods like the wind.

Jake gnashed his teeth. Leave it to the dashing aristocrat to woo Cori with his Southern charm. Hell's fire, after Jake had botched the encounter in her cabin, he had probably sent that saucy beauty running into Dal's arms as if he were her salvation from a lunatic. Jake was going to have to concentrate on portraying the suave gentleman instead of charging at Cori like an uncivilized heathen. It was obvious that Jake had been in the wilds too long!

"Dal seems to be beating your time," Terrance observed, watching the play of emotions on Jake's craggy

46

features. "But she's a hopeless cause, nonetheless."

"Where is she from?" Jake questioned, his gaze following the striking couple until they strolled out of sight.

"St. Louis or somewhere about, I think," Terrance replied. "Shouldn't we be getting underway?"

Muttering at Dal's appearance and its aggravating effect on him, Jake called down the speaking tube to alert the engineer in the hull. Beneath them, in the boiler room, the crew began heaving wood onto the fire.

"I fired that moron pilot Layton hired," Jake informed his new captain. "I hope you don't mind sharing duties as pilot and captain with me. We'll be short-handed until we reach Natchez to hire men I trust."

"Just to get the chance to be back on the river, I'll work two shifts back to back," Terrance insisted with a grateful smile.

Fondly, Jake patted Terrance on the shoulder. "My thanks. I'll ensure that you are well paid for the extra effort."

"I'm curious to see how much the river has changed since I navigated to Natchez," Terrance mused aloud.

"I hope it hasn't changed so much that neither of us recognize trouble before it strikes," Jake grumbled. "I'd hate to plow into a sandbar or sawyer. Layton would never let me hear the end of it."

"If Layton had set his stubby fingers on the wheel of this magnificent floating palace it would have sunk months ago," Terrance snorted derisively.

For the next few minutes, idle chatter was set aside to prepare the steamer for launch. The clanging bell signaled the steamboat's departure, and on the wharf, the roustabouts scurried across the gangplank, loading the last of the cargo. Passengers, laden down with luggage, threaded through the crowds, asking directions to their staterooms on the boiler deck.

While Jake and Terrance eased the vessel into the channel, Jake mentally kicked himself for bungling his pursuit of Cori Pierce. After his seclusion in the wilds, Jake felt like an inexperienced schoolboy compared to Dal. Jake had seen his long-time friend in action one too many times not to know that the foolish mistakes he'd made with Cori were going to put him at a definite disadvantage. If he didn't watch his step he might lose this challenge and the conquest of Cori Pierce . . .

What was I thinking? Jake scowled at himself. It was a ridiculous challenge in the first place. Two men who focused their sights on the same would-be bride were asking for trouble. There were dozens of eligible females on board this luxurious steamer. Jake had seen several debutantes strolling the decks. The whole point of acquiring a wife was to produce heirs, he reminded himself sensibly. If he lost Cori, all he had to do was set his sights on a healthy, reasonably attractive chit and pursue her. Maybe he should concede this absurd contest before conflict rose between him and his best friend. Cori certainly had appeared to be enjoying Dal's company far more than she had Jake's . . . except for that steamy kiss that caused an explosion of his senses.

And it was the memory of that jolting kiss that refused to let Jake gracefully bow out of the contest. The feel of Cori's delectable body molded intimately to his followed him like a shadow for the next few hours. Jake kept checking his timepiece in anticipation of escorting the lovely Cori Pierce to supper in the main saloon.

This time he would dazzle Cori with charm, he encouraged himself. Dal would meet with fierce competition. Grappling with that thought, Jake focused on the muddy Mississippi and bided his time. He wasn't backing off yet! Cori Pierce was a delightful prize, and Jake wasn't giving up just because Dal Blaylock had the same tantalizing interest in her, and that was that!

Chapter 4

All spruced up and dressed to kill, Jacob rapped on Cori's door and waited with his most beguiling smile—the one he had practiced on himself in his mirror. And what a devastating smile it was! Cori took one look at the sinewy Goliath who stood more than a foot taller than her five-foot-three-inch frame. It took only one glance at his muscular physique to remember how it felt to be enfolded in his swarthy arms, how his sensuous lips moved expertly over hers. He aroused sensations that had been impossible to ignore.

Even though Jacob Wolf was a confident man, Cori wondered if he knew just how intimidating and unsettling he was to those of the female persuasion. Because of Skully's tireless efforts, Cori had learned to counter every sort of man—except this one. The fact was, Jacob Wolf rattled her because of who he was and what he was and because of the phenomenal effect he had on her when he ventured too close. Lord, it was like standing beside a cannon, wondering when it would go off!

"You look lovely, Cori," he complimented with that deep rich Southern drawl that sent goose bumps across her skin.

With a nervous gulp, Cori withdrew the hand on which Jake had gallantly pressed a kiss. Thunderation! She had to get a hold on herself or she'd be drooling all over this handsome rake. She didn't even *want* to like him! Indeed, her crusade would become far more complicated if she did.

His forefinger lightly traced the enchanting lines of her face, marveling at how well she had disguised the bruise that discolored her eye and cheek. It was still noticeable, to be sure, but one had to look hard to see his knuckle print, his stamp of possession . . .

"Powder and stage makeup can do wonders," Cori commented, retreating from his touch. "Shall we dine? I'm famished."

Where was that bubbling laughter and the flirtatious smile he had observed while Cori was being escorted around the deck with Dal Blaylock? Apparently Jake made Cori wary and Dal put her at ease.

From the moment Jake accompanied Cori into the spacious saloon that had been filled with tables to serve the evening meal, Jake became more depressed. A flock of Cori's male admirers who had been on the journey downriver filed past. Noting her swollen eye, they paused to inquire about her bruise and to offer heartfelt sympathy.

"I ran into a wall," Cori replied to the monotonous question she'd been asked for the umpteenth time.

Jake sank a little deeper into his chair, feeling all of two inches tall.

After Cori responded to the burning question, she was treated to dozens of suggested remedies to relieve the pain and discoloration. This procedure of answering inquiries and listening to folk remedies continued for thirty minutes before Jake and Cori were allowed the privacy and luxury of enjoying their meal.

"Tell me something about yourself," Cori requested

50

between bites of leg of mutton and hominy.

His shoulder lifted in his characteristic shrug. "There isn't much to tell," he said modestly. "I was raised in Natchez by my grandmother after my parents perished in a fire that demolished a company steamer. I went west to fight with the Texans and have spent the rest of my life on the river. The past year I've been on the Missouri, clearing the clogged channel to extend service."

Jake took a sip of his mint julep. "And what about you?"

"I've never been to Texas or up the Missouri," she replied evasively. "Is the Missouri as tedious and dangerous as the rumors I've heard?"

Jake whittled at his braised brisket and popped a chunk in his mouth. "It's every bit as dangerous," he responded after he swallowed the morsel. "Where do you call home?"

"The Mississippi," Cori answered with a disarming smile.

There it was at last, that saucy grin. But Cori had employed the blinding smile to distract him and he damned well knew it.

"You aren't going to tell me anything about yourself, are you?" he asked.

"I didn't think it mattered all that much, since you proposed this afternoon," she shot back, but with a mischievous grin that took the sting out of her sarcastic remark. "I seriously doubt that, if you cared who I was, you would have asked for my hand."

Jake eased back leisurely in his chair to study the comely brunette for a moment. Cori Lee Pierce was a mystifying enigma. When he stared into her chocolate eyes, Jake could feel the magnetic attraction tugging at him. Oh, certainly, he had felt instant attractions to women before this. But the sensation seemed to delve deeper. Cori intrigued him with her cryptic comments

51

and her infuriating technique of leaping from one topic of conversation to another like a fidgety grasshopper. Her quick change of temperament also fascinated him. This chit, whoever and whatever she was, was complex, that was for sure.

The fact that there had been someone in her cabin and that she purposely lied to him about it left Jake's mind clouded with doubt. Was that unidentified companion a brother . . . a lover? And why the blazes did Cori consider her employer her enemy?

"You're staring, Jacob," Cori prompted, unnerved by that probing glance that sought out the hidden secrets in her soul.

Jacob mentally shook himself and broke into a wry smile. "I'm only trying to figure you out," he said frankly.

"I'm simple and uncomplicated," she replied with a nonchalant chortle. "What you see is what I am." One perfectly arched brow lifted as she regarded his arresting physique, wishing she could find one flaw to dwell on in her attempt not to like Jacob Wolf. "Are you having misgivings about your rash marriage proposal?"

"Are you going to accept mine or Dal Blaylock's?" he questioned point-blank.

Thunderation, he had done it again, had drilled her with unanticipated questions. For a moment Cori floundered in thought and fiddled with her silverware for lack of anything better to do with her hands while her mind whirled. "I . . . a . . . he . . . a . . . Dal didn't offer me one," she chirped uncomfortably.

"No?" Jake queried with obvious surprise.

Cori's animated features knitted in a bemused frown. "Why should he? We only just met and he isn't anywhere near as blunt and straightforward as you are."

"You prefer his style, I take it," Jake grunted sourly.

"He is a friend of yours? That surprises me. You're

52

absolutely nothing alike," Cori observed.

Jake leaned forward, his full lips thinning in a tight smile. "Do you have any idea how difficult it is to carry on a conversation with you when you refuse to stick to one topic without flying off to another in mid thought?" He glared at her. "Answer the damned question."

Brown eyes flashed with temper, something over which Cori usually had control unless physically threatened or mentally harassed. With Jake she felt both. "Forgive me for my many shortcomings. As for Dal Blaylock, it is not a question of preferring one style to another. The two of you are different and that doesn't make one of you better than the other. And in reference to your ludicruous proposal of marriage, the answer is no. I don't think the two of us are compatible enough to live under the same roof without killing each other!"

The instant Cori bolted to her feet, Jake snaked out a hand and snapped her back into her chair. The fierce tug threw Cori off balance. With a shocked squawk, Cori found her chair sliding out from under her. A pained groan erupted from her lips when her forehead collided with the edge of the table. Another moan tumbled free when she plopped on the floor amid the pool of her pink velvet skirt and ruffled petticoats.

The saloon suddenly became as quiet as the grave. Every pair of eyes was on the lady in pink, whose petticoats were twisted around her, exposing far more leg than was acceptable in mixed company.

A frustrated scowl rolled off Jake's lips as he bounded to his feet to assist the fuming young lady. Hurriedly, he reached down to hoist her off the floor.

Jake was quickly reminded of the adage about haste making waste. His abruptness caused Cori to slam her knee into the upended chair, provoking another howl of pain.

"Curse it! Don't touch me!" she yelped when Jake

tried to steady her on her feet.

He let go as if he were handling live coals and Cori grasped for the tablecloth to maintain her balance. To her dismay, the tablecloth, plates, and goblets of mint julep crashed to the floor. Mutton, potatoes and brisket splattered all over her expensive gown.

"You are a walking disaster!" Cori hissed furiously.

In a fit of temper, she snatched up a glob of potatoes and flung them in Jake's face. The crowd of bystanders gasped in unison at her daring. But Cori didn't give a whit if her employer fired her on the spot. She was so outraged that she was seeing the world through an angry red haze. Never in her life had she been forced to endure the presence of such a blundering galloot. In her estimation, Jacob Wolf was like a bull clambering around in a china closet. He broke or damaged everything he touched!

Vaulting to her feet, Cori wheeled around and stamped off. Jake was one step behind her, apologizing all the while.

"Go away and leave me alone," she railed as she rushed out the door and flew up the steps to the hurricane deck.

"I'm usually not this clumsy," Jake muttered in exasperation.

"Really? You could have fooled me," she snapped, taking the steps two at a time in her attempt to remove herself from harm's way.

"It's just that you make me uncomfortable with your evasiveness," he defended.

"And you make me furious!" Cori spouted. Her shrill voice indicated her temper had burst into flames.

"Please rejoin me for supper," Jake pleaded. He had never begged a woman in all his life, but damned if he wasn't imploring Cori. She had him setting all sorts of precedents and looking like an uncoordinated jackass.

"I have enough supper on my dress to sustain me until breakfast, thank you very much!"

54

"Hell's fire, woman, would you slow down a minute?" Jake exploded in frustration.

Cori slowed to a halt because she had no choice. The steely hand that gripped her shoulder refused to allow her to stir another step.

"I didn't want to dine with you," Jake admitted, wheeling to face him. "And I don't even give a damn about our stilted conversation. All I've wanted since the moment I laid eyes on you was this . . ."

The *this* to which he referred was a sizzling kiss that took the breath from Cori. The calamity at the supper table was instantly forgotten as soon as Jake lifted her off the deck and molded her into his muscular contours.

Fire leaped onto Cori's nerve endings as Jake's lips crushed hers. His tongue probed into the recesses of her mouth, stealing her breath, leaving her gasping for air. And suddenly Cori didn't care if she ever drew another breath. His explosive kiss was more than enough to sustain her while she swirled in the dizzying undercurrents of phenomenal desire.

The feel of his masculine body against hers sent wildfire spurting through her bloodstream. Cori couldn't have voiced a protest if her life depended on it. She was sinking into the dimensions of a dark, sensual world that lured her deeper into its supernatural spell.

To her surprise, she was suddenly kissing him back when she should have been clubbing him over the head for taking outrageous privileges. Her betraying body responded as it had the first time he had dared to kiss her. Pent-up emotion came pouring out like a swift-flowing underground spring that had just been tapped.

Never had a man evoked such dramatic sensations from her with his kisses and his possessive embraces. Usually Cori remained cold and unfeeling when amorously assaulted. But tonight she was like dry kindling ignited by this human torch. Jacob touched her and she tingled. He kissed her and she felt hot and shaky and completely out of control! Thunderation, what was the matter with her?

Jacob didn't know what had gotten into him, either. The previous moment he had been frustrated beyond words. And now it was as if he had come home from a long restless voyage that had spanned thirty-one years. This firebrand, as elusive as the wind, evoked needs in him that transcended physical desire. It was as if his very soul were reaching out to hers through this haze of boiling passion, calling to him, compelling him to satisfy this monstrous craving that had sprung out of nowhere.

Although Jake feared Cori was right in saying they weren't the least bit compatible, they definitely set off sparks in each other. She seemed to bring out the worst in him until she melted in his arms. Suddenly, this mysterious reaction between them felt ever so right.

Instinctively, his hands began to roam, to investigate the luscious swells and shapely curves beneath her trim-fitting gown. He resented the hindering garments that deprived his fingertips the pleasure of running over her soft skin, of discovering the location of each sensitive point . . .

"Jake! Don't you think you're rushing it a bit? My God, you've only just made a disaster of supper!"

Dal Blaylock's voice echoed from the shadowed stairway. His condescending comment was like a bucket of cold water tossed on a campfire. With an embarrassed shriek, Cori wormed for freedom. Steadying herself against the gingerbread lattice of the railing, she mustered what was left of her dignity and forced herself to meet Dal's disapproving stare.

Jake positioned himself in front of Cori like a shield and glowered at his oldest and dearest friend—rat that he was turning out to be. "I don't recall inviting you to interrupt us, Dal," he growled sarcastically.

"It seems someone should," Dal rapped out. It was fortunate the darkness disguised the color of his face.

"You are taking unfair advantage of the lady. She is fully aware that her position on board the *Belle* might be in jeopardy if she doesn't cater to your whims!"

Cori could feel Jake's massive body go taut at the insult. Before these two men came to blows, Cori thrust herself between them. "What happened simply happened," she declared for lack of logical explanation. "And as I stated earlier this afternoon, I am perfectly capable of taking care of myself. I don't need an endless stream of white knights rushing to my rescue." To Dal, she said, "Your concern is touching, but you must learn not to meddle in my affairs."

"But this afternoon, while we were strolling the promenade, you indicated that . . ." Dal tried to object.

"Never mind what I indicated then!" Cori cut in. "Pay attention to what I'm saying now. I am bound to no man. I have made no promise to anyone, nor do I intend to. I am free to see whom I wish, whenever I wish. I am no man's property! Have I made myself clear?"

"Perfectly," both men replied simultaneously.

Cori inhaled a deep breath and struggled for composure. "And now, if you gentlemen will excuse me, I have to tend my wound and change my clothes. Needless to say, I am canceling my performance tonight. My headache has just returned in full force, thanks to the two of you."

In a flash, Cori sailed down the deck and let herself into her room before slamming the door with a decisive bang.

"That was a low blow, Dal," Jake growled, finding himself in his first bona fide argument with his best friend. "I resent your remark very much!"

"And I sorely resent the fact that you are beating my time with her!" Dal sneered. "This afternoon, I had the distinct impression that Cori was warming to me, that she preferred my company. I treated her like a lady and now I find you pouncing on her like a dog on a bone!"

57

"You didn't hear her object, did you?" Jake smirked, determined to get Dal's goat. Sure as hell, he did.

"How the devil could she protest when you were smothering her with kisses? God only knows what else you were doing to her that I couldn't see from my position on the steps!"

"She kissed me back," Jake informed him.

"And she kissed me back this afternoon," Dal spewed in irritation.

"Then you were also taking advantage," Jake harshly accused. "It seems the pot is calling the kettle black!"

"I intend to ask for her hand in marriage tomorrow night after she accompanies me to dinner," Dal declared.

"*If* she accompanies you to dinner," Jake clarified.

"She has already accepted the invitation," Dal said smugly.

"And I already asked her to marry me," Jake announced, grinning in wicked delight when Dal staggered back as if he had been jabbed in the belly.

"When?" he howled in frustration.

"This afternoon, before I kissed her the first time," Jake needled his distressed friend.

"Well, if that isn't the most ridiculous . . ."

"All's fair in love and war, I believe you said," Jake snickered as he sauntered away. "She's going to marry me, Dal. You may as well accept that."

"We'll just see about that, *friend!*" Dal made the word sound like a curse. At the moment, that's exactly how he meant it.

"Indeed we shall, *friend,*" Jake retaliated.

"The battle is on!" Dal proclaimed as he stalked off in the opposite direction.

"That suits me just fine!" Jake remarked over his shoulder as he stomped toward the pilothouse to relieve Terrance.

*　　　*　　　*

A pensive frown creased Jake's brow as he sat at the small table in the long cabin that ran the entire length of the boat. Even the creak of stateroom doors that opened on both sides of the main saloon didn't faze him because he was immersed in thought. Blankly, he glanced toward the stern end of the room, where a small portion of the cabin had been partitioned off during certain times of day for the ladies to chat in privacy and enjoy the racks of books in the library. Jake lounged at the opposite extreme of the long cabin that was known as the gentlemen's social hall, where brandy smashes, milk punches, mint juleps, and eggnogs were handed back and forth across the heavily crowded bar.

Jake enjoyed his pensive reverie until a blonde by the name of Sarah Wade flounced forward, strutting her fine feathers. The past two days Sarah had attached herself to Jacob like a limpet to a rock the instant he returned from the pilothouse or an encounter with Cori. Although Jake had allowed Sarah to clutch at him like a leech each time he noticed Cori and Dal strolling about, the blathering girl was merely a prop to sustain his sinking spirits. But Sarah chattered like a magpie and Jake found himself preferring his awkward conversations with Cori to Sarah's incessant voice, which reminded him of a clanging gong.

While the widow Wade unveiled her life story, which was as riveting and interesting as a textbook, Jake focused his attention on his cousin Layton. His rotund relative, two years older than Jake, had shoved his barrel-shaped body up against a table that was surrounded by prospective investors. Champagne flowed like a river and Layton was putting on airs he would never possess. Jake could hear Layton boasting about the extravagant steamer, which exceeded all others in space and design.

Despite Layton's efforts, several of his guests were lured to the corner table where a man, who looked to be fifty or thereabout, bedecked in elegant clothes and expensive jewels, sat shuffling cards. Jake peered at the flashy character, whose rich baritone voice seemed to naturally draw attention. There was a melodic quality about the gambler's voice that was appealing to the ear.

In quiet amusement, Jake watched his cousin scowl as his companions abandoned him to take their chances with the mustached man whom Jake had tabbed as a gambler and a good one, no doubt. The rogue had that look about him, not to mention a warm, easygoing personality that attracted individuals like flies to sugar. Jake reckoned this particular gambler could be the life of any party; his mere presence and voice attracted attention.

Jake was well aware that dozens of fortunes had been won and lost on the river. Waterborne palaces like this one were a gambler's haven because of the ever-changing lists of passengers, many of whom carried large bankrolls. Long monotonous hours on steamers tempted many a traveler to the gaming tables. The more arrogant ones always seemed to wind up fleeced by a skillful gambler.

He recalled that on one journey upriver two years earlier, a young merchant, who had collected twenty-five thousand dollars from northern investors, found himself suckered into a game of poker. He lost the entire roll of cash, which wasn't even his to begin with. The poor man had been so horrified by what he'd done that in a moment of madness he attempted suicide. Jake had yanked the despairing gentleman off the railing and back to safety in the nick of time. Then he had challenged the seedy gambler, whom he suspected of cheating. Rather than face Jake's meaty fists and the Colt that was aimed at his chest, the gambler forfeited his winnings and departed the instant the steamer pulled ashore to wood up . . .

"A handsome man like you should be married," Sarah declared, squeezing Jake's arm to gain his attention. "Why, I have even been considering marrying again myself. It has been two years since my dear Henry died, and a woman needs a competent man to take care of her."

Jacob assessed the mildly attractive blonde of twenty-seven, wondering if she would be suitable marriage material if he lost Cori to Dal. The mere thought of settling for this chatterbox instead of the mystifying Cori Pierce turned Jake's stomach.

Although Jake had assured himself that one wife would serve as well as another, he couldn't quite picture himself tolerating Sarah Wade day in and day out. And no doubt, Jake had set his sights a mite too high when he declared the fiery Cori Pierce would be his bride. In the first place, she didn't appear to be interested in marrying, period! And in the second place, Dal was also beating down her door, vying for her attention. And last of all, Jake had made an ass of himself in every encounter with Cori. *Except when they kissed*, he reminded himself with a faint smile. In those instances, different kind of sparks flew . . .

His thoughts trailed off as Cori sailed through the door, waving to acquaintances and flashing smiles to rival the brilliance of the sun. Sarah was immediately forgotten, for Cori's stunning presence commanded the attention of every passenger in the cabin. The room was suddenly sizzling with electricity, and Jake was aching for this intriguing minx up to his eyebrows.

The orchestra burst into a fast-tempoed tune and a voice so clear and vibrant that it sent goose bumps skidding down Jake's spine filled the room. Lord, the woman had an incredible voice! Jake was amazed and impressed.

He sat there, stunned to the bone. He had heard glowing accolades about Cori's talents but he presumed that her arresting good looks had a great deal to do with the praise heaped on her. In fact, he figured Layton had hired her for her physical assets alone, even if she couldn't carry a tune. But it was readily apparent that

Cori was teeming with exceptional talent. She could indeed sing her way into the hearts of her audience while she flirted outrageously. She wandered through the maze of tables, caressing the shoulders of male patrons and accepting an occasional hug from those who had a tad too much to drink.

It was no wonder Terrance Sykes proclaimed this bewitching goddess to be a paradox. Sometimes she was as wary as a doe. Other times, like now, she was bubbly and seductive and playful. And occasionally, she was like ten passions seeking release at once.

"Ah, to possess that voice and such theatrical poise," Sarah sighed enviously. "The rest of us don't have a prayer when Cori sings."

Jake didn't bother to add that her curvaceous body was another of Cori's fascinating assets. Sarah was already jealous of what she considered to be her fierce competition. How well Jake knew that feeling. When Cori eased a hip onto Dal's knee during the last chorus of her song, Jake felt the jealous green monster straining against the chains in the dungeon of his mind.

And the situation grew worse, or better, depending on one's perspective. Cori's next musical selection was a fast-paced folk tune, to which she danced a jig. Hands came together to clap with the beat of the music while Cori sang and danced her way around the room like a winged fairy.

Applause bulged from the saloon when the song ended and the vivacious beauty in red silk bounded from a stool onto the bar that lined the adjacent wall. Not only could Cori sing like a bird, but she was so light on her feet that it seemed they never even touched the bar she employed as her stage.

The place was hopping until an unidentified passenger charged into the saloon sounding a shout of alarm. "There's been a robbery!" he trumpeted.

Bodies flew out of chairs in haste to pursue the thief.

Jake shot from the table and elbowed people out of his way to reach the boiler deck. In the distance he could hear one of the passengers cursing and swearing. Just as Jake rounded the promenade he heard a splash.

"There!" The victim shouted as he whipped out his pistol and unloaded it on the shadowed form. "That scoundrel! I hope he sinks to the bottom of the river before he can spend my money!"

Two more shots discharged on the shapeless object that sank into the murky depths like a grotesque sea monster retreating to safety.

"Are you sure that was the man who attacked you?" Jake demanded of the victim.

"Who else would leap overboard?" the victim snorted furiously. "The thief was wearing a black cape and a wide-brimmed hat that shadowed his bearded face. He appeared out of nowhere, rammed a pistol through my backbone and frisked me!"

The indignant passenger inhaled a frustrated breath and raged on. "When my assailant dashed down the deck, I chased after him. Then I heard the splash on the other side of the ship. That bastard is probably trying to swim ashore with my bankroll, damn him to hell!"

"Not again!" Layton muttered as he wedged his stout body through the clustered crowd. "I'm so sorry, Robert. We will do everything humanly possible to . . ."

"If you think I'm going to invest in this glorified pirate ship, Layton, you better think again," Robert spluttered in outrage.

"My pocket has been picked!" Someone shouted from the middle of the crowd.

Jake swung about to locate the source of the voice. The most recent victim, assuming he had been frisked during the mashing of bodies that congregated around the man who had been robbed, doubled his fist and thrust it into a nearby face. A fight instantly broke out, turning the group of passengers into an unruly mob.

"Enough!" Layton bellowed and then groaned as an unidentified fist plowed into his sagging jowls.

Jake didn't bother trying to break up the fight. Instead, he dashed around the corner to survey the opposite side of the steamer. It seemed inconceivable to him that the thief had leaped overboard in this particular stretch of the river. The current was swift and the spring rains had left the river high above its banks. Unless he missed his guess (and he doubted that he had), the sly thief had dumped an object overboard and then circled back to pick a convenient pocket before hell broke loose all over again. The river pirate could now slip back to his cabin and no one would be the wiser . . .

The sound of footsteps above him on the hurricane deck caused Jake to freeze in his tracks. He shinnied up the support beam like a chimpanzee and grasped the railing that surrounded the upper deck. Agilely, he hopped to his feet in time to see a billowing cape and a darkly clad body darting around the corner. Jake took off like a shot, skidding around the corner just as a cabin door creaked open and shut.

A dubious frown furrowed his brow when he realized how near he was to Cori's cabin. How well he remembered being miffed by the sound of an unidentified voice in Cori's room that first afternoon. In light of what had just happened, demons of curiosity danced in Jake's mind.

Purposefully, he stamped toward Cori's cabin and rapped on the door. He had already decided that if he received no answer he would break down the door. Something fishy was going on and he was bound and determined to get to the bottom of it!

When Jake was met with silence, he lowered his shoulder and prepared to ram through the door. With a full head of steam, he plowed forward . . .

Chapter 5

At the very moment that Jake came plunging toward the door Cori, garbed in a robe, swung open the portal to her cabin.

Jake barreled into the room like a charging rhinoceros. Cori's startled squawk broke the silence. She was mashed back between the wall and the swinging door. Jake's dull groan followed Cori's pained moan. He had crashed into the bed before he could stop.

Like a disturbed hornet, Cori buzzed out from behind the door that had smashed her nose against the left side of her face. She wasn't angry, she was positively livid with fury. With black eyes blazing, Cori breathed fire down upon the body of the man who lay sprawled on her bed.

"You clumsy imbecile!" she fumed, her voice growing higher and wilder by the syllable. "What the devil are you trying to do, kill me? Thunderation, you've blackened my eye, fractured my skull and kneecap, and now you've practically broken my nose!"

She paused to ensure her nose was all right. "I'll be lucky if I survive this jaunt down the Mississippi! I was hired to sing and dance, but I won't be able to speak or walk if you don't start taking a wide berth around me!" She sucked in an aggravated breath and plunged on.

"You are a human time bomb waiting to go off, Jacob Wolf. It is little wonder that you cleared the Missouri for travel. You are a one-man army!"

Jacob braced himself on both elbows and blinked bewilderedly at the pert brunette. "How'd you get back here so quickly?"

"Unlike you and the rest of the bats, *I* took the stairway," she flashed in her most sarcastic voice. "Do you behave like this often, Mr. *Were*wolf, or does this sort of thing only happen when the moon is full?"

"I was chasing a thief," Jacob announced as he pushed himself upright on the bed.

"Well, you won't find one in here. There is only me and my shadow, which, by the way, is as bruised and battered as I am, thanks to you."

A quiet rap rattled the door and Cori's eyes widened in alarm. Thunderation, the last thing she needed right now was for the individual on the outside of the door to come face to face with the gorilla of a man inside her room. "Go away! I'm in the middle of an argument with an idiot!" she shouted at the portal before resuming her tirade.

Damnation, Jacob Wolf had a terrible sense of timing. He was the last person she wanted to see at this moment. He was going to botch everything up if he kept barreling in on her when she wasn't expecting him. Sweet mercy, it was difficult enough as it was to handle Jacob when she *was* expecting him!

"Who do you suppose that could have been?" Jacob queried, studying her with deliberate scrutiny. He had seen that flash of panic in her brown eyes before she expertly masked her emotions.

"Probably Dal," she retorted. "I was supposed to meet him after my performance."

That shut Jacob up like a clam, thank the Lord.

Jake glared at her as he unfolded his powerful frame from her bed. "I don't appreciate your stringing Dal and me along at the same time," he muttered resentfully.

"I don't appreciate your bursting into my room, either. That makes us even," she shot back. "My life is my own and I answer to no man!" She made a stabbing gesture with her arm. "Now kindly remove yourself from my cabin so I can dress. My escort is expecting me. I only hope he recognizes me with my face swelled up like a pumpkin!"

Jake detested this feeling of helplessness that overcame him whenever he confronted Cori Pierce. She kept his emotions rocking up and down like a seesaw. He was suspicious and jealous and fascinated . . . and damned frustrated!

"Make up your mind which one of us you want," he scowled into her bewitching features.

"Don't dictate to me," she spouted.

"Are you going to stand there and tell me my kisses have no effect on you?" he challenged out of the blue. "For if you do, I'll call you a liar!"

Cori didn't deny it. She couldn't. He knew as well as she did that he unleashed forbidden desires in her that threatened to burn out of control. "They affect me," she begrudgingly admitted. "But I don't *like* the effect they have on me."

"Why not?" A roguish smile caught the corner of his mouth and his green eyes twinkled triumphantly.

They had passed the first milestone. Cori hadn't said she liked him and she probably never would, stubborn and strong-willed as she was. But at least she had confessed to feel something besides anger.

Cori presented her back and squared her shoulders. "You rattle me. I never feel safe when you're underfoot. It's like walking through a field of land mines, if you must know."

"And how do Dal's kisses effect you, Cori?"

She flinched when that deep resonant voice came from

67

so close behind her that she could feel vibrations on her skin. "That isn't any of your business," she squeaked.

"If I'm on one side of this triangle, it certainly is," he murmured as he traced the swanlike column of her throat.

He smiled wryly to himself when he felt her tremble beneath his light caress. Cori had a sensitive point just beneath her ear—her right ear, to be exact. Jake stroked that vulnerable spot again and received the same response. His lips followed, whispering their way down to the collar of her flannel robe.

"I think you had better leave," Cori whispered. Her hands gripped the back of the chair for support. Thunderation, if he didn't stop what he was doing she would melt all over him!

"I think I had better stay . . ." he murmured as his hands stole around her waist, pulling her against him, letting her feel his desire for her.

Cori's legs were about to fold up like an accordion. Valiantly, she battled to ignore the warm flood of pleasure his kisses and caresses evoked. Her heart hammered against her ribs, and an unfamiliar fire began to burn in the core of her being.

"I'm not . . ." She faltered and tried again. "I'm not what you think, Jacob, and I . . ."

"What do I think?" he queried as his greedy kisses flooded back up her neck to the vulnerable spot beneath her ear.

She not only heard his husky question, she felt it vibrating across her flesh, starting more disturbing fires. "I'm . . . not . . . experienced with men. I wouldn't know how to please you . . ."

"Let me be the judge of that, sweet witch," he replied, his voice raspy with unappeased passion.

Cori had known from the beginning that she was in way over her head in regard to Jacob Wolf. But the

68

situation had become progressively worse with each hour she had spent with him. And now, when he assaulted her with tantalizing kisses and titillating caresses she could feel herself sinking deeper and deeper.

Jacob Wolf was many things—a six-foot-four-inch headache, to be sure—but he had the most remarkably tender way with a woman. Cori had always prided herself in her ability to resist men's advances. But Jacob was an altogether different matter. He turned her inside out and her sharp wits always failed her when he ventured this close. He aroused her in the most incredible ways, leaving her wanting things she had cautiously avoided all twenty years of her life . . .

The world careened about her when his adventurous hands tunneled inside her robe to trace the underswell of her breast. Her nerves screamed as a tidal wave of arousing sensations washed over her. Each inch of flesh that he dared to touch burned as if it had been scorched by a hot branding iron.

Cori struggled to grasp at reality but it flitted away as Jacob's masculine scent invaded her senses, clouding logic. Every ragged breath she inhaled was thick with his tantalizing aroma. The feel of his masculine body pressed to hers lured her with intimate promises of mysterious pleasure. His tender touch destroyed the last of her defenses and transformed her will into his own . . .

A choked gasp broke from her throat when his hand cupped her breast and his thumb glided over the taut peak. Thought abandoned her entirely when Jacob turned her in his arms. His lips came crushing down on hers, stealing the breath from her lungs. She could feel his heartbeat thudding in accelerated rhythm, matching her own. She swore the floor beneath her feet shifted.

Faintly, Cori recalled the remark she'd made to Dal a few short days ago—the one about what happened between her and Jake simply happening without planning

69

or forethought. It was no one's fault, she realized. The chemistry between her and his swarthy giant just existed, like the moon's lure on the tides, like the wind's fierce tug on a high-flying kite. Even common sense seemed to have no bearing on this phenomenal response they had to each other. The fierce magnetism demanded reactions.

"I want you," Jake breathed hoarsely.

And indeed he did. He wanted Cori in a way he'd never wanted another woman. Male instinct tormented him. Fiery passion haunted him. He didn't give a damn if there was a thief running around loose on the *Mississippi Belle*. He had Cori in his arms and the sparks between them leaped back and forth like lightning darting from one cloud to another.

A team of wild horses couldn't have dragged Jake away from this tempting beauty. He was aware that it was too soon to expect intimacy from a woman like Cori. She openly confessed she knew nothing about what transpired between a man and a woman. And yet reason was no match for the unruly passion that gnawed at him. With each passing second, it became less a matter of *wanting* this luscious angel and more of an addictive *need* to have her in his arms. Holding her felt so incredibly right!

That thought penetrated his mind as he devoured her honeyed lips with ardent impatience. His hands glided beneath her robe, slowly pushing it from her shoulders until it lay in a pool at her feet.

An embarrassed blush blossomed on her cheeks as his all-consuming gaze measured her scantily clad figure. The frilly chemise hovered above the roseate buds of her breasts, revealing the trim indentation of her waist and the shapely flesh of her thighs.

Jake studied Cori's unrivaled beauty like a connoisseur of fine art scrutinizing a masterpiece. She was absolutely exquisite—just as he'd imagined she would be while he lay alone in his bed each night, visualizing what it would be like to make wild sweet love to her. Spellbound, Jake hooked his thumbs under the shoulder straps and drew the chemise to her waist, unveiling her silken flesh to his admiring gaze.

Awkwardly, Cori tried to cover herself, but Jake grasped her hands and pressed them to his chest. Nimbly, he unbuttoned his shirt and slid her fingertips over the dark matting of hair that covered his bronze skin.

"The only shame you should feel is that other women will never possess such exquisite beauty," he murmured as he bent his head to nibble at her quivering lips. "You're the stuff men's dreams are made of."

On their own accord, Cori's hands swam across the whipcord muscles, marveling at their strength. She had never dared such things with a man before, had never been pushed to this point of no return. But once she touched this sleek lion of a man, her inhibitions abandoned her. She became bold and more inquisitive by the second. She surrendered to his kiss and let the world glide carelessly away. Cori suddenly wanted nothing more than to explore the mysterious realm of passion she had denied herself for twenty years.

She didn't even remember taking his shirt off, but she must have since Jacob was no longer wearing one. Her wide eyes scanned his expansive chest, watching his muscles ripple and flex beneath her exploring caress. Touching him was like stroking a lean, powerful panther. Jacob was a magnificent sight to behold, incredible to touch. Caressing him prompted another wave of compelling sensations to undulate through her naive body, making her ache in a few dozen more places she never dreamed she had.

"Am I supposed to feel like this?" Cori gasped in a strangled breath, her eyes wide with wonder.

"How do you feel, Princess?" he queried as his skillful hands sketched intricate patterns on her breasts and ribs.

71

"Like a marshmallow that has been burned to a crisp on the outside and melted to its very core . . ." Cori gasped when his moist lips drifted over the dusky peaks to suckle at her breasts. "What are you doing?"

"What does it feel like I'm doing?" he whispered before flicking at the throbbing peak with his tongue.

"Driving me crazy . . ." Cori moaned when his hands trailed down her hips to stroke her trembling flesh while his tongue continued to tease the throbbing peaks.

"Driving you crazy with pleasure?" Jake murmured as he limned the satiny flesh of her thighs.

"Or something . . . I'm not sure what . . ."

Her breath stuck in her throat as his fingertips glided between her thighs to tease and excite. Sweet mercy, he had unleashed the wildest sensations imaginable. White-hot fire burned in the core of her being and Cori was helpless to contain her breathless gasp as his knowing fingers delved deeper to explore her womanly softness. He made her want him as if he were a mindless addiction. And when he drew her naked body against his, she could feel the throb of his manhood against her abdomen. The intimate contact caused an internal explosion and Cori felt herself trembling all over.

Just when she would have inhaled much-needed air to counter the dizzy feelings that swamped her, Jacob took her lips under his and kissed the last ounce of breath out of her. The hot, sweet ache channeled through every fiber of her being. Cori resigned herself to death by wondrous torment. Her body was still shaking like an earthquake, hounding her with a need she couldn't quite understand and was unsure how to go about appeasing.

When Cori instinctively arched against him, Jake shuddered uncontrollably. With an agility that usually escaped him when he was under this mysterious sorceress's spell, he hooked his elbow under her knees and lifted her into his arms. He carried her to bed and gently laid her down before stepping back to shed his trousers.

Owl-eyed and breathless, Cori gaped at the towering giant who loomed above her. She had never seen a naked man, and the jolt knocked what little breath she had left right out of her.

Jacob Wolf would put a Roman god to shame, she mused as her gaze sketched his awe-inspiring physique. He was a vision of invincible strength. His body rippled with finely honed muscles and bronzed flesh. Whatever he had been doing upriver on the Missouri he hadn't been doing it with all his clothes on, that was for sure! He was tanned all over like a brown-skinned warrior. All that marred his well-sculptured contours was the white scar that stretched across his shoulder—the visible reminder of his confrontation with an Indian war party.

A wry smile quirked Jake's lips as he watched Cori study him with feminine appreciation. She made him feel every inch a man. Obviously, she liked what she saw.

Before Cori could come to her senses and protest, Jake bent a knee and eased down beside her. "I think, sweet witch, that making love to you is going to be a new experience for me as well . . . I want you in ways I never thought it possible to want a woman . . ."

His mouth captured hers in a hypnotic kiss while his practiced hands investigated every part of her curvaceous body. He left not one inch of her satiny flesh untouched.

This gentle giant devasted her. Cori could no more have contested his intentions than she could have flown to the moon. This green-eyed magician provoked hot bubbling sensations that made mincemeat of her emotions and sensitized her innocent body. He made her want him madly, made her crave the intimacy of lovemaking.

Cori wasn't sure what had overcome her, but she was

73

suddenly as curious about him as he seemed to be about her. She yearned to memorize the feel of his hair-roughened flesh beneath her untutored fingertips. Her hands cruised over his broad shoulder to count his ribs and measure the padding of muscles that covered his hips.

Jake's muffled groan encouraged her to continue her bold explorations. Shamelessly, Cori tracked her hands over the masculine columns of his thighs and then enfolded his swollen manhood . . .

Whatever she had done, it must have been the wrong thing, she instantly decided. A low growl erupted from his throat as he pressed her to her back. Or perhaps it was the *right* thing to do, Cori mused as his sensuous lips devoured hers in a hungry kiss. She must have unwittingly aroused this giant past the limits of his self-control. She could hear his rough breathing, feel his hands swirling impatiently over her flesh.

Each answering caress caused flames to leap across her body. Cori swore she was about to go up in smoke. His ardent fondling and ravishing kisses stripped her of her sanity. She was like a helpless creature of need, a need so fierce and urgent that it demanded fulfillment.

As Jacob guided her thighs apart with his knee, Cori gave no thought whatsoever to resisting. Her body was his to command. He had made her want to be as close as a man and women could get . . .

A sharp gasp broke from her throat when his lithe body uncoiled upon hers. Pain stabbed through the haze of pleasure that enshrouded her and she pressed the heels of her hands to his rockhard chest to shove him away.

"No, Cori." Jake's voice was firm and yet amazingly gentle.

Frightened, she peered up into his rugged features, watching the lantern light flicker in the golden flecks that splattered his garnet green eyes.

"After the first pain of initiation I swear I'll never hurt you again," he promised as he bent to feather his lips over her quivering mouth. He moved, just so, penetrating the barrier to womanhood. He felt Cori stiffen beneath him and he waited until she adjusted to the unfamiliar feel of a man's body intimately invading hers. Exhibiting more patience and tenderness than he had ever displayed with a woman, he withdrew. Deliberately, he came back to her, offering another drugging kiss. And ever so slowly the pain became a wanton flame that filled her core with passion's mindless fire. He moved within her, gently at first, setting the sweet hypnotic cadence of love that was as ancient and mystifying as time itself.

Cori clung to him, bewildered by the swift-flowing current of passion that swept her up and carried her away from reality's shore. He brought her naive body to life with his tender lovemaking and riveted her with undefinable sensations that threatened to shatter her sanity. Suddenly, she was arching to meet his deep thrusts, craving to satisfy this sweet maddening ache that he had so skillfully aroused in her.

And then it came, like an internal explosion that devastated her senses and shattered her composure. The wild, breathless feelings that had piled upon one another burst like a volcanic eruption. Aftershocks undulated through her body as Jake shuddered above her and clutched her to him as if he meant to squeeze the life out of her.

Cori's journey back from the far-reaching perimeters of ecstasy was like the drifting of a weightless feather in the wind. She felt oddly content as she nestled against Jake's sturdy shoulder. Absently, she traced the cleft in his chin and the smile lines that bracketed his sensuous mouth.

"Is it always like this?" she surprised herself by asking. Cori blushed seven shades of red when Jake broke

75

into a rakish grin.

Studying the flush of color in her cheeks, he combed the dark tendrils of hair from her face. "Not always, no," he assured her huskily. "Sex is absolutely nothing like this."

Cori's thick black lashes fluttered up as she eased far enough away to assess his teasing smile. "I thought that was what we just had," she blurted out without thinking, embarrassing herself all over again.

"We made wild sweet love, naive little imp," Jacob corrected with a quiet chortle. "There's a difference." The roguish grin evaporated from his craggy features to be replaced by an expression Cori couldn't decipher. "And God forbid that you ever have to learn what that difference is . . ."

When his voice dropped to a seductive level and his expert hands began to rekindle the smoldering coals of desire, Cori forgot the questions that stampeded to the tip of her tongue. All she could remember was the ineffable pleasure she had discovered in Jacob's possessive embrace. He knew how to make a woman respond in total abandon, how to crumble her inhibitions and leave her wanting all he had to offer. When she was in Jake's embrace it was as if she were in a dark sensual dimension of time that defied rhyme or reason.

Jacob could spin a magical spell over her and create a universe of phenomenal sensations. Cori was hopelessly entranced by him. When he came to her again she welcomed him, confessing the pleasure he gave her. There was no pain, only wondrous feelings of rapture that exceeded her first experience with passion.

Her body cried out to his and her soul swelled with the splendor of being one with this magnificent man. And much later, when the fog of rapture faded, Cori propped herself up on an elbow to brush her forefinger over the muscular wall of his chest. She adored touching him,

76

reveled in the awesome strength that lay just beneath his bronzed flesh.

"You must have been with scores of women to be such an expert in loving . . ." she mused aloud.

Odd, the thought of another woman enjoying the same tantalizing pleasures he'd taught her struck an exposed nerve. Cori frowned at the unexpected stab of jealousy. She had no right to be possessive of Jake. *She had no reason to become intimate with him, either!* What had she done in a momentary lapse of sanity? Thunderation, it wasn't like her to succumb to a man just because he wanted her physically. She never had yielded before! Why had she now? And why to a man who stood squarely between her and her long crusade?

Jake noticed the conflicting emotions that chased each other across her exquisite features. He could feel her retreating. It was as if she had erected an invisible wall between them.

"Don't," he commanded, pulling her down onto his chest to peer straight into those chocolate brown eyes that mirrored mystifying depths of character. "I told you that what's between us wasn't lust. It's much more than that. Don't start regretting what happened between us. It's rare and special."

"Is it?" Her voice quavered with self-guilt and frustration. "We have barely known each other a week. When we're near each other things happen, things that leave me battered and confused." She tried to withdraw but Jake refused to release her. "I have a bruise for every time we've been together."

"I'm not usually so clumsy," he tittered as he smoothed away her skeptical frown. "It's just that you throw me completely off balance."

"I'm not so sure that's a good thing," Cori protested as another wave of guilt buffeted her. "Look where we wound up when we fell off balance this time!"

"Our lovemaking more than compensates for our blunders," he murmured softly, sketching her delicate features. "It doesn't get better than this, Cori."

"And I suppose you should know, being an expert with women," she muttered acrimoniously.

"Jealous?" he teased, arching a thick brow.

"Don't be silly. Why should I?" she said to save face.

"You have no reason to be," he assured her frankly. "I'll be the model husband after we marry."

Reality hit her like a sledgehammer. Jacob had seduced her, thinking that would force her to accept his proposal. Why that sneaky lout! While she had been lost to his skillful lovemaking he had been plotting to get himself a wife so he could fill his home with children! But because of who he was she couldn't marry him under any circumstances . . .

A wild desperate flicker replaced the mellow expression that had shadowed her eyes moments before. "I can't marry you!" she insisted. "No matter how you schemed to get yourself a wife, you are still my enemy . . ." Cori slammed her mouth shut when her runaway tongue outdistanced her brain.

"Enemy?" Jake frowned disconcertedly. Her remark reminded him of the mysterious conversation he had heard behind closed doors the first day he met her. "You sound as if you're a foreign country and we're engaged in a war!"

Cori squirmed away from his chest and groped for her robe. "I think you had better leave."

"Not until I know what you meant by that comment. And I won't stir a step until you tell me who was in your cabin that first day when you swore to me that no one was here," he said sharply.

Cori was becoming more flustered by the second. "I think it would be best if we didn't see each other again," she said with a finality Jake detested.

He opened his mouth to object but the rap at the door

interrupted him. "Hell's fire, what is this? A railroad depot? I never saw so much traffic," he grumbled, half under his breath.

Cori fled from bed and tossed Jake's clothes at him. "Give me a moment please!" Cori called to her visitor.

"Give me an hour," Jake mutterd sourly.

Cori glared him into silence and then stared at the door. "Who is it?"

"Dal," came the rich male voice from the deck.

Jake swore a string of curses.

Frantically, Cori grabbed a nearby gown and, with no regard for modesty, wormed into it in record time. Jake had just stood up to fasten his breeches when Cori yanked him down by the hair of the head, gesturing for him to crawl under the bed. Hiding from Dal Blaylock was the last thing Jake intended. He had staked his claim on this sassy beauty and she was his in ways no other man had ever enjoyed. But the pleading expression in Cori's eyes prompted him to slither under the bed and keep his mouth shut.

Inhaling a steadying breath, Cori squared her shoulders, pasted on a dazzling smile and marched toward the door. Without a backward glance, she sailed outside and looped her arm around Dal's elbow. "I could use a breath of air," she announced. "Would you be so kind as to escort me around the deck?"

"With pleasure, my love," Dal purred provocatively.

"With pleasure, my love," Jake mimicked sarcastically as he wiggled out from under the bed.

He heaved an exasperated sigh as he fastened his garments in place and eased open the door. Grumbling, Jake tiptoed outside to see Cori clinging to Dal. Damn it, he didn't understand that woman, not at all! She had been wild and passionate in his arms, pleasing him in ways he'd never dreamed possible, leaving him to wonder what the blazes he had been doing with all the other females he'd bedded the past decade. Whatever it was, it was nowhere near what he had experienced with that mystifying sprite.

The fact that Cori had yielded to him when she had obviously never allowed another man so close should have made her realize there was something unique between them. But no, she just pulled back like a turtle shrinking into its shell, refusing to admit that she cared for him . . . at least a little.

She *did* care for him, Jake encouraged himself. She must. And she had damned well better not reduce their lovemaking to simple feminine curiosity and an experiment with passion! Things *happened* when they were together. Maybe it wasn't love, but it was a damned sight more than lust! Jacob had certainly been around enough to know, even if Cori hadn't.

Jake was thoroughly frustrated. He was uncomfortable with his new role. In the past, woman had chased him until he allowed them to catch him—the ones he physically desired, that is. He could have had any female he wanted for a wife, but he had selected this stubborn, impossible minx. Now that he had decided to wed and give up his adventurous life he was being punished for all the women he'd loved and left along the way.

Well, I'm not giving up on Cori Lee Pierce, Jacob told himself firmly. He had wanted her the first time he saw her battling Kyle Benson. He liked her style, her spunk, and her irrepressible spirit. She aroused his desires and his admiration.

"One day, Cori Pierce . . ." Jake murmured to the silhouette that lingered beside Dal at the far end of the deck, "I'll hear you say you love me. I'll be damned if you and I are no more than enemies."

Still tormented by the sight of Dal and Cori together, Jake stomped off without the slightest idea where in the hell he was going.

Chapter 6

Discreetly, Cori eased up to the railing beside the elegantly dressed gambler who stood gazing over the river. For the first few minutes, while several passengers strolled past, Cori said nothing. And when she finally did speak, she didn't glance at the mustached man beside her.

"What have you found out about Layton's other prospective investors?" Cori queried quietly.

Skully Shelton braced his forearms on the railing. When a lone passerby was out of earshot, he replied. "They are all carrying huge bankrolls. I let Foster Noles win a thousand dollars from me last night before the commotion of the robbery interrupted our game."

"Is Ben Culver still interested in investing in the *Belle*?" Cori asked without sparing the gambler a glance.

"I think Layton has nearly convinced that conceited lout to sink a healthy sum into the streamer," Skully replied, his gaze fixed on some distant point.

"How is Mr. Culver at the gaming table?" Cori wanted to know.

"Fair competition," Skully reported with a frown. "He cheats."

A faint smile quirked Cori's lips. "Better than you do, Skully? I find that hard to believe."

"He cheats well enough to know when he's been had, I'm afraid," came the muffled reply.

"Which pocket contains his cash roll?" she quizzed him.

"Vest pocket, just above his heart. He packs a snub-nosed derringer in his right coat pocket, along with his expensive gold timepiece."

"What time do you plan to schedule a break in tonight's game?"

Cori pivoted to lean her elbows on the railing and tipped her head, allowing the breeze to caress the long sable mane that flowed down her back. She froze when her uplifted gaze locked with the man who stood above her on the hurricane deck.

Thunderation! She had hoped Kyle Benson had remained ashore in St. Louis after his fracas with Jacob Wolf. But no such luck! Where had that scoundrel been hiding himself the past few days? Probably in a dark secluded corner, snake that he was . . .

Cold blue eyes drilled down at Cori and she stepped away from the railing and out of view to prevent Kyle from glowering at her longer than necessary. She had already received the full effect of his bitter glance. No doubt he held her personally responsible for the loss of his position as captain.

"We'll stop at eleven o'clock to stretch our legs," Skully murmured before turning to amble off in the opposite direction.

Rattled by Kyle's appearance, Cori scurried away, eager to return to her own cabin without confronting Kyle. But as fate would have it, Kyle was stalking down the steps when Cori ascended them.

Raising a proud chin, she climbed the stairs, intent on ignoring Kyle's distasteful presence. Unfortunately, Kyle wouldn't let well enough alone. He roughly grabbed her arm and swung her around to face his vicious sneer.

"Take your hands off me!" Cori hissed, wishing she were armed with her parasol. She would have dearly loved to stab him.

"You cost me my job, bitch," he snarled into her brown eyes. "And you're going to regret it . . ."

"Benson! Take your hands off the lady."

Cori had purposely avoided Jake for two days after their amorous encounter in her room. She had refused to answer when he knocked at her door and she had surrounded herself with other admirers during meals. But in this instance, she was overjoyed to see this brawny giant.

"You have a bad habit of poking your nose in places it doesn't belong, Wolf," Kyle sneered contemptuously. "What's between me and the lady is none of your concern."

"I'm making it my concern," Jake swore as he stalked down the steps.

Kyle Benson was either a slow learner or an irrational fool. Cori wasn't sure which. In any event, he wheeled on Jake to return the punishing blows he had received in St. Louis. It was a critical mistake. Jake was poised and waiting to strike. He blocked the oncoming fist with his left forearm and delivered a right cross that slammed Kyle back against the banister. Once Jake had Kyle's full attention, he reared back and hit the scoundrel squarely between the eyes. With a muffled groan, Kyle tumbled down the last five steps to land at a young woman's feet.

Jake didn't bother to remove Kyle's unconscious form from the steps. He simply grabbed Cori's hand and hauled her up the stairs at a fast clip.

"You've been avoiding me," he accused, cutting right to the point, as was his custom.

83

"I've been extremely busy," Cori defended, attempting to wriggle her hand from his grip, but to no avail.

"Liar," he shot back. "You've had plenty of time to see Dal."

"I've been letting my bumps and bruises heal before I risked your presence again," she snapped testily.

The sight of this powerful mountain of a man caused a crosscurrent of emotions to flood through her like an underground river. She was helplessly attracted to Jake, despite her better judgment. And when the scent of his cologne invaded her senses, memories of their secret rendezvous rose like spirits from shallow graves. She and Jake had dared too much, and now she was paying the consequences by battling her stinging conscience and forbidden longings.

"What is going on between you and Kyle Benson?" Jake demanded, dragging her from her pensive musings.

"Nothing. We're the best of friends," she sassed him.

"Of course you are," he scoffed caustically. "That's why he keeps trying to attack you."

"He wants what every man wants from a woman," Cori spewed, her temper at a rolling boil.

"Except me," Jake clarified.

Cori glowered at him as he whisked her across the hurricane deck. "No? You took what Kyle Benson has been wanting since I hired on this ship, and I would never have let you . . ."

"*Took?*" Jacob pounced on her choice of words. "I took what you gave, if memory serves. Why are you so damned bullheaded, woman? You know as well as I do that there is something special between us."

"There is absolutely nothing between us," Cori retorted, tilting her chin to that proud angle that Jake had come to recognize at a glance. "All you are to me is a mistake I want to forget."

It wasn't true, of course, but pride and conscience put

the words to tongue. Cori didn't appreciate the fierce attraction she felt for Wolf. She was playing a dangerous game of intrigue on board this ship and her relationship with Jacob would thoroughly complicate her crusade. She wanted to forget their night together, to reduce it to feminine curiosity and recklessness. But Jake refused to observe a respectable distance between them, to let her feelings for him die a graceful death. She had given him the cold shoulder each time they chanced to meet, but he was immune to this treatment and he refused to leave her alone.

"I have made more than my share of mistakes," Jake growled at her, frustrated to no end. "You, however, are not one of them! I want to marry you."

"Thunderation, can't you get it through your thick head that I want nothing more to do with you?" Cori railed.

"Why? Because you're afraid you might accidentally fall in love with me?" he had the gall to ask.

"Of all the conceited, arrogant . . . oh!" Cori spouted furiously. "I detest your haughty air, your plainspoken manner, your . . . ouch!"

Cori missed a step when her foot became entangled with the leg of the lounge chair she had passed. "And I hate the way I'm always stumbling around when you're underfoot. You're turning me into a walking disaster, just like you are. Now go away and—"

"Jake!" Terrance Syke's voice boomed from the opened door of the pilothouse above them. "Come up here a minute. I don't like the looks of this bend in the river."

Cori breathed a sigh of relief, thinking the call to duty would be her salvation. She was wrong. Jake clamped a tighter grip on her arm and propelled her toward the steps that led to the top of the steamer.

"This conversation isn't over," he muttered, shoving

her ahead of him.

"I have nothing else to say to you," Cori flared.

"Good, then maybe you'll clam up and listen while I talk."

The instant Jake veered into the pilothouse, he stuffed Cori on the wooden bench on the back wall and brandished a lean finger in her defiant face. "Don't move."

As Jake pivoted, Cori made a face at his broad back and then childishly stuck out her tongue. Terrance bit back a grin. Jacob Wolf had never had trouble handling a woman. Until now, Terrance quickly amended. But Cori Pierce was and always would be a handful. Terrance was assured that his wager was safe. In fact, he was so certain that the odds were in this hellion's favor that he upped the bet that Jake wouldn't tame her, much less marry her.

"Make that fifty dollars, Jake," Terrance snickered before staring out over the river.

Jake's craggy features puckered in a sour frown. He knew exactly what Terrance was referring to, even if Cori didn't have a clue. "What the hell's the emergency?" he grumbled in question.

Terrance focused on the problem at hand. He gestured toward the gnarled trees that lined the west bank of the river where the channel swerved and then disappeared around a narrow, horseshoe bend.

"You suspect a sawyer," Jacob predicted grimly.

Terrance nodded in confirmation. "The river has changed its course since I last navigated it. This stretch looks different. The bank suggests the force of flood water has been tearing away at it."

Cori momentarily forgotten, Jake trained his experienced eye on the canopy of trees that now stood in the river instead of on the bank where it once had been. The Mississippi was notorious for flooding during spring rains and for going where it wanted to go. The current often became so fierce and powerful that it upended trees and gnawed at the shore, causing clumps of earth to slide into the swirling channel.

Rivermen like Jake and Terrance had a special kind of hate for the uprooted trees—the sawyers—that sank into the river. Sometimes the timber harmlessly rotted away. But all too often, a forest giant slid into the channel with clumps of earth still clinging to its tangled roots. The bombardment of other floating debris often broke off the smaller branches, making it difficult for a steamboat pilot to detect disaster until it was too late. These sawyers could slash open the bottom of a steamer and leave her and her passengers to face certain death.

When such a huge tree began to bob with the current, it was often forced down for several minutes before it resurfaced. Too many times, Jake had glanced at what appeared to be a clear stretch of channel only to see a sawyer break through the rippling water like a gnarled, bony hand of a hideous monster reaching up from the depths to claim its victim . . .

"There!" Jake erupted suddenly.

Cori's eyes widened as she followed Jake's gesturing arm to see a gigantic tree trunk bob up just twenty feet in front of them. Both men pounced on the wheel, swerving the vessel at a dangerous angle, attempting to veer away from the winding chute that pulled them downriver.

Below them, on the boiler deck and main deck, frightened shrieks and cries of alarm erupted. The unexpected lurch of the ship caused Cori to fly across the wooden bench on which she sat.

"Damn, look starboard!" Jake scowled. Hurriedly, he grasped the speaking tube to yell down to the engineer in the boiler room. "Reduce steam!"

The huge ship stalled momentarily, but the force of the current caused the vessel to swerve sideways, as if it had been caught in an oversized whirlpool.

87

"Men overboard!" came the terrified squawk from the main deck.

Leadsmen and roustabouts scattered like ants abandoning a contaminated den. Ropes were flung into the river to rescue the passenger and crewman who had been hurtled through the air when the steamer swerved to avoid colliding with the sawyer.

"Drop anchor," Jake ordered abruptly.

Another flurry of activity on the bow of the ship sent men scuttling to halt the steamer's progress before it plowed into the mammoth tree that rose from the river like a demon from the deep.

Cori pushed herself upright on the bench. Although they faced catastrophe, and although shouts of alarm echoed in the wind like a chorus of screeching banshees, her wide eyes were fixed on Jake. There had been times when she swore he was the most awkward creature on the planet. But this ordeal gave her a dramatically different view of the man. He was keen-eyed and competent, rising to the challenge with cool self-assurance. His reflexes were incredibly quick and his knowledge of the Mississippi and steamboats was clearly evident as he exchanged comments with Terrance.

Jacob Wolf had faced these perilous circumstances before. He knew exactly what to expect and how to counter calamity. The fact that he had lost his parents in a steamboat disaster made him all the more determined to ensure history didn't repeat itself. Jake took the safety of the crew and passengers very seriously. Newfound respect dawned in Cori's eyes as she watched Jake assume sole command of the wheel to bring the steamer about.

"Get every available man on deck to grab a pole," Jake ordered without taking his eyes off the swirling current he battled. "I want those damned sawyers staring up at me so I can see how much room I've got to slide safely between them."

88

"Between them? Hell!" Terrance crowed before craning his neck out the door to relay Jake's order. "If you try to cut through there, you'll sheer the paddle-wheels off this steamer."

"It's that or the sandbar," Jake grumbled, nodding his raven head toward the starboard bow. "The river left a reef when she cut this new channel. We'll be two days getting this lady out of that stretch of sand and debris . . . and maybe not at all . . ."

"And if you slice her hull, you'll also bury her and every passenger on board this ship," Terrance grumbled. "I'll take the sand."

Jake scowled when the force of onrushing water sent the vessel sliding sideways once again. "Look closer at the reef," he insisted.

Terrance did look and he didn't like what he saw one bit. A muted curse tumbled from his lips. "Damnation, there are snags all over that reef!"

Cori stood up to peer at the half-submerged barrier of sand that lined the bank. Sure enough, the gnarled branches of underwater trees clogged the quicksand.

"Sit down and back yourself into the corner before this ship comes about and throws you through the glass," Jake barked when he caught Cori's movement out of the corner of his eye.

Cori dropped onto the bench and sat as still as a statue.

"Get those sawyers up!" Jake roared down at the scrambling crew. "I can't hold her much longer!"

A chorus of heave-hos resounded on the main deck as the crew prodded the huge trees upward and kept them visible.

"As soon as you run the chut, the men will lose their grasp on the trees and they'll slam into the stern," Terrance predicted gloomily.

"Get another force of men on the stern to push them back," Jake demanded before reaching for the speaking tube. "Crack steam!"

The order to the engineer sent a huge puff of black smoke rolling from the stacks that bookended the pilothouse. The steamer lurched forward, slamming Cori's head against the wall.

Another wave of panic undulated through the crowd as bodies collided with one another. The groan of the engines and the creak of timber muffled all other sounds.

"Now!" Jake bellowed as he loosed the wheel and let it spin until the vessel righted herself in the river. Muscles strained to loft the snagging trees and the steamer shot forward.

This time Cori braced herself before the lunging steamer caused her to crack her skull again. She had only begun to relax when Layton Breeze's croaking voice wafted its way through the pilothouse.

"You fool! You're going to kill us all," Layton howled as he waddled inside with Kyle Benson one step behind him.

Jake didn't have time to spare his hysterical cousin a glance. He was bent on easing through the maze of disaster without ripping the hull from the steamer.

Layton traditionally fell apart during a crisis. While Jake quickly assessed situations, reviewed his options, and took charge, Layton proceeded to rant and rave and do nothing helpful.

"My God! We're going to perish!" he wailed, his voice clamoring like a gong.

The screech of tree trunks scraping the stern caused every individual on board to tense in wary dread. Crewmen grunted and growled as they shoved the sawyers away, trying desperately to prevent the trees from penetrating the hull.

And suddenly the *Mississippi Belle* was free, chugging merrily on her way as if nothing out of the ordinary had happened.

Cori slumped back against the wall, her eyes wide with relief and admiration at Jake's skills. She had just viewed Jacob from a new angle and she was incredibly impressed! While the rest of the world ran around like decapitated chickens, he assumed command. Jacob Wolf was the kind of man who rose to challenges and defied defeat.

When Jake stepped back to allow Terrance to take control of the wheel, Cori rewarded him with a smile that earned her a bemused frown.

"Are you all right?" Jake questioned.

"I'm in splendid shape, thanks to you," she said with another beaming smile that would have lit a stranded traveler's way through a blizzard.

Jacob didn't have the foggiest notion why the bewitching brunette was staring at him the way she was, but he liked it. Usually she bestowed suspicious glances and cautious frowns on him . . .

"It's a wonder you didn't kill us," Layton blustered as he fumbled for his kerchief to mop the perspiration from his brow and jowls. "You should have let Kyle navigate the river. He knows it like the back of his hand."

"Is that why you've been paying him double the going rate for captains?" Jake shot back, his green eyes cold and accusing.

Suddenly, Layton was on the defense, a position he sorely detested. He puffed up with so much indignation he nearly burst the seam of his tailored white jacket. "I believe in paying good help their due," he defended.

"With pay like that, your ex-captain could have bought the boat in two year's time," Jake snapped brusquely.

The tension in the pilothouse was as thick as hasty pudding. Cori's gaze bounced back and forth between Jake and Kyle and Layton, who were glaring mutinously at each other.

"Jacob?" an unfamiliar face appeared around the edge

91

of the door. "We have several injured passengers who need medical attention and we seem to be low on antiseptic and bandages."

"Just whose fault is that, I wonder?" Jake snorted sarcastically, glaring at his pudgy cousin.

Jake's gaze swung back to Barry Odum, the steward, who peered anxiously at him. "Have the linen napkins and tablecloths cut for bandages and assure our passengers that we will dock at Vicksburg to restock supplies and summon doctors to tend the injured. We should be in Vicksburg by six o'clock, barring another brush with calamity."

"Those napkins and tablecloths are worth a fortune," Layton declared in outrage. "I'll not have you cutting them to shreds."

"You have your orders," Jake said to Barry.

When the young man wheeled away, Jake grasped Cori's hand and pulled her protectively against him before he brushed shoulders with Kyle on his way out. The animosity between Jake and Kyle was clearly evident. Both men were barely tolerating each other.

"I demand that you put Kyle back in charge of this ship," Layton spouted.

"No, he's off the payroll," Jake blared at his flush-faced cousin. His gaze shifted to Terrance Sykes. An ornery smile pursed Jake's lips. "If either of these two men make a move to grab the wheel, shoot them. I'll be back to clean up the mess later."

Leaving the threat dangling in the air, Jake shepherded Cori outside and hustled her down the steps to the hurricane deck.

It was a most impulsive thing to do, Cori knew. But emotions were running high. She wasn't sure why she was stung by the compelling urge to plant a kiss on Jake's sensuous lips, but she did—right in front of God and anybody who cared to watch.

The steamy kiss set Jake back on his heels. It was the first time this mysterious minx had initiated an embrace. He usually found himself fighting his way through her defenses to unlock the passions she tried so hard to hold in check.

"What did I do to deserve that?" Jake queried with a roguish grin. "Whatever it was, I'll be sure to do it again if it will earn me a dozen more kisses like that one."

Remembering herself, Cori glanced around at the curious faces that peered back at her. Upon seeing Dal Blaylock's annoyed scowl, Cori turned beet red. And upon seeing Cori's reaction to Dal's reaction, Jake growled thunderously.

"Is it so important what *he* thinks?" Jake muttered at her. "What am I? The gigolo no one else knows you have while the gallant Dal Blaylock courts you in public?"

"You just don't understand," Cori replied with a frustrated sign, unable to sort out the tangled emotions that hounded her.

"How can I when you're so damned mysterious?" he countered in a most unpleasant tone. "I wound up in your bed and yet you parade the decks on Dal's arm, flirting with him and avoiding me as if I'd contracted leprosy."

"Would I have kissed you just now if I . . ."

Jake cut her short with a derisive snort. "Would you have spent two days playing your cat-and-mouse games with me if you were proud of this thing between us? Do you have any idea how hard you are on a man's pride?"

"Thunderation! I haven't even figured out what is between us," Cori erupted, struggling to keep her voice below a roar.

"I already told you," Jake grumbled. "I want you to be my wife. Does that sound as if all I want from you is a tumble in the sheets?"

His blunt question put another blush on her cheeks. "I

can't marry you." She looked away, refusing to meet his piercing stare.

"You *can't* or you *won't?*" he demanded to know.

"Both." Cori blinked, exasperated by the sting of tears that clouded her eyes.

Frustrated, Jake towed Cori toward her cabin and would have escorted her inside if she hadn't plastered herself against the door like a barricade.

"Now what the sweet loving hell is going on?" he scowled at her.

"Nothing."

"Then why can't I come in?" Green eyes narrowed on her alarmed stare. "Who's in there that you don't want me to see?"

Cori swallowed the lump that clogged her throat. "No one," she lied, and not very convincingly, she was sorry to say.

When Jake reached for the door knob, her hand folded over his. "Can we go to your cabin? Please?"

He knew she was hiding something, and yet the temptation of being alone with her after a two-day abstinence was too great a temptation.

Heaving a sigh, Jake guided her along the deck to his room in the texas. Cori inhaled a thankful breath, relieved that he hadn't forced her to open the door. At least she had prevented him from learning more than he needed to know. There was too much at stake, Cori reminded herself. Even though her emotions played tug of war with each other, she knew she could never be honest with Jacob. And because she couldn't, they had no future. He represented what she had despised for long tormenting months. And yet, despite the insurmountable obstacles between them, she did care for Jake, more than he would probably ever know. Exactly how much? Cori didn't dare delve too deeply for fear of what she'd find. Jacob Wolf already mattered more than he should have.

Knowing that was unsettling enough!

Cori felt as if she were walking an emotional tightrope, torn by an obligation she felt honor bound to complete and frustrated by a man from whom she would forever have to withhold secrets from her past.

Thunderation! Of all the men who traveled the river, why did Jacob Wolf have to be the one to awaken her slumbering passions and leave her wishing she could offer more than was humanly possible for her to give? What rotten luck she'd had when she ran headlong into this muscular hunk of temptation!

Chapter 7

When Jake kicked the door shut with his boot heel, Cori pivoted in front of him and squared her shoulders, staring at him with somber directiveness. "I have a proposition for you," she announced. "If you will ask no more questions and make no other demands, I will consent to being your mistress for the duration of the journey."

Jake stared at her with his jaw sagging on its hinges. There had been a time in Jacob's life when he would have been perfectly satisfied with such an arrangement. Women had schemed to become his wife rather than settle for a casual affair. But during this new phase of his life, Jacob Wolf—converted rogue and former adventurer—had new objectives.

It infuriated him that this saucy spitfire would stoop to becoming his mistress just to protect her secrets. It annoyed him that their roles had somehow been reversed. If anyone had suggested an affair it should have been *him!* But now the shoe was on the other foot and Jake sorely felt the pinch. He had begun to care for this shapely brunette in ways he had never felt about another woman. He found himself cursing the blundering remark he'd made about all women being the same. That had been the shining example of famous last words. Women were definitely *not* all the same. Cori Lee Pierce was in a class all by herself and Jake had been intrigued by her.

Jake supposed he deserved to be hounded by feelings of indignation after Cori voiced her proposition. He had offered similar ones in the past and now he was getting a taste of his own medicine. Ah, what irony, thought Jake. This time a woman wanted his body and not his name. Hell's fire, that was a switch!

"No!" he ground out, his green eyes flaring with frustration.

Although Cori was far better at repelling advances than instigating them, she took a step closer. Tentatively, her hand uplifted to trace the cleft in his chin, the sensuous curve of his lips. "You arouse me, Jacob, isn't that enough, just knowing that?"

"No," he muttered, fight the overwhelming need to capture this infuriating female in his arms and forget why she exasperated him to the extreme.

Long velvet lashes fluttered up to meet his obstinate frown. "I am offering you all I can give."

"It isn't enough," he pouted.

She pushed up on tiptoe to press her lips to his. He was rock-hard muscle, taut and unyielding, but male desire was warring with his mind and body. Cori could feel his trembling frustration beneath her exploring hand, one that glided over the broad expanse of his chest.

The fact that Jake allowed her to kiss him without responding was a blow to Cori's pride. The one time she wanted a man to react, he didn't. Mustering her courage, she tried again. Her arms slid over his muscular shoulders, drawing his head to hers. Her supple body melted into his, hungry for the intimacy they had once shared.

When her petal-soft lips whispered over his and her breasts pressed wantonly against his chest, Jake felt himself losing the battle of mind over body. *Oh, what the hell*, his male instincts screamed at him. *Take what she's offering and be content with it. It's this or nothing, you fool.*

With a tormented groan, his arms encircled her. He kissed her then, with all the pent-up emotion that boiled inside him. Damn her secrecy and her stubbornness. She excited him, made him ache up to his eyebrows. One touch, one kiss, and he was on fire for her.

Cori felt as if she had been swept up into the vortex of a hurricane. The world was whirring around her, knocking her off balance. This one man—a man she couldn't have—was the only one who affected her so. When she was in his sinewy arms nothing else mattered quite as much. It had been this way the first time he'd kissed her. Every time thereafter it got worse. Wild, helpless feelings that defied logic assaulted her . . .

"How's that for second best?" Jake muttered, his voice thick with unappeased passion.

His bitter remark cut through Cori like a double-edged dagger. He didn't understand and she couldn't explain without betraying her motives. "You are second to no one and you damned well know it," she snapped in frustration.

"Am I?" His mouth twisted sardonically. "Then why this obvious fascination for Dal Blaylock?"

Cori wanted to clobber him and hug him all in the same moment. "I made you an offer, the only one I can give. Take it or leave it, Jake," she demanded tersely.

"Damn you," Jake growled at her.

Cori wasn't the only one who was buffeted by conflicting emotions. Jake wanted to shake this elusive sprite until her teeth fell out. At the same time, he wanted to ravish her with kisses that stripped all thought from both their minds.

When Cori tried to fling herself away from him, Jake yanked her back. "My mistress then," he scowled at her, even though his big body shuddered with the ardent needs she so easily aroused in him. "By night you will be *mine*. By day you will be *his*. And God help you if you ever do fall in love with me, Cori Pierce." His green eyes were like chips of ice. "For if you do, I will scorn your love and take a wife who appreciates a man who is willing to offer fidelity and forever . . ."

Angry words spoken in torment, that's what they were. At that precise moment, Jake almost hated this gorgeous pixie who had turned him wrong side out. She had made him agree to her bargain, even though he wanted more than her body, wanted to be more than the time she was killing while she played this enigmatic game of hers.

"Get undressed and climb in bed," he ordered frostily. "And after I've pleasured myself with you, you can trot off to Dal."

His tone dripped icicles. His harsh words cut her to the quick. He made her feel cheap and heartless, and yet she couldn't disclose her purpose. Jake didn't understand the torment she was enduring because of her crusade, one that was in direct conflict with this compelling need to be with him.

"I . . . a . . . I've changed my mind," she choked out, biting back the humiliated tears that welled up in the back of her eyes.

"You made this bargain, vixen." His gaze glittered dangerously down on her. "Lie down."

When he made a grab for her, Cori leaped away like a mountain goat and collided with the washstand. The pitcher teetered on the edge and crashed to the floor, sloshing water everywhere. With a growl, Jake pounced and Cori shrieked in alarm. He was furious with her. She could read the anger in the rugged lines of his face, in the twist of his lips.

In her haste to escape, she sent the tuft chair toppling behind her. Jake's muted scowl was followed by a resounding thud. Cori braved a glance over her shoulder as she twisted the door knob. Jake lay on the floor, his arms and legs entangled with the legs of the chair. The look he flung at her was worth a thousand words, none of which Cori dared to ask him to translate. She was sure they would have burned off her ears.

Shiny tears glistened in her eyes as she met his glare. She opened her mouth to say . . . What? Cori didn't have the slightest idea.

Jake's deep resonant voice rumbled toward her like thunder. "Be here tonight, she-cat, after your musical performance . . ." The words dropped like stones in the silence. "If you aren't here to pleasure me as you proposed, I'll come find you, even if I have to break down your cabin door . . ."

A goading smile grazed his lips as he rose to his feet and uprighted the chair. "And we both know to what extent you are willing to go to protect this damned secret of yours." He looked at her long and hard. "One day, I'm going to discover what terrifies you so much that you are willing to offer me your body to ensure your mysterious secret."

Even though it was her own fault, Cori resented the corner into which she had been backed. "I hate you, Jacob Wolf!" she hissed like a disturbed cat. "You *are* a wolf, curse your miserable hide!"

"But Little Red Riding Hood you are not!" he hurled insultingly. "Nine o'clock. Be here in my bed!"

The dam of tears she had so valiantly held in check burst free as his words rolled over her, angry and threatening. Cori flew out of the cabin and slammed the door behind her. Blindly, she whizzed back to her room, wiping away the tears that burned down her cheeks like floodwaters rushing over a riverbank.

It served her right, she knew. Her unpleasant encounter with that big ape only proved that wanting a man brought disaster. Perhaps if she and Jake had met at another time and place, if the tragic incident that had changed her life ten months earlier hadn't occurred . . .

Flashbacks from the past sent another stream of tears boiling from her eyes. Jacob Wolf and his cursed family were her enemy, she reminded herself bitterly. She had been a fool to make such a ridiculous proposal, to seek a few moments of pleasure in his arms despite the obstacles between them. And damn him to hell and back for making such cold demands on her in a fit of temper. He had taken something warm and tender and spoiled it all. Thunderation! Why was she so drawn to that infuriating man? Whatever the reason, she was every kind of fool for wanting him.

Tonight when she returned to his cabin, she would be as cold as stone when he touched her. And when she refused to respond, he would demand that she never come back again. Maybe then this mystifying spell would be broken and she could bury his memory, could forget the turmoil.

Clinging to that thought, Cori stormed into her cabin, looking for something to throw. She grabbed the first thing she passed, the delicate model of a ship. The wooden sculpture sailed into the wall and sank to the carpet in a zillion pieces.

"Are you, by chance, upset?" came the amused voice from behind her.

"I don't want to talk about it," Cori muttered, wiping away the sediment of tears.

"Him again." Quiet laughter wafted across the cabin. "I honestly think the two of you would be better off if you did get married. Then you would have a license to fight."

Cori glowered at the taunting face across the cabin. "And just where would that leave you and me?"

Her companion shrugged noncommittally.

101

Cori let out her breath in a rush. "You know as well as I do that I can't marry Jake, not for any reason. You are merely making those ridiculous suggestions to harass me."

"If you're smart enough to figure that out, then you also know I would prefer that you spend all your time with Dal Blaylock. He's much safer," came the curt reply.

Silence stretched between them.

"Ben Culver will be relieved of his bankroll at eleven o'clock," Cori announced, dropping the controversial subject like a hot potato.

"Where will we make the exchange?"

"The promenade of the hurricane deck," Cori replied, her tone thoroughly deflated from her confrontation with Jake.

Jacob picked up the pieces of the shattered porcelain pitcher and cursed the tormenting image that floated above him. In fury and frustration he had spoken cruelly to Cori. He had wanted more than she intended to give. And to share the company that misery loves so well, Jake had struck out to hurt and insult her. It crushed him to know that dark-haired hellion didn't trust him enough to take him into her confidence. Knowing she was hiding something from him drove him mad with curiosity. Knowing he needed more than a secret rendezvous tore him to pieces, bit by exasperating bit.

Jake had but to close his eyes and he could see that dazzling minx sashaying across the deck on Dal's arm, plying him with sunny smiles and laughing at some witty remark he'd made.

Jake needed to find himself a dependable wife and forget Cori Pierce even existed. Dal Blaylock was welcome to that troublesome sprite! *And I don't have time to spare that firebrand another thought,* Jake scolded himself fiercely. He had to check the steamer for damages and examine the injured passengers and crew. The instant they reached Vicksburg he had to collect supplies that Layton had overlooked and also summon physicians to tend the wounded.

Heaving a heavy sigh, Jake put the finishing touches on the room that he and Cori practically demolished during their squabble. Whipping open the door, Jake stepped outside, determined to erase all thoughts of Cori Pierce from his mind. But it was damned hard when he spied Cori and Dal at the far end of the deck, encircled in each other's arms.

Jake scowled murderously when Cori stretched up on tiptoe to press a tempting kiss to Dal's lips. Damn her fickle hide! She was driving him stark raving mad! That witch must have been a harlot in another lifetime, he thought resentfully. Once Jake had introduced her to passion she was eager to enjoy a little variety in life. Why, she was probably offering Dal the same proposition she had voiced to him only a half hour earlier! Jake could have cheerfully choked her without the slightest regret. That mean fickle woman was tramping all over his pride.

She hated *him?* Ha! *he* hated *her* worse! And when she crept into his room tonight, he was going to show her the difference between lust and lovemaking. He would take from her without giving anything whatsoever in return. She would regret this bargain of hers, just see if she didn't!

Chomping on that spiteful thought, Jake stamped down the deck, sparing the chummy couple, who were locked in each other's arms, one mutinous glance. And to his further frustration, Cori had the audacity to smile sweetly and wink at him.

At that moment, Jacob Wolf wanted to grab hold of both Cori and Dal and heave them overboard. Never in his life had he been so frustrated and miffed by the unexplainable and contradicting behavior of this woman!

A contented smile pursed Dal Blaylock's lips as he watched the light and love of his life twirl in her blue satin skirts and then belt out the high notes of the lively tune she was singing for her audience. His gaze left her momentarily to gauge the crowd's reaction. The other passengers were as spellbound as he was, Dal noted. All except one. Jacob Wolf was propped negligently against the saloon door, glaring poison arrows at the mystifying nymph whose lovely voice could tame the most savage beast.

Casually, Dal eased from his chair and ambled over to Jake, who didn't look the least bit pleased to see him. "How is your pursuit of the delightful Miss Pierce progressing?" he inquired with a taunting grin.

Jake glowered at Dal. "Well enough," he grumbled, pride refusing to divulge that he feared he was losing ground. Jake was sorely tempted to announce that he and Cori had been as close as two people could get. But bitter though Jake was, he had far more scruples than to seduce and tell. He had lived down the lane from a tattletale all his life, and Jake would be damned if he would stoop to Layton's annoying tactics.

"She is absolutely breathtaking, isn't she?" Dal's lovestruck gaze fastened on Cori as she danced her way across the room and paused to ease into one of the male passenger's laps.

"Absolutely," Jake grunted, his sour tone belying his words.

One blond brow elevated curiously. "Surely you and the bewitching young lady aren't at odds," he taunted his long-time friend. "What a pity that would be."

104

"I'm overwhelmed by your sympathy," Jake snorted sarcastically.

"Come now, Jacob, what did you expect?" Dal chuckled as he eased back against the wall, crossing his arms and legs in front of him. His gaze was magnetically drawn back to Cori and he sighed appreciatively. "I rather think she likes me, and I'm positively certain I'm bewitched by her. Surely you don't expect me to give her up without a fight."

This conversation was turning Jake's disposition pitch black. "I have things to do," he mumbled, turning away from the beguiling beauty who had earned the rapt attention of every passenger in the main cabin.

"Don't worry about Cori being swamped by over-zealous suitors. I'll see that she is returned to her room unmolested." Dal snickered.

"Yourself included?" Jake smirked.

The snide remark caused Dal to jerk straight up. "My intentions are honorable where the lady is concerned," he snapped. "I trust you can say the same for yours."

A curious frown plowed Dal's brow when Jake's broad shoulders lifted in that customary shrug. Although he was too much the gentleman to come right out and demand to know how far Jake's courtship with Cori had progressed, Dal was dying to know. He knew Jake had kissed Cori because he had witnessed their embrace. Damn, he would give most anything to know exactly how Cori felt about Jake. But she had refused to commit herself and that frustrated him to no end. He, like Jake, wasn't quite sure where he stood with the elusive Cori Pierce.

"As I said, I have things to do," Jake repeated before he ambled out the door.

Dal stood there pondering Jake's evasiveness. The brawny giant had neither admitted or denied that his pursuit of Cori was honorable and within the limits of propriety. He fixed an accusing stare on Cori, wondering just how generous she had allowed Jake to be with his affection.

The time had come to force Cori to make her choice, Dale decided. His good nature was wearing a mite thin and he resented the fact that he and Jake were both enamored with the voluptuous brunette who would state no preference in her suitors.

Well, she was going to have to choose, and quickly, Dal mused. He wasn't about to let this amorous competition spoil his friendship with Jake. Cori was ruining the relationship between Dal and Jake, and one of them needed to bow out. Dal didn't want to be the one to retreat, not when he was utterly fascinated with that delectable pixie.

Grappling with that thought, Dal returned to his seat to enjoy the remainder of the performance. Tonight he was going to press Cori for an answer. What had seemed a challenging game in the beginning had become far more serious than Dal dreamed possible. The conflict between Dal and Jake had grown by leaps and bounds. One of them had to lose the lovely Cori Pierce. Dal wanted to believe she cared for him. Her kisses suggested that she felt the same physical attraction, as well as the possibility of a deeper, more meaningful relationship.

"May the best man win," Dal murmured, lifting his glass to toast the vivacious brunette who was receiving a round of well-earned applause. "I'm sorry you have to be the loser, Jake, but not half as sorry as I'd be if it were me . . ."

All this kissing was making Jake sick, especially since he wasn't the one doing any of it! He stood in the shadows on the hurricane deck, watching in restrained frustration while Dal and Cori clung to each other like two lost souls who had just found each other in eternity. Curse it!

After Cori's riveting performance, which put the audience on its feet in applause, she had sailed from the saloon on Dal's arm. If she was still upset about the unpleasant encounter in Jake's cabin, she was doing one helluva job concealing it.

Jake slumped dejectedly against the railing. He had the unshakable feeling that his angry words and cruel demands had sent Cori right into Dal's waiting arms. He was going to lose her; Jake could feel it as he watched Cori melt against Dal.

Too disgruntled to watch for another second, Jake spun away to stare at the moonlight that sparkled across the river. He ached all over. He despised himself for his poor handling of the situation. He detested Cori's attraction to Dal when he longed to be the only man she yearned to spend time with. Jake supposed he deserved this mental anguish after he'd taken so many women for granted all these years. And he reckoned he shouldn't condemn Cori for rationing out time to a variety of men, especially when she drew men like metal to a magnet. She was only twenty, after all. And she had been innocent until Jake had introduced her to the world of passion.

The thought of what they had shared tormented Jake beyond words. It had been rare and special and . . . Jake expelled a disconcerted scowl. He should wash his hands of that fickle minx. He certainly would if he could. Even knowing how Dal felt about her didn't prompt Jake to do the gentlemanly thing and back away. The simple truth was that he wanted her desperately—in his life as well as in his bed. And damn her for clouding his mind when he should have dashed off and proposed to the first female who'd have him!

I can have any woman I want, Jake assured himself confidently. Except Cori . . . And wasn't it just like a

107

man to want what he couldn't have when he finally decided to settle down and take a wife? To punish him, this mysteriously intriguing witch had been sent up from the jaws of hell. He was paying retribution for every sin he'd ever committed, plus a few dozen more that he hadn't even gotten around to yet!

"Damn her," Jake muttered as he stuffed his hands deep into his pockets and stamped toward the pilothouse. That fickle female was tying his emotions in knots!

Chapter 8

With her heart thumping beneath her ribs, Cori walked toward the texas like a condemned prisoner approaching the gallows. She doubted Jake would be in a better frame of mind than he had been when they last spoke.

Rattled by that thought, Cori raced across the empty cabin and poured herself a drink of brandy from Jake's private bottle. She wheezed to catch her breath and then downed another drink of courage. It wasn't enough. Cori poured yet another snifter and inhaled it in one swallow.

Maybe he intended to stand her up, she mused as she guzzled another drink. Maybe he had decided to humiliate her by leaving her waiting for an hour before he arrived to announce that he didn't want what she had to offer after all. Cori took another drink.

But what if he did come, intent on being cruel and abusive? Cori swallowed another drink . . . or three. By now she had stopped counting.

What if Jake decided to throw himself at her and teach her the difference between animal lust and tender lovemaking? She couldn't bear the thought of seeing a sweet dream transformed into a nightmare. Cori poured another snifter level full and gulped it down like a python. Damn, she never should have made such a bargain! Jake was going to make her very, very sorry . . .

Minutes passed and the brandy took effect. A silly smile hovered on Cori's lips as she ambled around the room. She was feeling no pain now. Jake could do what he wished and it wouldn't faze her. How could it? Even her nose was numb and her previously tender forehead and cheek seemed to have miraculously healed, despite the bumps and bruises she had sustained.

The door whined as it swung open. Jake stepped inside. Cori lifted her hand and graced him with a sluggish smile.

"Would you care to join me in a drink?" she slurred over her thick tongue.

"A drink of what?" Jake snorted in disapproval. "You polished off the whole damned bottle!"

So this was how she intended to get through this prearranged tête-à-tête! Stumbling drunk, damn her!

Cori glanced down at the empty flask. "Oh dear," she mumbled, holding the bottle up to the lantern light. "There's only one sip left."

"How generous of you to offer me the last drop of my own private stock, my dear Cori," he smirked sarcastically. "I knew you were fickle, but I had no idea you were also a lush."

The insult slid off like water rolling down a duck's back. "I thought perhaps you decided not to come so I helped myself to a drink," she babbled drunkenly.

"Helped yourself to the *bottle*, you mean," he contradicted with a snort. In two long strides he was upon her, snatching the glass away and setting it on the table with a decisive clank. "Are you trying to wash away the taste of Dal's kisses or numb yourself to mine, minx?"

Dark eyes blinked up into his scowling face. "Do you really care, as long as I keep my part of this bargain?" Her glazed gaze wobbled around the dimly lit cabin. "Where's

110

the ropes and chains and whips? I'm ready to get this over with."

Jake might have laughed at the comical expression of martyrdom that clung to her features if he hadn't been so frustrated. But he didn't, because he was . . .

"You want me to make you hate me more than you already do, don't you?" he muttered at her.

Cori frowned. His rapid-fire speech was difficult to follow in her intoxicated condition. It took her a moment to puzzle out what he's said. "No," she replied belatedly. "I only want what we had the first time."

Her sluggish comment drained the anger from his taut body. Tenderly he cupped her chin, lifting her bloodshot eyes to his probing stare. "What about Dal?"

"I'd rather not invite him in. I'd like to have you all to myself," she slurred.

Despite himself, Jake grinned. He wondered if she even knew what she was saying. Drunk as she was, he doubted she would even remember this night at all.

"Do you want me?" he questioned softly, his hand drifting to that sensitive spot beneath her ear.

"Yes," she squeaked as a herd of goose bumps stampeded across her flesh. "The way it was . . ."

"Like this?"

His sensuous lips courted hers with intimate promises and he felt Cori melt against him the same way she had when Dal had . . . Jake squelched the tormenting thought. No matter what, he was going to brand his memory on her fuzzy mind. And when she flew back to Dal's outstretched arms, it would be Jake's face that rose above her, Jake's touch that warmed her blood.

All thought of punishing Cori by subjecting her to rough, humiliating kisses vanished from his mind. When she was in his arms Jake had only one purpose—to recreate the magic that he'd discovered with this dark-eyed vixen. He could feel the sparks leaping from his

111

body to hers and back again, feel the longings unfurl deep inside him. He hated her mysteriousness, her two-timing games with Dal. And yet he adored this elusive creature who turned him every way but loose. She had him questioning his sanity, but when he felt her luscious body molded familiarly against his, nothing else mattered but loving her.

The kiss Cori offered him in return carried enough heat to melt the moon and leave it dripping on the black velvet sky. Jake's composure withered and his hand slid down her ribs to her hips, bringing them familiarly against his, letting her feel how quickly and easily she aroused him.

Between the excessive amount of brandy she'd consumed and the intoxicating taste of Jake's kisses, Cori was hopelessly drugged. Her mind bowed before the wanton needs of her body. An uncontrollable urge to touch him overwhelmed her. She longed to explore his magnificent body, to commit every inch of his muscular flesh to memory, to return the cresting pleasure that rolled over her like a tidal wave.

A ragged sigh escaped her lips as she tunneled her hand beneath his shirt to sketch intricate designs on his hair-matted chest. Her lips followed, whispering over his bronzed skin, worshiping the feel of his muscled skin beneath her featherlight kisses. Her adventurous hands trailed lower, removing the belt and breeches that blocked her path. Languidly, she investigated the lean curve of his hip and the hard column of his thighs.

Cori was again reminded of the comparison between a sleek panther and this incredibly well-built man. Jacob was solid muscle, a glorious sight to behold, to touch. And touch him Cori did, without one whit of reserve. When he trembled beneath her brazen touch she marveled at this strange power she seemed to hold over him. It filled her with a sense of wonder and confidence.

112

Her soft lips skied over his shoulder, tracing the erotic path her hands had blazed. When Jake shuddered again, Cori smiled against his hair-roughened flesh. She delighted in devastating him as thoroughly as he devastated her. She reveled in knowing his steel-honed body better than she knew her own.

A choked gasp broke from Jake's throat when Cori's inquisitive hand brushed intimately against him. He was on fire for her, but he promised himself he wouldn't rush this splendorous moment. When he came to her, he wanted her to be as hungry for him as he was for her. His trembling hands loosed the stays on her gown, and he made short shrift of leaving the garment in a rumpled heap on the floor. Just as quickly, he removed the chemise that shielded her luscious flesh. Then he treated every inch of exposed skin to warm, greedy kisses that were meant to return the intense pleasure she had aroused in him.

Fire spiraled in Cori's blood when Jake plied her with the kind of expert kisses and caresses that she had yet to master. But she strived to emulate his experienced touch, to return the ardent pleasure he gave. His hands, like hers, were wandering everywhere at once—enticing, sensitizing, tantalizing.

Cori didn't remember how they had gotten on his bed, but they were there, lying flesh to flesh, kissing and caressing each other as if there were no tomorrow. Breathing was practically impossible; her heart was thudding in frantic rhythm. Speaking was difficult, but Cori found herself whispering her need for him over and over again.

When his left hand moved to shackle her wrists, restraining her from caressing him, Cori groaned in disappointment. But when his right hand and moist lips swirled over the rose-tipped crests of her breasts, she melted into a puddle of simmering passion. His tongue

113

flicked at the throbbing peaks, causing a coil of hungry need to unfurl inside her. Instinctively, she arched toward his teasing kisses and titillating caresses, reveling in the rapturous sensations he evoked from her.

A strangled gasp rattled in her throat as his kisses and caresses floated over her belly to sensitize the tender flesh of her thighs. Her body quivered as if it had been besieged by an earthquake as his knowing fingers stroked and excited. He left her writhing in unfulfilled need, made her cry out for him to take possession, to satisfy this monstrous craving he had instilled in her.

Frantic and half out of her mind with frustrated passion, Cori jerked her hand free to guide him to her. She had been reduced to begging for him like a shameless wanton. But she didn't care if he knew how wildly she wanted him. Pride and conscience were no match for this maddening ache that demanded appeasement.

Jake had intended to go on caressing her indefinitely, but the flame of passion in her ebony eyes entranced him. When she stroked him with impatient urgency and whispered her need for him, the wall of restraint crumbled as if it had never even existed. Her silky body glided provocatively against his, eager to accept him. Jake trembled with gigantic needs that drove him over the edge. His lips crushed down on hers as he settled exactly upon her, ending the torment of being so close and yet so maddeningly far away. But suddenly he wasn't the possessor but rather her possession. He was hers to command, and he matched her eager thrusts as she clutched him to her and gave herself up in wild abandon.

Riveting sensations bombarded Jake as they moved together as one beating, breathing essence, sharing the magic of passion that threatened to devour both of them. Mindlessly he drove into her. He was a creature of breathless need, a prisoner of his own ardent desires. It amazed him that this one remarkable woman who frustrated him to no end was also the one who satisfied him as no other female ever had. Jake wondered again, as he had the first time he and Cori made love, what he had been doing when he wound up in bed with other women. It sure as hell wasn't anywhere near what he experienced when this high-spirited sprite was in his arms. She made him feel as if he were skyrocketing straight into the sun. She was the flame that set him afire, the fever he couldn't cure. She stupefied him with her reckless abandon, matching him with her uninhibited passion . . .

And then it came, like a churning thunderstorm unleashing its full force, devastating all within its path. Jake held on for dear life as a multitude of indescribable sensations exploded inside him . . . Gradually, the haze cleared and Jake propped his elbows on either side of Cori's shoulders to peer into her heavily-lidded eyes.

A contented smile tripped across her lips as she stared up into the craggy face that formed the perimeters of her intoxicating dreams. Cori knew they couldn't enjoy a future together, but the present . . . ah, how she reveled in the way this sinewy giant affected her when he took her on that wondrous journey across the far horizon. He made her feel . . . well, it was something so mystical that it surpassed description. It was simply there, like the moon in the midnight sky and the sun beaming down at high noon . . .

Cori's bewitching features puckered in a drowsy frown. What was this sweet, compelling emotion that tugged at her heartstrings and inflammed her very soul? "Kiss me quickly," she murmured. "I don't want to think."

A roguish smile flitted across Jake's lips as he complied with her breathless request. "Why not, sweet nymph? Afraid of what you might discover if you delve too deeply?"

She heard the murmur of his words as if they had come

115

to her through a long dark tunnel. The world was fading from view and she was flitting into another dimension. Too much brandy and Jake's unrivaled lovemaking had taken its toll on her mind and body. Her tangled lashes fluttered against her cheeks and she drifted off to sleep, letting her dreams take up where the reality of Jake's splendorous lovemaking left off . . .

When Cori slumped beneath him, Jake eased away. His green eyes lingered on her slumbering features, mystified by the maelstrom of emotions that swirled inside him. Tenderly, he reached out to trace the elegant curve of her brows, the tainted cheek that still bore the faint mark of his accidental blow, the discolored bump on her forehead that he had inadvertently caused at dinner.

Lord, he'd only met this hellion the previous week, but it seemed as if he had known her forever, as if she'd been a part of him that he'd just now realized he'd overlooked. Cori—the enchantress who sang and danced her way into a man's heart. Cori—all fire and temper and mystery. Cori—his secret lover . . .

Jake expelled a weary sigh and closed his eyes, anxious to follow Cori into erotic dreams. "I'm sorry you have to be the loser, Dal," he murmured to himself. "But I can't give this sweet witch up. She means too much to me . . ."

Slowly, Cori was lifted from the peaceful arms of sleep by tempting kisses that teased the vulnerable point beneath her ear. Instinctively she moved closer to the pleasant sensations, smiling in lazy satisfaction. Her arms curled around Jake's neck to toy with the raven hair that capped his head and her lips sought out his, offering a burning kiss.

The memory of their lovemaking hovered around her like a fog, and Cori was hesitant to break this wondrous spell. Despite their heated exchanges and the clumsiness

116

that plagued both of them when they were near each other, their passionate lovemaking more than compensated for their arguments and blunders.

"I need to make love to you again," Jake whispered against the swanlike column of her throat. "It seems hours ago that we . . . Argh!"

Cori bolted upright so quickly that her shoulder collided with Jake's chin. "Hours?" Wide-eyed, she gaped at him. "Thunderation, what time is it?" she croaked.

"What the hell difference does it make?" Jake muttered over his tongue, the one he had inadvertently bitten when Cori rammed him in the jaw. "Night is night."

"Oh my God!" Cori was out of bed in a single bound, rummaging through Jake's coat pocket to retrieve his timepiece. Skully had set the time of the robbery at eleven o'clock. If she was late, he'd strangle her!

A muddled frown clouded Jake's brow when he noticed Cori had gone directly to his left pocket, as if she knew exactly where to locate his watch. What an incredibly observant female she was!

"Ten thirty! Damn." Frantic, Cori tossed Jake his timepiece and dived into her clothes.

"What the blazes is wrong with you?" Jake demanded as he snatched up his breeches.

"I have an appointment," she said as she wrestled with the stays on the back of her gown.

"With Dal no doubt," Jake scowled sourly. "I'm going with you. It's time he knew the two of us have been . . ."

"No!" Cori flung up a hand to forestall him. "Please, Jake. I kept the bargain and you promised not to interfere or ask any questions."

"I never agreed to that technicality," he all but yelled at her. "What kind of woman are you anyway? You persist in playing a man and his best friend against each other. You damned well better tell Dal how it is between us or so help me, I will!"

Cori grimaced at his booming voice. "You just don't understand how things are."

"So you keep saying. I'd like to know just what the hell it is I don't understand," Jake grumbled, his handsome face knotted in a frustrated frown.

When Cori dashed toward the door, Jake bowed his neck and charged after her, garbed only in his unfastened breeches.

"You have to stay here," Cori yelped in panic. "Please!"

"Let's not forget who owns and operates this ship!" he snapped. "I can come and go anytime I please!"

"Of all the things I keep letting myself forget, that isn't even on the list," she grumbled acrimoniously.

"What the sweet loving hell does that mean?" he wanted to know that very second. "Hell's fire, Cori, you're driving me nuts with your remarks and your behavior."

Her back to the door, Cori reached behind her to twist open the knob. Her pleading gaze stopped the looming giant dead in his tracks. "God help me for saying so, but I do love you. Scorn me for it if you wish, but it's the truth." Cori swallowed with a gulp, cursing herself for blurting out what she had been afraid she had known to be true from the moment Jake dared to kiss her. Some women needed time to analyze their emotions and sort out the secrets in their souls. Others simply knew when the love bug had bitten them. For Cori, time had nothing to do with that mysterious emotion called love. To be sure, Cori had fought the feeling tooth and nail. But nothing smothered the tender feelings Jacob Wolf had drawn from deep inside her. Her forbidden love for him was a curse, she knew. But the confession, too long contained, simply popped out the instant she opened her mouth.

While Jake stood there, thunderstruck, gaping at her as if *she* were the crazy one, Cori plunged on. "And because I love you, I ask you not to question me or follow me."

"How much?"

Cori blinked. "How much what?"

"How much do you love me?" he questioned with a piercing stare.

"I have to go."

"Damn it, answer me!" Jake blared at her. "Do you love me more than Dal?"

"More . . ." Her confession whipped around the door as she shut it behind her.

Blankly, Jake stared at the image that was emblazoned on the portal. Even now, he could see those brown eyes peering beseechingly up at him with a mixture of emotions he couldn't decipher.

Jake frowned. Had she blurted out her confession just to knock him off balance and make good her escape? Was Dal waiting for her, expecting that which she had so passionately offered to Jake?

Curiosity had killed many a cat. But felines didn't have the corner on inquisitiveness, not by any means. Jake's mind was whirling with unanswered questions and dark suspicions. He couldn't just sit in his cabin twiddling his thumbs. After all, he had made no promises about following her. Cori had requested that he didn't come after her, but he hadn't vowed to stay put.

Spinning about, Jake scooped up his discarded shirt and haphazardly fastened the buttons. Hurriedly he tugged on his stockings and boots and scowled when his left foot found the wrong boot. When feet and boots were sorted, he shrugged on his coat and quietly eased open the door.

In the shadows, he spied Cori emerging from her cabin at the far end of the deck. And there, lingering by the railing, was Dal, just as Jake had predicted. With a playful giggle, Cori bounded toward him. She threw back her head, allowing the sable tendrils to tumble recklessly around her as Dal swung her in a dizzying circle and dropped a hungry kiss to her lips.

Jake stamped toward the bow of the ship. Terrance called down to him as he stormed across the deck. When Jake pivoted, he caught a movement out of the corner of his eye. His gaze narrowed dubiously when a darkly clad, heavyset man in a wide-brimmed hat skulked along the deck, heading off in the opposite direction.

"I'll be back in a minute," Jake promised Terrance.

Cautiously, Jake inched along the wall of the texas. He couldn't say for certain from which cabin the mysterious man in black had emerged, but he could hazard an educated guess. Earlier that day Cori had refused to admit Jake into her cabin. Someone had been there; Jake would have bet his fortune on it. And that someone could very likely have been the unidentified passenger who had just disappeared around the corner that led to the stairwell. This scoundrel, whoever the hell he was, had some evil hold on Cori, Jake predicted bleakly. She feared this rascal to the point that she would divulge nothing about him to Jake. That bastard was somehow using Cori for his wicked scheme. Robbery perhaps? Was he blackmailing her into silence?

The thought resounded in Jake's mind like a pealing bell. Good God almighty, that sneaky weasel had to be using Cori as his cover while he stalked the *Belle* in search of his victims.

Hell-bent on his purpose, Jake crept down the deck to the darkened stairway. On the opposite end of the hurricane deck he could hear Dal's purring voice and Cori's answering murmurs. Curse her to hell and back! Jake lingered, having half a mind to stomp over and tell Dal that Cori was off limits, that she . . .

A startled voice erupted from the boiler deck, spurring

Jake into action, leaving him cursing the fact that he had dwelled too long in thought. Spinning about, he leaped down the steps while cabin doors opened and bodies flooded out of the main saloon. Jake found himself propelled into the middle of a milling crowd.

"I've been robbed!" Ben Culver hooted in dismay. "He even took my gold timepiece! My family's heirloom! My money!"

The pudgy Layton Breeze battled his way through the wall of humanity to console his prospective investor. With a growl, Jake shoved bodies out of his way to reach Ben Culver. And then Dal Blaylock came rushing down the steps to lend assistance. Actually, Jake was surprised Dal had been able to pry himself away from voluptuous temptation to answer the call of alarm, lusty rake that he was!

"Which way did he go?" Layton interrogated the robbery victim.

One shaky arm shot toward the steps. "That way, I think. Hell, I don't know! He pounded me on the head with a pistol and took off. I lost my bearings. Maybe he went that way." He gestured in the opposite direction.

People scattered when a splash erupted below them. Jake hurled himself toward the railing to see a dark blob bobbing in the moonlight.

"Man overboard," one of the roustabouts yelped.

Unfortunately, the steamer was cutting through the water at a fast clip and the "man overboard" disappeared into the gloomy darkness.

"I'm not investing in this thief trap!" Ben Culver snarled at the peaked Layton Breeze. "The deal is off. Find yourself another pigeon. Anyone who sinks his money into this ship will lose his fortune or have it stolen from him. Your company will probably be bankrupt in six months, Breeze. I will never ever suggest that any of my friends sail with you or ship their cargo with your line!"

"Now, Ben, you're distressed," Layton soothed. "Don't make any rash decisions just now. You know these things happen on steamers occasionally. It is impossible to have police jurisdiction in the middle of the Mississippi River."

"Then hire guards, for God's sake!" Ben crowed. "Your company's reputation is at stake here!"

"I'll hire a competent guard first thing in the morning," Layton promised.

While the two men were engaging in conversation, Jake squeezed his way through the crowd and circled the boiler deck, listening intently for footsteps below and above him. He had the instinctive feeling that the "man overboard" was a ruse. The fact that the *Belle* was pulling ashore to wood up left him wondering if the real culprit was waiting to slip off the ship when the roustabouts scurried ashore to gather cordwood.

Jake leaned over the railing to monitor the silhouettes that milled around as the gangplank was set upon the lower deck. He was contemplating shinnying down to the main deck when two shadows stretched out across the water. Jake glanced up to the hurricane deck to see two figures on the promenade above him.

Like a discharging cannonball, Jake shot up the supporting beam and swung a leg over the railing of the hurricane deck. Lo and behold, the darkly clad man passed Cori, who had been abandoned by the gallant Dal Blaylock, who had gone thief hunting. After bumping Cori broadside, the mysterious stranger disappeared around the corner. Cori murmured something indecipherable and then hugged her cloak tightly about her, as if she were warding off the evening chill.

Scrutinizing green eyes narrowed on the comely brunette who lounged against the railing. In swift precise strides, Jake stalked toward her.

"Who was that man?"

Cori smiled innocently at him. "I don't know. He simply bumped into me on his way around the corner and then apologized for his clumsiness."

Another dazzling smile hovered on her lips and Jake frowned suspiciously at her. "You know perfectly well who he was, don't you, minx? And don't you dare tell me he's another question I'm not supposed to ask!"

For a moment, the comely sprite stared blankly at him. Hell's fire, what an adept little actress she was. She was standing there so innocently that he expected her to sprout wings and a halo any second.

With a mutter that was reminiscent of a growling wolf, Jake stormed around the promenade to give chase to the mysterious thief. Halfway down the opposite side of the deck stood the elegantly garbed gambler whom Jake had frequently noticed at the gaming tables. Skully stood puffing on his cigarillo, gazing ponderously across the silvery river. At the far end of the deck was a mob of passengers who had joined in to search the ship.

When Jake whizzed by, determined to apprehend the elusive scoundrel, Skully grabbed his arm. "I'd like a word with you, Mr. Wolf, if I may."

Frustrated, Jake scanned the crisscrossed shadows and the clump of bodies that clogged the stairway.

"I'm not contradicting Ben Culver's story, you understand," Skully began tactfully. "Indeed, he may well have been robbed when we paused in the middle of our poker game to stretch our legs." The gambler broke into a wry smile. "But the fact is, Ben lost quite a bundle to me and then stomped off, half mad. After the robbery a few night ago, I wonder if perhaps Mr. Culver preferred to place the blame on an unpoliced steamer rather than admit to his bad luck at cards."

Skully puffed on his cheroot and then flicked his ashes over the rail. "He cheats at cards, Mr. Wolf. It leaves me to wonder if he isn't a liar as well . . . I just thought you

123

ought to know . . ."

Jake expelled an exasperated sigh. Maybe he was dashing to all sorts of wrong conclusions. Maybe he wanted there to be a Mr. Mysterious who had some secretive hold on Cori so Jake could explain her curious behavior. Perhaps Dal had intended to rendezvous in her room earlier that afternoon and Cori just didn't want Jake to know it. Maybe she had just let him think there was someone else awaiting her, just to throw him off track. How the hell did he know what was going on around here? That woman had turned his world upside down so many times that he wasn't sure which way was up these days!

When Jake stormed off to find his babbling cousin Layton and the irate Ben Culver, Skully half-collapsed on the railing and breathed a sigh of relief. That was too damned close for comfort, thought Skully.

After a few minutes, passengers scurried back to their rooms and the decks were abandoned. When the coast was clear, Skully ambled over to the supply room and eased open the door.

"Be careful," he warned the man who lingered by the wall. "Jacob Wolf is no fool."

When his companion stepped outside, Skully stared curiously at him. "Did you make the exchange?" he questioned quietly.

The darkly clad man nodded affirmatively before he slinked back in the direction he had come.

By the time Jake made his way back to the pilothouse, the decks were clear and there was no sign of the suspicious man in black. All was quiet on the *Belle*, quiet but hardly peaceful. Demons of curiosity and hounding frustration nagged at Jake as he took the wheel and allowed Terrance a few hours of sleep. While Jake scanned the river, avoiding sandbars and gnarled tree limbs, his thoughts kept drifting back to what Cori had said before she dashed from his cabin. He wanted to believe her confession, but he wasn't sure he could trust her. She was a walking contradiction. What game was she playing with him and Dal? Lord, he'd give most anything if he could read that woman's mind!

A slow smile worked its way across his lips, remembering the splendor he and Cori had shared in the privacy of the texas. That was not the response of a woman who pretended passion, Jake assured himself. Cori must care for him, no matter what sort of trouble she might have embroiled herself into. A woman couldn't feign that kind of arden passion, especially a woman as inexperienced at love as Cori was.

She cared for him in her own weird way, Jake encouraged himself as another smug smile surfaced on his lips. Poor Dal, he may have received a few kisses from the lady in question, but Jake had her true affection. Sooner or later Cori would let Dal down gently and reveal her preference. And she was going to marry Jake. Dal would have to find himself another bride.

Chomping on that confident thought, Jake scanned the river. He tucked the image of the darkly clad man who had been prowling the deck into the far corner of his mind. Soon he would be strolling the promenade of the *Belle* with the feisty brunette he had selected for his bride. Cori wouldn't deny what she felt in her heart. They were good together and she knew it. Things happened when they were together. All sorts of sparks flew. Jake had found the one woman who would make his life a delightful escapade. He wouldn't have to venture off into the wilds to find challenge and excitement.

Now, if Dal would just back off and stop confusing the issue! Jake mused as he stared down the churning river.

Chapter 9

There was a new look to the *Mississippi Belle* as she chugged toward Memphis. After the last holdup, Layton had hired Kyle Benson to patrol the decks from dusk until midnight. Although Jake had adamantly objected to having the hot-tempered ex-captain armed and with the authority to shoot to kill, Layton won out. He had taken a poll of passengers who wished to have an armed guard on duty for their protection. Public opinion, unfortunately, was on Layton's side.

Jake would much have preferred to deputize himself or Dal for the duty. Dal sided with Jake, arguing that innocent bystanders were liable to be shot by posting a man like Benson on guard. And Jake found himself saddled with more than enough duties to preoccupy him without having to keep a watch on Benson.

To complicate matters, Terrance Sykes came down with the grippe and Jake was left to man the pilothouse for hours on end. When he swore he would fall asleep at the wheel, Terrance rallied long enough to relieve him while Jake enjoyed a few precious hours of rest.

Jake slowly roused from the catnap he'd taken to tide

him over for his extended shift at the helm. With an exhausted groan, he pried himself out of bed. Absently, he massaged his stiff muscles and expelled a weary sigh. Thoughts of Cori tripped across his mind, leaving him wishing he had a few spare moments to spend with her. But as fate would have it, Jake's obligations in the pilothouse left Dal free to occupy all Cori's time.

Being a brilliant conversationalist and an interesting companion, Dal had indeed monopolized Cori's time. To Jake's chagrin, he noted the twosome had become inseparable the past two days. Jake rarely saw one without the other. And even though he tried to reassure himself that Cori felt something special for him, it became increasingly difficult for him to believe.

The timid rap at his door jostled him from his musings. Stiffly, Jake opened the door. His brows jackknifed in amazement when he found Cori staring up at him with a bewitching smile.

"May I come in?"

"Are you sure you can spare the time out of your busy social schedule?" he couldn't help but ask in a sarcastic voice.

Her lovely face fell at his snide question. "I didn't come to fight with you, but if you're going to be argumentative . . ."

His hand clamped around her forearm. Impatiently he ushered her into the cabin and shut the door behind her.

"I wanted to make sure you were all right," Cori murmured, trying to still the wild beat of her heart.

Just staring at this ruggedly handsome rake set her pulse racing. She had missed seeing him. Each time she'd called on him he had been at the wheel . . . except now.

"I didn't want you to think I was trying to ignore you. The truth is, I've missed you, Jacob," she admitted honestly.

"Pray, tell me how you could have found the time to

miss me with Dal following you around like your shadow?" Jake grunted. Mental anguish and physical exhaustion were wearing heavily on his disposition.

"You are a most impossible man," Cori grumbled, peeking up at him through long black lashes. "If you're going to be a surly wolf, I'll take my leave and you can find something else to chew on besides me."

Before she could make a hasty retreat, Jake's powerful body flattened hers against the wall. "Kiss me back into a good mood," he challenged her, his sensuous lips only a hairbreadth away from hers.

A saucy smile lingered at the corners of Cori's mouth as she looped her arms over his broad shoulders. "What you need most, I think, is a decent night's sleep."

"No," he contradicted, his voice thick with caressing huskiness. "What I need most is you in my bed. I'll gladly forgo sleeping."

His mouth slanted across hers and the warm familiar sensations channeled through every fiber of her being. This brawny rake had become her addiction. She had tried not to think about him, tried to call a halt to this affair that would hopelessly complicate matters. But *not* thinking about him when he had taken up permanent residence in her mind was impossible.

Cori had listed all the consoling platitudes about why she should avoid Jake. She should have let him think passion had provoked her confession of love and she should have kept her distance from him. But like a moth compelled to a flame, knowing she would get her wings scorched, Cori still sought him out. She had discarded her pride and her convictions and allowed her heart to rule her head.

A muffled groan rumbled in Jake's massive chest when Cori's hands drifted inside his shirt. The fire that blazed in her kiss melted him into senseless puddles. He needed to relieve Terrance and yet he couldn't let Cori go, knowing Dal would be waiting to distract her again.

"I want you," Cori whispered as his hands migrated over the tips of her breasts, causing tingling sensations to skitter through each nerve and muscle.

"Tender lies," Jacob muttered, even though he was unable to stop the flow of his seeking caresses.

"Believe what you see in my eyes," she murmured, lifting her gaze to his. "Don't believe what you are prone to think . . ."

He *thought* the fickle chit was two-timing him with Dal. But he saw the flicker of passion in those fathomless depths. "Hell's fire, Cori, I swear I'll never figure you out," he breathed in barely controlled desire. Then he kissed her hard and desperately.

Jake had just given up all thought of restraining his incurable need for this feisty sprite. His body buckled to the burning needs and he clutched her urgently to him, tasting her, touching her as he had longed to do the past two days.

A knock resounded on the door, forcing Jake to pry his lips away from Cori's luscious kiss.

"Damn, can't a man have a little privacy around here?" he grumbled at whoever was on the other side of the door.

"Sir," Barry Odum called hesitantly. "Mr. Sykes is a mite under the weather again. And speaking of weather. There's a storm brewing. Mr. Sykes said he could use your help. He said if you would have come to relieve him about five minutes ago that would have been about right. That's when his face turned purple and his knees folded up under him."

Jake had the exasperated feeling that Fate and Mother Nature had linked hands to keep him away from this tempting minx. It wasn't the first time Jake had the unsettling feeling this unusual relationship with Cori wasn't meant to be. Never in all his life had a courtship progressed in such a tangled, confused manner!

"I better go," he said, dragging himself away from the devil's own temptation.

"May I come with you?" Cori questioned hopefully. "Time is so short."

"I can't afford distractions." Jake shrugged on his coat over the clothes he'd slept in. A muddled frown puckered his brow when Cori's last remark soaked in. What the hell did she mean about being short on time? Only God knew, and even He probably didn't understand this paradox of a woman!

"I'll be as quiet as a church mouse," she promised faithfully.

Jake regarded the saucy imp for a moment. His eyes measured her curvaceous figure, wishing he had time for a dozen more tantalizing kisses and caresses. Cori Lee Pierce was many things, most of which he couldn't begin to understand. But quiet? That wasn't among her saving graces. And yet the chance to be near her outweighed logic. The fact was, Jake was happier when he was with her than when he was without her, especially knowing Dal was so eager to take his place.

"As you wish," he murmured as he escorted her out of the texas and up to the pilothouse.

A cold gust of wind slapped them in the face as they climbed to the top of the ship. Waves lapped against the *Belle*, making her pitch and roll with the angry river. Jake wrapped a supporting arm around Cori as another gale whipped over the ship.

The instant the twosome veered into the pilothouse Terrance breathed a feeble sigh. He was draped over the wheel, barely able to hold up his tousled head. His face was a putrid shade of green and his lips were a pathetic shade of blue.

"Damned sorry about this, Jake," Terrance croaked like a sick bullfrog.

130

"Get Terrance to his quarters," Jake ordered Barry Odum. "Then send for some warm broth for our ailing friend."

"No food," Terrance chirped, growing ill just thinking about pouring broth into his churning stomach. "Just shoot me and put me out of my misery."

When the young steward hauled Terrance away, Cori glanced questioningly at Jake. "Is there anything I can do to help?"

He nodded grimly. "Keep a sharp eye out for snags and sawyers while we're fighting this wind."

A bolt of lightning flashed from the boiling black clouds that scraped the river. Thunder boomed like a cannon. Cori flinched. She didn't like the looks of the brewing storm or the eerie dampness in the air. On a previous trip down river they had faced a violent thunderstorm. Cori vividly remembered thinking all the passengers, herself included, would be drowned when the steamer was swamped and buffeted by cyclonic winds . . .

Another sizzling lightning bolt struck a tree on the east bank of the river and flames instantly leaped along the branches. Cori very nearly jumped out of her skin when a clap of thunder crashed above them. To compound the feeling of impending doom, rain and hailstones pelted the steamer like drumming fingers. Sheets of rain and hail danced across the decks, and the curses of the crew and roustabouts on the main deck mingled with the wailing gales. The downpour cut visibility so severely that Jake could barely see twenty yards in front of him. The steamer dipped with the swells of the river, and it became increasingly difficult to maneuver the lumbering vessel in the crosswind.

Jake detested windstorms that caused the water to become choppy and turbulent. The surface of the river warned a pilot of approaching dangers, ones that became invisible during violent storms. Slanting ripples offshore

131

indicated there were bluff reefs of sand just below. A dimple in the water warned of rocks and buried trees that waited to wreck a ship. Boiling rings undulating on the surface indicated a sand bar that had begun to dissolve. Slick spots with circles and radiating ripples suggested the bottom of the river was building with sediment and becoming dangerously shallow. But the action of gusty winds on the water distorted the warning signs and left the river pilot to navigate on only a prayer.

The steamer suddenly lurched and thrashed its paddlewheel. "Hell's fire," Jake muttered. He snaked out an arm to reach for the speaking tube to shout orders to the engineer. "Crack steam. Give me all she's got!"

Cori froze as the huge steamer ground against an unseen bluff reef whose steep narrow sides were so near the surface that it snagged its unsuspecting prey.

"Cori, take the wheel," Jake ordered abruptly.

"Me?" she croaked, frog-eyed.

"You," he barked urgently. When Cori hesitated, he grabbed her taut arm and yanked her in front of the wheel. "Hold her steady."

"But I . . ." Cori squeaked, only to be cut short by Jake's annoyed snort.

"Just do it, damn it," he bellowed at her and then charged out into the hail and rain to shout orders to the crew below.

With her arms as stiff as petrified wood, Cori clutched the wheel that rebelled against her firm grasp. The wind and waves tugged at the vessel, and Cori had to brace her feet to prevent herself from being flung aside. Never again would she underestimate a pilot's strength or skills, she swore as her heart pounded against her ribs as if it meant to break one or two of them. Jake had made the task of steadying the wheel look easy. It was anything but!

Her frantic gaze darted to the man who was soaked to

the bone and who was leaning out over the rail to bellow orders. Cori feared he would be blown overboard, leaving her in sole control of this ship.

"THUNDERATION!" Cori yelped when the wheel, as if it possessed a mind of its own, threatened to spin like a top. She skidded sideways, trying valiantly to control the vessel whose boilers were rolling with a full head of steam while the buried reef prevented it from making progress.

At Jake's demand, every available man on the main deck had grabbed a pole and plunged it into the reef that grounded against the starboard side of the ship. Timbers groaned and the vessel shuddered.

As if there wasn't trouble enough, the storm unleashed its full fury and whistling winds bombarded the snagged steamer. The swirling gale whipped at the ship, leaving her rocking and dipping at dangerous angles.

A terrified yelp erupted from Cori's lips when the wheel spun out of her hands, throwing her against the wall of the pilothouse. Cori prayed. Oh, how she prayed as she scraped herself off the floor to lunge at the whirling wheel. Pain cracked against her knuckles as she tried to clutch the wheel and maintain a steady position.

The lumbering steamer suddenly lurched forward under the power of the raging fire in its boilers. Although cyclonic winds rattled the window panes of the pilothouse and every object that wasn't nailed down skidded across the decks, the steamer dipped and dived its way back into the roaring chute of the channel.

Clamped to the wheel like a statue, Cori stared straight ahead without the slightest idea what danger signs she was supposed to be watching for. Her knees threatened to fold up like an accordion, but she held firm, refusing to buckle to her chaotic emotions.

A wry smile pursed Jake's lips as he stepped back into the pilothouse, leaving puddles behind him. "That was the finest piece of piloting I've seen in a while, Cap'n

133

Pierce," he complimented Cori, whose face was as white as flour and whose stance indicated that fear held her stiff as a board. "You spun the wheel at just the right moment to loose us from the reef."

He planted a cold kiss to her blue-tinted lips and wedged her out of the way to resume command of the wheel. Cori collapsed on the wooden bench and her hands shook with the aftereffects of the battle. She peered unblinkingly at the muscular giant, whose soggy clothes revealed his masculine physique to her wide-eyed gaze.

"I wasn't doing the piloting," she squeaked in a voice that sounded nothing like her own. "It was my guardian angel. I was picking myself up off the floor at the time."

Jake spared her a startled glance, but he had no time to respond to her comment. A fierce gale assailed the steamer as she lumbered around the bend. Jake could feel the ship skidding sideways and rolling with the waves that threatened to shove them against the shore. When the wheel strained against his hands, he gritted his teeth and held it firm.

For half an hour, Jake battled the storm and the steamer that was tossed by turbulent winds. But at long last the storm blew ashore and left the *Belle* to nurse her bruises.

In the calm that followed the storm, a flurry of activity broke out on all three decks. Dal Blaylock appeared at the pilothouse, his eyes wide with alarm.

"I've been searching every nook and cranny for you, Cori," he declared as he hoisted her to her feet and shuffled her toward the door. "Are you all right, my dear?" His gaze swung accusingly to Jake, who was standing in a puddle glaring back at him. "I doubt Jacob needs a distraction. I'll accompany you back to your cabin."

Before Cori could accept or reject the offer, Dal

shepherded her along the slick deck. His arm stole around her waist, tugging her closer.

"Did you tell Jacob?" he murmured against her ear.

"Tell him what?" Cori blinked bemusedly. She had just recovered her powers of speech and mobility and Dal had thrown her off balance again.

"You know what, sweetheart," he purred seductively. "If you would prefer that I tell him, I will."

Cori massaged her throbbing temples. "Could we talk later, Dal? After the two hours I've just endured, I've developed a horrendous headache."

He dropped a kiss to her heart-shaped lips. "Very well, my love. I'll meet you after your performance tonight." Gallantly he lifted her limp hand, pressed a kiss to her wrist, and bowed over her like a knight offering his respects to his queen.

Dal Blaylock was indeed the epitome of gentlemanly behavior. He had charm galore. His handsome blond features, his muscular physique, and chivalrous manner could easily tug at a woman's heart if she wasn't guarding it closely.

For a long pensive moment, Cori assessed the dashing rake who very nearly matched Jacob Wolf's size and stature. Thunderation, things were getting so complicated she scarcely knew what to do!

"I love you, Cori," Dal whispered before he took his leave.

On wobbly legs, Cori entered her cabin to find Skully lounging in the tuft chair.

"Where in the world have you been, girl?" he questioned in concern.

"Steering the steamer," she replied before sprawling on the bed.

"What?" Skully crowed like a plucked rooster. "Why the blazes were you . . . ?"

"What do you want, Skully?" Cori snapped, cutting

135

him short. "I have a splitting headache and I could do with some rest."

"I think it's time to make another strike," he announced with great conviction.

The third party in the room piped up then. "The steamer is being patrolled by Kyle Benson, in case you've forgotten."

"I haven't."

Despite her headache, a sly smile pursed Cori's lips. She pushed herself upright to peer at Skully. "I do believe Skully is right. We know Benson's procedure after monitoring him for the past two days."

Skully grinned at the twinkle of mischief in Cori's ebony eyes. "I suppose you have a suggestion as to whom our next victim should be."

"Indeed I do." The smile that pursed her lips grew wider and her eyes danced with wicked amusement. "Layton Breeze himself. He convinced Dorian Flanders to invest in this steamer just last night. I know Layton is carrying a bulging bankroll."

"Do you think you can pick his pocket as easily as you did a few of his other investors?" Skully quizzed her.

She nodded negatively. "The roll of cash is too large. He would feel it being tugged from his pocket, especially since he wears such snug garments."

Skully stroked his mustache thoughtfully. "Perhaps we should try a different approach," he pondered aloud. "Layton considers himself quite the lady's man. *And* he has shown a fascination for Cori, even if she has tactfully avoided his advances without insulting him." His gaze circled to Cori and a thick brown brow lifted in question. "Are you willing to take Mr. Breeze on the ride of his life, my dear?"

The impish grin evaporated from Cori's lips. The memories came rushing back like a tidal wave. "It would be a pleasure to strike Layton. After all, he's the one responsible."

136

"And what about your dear friend Jacob Wolf?" the third party wanted to know.

Cori glanced the other way. "Having come to know him, I don't believe he was involved in Layton's dastardly dealings. I think we should leave Jacob out of this entirely."

"That isn't what I meant," came the quiet reply.

Skully frowned, his eyes quiet and watchful. "Just exactly what is going on with you and Jacob Wolf, Cori?"

"Jacob has nothing to do with this matter," she replied evasively. "We swore to have our revenge on Layton and we shall, despite my . . . ," she paused, carefully formulating her words, "my friendship with Jacob."

Another frown furrowed Skully's brow. "Under the circumstances, you must know nothing could ever come of a courtship between the two of you. It would be dangerous and extremely complicated."

"I thought it would be delightfully ironic," their companion chortled before dropping down on the bed beside Cori. "She could marry Jacob and our revenge would be even sweeter. And the amusing part of all is that he and his conniving family would never have to know they'd been *had*."

"I couldn't do that to him," Cori protested. "He's . . ."

"I think Cori cares far more for him than she willing to admit to us," the third party declared with firm conviction.

Skully eyed the pert brunette with wary trepidation. "Good God, Cori, you can't be serious about the man! Every time he comes within ten feet of you disaster strikes. You've just recovered from the bumps and bruises he's caused you."

Her chin tilted to a characteristically defiant angle. "I do not wish to have this discussion."

"Why? Because I struck a sensitive nerve?" her companion teased unmercifully. "Ah, the irony of it, dear Cori. How often have Skully and I heard you declare that no man would suit you, that you intended to live out your life without a husband to hamper you."

"I never said I was going to marry Jacob, only that . . ." Cori corrected and then closed her mouth before she revealed the secrets in her soul.

"That you what?" her companion prodded relentlessly. "That you are falling in love with him?"

"Oh Lord," Skully groaned.

"Are we going to plan to pry Layton loose from his roll of cash or needlessly harass me?" Cori spouted.

"Ease up on Cori," Skully advised their mischievous companion. "What she feels for Jacob Wolf is her own affair." His penetrating gaze focused on Cori's beguiling features. "She knows she must break off her relationship with him when we reach Natchez."

"She knows, but she's had difficulty remembering that," their companion snickered. "It would certainly *un*complicate my problem if she would avoid him like the plague."

"You're being childish," Cori parried with a frustrated sniff. "It's because of you that I've had all sorts of . . ."

"Now, let's not fight, shall we?" Skully intervened with a smile. "The both of you have duties to perform and squabbling won't solve problems. When Layton Breeze winds up robbed on his own ship that should put the finishing touches on our mission here. If we scare him badly enough, maybe he'll sell this steamer, thinking it has become a jinx to him."

Skully settled back in his chair and lit his cheroot from the lantern. "The clientele of the *Belle* has already declined considerably since the robberies began. All that lures passengers to this steamer is Cori's nightly concerts. And soon she will quit her job. By the time we finish with Layton, he'll be ready to sell out." An ornery grin pursed his lips as he bit down on his cigar. "And to further frustrate Layton, I have set my sights on that

138

foppish Englishman, Lord Dumphrey."

"Lord *Hum*phrey," Cori corrected.

"*Dum*phrey," Skully emphasized. "He has been educated past his intelligence and he knows more than he will ever be able to understand. It will please me to no end to bring that haughty dandy down a notch or three. He has visions of investing in this steamer, but he won't have enough money left to buy a cup of tea when I get through with him."

"And bankrupting Layton isn't going to be enough to suit me," Cori muttered bitterly, circling back to the previous topic of conversation. "I want him to pay his full due."

"First we must break Layton financially," Skully reminded her. "Then we will call in our personal debt. One step at a time, my dear. One step at a time."

A mischievous smile quirked Skully's lips as he leaned forward. "Now here's what we'll do tomorrow night at ten o'clock." His gaze sobered when it settled on Cori. "Last time we planned a robbery you were on some secretive mission that you refused to divulge to us. But this time, young lady, you had better not be late . . ."

Chapter 10

To Jake's relief, Terrance's case of the grippe proved to be short-lived. By the following morning, Terrance had regained his color and had gobbled down an enormous breakfast. Though still a mite peaked and weak, he proclaimed himself fit enough to man the wheel. Shuffling Jake out of the way, Terrance insisted that his employer crawl into bed to rest.

Jake did exactly that. It was eight hours later that he awoke from sleep, chilled from his exposure to the elements, swallowing over a scratchy throat. His eyes watered every time he blinked and his skull pounded with a nagging headache.

After soaking in a warm bath, he fastened himself into a clean set of clothes, ambled down to the boiler deck, and seated himself in the saloon, intent on ordering one of everything on the menu. He had hoped to invite Cori to join him for his meal, but she didn't answer the knock on the door. Jake rather expected to see her on Dal's arm, but to his surprise Dal was also dining alone.

Jake had just dived into a heaping platter of filet of chicken with truffles and a huge pile of beans and potatoes when Dal planted himself in the chair across from him.

"You're looking a bit rough around the edges," Dal observed. "It appears the storm took its toll on you."

"I've survived worse," Jake said hoarsely and then soothed his sore throat with a mouthful of potatoes.

"You always were resilient," Dal complimented as he carved into his green apple pie, savoring the delicious pastry. "You have the ability to bounce back after the worst of blows. I hope you will recover quickly from this latest one."

Jake was out of sorts because he was enduring poor health. It made him cross and impatient. "Get to the point, Dal. I'm in no mood for idle chatter."

"So it seems." Dal squirmed uneasily in his chair. "I had hoped to catch you in a better frame of mind, but delaying this will only . . ."

"You're babbling again," Jake snorted as he whittled at his chicken.

Dal inhaled a deep breath and expelled his announcement in a rush. "I proposed to Cori last night and she accepted."

The news shocked Jake so thoroughly that the knife in his right hand shot through the chicken filet, slammed into his coffee cup and sent dishes toppling.

He fixed his bloodshot eyes on Dal, who grimaced at the frown on his friend's face. "She can't marry you because I think she's in love with me," Jake growled.

"Not to hear Cori tell it," Dal parried. "She assured me that it was me she loved. I honestly believe she does!"

Jake had never felt so furious or betrayed in all his thirty-one years. Damn her tender lies, her wicked deceit! Cori's confession of love had been a ploy to keep him locked in his quarters while she flitted off to cavort with Dal. Damn that witch to hell! And double damn *him* for being such a gullible fool. He had decided to marry and settle down and he had picked Cori for his bride. But the first time he laid eyes on that feisty firebrand he had

141

refused to heed Terrance's advice. Jake had arrogantly thought he could persuade her to accept his proposal, but his rival had as much to offer Cori and far more time to devote to his courtship.

While Jake was taking double shifts at the wheel, Dal was plying Cori with promises of a sunny future, heaping compliments on her left and right. That cunning witch had come to Jake's bed and then turned around and accepted Dal's proposal! Curse her lovely hide! He had been her gigolo, the time she was killing, her experiment with passion!

"Now Jake, I know you're upset," Dale murmured compassionately. "I would be too if it had been the other way around. But last night things went a mite too far and . . ."

Dal's last remark suggested things Jake didn't want to hear, things that cut him to the quick. He had no reason to think Dal would lie about such things, and yet the competition for Cori's affection was fierce. Jake wasn't sure how far Dal would go to ensure that he won Cori's hand. Just look how far Jake had gone, hoping their intimacy would ensure her acceptance of his proposal.

"That fickle little bitch," Jake scowled furiously.

Dal jerked upright in his chair. "I will not have you dragging my fiancée's name through the mud, friend or no!" Dal snapped, his golden eyes flashing contempt. "I love her and she loves me."

"Oh really?" Jake snorted explosively. "That's not the story I heard. Not too long ago she swore it was me she loved." Jake didn't add that Cori had been in his bed making wild sweet love to him as well. He should have, but he simply couldn't bring himself to mortify Dal when the man had insisted Cori had accepted his proposal.

Dal did a double take and then recovered his composure. "Things change rather quickly at times," he mumbled awkwardly. "I had hoped there would be no bitter feelings between us, but . . ."

"The only bitter feelings are between her and me," Jake grunted in an abrasive tone. "She should have told me herself."

"You've been at the wheel more often than not the past two days," Dal pointed out. "And quite naturally, Cori is apprehensive about announcing her preference. What did you expect?"

"A little honesty would have been nice," Jake sneered. Blazing green eyes seared Dal's handsome features. "And I cannot help but wonder, dear friend, just how honest she has been with *you*."

Dal's blond brows puckered into a wary frown. "And what, exactly, are you suggesting?"

"She and I . . ." His voice trailed off into a muffled curse. Angry and bitter though he most definitely was, he still couldn't tell Dal that he and Cori had been intimate. Cori was the most deceitful two-timing witch ever to float up from the pits of hell, but it was hardly Dal's fault. He had been taken in by Cori's flirtatious smiles and alluring charms, just as Jake had been.

Jake wondered if this proposal and Cori's acceptance was her way of brushing him aside. Know how cunning Cori was, Jake suspected she would dump Dal in the same cruel manner by latching onto another man. Then she would let her latest beau break the bad news to her present fiancé.

"Eat your chicken and calm down," Dal advised when Jake looked as if he were about to explode. "Feeding my frustration always seems to help me."

"The only thing that will ease my temper would be feasting on Cori Pierce's fried heart," Jake snarled spitefully.

That said, he bolted from the table, causing his chair to rear on its hind legs and crash to the floor.

"What are you going to do?" Dal questioned in alarm.

Jake looked like black thunder. "*What* am I going to do *when?*" he muttered venomously. "Do you mean *before* or *after* I stab, shoot, and poison that lying minx?"

Dal couldn't recall seeing Jake so furious . . . ever! His craggy features were skewed in a sneer that would have sent an alligator slithering into the murk.

"Now, Jake, you leave Cori alone or I will be forced to defend her," Dal warned. "I would detest squaring off against my best friend."

"If I promise not to kill her, will you let me have a few moments alone with her?" Jake growled down at his peaked friend.

"Considering the mood your in, I'm not sure I can trust you not to kill her first," Dal grumbled as he unfolded himself from the chair.

Jake's steely hand clamped on Dal's shoulders, stuffing him back into his seat. "Ten minutes is all I ask," he gritted out. "When I hear the words from her own lips, I'll accept your engagement."

Dal surveyed Jake's frown for a long indecisive moment. "Do you swear you won't hurt her?"

"Even though I have the compelling desire to tear her limb from limb, I'll restrain myself," Jake promised in a growl.

Warily, Dal nodded his consent. He had never known Jake to strike a female, except for the accidental blow he had leveled on Cori in St. Louis, but there was always a first time, and Jake was mad as hell, after all. "I'm holding you to your word, Jacob. No matter how angry she makes you, you had better not harm a hair on her head."

After Jake had spun around and stormed off, Dal began to worry. He shouldn't have consented. Jake was in a ferocious fit of temper, and since he was, Dal had no recourse but to follow after him. He would allow Jake his privacy, but he vowed to be within shouting distance

144

should Cori require help. Unfortunately, should she be in need of assistance, Dal had the inescapable feeling he would need a platoon of able-bodied soldiers to bring Jake in hand. When Jake was fighting mad he was as formidable as a mob of ten good men!

Cori had just stepped onto the landing of the curving staircase that joined the hurricane deck to the boiler deck when Jake's ominous form appeared at the foot of the steps. Even the crisscrossed shadows of the night didn't conceal the hot sparks that leaped from his eyes or disguise his foreboding stance. He looked like black thunder.

A cautious frown knitted Cori's brow as Jake stalked toward her like a deadly hunter advancing on his prey. "Jacob, it's good to see you again," she commented, hoping to replace his venomous glare with a smile. It didn't work worth a whit.

"I'll just bet it is," Jake growled sarcastically.

Even when he halted a step below her she was still forced to glance up to meet his eyes. It was not a pretty sight. Those green pools churned like a hail-filled storm cloud.

"You could have told me yourself," he said in the most unpleasant tone imaginable.

Her delicate brows furrowed. "Told you what?"

His curled fingers hovered around her swanlike neck when she stared so innocently at him. He truly wanted to strangle her.

"Don't pretend ignorance," he snapped like a rabid wolf. "I'm referring to the fact that you accepted Dal's proposal last night, as if you don't know!"

"I did?" Cori blanched and then looked away, anywhere except into Jake's murderous green eyes. "Oh, I did, didn't I?" she mumbled awkwardly.

Jake looked as if he wanted to hit her. Quite honestly, Cori was surprised he didn't. In all his life, Jacob had never been so furious, disappointed, or frustrated, and never ever had he endured all three at once. Cori was behaving as if she had already forgotten she had agreed to spend the rest of her life with Dal. One would have thought her acceptance of marriage was of little consequence to her. Curse her, how could she be so cold and callous? What kind of woman was she? One without a heart, Jake thought contemptuously.

"If you're going to marry Dal, what was that hurried little confession you offered to me the other night?" he thundered. "Was it your ploy to escape me so you could fly into your fiancé's arms?"

"No," Cori hastily assured him. "I meant what I said, Jake, I truly did."

Jake stared at the shapely brunette in royal blue satin as if she had sprouted an extra head, one equipped with devil's horns. "You love me and yet you are going to marry Dal?" he muttered in disbelief.

Cori inhaled a ragged breath and slowly exhaled. "Yes, I guess I am."

"You *guess?*" Jake growled acrimoniously. "Marriage isn't a guess; it's a commitment. And from the sound of things, you don't know the meaning of love or commitment." The heated glare he hurled at her was hot enough to melt rock.

Cori reached up a trembling hand to smooth away his disdainful frown, but he slapped at her fingertips.

"Don't touch me or I swear to God I'll choke the life out of you!" Jacob spewed in barely controlled fury.

Something inside Cori shriveled up and died when Jake scowled at her. "Jacob, I'm sorry. I know you don't understand and I know you probably don't believe that I wish things could have turned out differently, but . . ."

"No, I sure as hell don't believe it!" he retaliated in a

whiplash voice. "I would have married you and laid the world at your feet. You would have wanted for nothing." His lips curled and thinned to such extremes that Cori swore they would snap under the pressure. "And what did you tell your fiancé when he discovered he wasn't the first man in your bed?" Hollow laughter reverberated in his swelled chest. "I'm sure you were ready with an explanation. Knowing how easily those tender lies trip off your lips, I'm sure you found a way to solve Dal's curiosity without . . ."

"Stop it!" Cori railed at him, tormented beyond words. "Did Dal tell you that?"

"He hinted at it," Jake scowled, haunted by the thought of Cori lying in Dal's arms.

Cori got a grip on herself. "I told you in the beginning that I couldn't marry you. I love you and that's the truth. I probably always will, but I can't . . ."

Jake jerked her off the steps and into his arms. A few moments earlier he had sworn he detested her touch, loathed the very sight of her. But his emotions were so twisted and tangled that he was suddenly contradicting himself. Like a starved beast, he devoured her quaking lips. He felt the need to kiss her and to go on kissing her until he got this infuriating witch out of his system.

How could a kiss that had once been so sweet turn so sour so quickly? he wondered as he ravished her. She was like a poison in his blood. Yet he vowed he would hold this minx to him until he could no longer tolerate another taste of her lying lips and venomous kisses.

Never had Jacob been so rough and abusive. The tenderness he had once displayed was now gone. He plundered her lips and stole her breath without offering to give it back. Instinctively, Cori fought him, struggled to pry herself loose. But despite the anger and frustration the flame of desire began to burn. Her traitorous body melted into his and she accepted his bruising kiss,

147

wanting the gentleness she had once known. A steady stream of tears rolled down her cheeks as he made a mockery of the tender embraces that had once formed the perimeters of her dreams.

Jake hated her. He didn't understand this enigmatic sorceress. She was a walking paradox. She had expressed her love for him and then, in the same breath, had denied her affection by announcing she could never marry him. She was driving Jake stark raving mad, that's what she was doing! And if she did follow through with her marriage to Dal, Jake knew he could never tolerate any social function that Dal and his bride attended. It would kill him to watch Dal dote over her.

Against his will, despite all else, Jake found himself yielding to the bubbling sensations of passion. Even the bitter feelings that prompted him to launch his abusive assault buckled beneath his obsessive hunger for her. He had wanted to hurt her, to punish her for the hell she was putting him through, but his body betrayed him. When Cori's arms automatically slid over his shoulders, a groan of unholy torment rumbled in his chest. Suddenly he was kissing and caressing her in that old familiar way again, with a tenderness this deceitful vixen didn't deserve.

"I love you, Jacob," Cori whispered brokenly. "No matter what happens. No matter what I must do, always remember that. One day you will thank me for having the sense to say no to you."

"Damn you, Cori," Jacob bellowed in abject frustration.

"No, damn you, Jake!" Dal Blaylock's rumbling voice echoed in the stairwell. "Let her go!"

Jake did, and none too gently. Cori's rubbery legs were unprepared to support her when Jake unceremoniously dropped her back to her feet. With a startled squawk, Cori collapsed on the step amid a pool of royal blue satin and white lacy petticoats.

"What are you trying to do? Break both her legs?" Dal

snorted as he stamped up the steps.

"I promised not to kill her," Jake muttered, staring down into Cori' misty brown eyes. "But I didn't say I wouldn't maim her permanently."

Dal shoved his shoulder against Jake's hip, bodily moving the looming giant out of the way. He scooped Cori into his arms, cuddling her protectively against him. "You had your ten minutes," he snapped brusquely at Jake. "Now leave her alone."

"Put me down!" Cori wailed, so frustrated that she couldn't think straight. When Dal set her on the step, Cori rearranged her twisted garments in angry jerks. "Both of you leave me alone!"

"Gladly," Jake sneered at her. "Good riddance, Cori. I would say it has been a pleasure knowing you, but unlike some of us, I am not prone to lies."

Cori cursed under her breath as Jake stomped off like an enraged grizzly. Her heart was dangling around her knees. She had been snared in a trap of her own making and she couldn't untangle herself from it. Obligations forced her to let Jake go when she wanted to call him back. Circumstances beyond her control prevented her from enjoying her heart's desires. Personal sacrifices had to be made during her noble crusade. Letting Jake go was her sacrifice, but it nearly killed her to watch him storm away. She knew she would never revel in the splendor she had found in his arms, knew he would hate her all the days of his life.

"I'm sorry you had to endure that unpleasant encounter, sweetheart," Dal murmured consolingly. "Jake will get over it. Just give him a little time."

"Oh, hush!" Cori blurted out in exasperation.

Dal blinked in astonishment. Seeing the flood of tears pour down her cheeks he frowned suspiciously. "Do you still care for him?" he demanded to know.

"How dare you suggest that you and I . . ." Cori

149

gnashed her teeth. "You had no right to make insinuations to Jake!"

"I was only trying to let him down gently," Dal declared, studying the frantic expression that claimed her flushed features. "But I'm beginning to wonder just what *has* been going on between the two of you. You really can't make up your mind, can you, Cori?"

"Will you stop drilling me with questions? Can't you see I'm upset?" Cori sobbed hysterically.

Dal looked as if someone had punched him in the midsection. "You do love him, don't you?" he blurted out in grim speculation. "And what about me? Were those confessions of undying love that you whispered last night just more of your wicked lies? Was it the security and position I can offer you that prompted you to accept my proposal? You know perfectly well that Jake has as much to offer as I do!" He raked her with a disdainful glance. "I'm beginning to think you love whoever you are with at the moment!"

"Stop hounding me!" Cori cried. "I need to think."

Dal glared at her, suddenly unmoved by the river of tears that trickled down her cheeks. "You'll have plenty of time to think, little witch. A lifetime in fact. Don't bother retracting your acceptance of my marriage proposal. As far as I'm concerned, I never even asked!"

Dal stormed off in the same direction Jake had taken, and Cori plunked down on the step and cried her eyes out. Nothing was working out the way she had planned. She had confronted two endearing men, both of whom any woman on God's green earth would have delighted in claiming as a husband. But Cori had driven them both away and she couldn't explain to either one of them without revealing her true purpose for being on the steamer.

"Thunderation," Cori spluttered. "Thunder . . . thunderation!"

A low rumble of laughter wafted its way down the steps. Cori jerked around to see Kyle Benson smiling maliciously at her.

"What a pity you lost both your meal tickets," he smirked caustically. "Forgive me for withholding my sympathy, but the fact that you and your two haughty suitors are miserable makes me deliriously happy."

Cori had never had any regard for Kyle Benson, who reminded her of a human scarecrow with his tall, lanky frame and ill-fitting clothes. But at the moment she hated him twice as much as before.

It was a foolhardy thing for her to do—taking her frustration out on the smirking galloot. But Cori had the uncontrollable urge to hit something. Since it was within striking distance, Kyle's face seemed the most logical thing to clobber.

Cori was on her feet in a single bound. She marched toward him and, quick as a coiled snake, struck Kyle across the cheek.

"Both Jake and Dal are four times the man you could ever hope to be," she spewed like a geyser. "Even if you were the last man on earth I would never accept the lurid offers you made in St. Louis!"

Anticipating his response, Cori ducked under his blow and then shot down the steps toward the saloon before Kyle could pounce on her. She was in the main cabin, calling to the orchestra to accompany her with a lively tune before Kyle could drag her outside and beat the tar out of her.

Cursing vehemently, Kyle examined his stinging cheek and watched Cori paste on a dazzling smile for the benefit of her audience. Someday, he vowed stormily, he was going to find a way to repay that sassy termagant for scorning his affections. She thought she was too good for the likes of him, but he would have his revenge by taking her. He would humiliate that high-strung hellion, just

151

see if he didn't!

While Cori plunged into song and dance to relieve her frustrations, Jake and Dal were at the bar, matching each other drink for drink.

"Damned deceitful little virago," Dal scowled into his glass. "We both ought to charge off and marry the first two available females we can lay our hands on."

Although Dal had arrived to declare that his engagement was off, Jake was still fuming. He was appalled at himself for being taken in by Cori. The fact that she had duped him and his best friend was a double blow to masculine pride.

Jake honestly wondered if Cori hadn't planned it all. She had pitted best friends against each other to rid herself of unwanted marriage proposals. She was a habitual flirt who delighted in stringing men along and then dropping them like hot potatoes. Instead of graciously declining both marrige proposals, she had cunningly stabbed them both in the back and then twisted the knives as deep as they would go. No doubt that witch was even now enjoying a hearty laugh at Dal and Jake's expense. She had staged that little scene on the steps and worked up a few crocodile tears for the occasion, damn her.

"We should have listened to Terrance," Jake muttered before downing his tankard of brandy in one swallow. "It looks as if he won the wager."

"I'll never question that man's opinion again," Dal grumbled and then threw back his blond head to guzzle another drink. He poured himself another and swallowed hard. "I'm going to find myself a devoted, homely woman who'll appreciate me. Her looks will be her chaperone and I won't have to worry about some other man stealing her away from me."

"If she's as ugly as original sin, I'll like her even better," Jake chimed in before pouring another brandy down his gullet. When Cori's vibrant voice filled the saloon, Jake scowled sourly. "I need another drink."

"Take two," Dal offered generously, slopping whiskey into Jake's empty glass.

Jake took three drinks as fast as he could inhale them. "To our wedding day." He lifted his glass in toast.

"To dull, uncomplicated wives," Dal mumbled.

Without his usual coordination, Jake slid off the bar stool and wobbled along the wall. He propped himself against a nearby chair and waited for the roaring applause to die down. With malice and forethought, he made a beeline toward the voluptuous brunette in blue satin, the one who had stolen the hearts of her audience.

Apprehensively, Cori monitored Jake's approach. She was out of breath from her rigorous dance, and the wary anticipation of confronting Jake again wasn't making breathing easier.

"As always, minx, you've charmed your crowd of admirers," Jake slurred with mocking disdain.

"Thank you," she murmured awkwardly.

"And by the way . . ." He half turned, as if the idea had just occurred to him, "You're fired. When we reach Natchez, gather your belongings and get the hell off this ship."

Having said his piece, Jake staggered out of the saloon, leaving Cori to compose herself as best she could before continuing her performance. All the while she sang, she felt like screaming in frustration. But she was a trained performer and perform she did, even though she was bleeding invisible tears behind the mask of her carefree smile.

153

Chapter 11

While lounging in the men's social hall, Layton Breeze smiled triumphantly and patted the oversized cash roll in the vest pocket of his white jacket. He had succeeded in persuading Dorian Flanders, the wealthy merchant from New Orleans, to invest in the steamer. In another few months Layton could assume complete control without tangling with his meddling cousin. It had become Layton's aspiration to split the company and crawl out from under Augusta and Jake's thumbs. It had always infuriated Layton that Augusta put Jacob in charge, leaving Layton second in command. Despite his pleas, Augusta continued to show favoritism. As matriarch of the family, her wishes were observed until Jacob convinced her otherwise. But Layton intended to break away and form his own company, utilizing as much of the corporate money as possible. After all, he was entitled to half the fortune, he reminded himself.

With the aid of a few more investors he could claim the *Mississippi Belle* as his own and take control of one of the other steamers the family owned. With Kyle Benson's assistance, Layton could ensure that passengers rushed to his ships rather than to the competition. And given time, Layton had visions of driving Jacob out of the business as well.

If only he could stop this rash of robberies that plagued the *Belle*, he mused sourly. Business had been booming until the last few months. Now the *Belle* had developed a bad reputation, even though passengers were still drawn by the delightful chanteuse who sang and danced her way across the main cabin. But business would escalate once again, Layton consoled himself. Sooner or later he would catch this ring of thieves that worked the river.

Chomping on that encouraging thought, Layton pulled a tray of appetizers toward him. Since his favorite pastime was eating, he chose to gobble the snacks as a method of celebrating the acquisition of the cash that now bulged from his pocket.

Somehow or another, Skully had lured him into a poker game between bites. Layton wasn't even sure how Skully had done it. The gambler had stopped by to engage him in conversation and before Layton knew it he had been dealt a hand. One thing had led to another, and soon there were a half-dozen men involved in the high-stakes game. Layton enjoyed gambling and Lady Luck had been sitting on his shoulder during the evening. To his amazement, he won several thousand dollars to add to the cash he had collected from his investors.

Strutting like a proud peacock, Layton ambled from the saloon after Skully suggested the players stretch their legs for a half-hour before resuming the game. Layton swaggered onto the deck to inhale a breath of air and gloat. He was in fine spirits this evening.

"Mr. Breeze, I wonder if I might have a word with you."

Layton pivoted his rotund body to find Cori Pierce peering beseechingly at him. He'd had his eyes on this gorgeous pixie since he'd hired her to entertain his

155

passengers, but he had never pushed for sexual favors from her. Oh yes, Layton had dropped a few hints, suggesting that he wouldn't be averse to sharing a few private moments with her, but Cori had skillfully eluded him. He knew, after Kyle's unpleasant experience in St. Louis, that this shapely sprite refused to be coerced into bed. But that hadn't stopped Layton from fantasizing about her. Indeed, he had imagined them doing all sorts of tantalizing things together on dozens of occasions.

"Of course, my dear," Layton purred as he slid a stubby arm around her trim waist. "You could have more than a word." His puffy eyelid dropped into a suggestive wink. "You know all you have to do is consent . . ."

"You are a married man," Cori reminded him. "I doubt very much that your wife would approve of such things."

When Layton grinned, his sagging jowls elevated a noticeable two inches. "Then we just won't tell Sylvia." He gave Cori a playful pat on the arm. "All these months you could have been enjoying extra privileges as my employee." He winked again. "The door to my cabin is always open to you. If you're so inclined, my dear, you might be surprised to learn that I give a pretty good performance myself."

"I shall keep that in mind, Mr. Breeze," she murmured, forcing herself not to gag at the disgusting invitation.

"*Layton*, please call me Layton," he insisted, with what Cori assumed to be his attempt at a charismatic smile. She'd seen better, more pleasing grins on the faces of mules.

"But I may no longer be your employee." Cori sighed for dramatic effect. "Your cousin fired me this evening."

"What?" Layton peered bug-eyed at the bewitching brunette.

When Layton would have lingered on the boiler deck,

156

Cori ambled toward the steps. As anticipated, Layton followed after her.

"I believe it was our personal conflict that compelled Jacob to dismiss me." Cori reached into her purse for a handkerchief and dabbed at the tears she had worked up for the occasion. "We had a disagreement and he became angry with me."

"Now don't you worry your pretty little head about it," Layton cooed, giving her a consoling pat on the shoulder. "I'll handle that cousin of mine."

Through the shiny tears, Cori mustered a grateful smile. "You have been so good to me, Layton," she sniffled. "How can I ever thank you?"

Layton's gray eyes flicked over Cori's arresting figure. "An appreciative kiss would do for starters," he whispered, his puffy lips puckering in invitation.

Cori caught the movement in the shadows. As much as she detested the thought, she knew she was going to have to kiss this plump toad so he would be distracted. Her accomplice was lurking in the darkness, waiting to strike.

When Layton swayed toward her, his pot belly brushing against her abdomen, Cori steeled herself against his repulsive physical contact. She forced herself to accept his slobbery kiss and the chubby arms that fastened around her.

While the couple stood in the shadows of the stairwell, the darkly clad thief pounced on them. The barrel of a pistol rammed into Layton's spine, jerking him from his fantasy come true.

"Monsieur Breeze," the thief growled in a heavy French accent. "Remove your arms from the lovely *mademoiselle* and raise them over your head, *tout de suite.*"

Layton turned pea green as he raised his trembling arms over his head. His eyelids batted frantically as the pistol wedged deeper between the rolls of flab that encircled his ribs.

While the victim stood stock still, reaching for the stars, the darkly clad thief slid his gloved hand around Layton's oversized belly. Nimbly, the bandit removed the roll of cash that bulged in Layton's vest pocket.

"You should not be so foolish as to strut about with so much loot, *monsieur*," the thief clucked in mocking disapproval.

When Layton opened his mouth to object to the insult, the barrel of the pistol jabbed him into silence.

"*Merci, monsieur*. I will try not to spend all your money in one place."

With a taunting salute, the river pirate disappeared into the shadows. His footsteps clicked against the steps as he made his hasty escape.

Layton let out a howl that would have raised the dead. Cursing fluently, he waddled off on his tree-stump legs in hot pursuit. When he heard the splash in the water below, he scuttled toward the railing just in time to see the dark silhouette sinking into the depths, as it had on every occasion when an unsuspecting victim was relieved of his bankroll.

Jacob had retired to his room to nurse his sore throat and churning stomach, which had rebelled against the whiskey he'd consumed. When he heard the familiar cry of alarm, he bolted from his cabin to see Layton clomping across the boiler deck. To his shock, he watched Cori whiz past him, intent on circling the promenade.

In the past, Jacob had always pursued the wily thief. Now he decided to take a different approach. This time Jake wheeled in the opposite direction than Cori and Layton had taken and raced back up the steps. In the shadows of the hurricane deck, Jake saw a cabin door ease shut.

158

A suspicious frown clouded his brow as he silently crept along the deck. He swore the portal that had swung shut was the one that gave entrance to Cori's cabin. Jake instantly remembered thinking he had seen someone enter her room before—both the first and second time he had witnessed a robbery.

After the frustrating events of the evening, Jake had sworn that Cori was the lowest form of life on earth, and being furious with her already, he was quick to suspect that she was somehow connected with the elusive thief who had been plucking passengers clean. If that deceitful sorceress would pit two best friends against each other for her own wicked delight, she would also stoop to playing the accomplice of a thief, he reckoned.

While Jake stalked toward Cori's room, shouts resounded on all three decks, but Jake had set his sights on Cori's room, the one he swore had become the refuge for the cunning bandit who had pretended to dive overboard.

Although Jake wasn't feeling up to snuff, he gritted his teeth, mustered his strength, and prepared to do battle. He burst through the door, and sure enough, his darkest suspicions proved correct. There, hovering over Cori's dresser was the darkly clad villain who had plagued several passengers the past week.

The surprised thief wheeled around, fumbling to grasp his pistol. But Jake hurled himself forward, wrestling the weapon away. A pained grunt erupted from Jake's lips as a doubted fist connected with his jaw. An uplifted boot struck him in the groin and he automatically buckled to protect his privates from another disastrous blow.

In the bat of an eyelash, the thief sprang toward the door, but Jake had recovered quickly enough to snake out a hand and grasp the man's trailing cape. With a snarl and a fierce jerk he yanked the escaping thief backward. The bandit swung his fist wildly, landing another blow to

Jake's left cheek. He made a frantic attempt to retrieve the weapon Jake had dropped when struck in the crotch.

Muted hisses and growls erupted from both men as they struggled for control of the pistol that skidded across the floor after colliding with a scuffling foot. The struggle for possession of the weapon seemed to go on forever. At last Jake got a firm grip on the weapon and whipped it up, only to have it knocked free by the thief's flying foot. The fight started all over again, but this time Jake switched tactics by sprawling on the riverboat pirate, squashing him flat.

The bandit's breath came out in a whoosh and his bearded face was mashed into the rug. Claiming the advantage, Jake reached out to grasp the pistol. Roughly he rammed the weapon into the scoundrel's ribs and then rocked back on his haunches.

"Get up!" Jake snarled maliciously.

Reluctantly, the bandit did as he was told, or at least he was in the process of rising when Jake impatiently grabbed him by the nape of his neck and yanked him upright.

A murderous frown puckered Jake's brow as he peered down at the shadowed face beneath the mop of black hair, mustache, and beard. The thief's hat had been knocked off long ago, but even without it, Jake didn't recognize the man he had captured.

"What are you doing in Cori's room?" Jake sneered in question.

"What are *you* doing in *mademoiselle's* room?" the insolent thief snapped in the same derisive tone.

"She's in on these escapades of yours, isn't she?" Jake growled, giving the bandit a hard shake.

"No, *monsieur*, she is not," the bandit declared with perfect assurance. "And I haven't the slightest idea what escapade you are referring to."

"Of course you don't," Jake smirked, his fingers

digging deeper into the thief's throat. "Where's the stolen money?"

"I have no money," the bandit croaked.

"I'm in no mood for games," Jake snarled, his temper very nearly depleted. "Hand over that damned money . . . now!"

"I told you, I haven't any money," the thief gasped as Jake's curled fingers dug into his vocal chords.

Jake was already angry from his confrontation with Cori and his battle with the symptoms of the grippe. Now he lost the last shred of his temper. With a vicious growl he grabbed the lapel of the thief's cape and the collar of the shirt beneath it. With a quick tug, he ripped the garments loose.

"Hell's fire!" Jake squawked, further irritating his raw throat. His eyes bulged from their sockets. He had expected to see a man's bared chest beneath the shredded garments. What he saw instead, despite the dim light that peeked through the partially opened curtain of the dark room, was the heaving breasts of a woman!

Shock held Jake immobilized for an instant. It was a half-instant too long. The bandit shot toward the door, clutching her padded garments around her.

Jake did, however, recover in the nick of time. With a hoarse growl, he launched himself at the bearded female.

Again the thief landed face down, muttering curses into the carpet. Still snarling, Jake shoved the bandit to her back and plunked down on her belly. With no gentleness whatsoever he ripped the stage mustache and beard from the woman's face and received another jolt that left him crowing in disbelief.

"Cori?" Jake choked out, afraid to trust his eyes. His hand clamped onto the mop of black hair, giving it a quick yank. Sure enough, a waterfall of sable tendrils tumbled from beneath the matted wig.

"How in hell did you . . . ?" Jake glanced toward the

161

closed door, gesturing in the direction of the promenade where he had seen this elusive minx only ten minutes earlier. "I thought I just saw you . . . How did you . . . ?" He was so stunned he couldn't form a sentence to save his life. "You were just . . ."

The creak of the door brought quick death to his jumbled comments.

"Lord, that was close! I almost . . ." the unexpected intruder came to a skidding halt and gasped at the sight of the man atop the darkly clad bandit.

Jake received a third jolt, one that left his overworked heart hanging in his chest like a ton of lead. His wild-eyed gaze riveted on the face of the intruder and then swung back to the woman he had pinned to the floor. He couldn't believe what he was seeing!

Below him were the exquisite features of Cori Pierce, the caped bandit who had been preying on unsuspecting passengers on the *Belle*. And across the room was the identical face of Cori Pierce. The woman had the same stunning features—right down to the eyelashes! Hell's fire, his rising fever was causing him to see double. Either that or there really *were* two Cori Pierces on the *Belle*.

When the second Cori Pierce, who stood in the doorway, wheeled to make her escape, Jake snatched up the pistol and aimed it at her departing back. "Since the whole world assumes there is only one of you, the other one won't be missed." The click of the trigger dropped like a stone in the silence. "Take another step, honey, and you're as good as dead."

The second Cori Pierce froze in her tracks and gulped over the lump in her throat.

"Turn around and shut the door behind you," Jake snapped.

She did.

"Whose hairbrained scheme was this?" he demanded gruffly.

162

Both Cori Pierces glanced at each other and pointed an accusing finger. "It was hers," they replied in unison. Their voices were as identical as their faces and figures.

Exasperated beyond words, Jake unfolded himself, dragging the bandit up with him.

"Which one of you is the real Cori Pierce?" he asked, glaring at one face and then the other.

"Neither of us," they answered simultaneously.

Jake was on the verge of pulling out his hair. The shock of discovering Cori was the elusive bandit set him back on his heels. Learning there were two women who fit the same description knocked him to his knees.

Since he was getting nowhere with his questions, Jake phrased his next one to gain a definite answer, or at least he hoped it would. "And which of you lovely ladies is the one I seduced?"

The second Cori Pierce, the one who stood by the door, gasped in stunned disbelief. The blazing brown eyes of the thief whom he held captive in his arms glared murderously up at him and proceeded to slap him across the face. Jake didn't flinch when her hand collided with his cheek the first time. He didn't complain when she struck him again in the same spot. The third time she tried to slap him he caught her hand in midair. Two whacks on the face were enough compensation for the times Jake had accidentally caused bodily injury to this hellion.

"Damn you," Cori hissed poisonously, mortified to no end.

Still keeping a firm grasp on the wriggling bundle in his arms, Jake glanced at the other young woman whose jaw sagged on its hinges. "Go fetch Dal Blaylock," he ordered abruptly.

Cori's identical twin gasped in dismay. "Please don't drag him into this," she pleaded. "He's suffered enough and I couldn't bear to have him know . . ."

"Fetch him!" Jake bellowed sharply, his scratchy throat momentarily forgotten. "Or you will no longer have a sister."

Two identical faces riveted on each other before the young woman beside the door nodded begrudgingly and made her hasty exit.

"What's your sister's name?" Jake questioned as he herded Cori across the cabin and stuffed her into a chair.

Cori glowered into the green eyes that drilled into her. "Lori Ann," she replied, her voice quavering with frustration.

"And where's the money you stole from my cousin?"

"I dropped it in the supply room on the other side of the deck," she muttered in confession. "Lori retrieved it and stashed it in her gown."

"Why?" Jake growled in exasperation.

"That's a stupid question. Where did you expect her to stash the money?" Cori sassed sarcastically. "She couldn't very well clamp the bank roll in her hand and waltz off across the deck, now could she?"

He was making no headway whatsoever, and that exasperated him.

"You know damned well what I meant," Jake snapped. "Why did you stoop to banditry in the first place?"

Cori tilted a belligerent chin. "What difference does it make why? A thief's a thief. So hang me," she challenged him.

"I was leaning more toward a public execution in front of a firing squad," Jake sneered into her smirk.

Wary though she was of this fire-breathing dragon, her notorious temper caused a flood of words to flock to the tip of her tongue. "Then do your worst. What do I care?" she hurled at him. Stubborn pride refused to allow her to be intimidated by his beastly threats.

Jake jerked her out of her chair so quickly that it made her head spin. Her feet dangled off the floor as he stuck

164

his face into hers. "On second thought, killing you would be too merciful," he growled into her bulging brown eyes. "I think you deserve long-suffering torment. And so help me God, I'll see that you get exactly what you deserve for your deceit and your crimes!"

Cori could tell by the look on his face that it wouldn't take much to provoke him to strike her. Stubborn and rebellious though she was, she well remembered the feel of his fist lancing off her cheek that day in St. Louis. Hating to admit defeat but seeing no possible way to avoid it, Cori finally slumped against him. It was a demoralizing blow to know the man she loved hated her with every fiber of his being. Thunderation, if she could have wriggled loose, she would have seriously considered throwing *herself* overboard instead of the weighted sacks she had tossed into the river each time she robbed her victims.

All hope of escape was dashed when the door swung open. Her sister and Dal Blaylock sailed into the room. Curse it, fumed Cori. Now she *and* her sister were trapped like rats!

Chapter 12

Stunned amazement claimed Dal Blaylock's features when he peered at the identical twins. Thunderstruck, he struggled to inhale a breath. So great was his shock that his legs folded up and he staggered to maintain his balance. His mouth fell open and unintelligible syllables gurgled in his throat.

"There's two of them!" Dal chirped when he had finally recovered his powers of speech.

"How astute you are," Jake chuckled, watching Dal's expression mirror the shock Jake had experienced a few minutes earlier. "It seems our elusive river robbers have been silently laughing at us while they played their cunning little game of intrigue. You and I were so busy stewing over who would win the heart of the hopeless coquette that we never once guess the 'lady' in question had a double who was also a professional pickpocket." His mocking gaze slid over Cori. "I shudder to guess how many other unsavory talents you possess."

Dal's reaction was similar to Jake's. After the initial shock wore off, anger and humiliation set in. He muttered several salty curses and then exploded with, "Of all the dirty rotten lowdown tricks!"

He wheeled on Lori, causing her to blanch. "You little

166

fool! Did you think your beauty compensated for such stupidity? Did you ever stop to consider what would happen when you got caught? You could have found yourself staring down the barrel of Kyle Benson's weapon." Then Dal trained his fuming glower on the young woman who clutched at her ripped cape and gaping shirt. "That trigger-happy guard would have killed one of you!"

"He wouldn't have had the chance," Cori snapped at Dal. "We know every move he makes while he's patrolling the decks. At ten o'clock Kyle is on the boiler deck, on the bow to be specific. At ten minutes after ten he struts into the saloon to fetch a drink. He lingers there for seven or eight minutes before circling the hurricane deck."

Jake gaped at Cori, amazed that she and Lori had so perfected their crime. "How the blazes did you pull off these capers?" he had to know.

"We studied the habits of our victims and then struck when they were most vulnerable," Cori explained. "With some of them, it was a simple matter of lifting their bankrolls while we performed in the main cabin."

"You fleeced them when you plopped down on their laps, I suppose," Jake muttered in grim realization.

"Either that or we picked their pockets when we bumped into them in the crowd," Lori quietly confessed. "When we robbed our victims at gunpoint, I tossed a weighted feedsack overboard and then passed my sister on the way around the deck and . . ."

Jake remembered seeing the darkly clad man bump into Cori (or was it Lori?) a few nights earlier. "Then you handed the money to your twin and scampered back to the room and no one was the wiser," he finished for her. His gaze darted to Dal. "I believe Lori had Layton's bankroll rucked in her bodice. Retrieve it."

Lori squealed as Dal's fingertips dipped beneath the

167

neck of her gown and extracted the roll of cash that was nestled against her bosom.

"Why?" Dal quizzed Lori. He was met with stubborn silence. "If you needed money, why didn't you ask me for it while you were stringing me along with those false confessions of love?"

"I mean what I said!" Lori protested hotly.

"Of course you did," Dal snorted. "Jake and I were the time you and your scheming sister were killing between robberies." His lips curled as he glowered flaming arrows at Lori Ann. "You had your laugh and now Jake and I are going to have ours. And may I remind you Cori . . . Lori," he hastily corrected himself. "He who laughs last laughs the longest and the loudest!"

Jake loosed Cori from his grasp and ambled over to retrieve the wad of cash that Dal was brandishing in Lori's face. "If you will excuse us, ladies . . . and I use the term loosely . . . Dal and I need to adjourn to decide on the proper brand of punishment you two so richly deserve."

While Jake glanced back at Cori Lee, Dal leveled a mutinous glare at Lori Ann. Without another word the men filed out, slamming the door shut with a decisive thud. The sound reminded Cori of a judge's gravel pounding out a sentence of doom.

"Now what?" Lori wailed, her face in her hands.

"We wait a few minutes and run for our lives," Cori decided.

"He hates me," Lori sobbed despairingly.

"Can you blame him?" Cori muttered as she hurried over to fetch another shirt.

Lori glared at her sister's back. For the most part, the twins got along superbly. But in this moment of extreme duress, Lori's temper was flaring. "It's your fault that Dal doesn't believe I honestly care about him. You had to go and get mixed up with that Wolf!"

168

Cori pivoted with an answering glare. "And you kept insisting that I marry him," she parried sharply.

"You know perfectly well that I was only badgering you for the mere sport of it," Lori snapped.

"We made a pact not to be courted by two men at the same time, but you let that sweet-talking Dal Blaylock sweep you off your feet," Cori accused.

"And you should have told me that you and Wolf . . ." Lori slammed her mouth shut. Enough said. They both knew what had transpired between Cori and Jake. He had certainly made it clear enough.

"And imagine my surprise when Jacob informed me that I had accepted Dal's marriage proposal!" Cori shot back, fighting down her blush. "You should have told me!"

"I didn't have time. We've been meeting each other coming and going and switching places too quickly for lengthly conversation," Lori countered. "We have done all the damage we can do to Layton, and I had decided to settle down with Dal in Natchez. We had already decided this was to be our last trip down the Mississippi, and Skully . . ."

"Don't you dare bring Skully's name into this," Cori ordered, waving her finger in her sister's face.

"I'm not stupid," Lori declared indignantly.

"You could have fooled me after you accepted Dal's proposal without consulting me," Cori countered. "We agreed that nothing was more important than this crusade. But you let your heart rule your head. And according to Dal, things went a little too far . . ."

Lori's face turned blood red. Muttering, she plopped down in the chair and expelled a frustrated breath. "It seems we both let our hearts rule our heads. But that is of little importance now," she said bleakly. "We'll be lucky if we escape with our necks."

Glumly, Cori plunked down on the edge of the bed.

Lori was right. The past was inconsequential now. They had roused two sleeping lions who at this very moment were putting their heads together to decide on the punishment they would dole out. Knowing how vindictive both men were, Cori expected no mercy. If she and Lori didn't make good their escape they could anticipate rotting in prison . . .

While Cori Lee and Lori Ann speculated on their grim future, Jake and Dal were immersed in conversation. They struggled to resolve their dilemma of twin thieves, lovely but infuriating twins who were as guilty as sin!

Dal shook his blond head in dismay and exhaled a long sigh. "Never in my worst nightmare would I have dreamed that imp . . . those imps," he amended "would get themselves involved in such a devious plot. I've had a few run-ins with wily scoundrels, but those two . . ." He raked his fingers through his hair and let his arms drop heavily by his side. "They even went so far as to paint bruises on Lori's face to ensure they continued to look exactly alike. And worse, they garbed themselves in padded garments, stack-heeled boots, and various disguises to conceal their identities," Dal muttered sourly. "What are we going to do about them?"

Jake shrugged a broad shoulder and stared out over the river, seeing the lights of Memphis in the distance. "If we expose them for what they are, Layton will have their heads for hoodwinking him. And Kyle Benson . . ."

Jake broke off into a wordless scowl. He shuddered to think how Benson would employ the information to satisfy his obsessive lust for Cori. Layton would demand severe restitution for ruining the *Belle's* reputation, not to mention how outraged he would be to learn he had hired master criminals to entertain and rob his passengers and prospective investors. And why had the twins concentrated on Layton's investors? Jake couldn't puzzle that out.

"Do you still love her?" Jake asked after a moment.

Dal jerked up his head, muttered under his breath and then nodded begrudgingly. "Despite my wounded pride, my stunned amazement, and everything else, I do. But damned if I know why!"

"And you're willing to keep their secret until I can devise a way to work this out?"

Dal's blond brows formed a single line over his golden brown eyes. "What do you have in mind?"

"I'm proposing that we employ our recently discovered knowledge to ensure these two hellions toe the line."

Dal peered quizzically at the wry smile that quirked Jake's lips. "I don't follow you."

"If Layton suspects there are twins, he might become suspicious and put one and one together. Brains aren't Layton's largest commodity, but he might begin to wonder if they were in on the thefts. If you recall, Cori was always somewhere in the vicinity when the victims were relieved of their cash. Layton might begin to see the pattern if he has time to consider it. As for me, I won't be satisfied until I know why those she-males have targeted the *Belle*. Both of them refused to say why they did it. That makes me suspicious."

Jake stared across the moonlit water. "Three times now Cori has referred to me as the enemy, and I want to know why. Unless I miss my guess, they have ulterior motives for preying on the *Belle*."

"And what is to prevent either of them from attempting escape if we don't disclose what we know to the proper authorities?" Dal questioned.

A mischievous grin worked its way across Jake's craggy features. "It's simple, my friend. If one of them does try to flee, we'll make it known that the other sister will be left to serve a double sentence. If we keep them separated, they can't scheme to elude us."

"You are suggesting blackmail?" A sly grin caught the corner of Dal's mouth. "What an ingenious way of keeping those lovely little thieves under thumb," he chuckled delightedly.

"Blackmail does have its advantages," Jake snickered.

Before he could unfold the details of his plan, the door to Cori's cabin flew open and both women shot across the deck. It seemed Cori and Lori intended to scamper away to hide until the steamer arrived in Memphis. No doubt they would lose themselves in the crowd, never to be seen or heard from again.

Unfortunately for the fleeing twins, their captors fell into hot pursuit. Despite their struggles, Dal grabbed Lori and Jake latched onto Cori, dragging them in opposite directions. As Dal towed his hostage into the twin's cabin, Jake dragged Cori to his own quarters.

Standing between her and the door like a human barricade, Jake glowered at the fuming brunette who had reassummed her masculine disguise. "I have a proposition for you," he announced.

Cori swore under her breath. She had been so certain Dal and Jake had stormed off to find Layton and reveal the names of the thieves. She had assumed wrong. Thunderation! Now she was right back where she started—in serious trouble.

"What sort of proposition?" she questioned with consternation. "Don't tell me you're actually going to be gracious enough to allow me to choose my own method of death."

"Method of *torture*," he corrected with an ornery smile. "You can give yourself up to Layton and his new henchmen, Kyle Benson, or you can return all the stolen money and do exactly what I tell you."

"I'd rather die!" Cori snapped rebelliously.

172

"That isn't one of your choices," he countered matter-of-factly.

Cori was so frustrated she could have bit nails in two. "I am not about to make any decisions without consulting my sister."

Jake strode purposefully toward her, backing her into a corner. "You are in no position to make stipulations," he reminded her. "If you wish to see your sister in Layton's hands, suffering all the tortures of the damned, that can easily be arranged." A satanic smile hovered on his lips as Cori flinched at his unpleasant plans for Lori. "I'm sure you would suffer nine kinds of hell knowing your dear sister died while you were forced to go on living. If you don't follow my demands to the letter, I will see to it that Layton and Kyle take out their anger on Lori as if she alone were responsible for the robberies."

Cori studied Jacob's goading smile. He not only looked as if he would follow through with the threat, he behaved as if he would derive pleasure in watching Lori suffer. Losing Lori would devastate Cori. Seeing Lori suffer would indeed be worse than death!

From what Cori could ascertain, the situation was hopeless. She was at Jake's mercy, and he had no compassion left for her now that she had deceived him. She supposed she should be thankful he was willing to keep the secret from his cousin. *Why* he would, Cori didn't have the slightest idea. As far as she knew, blood was thicker than water.

"Why are you doing this?" she quizzed him.

A devilish smile pursed his lips. "Because I will have you exactly where I want you," he informed her glibly. "You will become my submissive slave and mistress who obeys my every wish. Your sister's life hangs in the balance. And to ensure that she doesn't suffer for the both of you, you will do my bidding until I tire of repaying you for the hell you've put me through."

So he hated her that much, did he? It was *humiliation* that she was to endure for hornswoggling him, for the mortification she had caused him. Well, wasn't he the sly one! he intended to force her to humble herself while holding the threat of Lori's execution over her head. The scoundrel! *He* was the one who deserved to be shot, not her!

"And what, my royal master, will prevent me from burying a knife in your back while you sleep?" she hissed at him.

Jake shrugged off her contemptuous tone and venomous glare as if they had no affect on him. "You seem to forget that Dal knows exactly what has transpired tonight. In the event of my untimely demise, he would see to it that my wishes were carried out."

"I hate you!" Cori spewed, eyes blazing.

"No, you love me," he taunted her unmercifully. "How quickly you have forgotten those tender lies you offered me not so long ago." He stroked the cleft in his chin and smile sardonically. "Now, let me see, what was that touching little lie you spouted at me? Ah yes, I believe you said you loved me, no matter what I thought about you, no matter what you felt you had to do." Jake curled his finger beneath her chin, forcing her to meet his goading grin. "What a talented actress you are, my dear. I'm sure with your exceptional theatrical abilities you will have no difficulty pretending to enjoy my attentions."

Cori slapped his hand away as if it were a pesky mosquito and then spun to face the wall. Calmly, Jake strode toward the door. "I will be at the wheel for a while, my dear Cori. Make yourself at home." He opened the door and leaned heavily upon it. "And do, while I'm gone, rehearse your tender lies. When I return, I'll be anxious to hear of your deep abiding love for me. The same, of course, that I feel for you . . ."

174

As if a jailer had clanged her cell shut, she heard the key turn in the lock, imprisoning her in the texas.

Cori dropped numbly into the chair and soundly cursed herself for involving her sister and Skully in this lame-brained scheme to bleed Layton Breeze dry. She hadn't even considered meeting with calamity when she was fighting a noble cause. But she had met catastrophe head on. And disaster's name was Jacob Wolf! He would make her pay ten times over for deceiving him and robbing his family's company.

"Thunderation," Cori muttered dejectedly. Crime not only didn't pay, but the punishment Jake had designed for her was worse than all the tortures of the damned. And the worst part of all was that she truly had fallen in love with that vindictive rascal. Her hell on earth was knowing that he would never ever believe her . . . Tender lies . . . that's what he'd called her confessions of love.

Cori slumped and her spirits scraped rock bottom. She would probably spend the rest of her life regretting the day she'd met that green-eyed rake. As vengeful as Jake seemed to be, he would probably find some clever way to ensure she suffered for humiliating him throughout eternity, too!

Sweet merciful heavens, how was it possible that, when a woman assumed things were as bad as they could get, things managed to get even worse?

Chapter 13

Cori had been sitting in the texas for half an hour, analyzing the disastrous situation and reviewing her options. She assumed Jacob would be on duty for at least two hours while Terrance caught a catnap. She also knew they were nearing Memphis. If she didn't escape and take Lori with her, they were doomed to a miserable fate.

Muttering several unladylike curses, Cori paced the floor like a caged tiger. She had to take the risk of escape. Her somber gaze circled to the locked door and a slow smile worked its way across her lips. According to Skully, there wasn't a lock that couldn't be picked. He had trained her in all the unseemingly arts that he felt she and Lori needed to carry out their scheme to torment Breeze Steamboat Company—from picking pockets to picking locks. And if ever there was a lock that needed to be picked it was the one that held her captive in the texas.

Determined of purpose, Cori tugged a hair pin loose and turned her attention to the lock. If she and Lori could escape, they could get a message to Skully later and then hide out in Memphis until the coast was clear. The town now boasted a population of about twenty thousand. They could don disguises and lose themselves in the crowd . . .

The click of the lock put a triumphant smile on Cori's exquisite features. Imprison her in his cabin, would he? Jacob Wolf could never hold her for very long, Cori thought smugly. What had been between them was officially over. It had to be. Jake despised her and she was every kind of fool if she kept carrying this torch for him. She had known from the beginning that falling in love with her enemy could prove disastrous and it most certainly had!

Cautiously, Cori eased open the door and peeked out into the darkness. She inched along the outer wall of the texas toward her own cabin.

A dim light flitered through the curtained window. Apparently Lori was still awake, stewing over the catastrophic events of the evening. Poor Lori, Cori mused sympathetically. She had fallen hard for the suave Dal Blaylock. She was probably as crushed by his contempt as Cori had been when Jake taunted her.

Squatting down, Cori prepared to pick the lock, but the knob twisted in her hand and the portal swung open. Cori didn't know who was more surprised by what they saw, she or the two occupants in bed. It was too close to call.

Two pair of shocked eyes blinked at Cori, who was so startled that she collapsed to her knees in the doorway. There, shielded by the quilt that was haphazardly draped over them, were Lori and Dal, snuggled up together like two bugs in a rug.

Damn that Jacob Wolf! He had led her to believe that Lori was to be sacrificed for Cori's criminal activities. But Lori looked anything but tortured! Embarrassed at being caught in bed with Dal was what she looked. Double damn that Jacob Wolf. Cori had wasted a perfectly good half hour stewing over her sister's fate.

Composing herself, Cori gathered her feet beneath her and eased the door shut. Spying Dal's discarded pistol among his clothes, Cori quickly retrieved it and pointed it

177

at his bare chest.

"Don't kill him!" Lori yelped, pressing herself in front of Dal.

"How'd you escape?" Dal croaked.

"I had to pick the lock, but it seems my dear sister was able to come and go as she pleased." Her narrowed eyes fastened accusingly on Lori. "Obviously, she chose to stay . . ." Her gaze darted sideways, and she noticed the roll of cash that was lying atop the bureau, the roll that had previously been tacked to the bottom of the dresser drawer.

Aware of where Cori's gaze had strayed, Lori hurriedly explained. "Dal said if I would return the stolen money, all would be forgiven, provided I consented to marry him." Her loving gaze swung back to the handsome blond who had stolen her heart. "I don't want to leave him, if that's what you're planning. I love him . . ."

It was obvious Lori had convinced Dal that her affection for him was enduring, no matter what had transpired the past week. He was staring at Lori in a way that Cori wished Jake would stare at her.

That was never going to happen, Cori told herself realistically. Jake had made it clear that he wanted revenge for her attempt to victimize Layton and his investors. Jake had convinced himself that Cori offered lies, not love. He had vowed to torture her with mental anguish. If he could no longer use Lori as a weapon against Cori, he would simply find another way to keep her in chains. Cori knew that as well as she knew the sun rose in the east.

"Will you ensure Jake doesn't use Lori to get back at me?" Cori questioned Dal somberly. "Without your solemn promise that she'll be safe, I'll be forced to take her with me, whether she wants to go or not."

Dal was trapped between a rock and a hard spot. He had promised to follow Jake's orders, but when he and Lori were alone, one thing had led to another. They had lashed out at each other, but in the end their affection for each other smothered their anger. Lori had agreed to hand over the stolen cash when he presented her with the choice of serving a prison term or becoming his wife. And to assure him that she honestly cared for him, she had . . .

Difficult though it was, Dal tucked the tantalizing memories of the past hour in the corner of his mind. Although he and Lori had resolved their differences, Jake and Cori hadn't or she wouldn't have been here, intent on escape.

If Dal allowed Cori to flee, Jake was going to be positively furious. *As if he had a choice,* Dal reminded himself grimly as he peered at the pistol that was now aimed at the top of his head. Cori had every intention of leaving the ship, and Dal was not suitably dressed to give chase. The fact that Lori wanted to stay and risk Jake's wrath was proof that she cared. Lori hadn't given in to him just to save her lovely neck. Dal knew that for certain.

"Jacob won't harm her," Dal assured Cori. "He may be even more spiteful and vindictive if he ever catches up with you. But I think he will respect my request to let Lori go free since she returned the money."

"You have more faith in your friend than I do," Cori smirked cynically. Her ebony eyes riveted on her twin. "Jacob will look at you and see me. That will remind him how much he loathes me and I don't want him to take out his frustration on you."

"I'm willing to take the risk to be with Dal," Lori insisted. Her dark eyes drifted back to Dal and she melted like butter. "I'm sorry, Cori. He means as much to me as our . . ."

Cori knew what her sister refused to say in Dal's presence. Her feelings for Dal were now as strong as their

179

noble crusade for justice and revenge.

Damn, their plan had worked superbly for almost ten months—until Jacob Wolf and Dal Blaylock swaggered onto the *Mississippi Belle*. Now everything was a tangled mess.

Resigning herself to the fact that she had to strike out alone, Cori strode over to the bureau to extract enough cash to sustain her until she could find work. She prayed Dal's friendship with Jake was strong. If not, Lori would find herself up to her neck in trouble. Cori made a mental promise to sneak to Natchez and ensure all was well with her twin. If not, she and Skully would devise a way to rescue Lori from her predicament.

Jake had been right. Nothing would torment Cori more than seeing her sister suffer for the scheme Cori had devised for revenge. And damn his soul to hell if he took his frustrations out on Lori! Cori prayed Dal could intervene and prevent Jake from dragging Lori off to jail for her crimes. But it wasn't a crime, Cori told herself firmly. It was restitution. Layton Breeze had, with malice aforethought, schemed to . . .

"If you're going you had better go now," Lori prompted. "If there was even a remote chance that Jacob Wolf might come chasing after me, I know I would want a head start!"

Accepting that good advice, Cori spun toward the door, her dark cape rustling about her. Jake had been furious with her when he discovered the truth. Cori wasn't sure she wanted to be on the same continent with him when he realized she had picked his lock and fled. There wouldn't be an appropriate word to describe how angry he would be this time!

Her worried gaze circled back to her sister, wondering if Dal wasn't a mite too confident in thinking he could protect Lori from Jake. He could be extremely frightening when he was in a full-blown rage.

180

"I'll take good care of her," Dal assured Cori, interpreting her apprehensive stare.

"And if worse comes to worst, tell Jake this was all my idea and Lori would never have participated if I hadn't forced her into it."

And then Cori was gone, stealing quietly into the night. She had taken time to snatch up her stage mustache, beard, and wig, intending to remain disguised as a man until she reached Memphis. Then she would conceal her identity behind another disguise, just in case Jacob came looking for her. And God help her if he found her! Cori shuddered at the unnerving thought. She didn't want to think about that just now. She had an escape to make.

As the steamer eased into port, Cori lost herself in the flood of roustabouts who surged from the main deck to unload and replace cargo with stacks of cotton bales that were piled on the wharf. Only when she had scurried up the steep banks toward town did she breathe a sigh of relief. But it was short-lived. A group of hooligans suddenly emerged from the shadow of the trees and congregated around her. They eyed her fashionable garments as if she were a wealthy gentleman, ripe for the picking.

Of all the rotten luck! Cori muttered as she clutched the pistol she brought with her. For eight months she had been robbing Layton Breeze's prospective investors. Now it looked as if she was going to become the victim instead of the bandit. Damn, nothing had worked out as she had anticipated!

When the steamer had been secured at the docks, Jake left the pilothouse to oversee the loading of cargo and boarding of passengers. The symptoms of the grippe were still nagging him but he forced himself not to break

181

stride. He kept telling himself he didn't have time to become ill. He had a ship to run and the problem with the twins to resolve.

As he climbed down the steps to the hurricane deck and ambled past the texas, a pensive frown furrowed his brow. He couldn't help but wonder how that dark-haired hellion was enjoying frying in her own grease. Jake wanted to scare the living daylights out of Cori, to make her suffer for humiliating him.

The opportunity of tormenting her was too good to bypass. Assuring himself that the taste of revenge would relieve his sore throat, Jake reversed direction. He intended to burst into the texas and harass Cori once more for good measure. When he finished with her she would be begging for mercy and repenting for her daredevil crimes. Jake had that vixen right where he wanted her . . . or so he thought . . .

A muted growl exploded from his lips when the unlocked portal swung open. To his outrage, he found himself staring at an empty cabin.

Jake fixed his blazing green eyes on the door a few cabins away from his own. No doubt Cori had escaped and darted off to save her sister. Dal was probably lying in an unconscious heap, tied up in knots.

Envisioning the worst, Jake dashed toward the cabin and barged inside. He stumbled upon the same scene Cori had witnessed—two naked bodies entwined under the same quilt. It was apparent to Jake that Dal had buckled to his desires. He was hopelessly enamored of the delectable minx who shared the identical voice, face, and body of her lovely sister. Damn! Jake should have known better than to let Dal handle Lori Ann. Dal's idea of *handling* that gorgeous sprite was not at all what Jake had in mind!

"You're a lot of help." Jake scowled bitterly at Dal and then turned his venomous snarl on Lori. "Where is she?"

"Where's who?" Lori questioned in feigned innocence, shielding herself from Jake's smoldering glare.

"Don't play ignorant with me, damn you," Jake snapped, causing Lori to shrink away from his lightning voice and thundering growl. "Where's that cunning sister of yours?"

When Lori tilted a defiant chin, Jake stomped toward the bed as if he meant to snatch her up and shake the information out of her.

Dal shot upright, positioning himself in front of Lori. "Don't lay a hand on her, Jacob," he all but shouted. "Lori returned the stolen money." His outthrust arm indicated the wad of cash, minus the amount Cori had taken to pay her living expenses. "I assured Lori that we wouldn't press charges if the cash was returned to its proper owners."

"Et tu Brute?" Jake muttered at his so-called friend. "And don't tell me you didn't know Cori escaped. She wouldn't have left without trying to take her beloved sister with her."

Jacob looked as if he wanted to strangle the both of them. His face was puckered in a furious sneer that did his handsome features no justice.

"Now calm down, Jacob," Dal insisted. "You got the money back. Lori is repentant of her crimes, aren't you, Lori?" He turned his blond head to glance at the wary brunette. "Tell Jake you're sorry."

"I'm sorry," she murmured over Dal's broad shoulder.

"There, you see?" Dal broke into a beaming smile. "All is forgiven and forgotten. We'll divvy up the money to the victims and that will be the end of it."

"That *won't* be the end of it!" Jake contradicted in a harsh tone. "Your idea of justice is getting this wench in your bed and I . . ."

"You will not refer to my fiancée as a wench!" Dal snapped, offended. "Apologize this instant."

"All right," he conceded sarcastically. "Your idea

183

of justice is getting this *thief* in your bed."

Dal found himself forced to rely on Cori's suggestion. Jake looked like boiling fury standing there with his lips curled and his huge chest heaving with each frustrated breath he inhaled. His temper was rising to match his soaring fever. Nothing could have been worse than for Jake to be furious and ill all at the same moment. One condition was seriously aggravating the other.

"It wasn't Lori's fault," Dal defended her. "Cori planned the entire scheme. Cori performed all the robberies. So all Lori is really guilty of is withholding information against her sister. Her crime is loving her sister enough to keep the silence."

"Just as I suspected," Jake muttered hoarsely.

"Please let it be over," Lori implored, clutching the quilt beneath her chin. "I love Dal, and more than anything, I want to marry him and begin our new life together."

"A likely story," Jake sniffed. "How easy it is to repent and beg forgiveness after you've been caught." His watery green eyes bore down on Dal. "And you let lust do your thinking for you! I asked for your help and you betrayed me."

"It's over," Dal declared testily. "You have the money back. Be content with that."

"It will never be over while that devious little witch is running around loose," Jake countered as he turned toward the door. "That woman is completely out of control and I won't rest until she *is* under control!"

Slamming the portal behind him, Jake stamped across the deck. He felt forsaken by his best friend. Dal was ready to drop the matter because he had what he had wanted. Jake had nothing but a five-foot-three-inch headache, a raw throat, and a queasy stomach. Damn it, when he got his hands on Cori Pierce he was going to ensure she suffered all the torments of hell.

Since Dal had become Lori's knight in shining armor, Jake had no other choice. Dal had fallen head over heels for that lovely imp and he was prepared to defend her to the death. Damn Dal and his Southern chivalry! Damn Cori and her daring shenanigans! And damn the grippe! What Jake really needed was to crawl into bed and recuperate. Instead, he was forced to dash off on a wild-goose chase in the middle of the night!

A frustrated sigh tumbled from Jake's lips as he took the steps two at a time to reach the main deck. Dal had found himself a bride and all Jake had gotten from this ridiculous challenge of theirs was trouble with a capital T. Dal had been offered confessions of love and Jake had been plied with lies and deception. He wasn't going to be satisfied until he knew why Cori had preyed on the *Mississippi Belle*, why she had referred to him as the enemy. Damn the money. Damn the banditry. Damn, damn, damn! Jake wanted answers to the questions that were buzzing around his fevered brain.

Jake stormed across the gang plank like a charging rhinoceros, searching the faces in the torchlight. Somewhere in Memphis was a female garbed in men's clothes. And when Jake got his hands on that minx he was going to . . .

A pistol shot shattered Jake's vengeful thoughts. His gaze swung toward the sound, which was followed by several muffled curses. On the cliff above him he heard a woman's shriek. His heart stalled in his chest when he recognized Cori's voice.

Frantic, Jake scrambled straight up the slope to see three burly men wrestling the pistol from the victim they had erroneously assumed to be a gentleman. Her feminine shriek had momentarily stunned the brigand, but now they seemed to have intentions other than divesting her of her money.

Jake rumbled toward them like a locomotive. His

185

outstretched arms fastened around the surly group, taking all of them to the ground with him.

Cori groaned painfully as she was squashed between three foul-smelling bodies. She swore this group of hooligans had never engaged in bathing of their own free will. Getting rained on was as close as they'd ever come to being clean. They stank to high heaven, and their offensive smell was being smeared all over her. Lord, what a night this was turning out to be!

When first approached by the hooligans, Cori had tried to offer them the money in her pocket, but one of them had pounced on her. Naturally, she had drawn her pistol to protect herself. Seeing the flash of silver in the moonlight, one of the thieves had attempted to knock the weapon from her hand, causing it to misfire. And then the fight was on. All three men had swarmed her and she had squealed in a voice that was decidedly feminine. What a mistake that had been! Groping hands had fallen upon her and she had found herself in serious trouble.

And then the last man she'd ever wanted to see again came barreling up the cliff to tackle her and her assailants. Cori suddenly had twice as many reasons for wanting to escape. She had the unshakable feeling that Jacob Wolf was out for blood. He wouldn't have been satisfied knowing Cori had been attacked and killed by thieves. The irony wouldn't have been enough for him. Oh no, Jake wouldn't be happy unless she suffered by his hands. He wasn't about to permit these three baboons to steal his thunder when he was entertaining visions of killing her himself . . .

Pained grunts erupted from the five bodies wallowing in the mud hole into which Jake had knocked them. Cori pressed her face against the closest shoulder, hoping to avoid the flying fists. How well she knew that Jake's fist packed a powerful wallop. She didn't want to be on the receiving end of one of his blows ever again. Neither did she wish to be clobbered by any of the three burly brutes who had accosted her.

Thunderation, she would have preferred to be home sick in bed, anywhere except in the middle of this pile of jabbing knees and swinging fists! And if anyone needed to be home sick in bed it was Jacob. But thanks to Cori, Jake also wound up in a brawl that taxed his strength.

When the body above her rolled sideways, dazed by one of Jacob's punishing blows, Cori clawed her way out from under the stack of men. With a quick jerk she freed her left leg, the one that had been entangled in the mass of appendages that were wrapped around each other like knotted ropes.

Cori's first impulse was to bound to her feet and run for her life. But she didn't have the heart to leave Jake outnumbered three to one. Two-to-one odds would keep Jake occupied while she escaped, she reckoned. Glancing frantically around her, Cori spied a broken tree limb that would serve as a makeshift club. Clutching the branch, Cori took careful aim at the moving heads. Having randomly selected one to pound on, Cori reared back to strike.

As fate would have it, Jake's skull accidently got in her way. Horrified, she watched Jacob slump atop the three men who had assaulted her. She did, however, recover from her shock in time to give all three ruffians a good clubbing.

Hurriedly she vaulted to her feet and shot through the cluster of trees that hugged the hill.

By the time Cori made her escape, a crowd had gathered. She spared a quick glance over her shoulder to ensure that someone would come to Jake's rescue now that she had incapacitated him. She didn't dare head toward town, not with Jacob only minutes behind her. Intent on losing herself in the woods, Cori plunged deeper into the thicket of trees. Lord, she dreaded the

187

thought of Jacob rousing to consciousness and pursuing her. No doubt he would suspect her of purposely splitting his skull. Jake had been furious before. There was no telling how outraged he would be when he awoke! Cori shuddered at the thought.

Breathlessly Cori battled her way through the dense underbrush. If not for her stage mustache, beard, and cape, she swore her skin would have been slashed to pieces. Thorns and branches leaped out to snag her clothes and hamper her escape, but Cori gritted her teeth and ran for her life . . . worthless though she knew it would be if Jacob Wolf caught up with her. God help her if he did! She was definitely going to need all the divine assistance she could get.

Chapter 14

Jake awoke and groaned miserably. He propped himself up on all fours while the citizens who had come to lend a helping hand subdued the three ruffians whom Cori had also clubbed over the head.

"Go fetch the constable," somebody shouted.

Footsteps echoed in the night and the sound of shuffling feet filtered into Jake's pounding brain.

"Are you all right, Mr. Wolf?" one of the roustabouts from the *Belle* questioned.

Hell no, he wasn't all right. His throat was raw and he was chilled from wallowing in the mud. The dull headache he'd endured all evening was now throbbing agony, thanks to that cursed Cori Pierce or whoever she really was. Only God knew for sure!

"I'm fine," Jake lied. His voice sounded like the screech of an owl. "Where's the victim these three thugs accosted?"

The roustabout gestured toward the clump of trees. "He tore off in that direction."

Staggering, Jake rose to full stature. He glared at the canopy of trees and headed toward them. Pausing momentarily, Jake listened for the sounds of thrashing. When he had guessed Cori's direction, he charged

189

forward, determined to catch up with her if it was the last thing he ever did. And the way things were going, it probably *would* be the last thing he ever did!

Lord, what had he done to deserve the hell that woman had put him through? Oh, certainly Jake had seen wilder days, but he had never victimized another living soul and he had never purposely hurt another human. He hadn't exactly been a saint where women were concerned, but certainly he didn't deserve to get mixed up with that ebony-eyed witch, did he?

Envisioning his fingers curled around Cori's swanlike throat, Jake fought his way through the entangled bushes. Curse that woman! When he got his hands on her he was going to strangle her, shoot her, and then skin her alive!

Cori gasped in fear as she glimpsed the form of a man in the crisscrossed shadows. She had hoped Jacob would be indisposed for several minutes before he pursued her again. No such luck. He was hot on her heels and he was snarling like an enraged grizzly bear. Damn. . . .

Cori swiveled her head back around and she spied a creek gleaming like silver in the moonlight. Calculating the width of the rivulet, she prepared to leap onto the opposite bank.

It was wider than she thought. She managed to jump halfway across and landed with a splash in mid-stream. Braving another glance over her shoulder at Jacob, who looked furious enough to tear her to pieces with his bare hands, Cori scrambled toward the opposite bank and clawed her way up the slippery slope. The recent rains had left the incline slick as glass, and Cori reached up to clutch at the mass of leaves and branches that lined the rim of the gully. When she tried to hoist herself up, the loose leaves and limbs gave way and she found herself

190

clawing at the air.

With a surprised shriek, Cori toppled backward, landing flat on her back in the knee-deep creek. That was when Jacob showed up.

Terror filled Cori's eyes as Jake's fists clenched around the lapels of her cape. He yanked her roughly out of the water, the moonlight slanting across his craggy features. This was definitely not the face of a happy man, Cori realized as he bared his teeth and growled at her.

"You little witch!" Jake seethed, gasping for breath.

"Kill me and be done with it," Cori hissed at him. She resigned herself to a battle lost, but she vowed to take her secret with her to her grave.

"I want some answers first!" Jacob boomed, shaking her until her teeth rattled.

"No, yes, yes, and no," she sassed him in mocking retort. "There are your answers to whatever stupid questions you wanted to ask. Now get this over with!"

She was purposely antagonizing him, daring him to do his worst. Jake was sorely tempted to do just that. Hell's fire, of all the women in the world, why did this she-male have to wander into his life to torment him to no end?

"Why did you prey on my family's steamboat company?" Jake growled. "Why this particular ship? Why am I your declared enemy? Damn it, you better tell me!"

She didn't of course. She simply glowered defiantly at him.

Muttering, Jake swung her down into the creek, submerging her in the water. He held her under until he knew she needed a breath of air.

"Why?" he demanded as he lifted her face from the creek.

"Curse your soul!" Cori flashed furiously.

Jake shoved her down again. He was going to drag answers from this obstinate sprite if he had to keep this up for the rest of the night!

It did take a while. Cori was defiance personified and Jacob was determination in the flesh. The procedure continued until her strength was almost depleted.

"Enough!" Cori choked out. "I'll tell you."

It was several minutes before she could breathe normally enough to talk without sputtering and gasping for air. And while she wheezed and coughed, Jake hooked his arm around her waist and sidestepped up the slope. Anchoring his hand on a low-hanging limb, Jake hoisted himself and Cori onto flat ground. Before she gave any thought to escape, he sank down on top of her in the thick carpet of grass.

To say he didn't trust this wily vixen was an understatement. As long as he had her sprawled beneath him, her wrists shackled in his fists, he didn't anticipate an escape attempt. But never again would he give this shrewd termagant the benefit of the doubt.

"I'm waiting," Jake persisted, just in case she thought he forgot the whole point of this tortuous investigation.

"I can barely breathe with you sitting on me," Cori croaked. Damn, she hated being held down!

Jake relented enough to shift his weight to her hips instead of her belly. "Start talking," he commanded in a whiplash voice. "I've run clean out of patience, woman."

Cori was already infuriated, and when she started talking, the words rushed out in a spasm of hisses. "Your cousin killed my father and stole our steamer! I wanted to steal back ever penny of the investment Layton swindled from us. And when I had enough cash to drag your all-powerful family to court, I wanted Layton to rot in jail for his dastardly crime!"

The emotion Cori had buried beneath layers of bitterness and revenge erupted. She knew she would never enjoy the satisfaction of besting Layton Breeze, not when Jacob Wolf stood in her way. Tears streamed down

192

her cheeks as memories of her father rose within her. Cori had sworn to avenge Michael Shelton's death, and now her visions of revenge were scattering like ashes in the wind.

"You and your money-hungry family destroyed my family. You left us without a father, left us destitute," she raged through the onrush of tears. "My father sank all the money we had into the *Mississippi Belle* and we had nothing left to call our own after Layton stole it away from us. I wanted part of that one hundred thousand dollars back, enough to fight Layton in court and see him punished for what he did!"

Bewildered, Jake peered into her tear-stained face. He had never seen this strong-willed hellion come apart at the seams. She had always appeared the epitome of self-control. But once she had revealed her secret, all the emotion that boiled inside her had erupted like a volcano.

Thinking back, Jake recalled that Layton hadn't said how he'd acquired the *Belle*. But a weasel though Layton was, Jake could scarcely believe his cousin was capable of murder. Greedy to the extreme? Yes. Arrogant without reason? Most definitely. But murder? Jake seriously doubted it and he proceeded to tell Cori so.

"Defend him, why don't you?" Cori scoffed through the flood of tears. "I knew you would. But Layton *did* kill my father. Layton hired thugs on the wharf to discourage passengers from boarding the *Belle* while it was in my father's charge. He passed rumors that my father was incompetent and the *Belle* wasn't seaworthy, that it was a deathtrap. He lowered his ticket prices to undercut competition, but still it wasn't enough to bankrupt my father."

Cori inhaled a shallow breath and plowed on. "Layton was envious of the ship. He wanted to own the finest steamer on the Mississippi. Twice he insisted on buying the *Belle* for a third its cost and twice my father rejected

193

the ridiculous offer."

Her lips trembled as the haunting nightmare rose above her. "The third time my father met with Layton he didn't come back. I went searching for him . . ." Choked sobs burst from her throat. "I found his body behind his office on the dock. He'd been shot in the back and there was a bloody gash on his right cheek. The deed to the *Belle* was missing from his desk, along with the cash he had on hand. No doubt Layton forged the bill of sale without paying a cent. He merely murdered my father to get what he wanted."

Jake stared somberly at the tortured expression on Cori's face. "Are you certain that robbery wasn't the motive for the killing?" he questioned hoarsely.

"Of course it was made to look that way," Cori gritted out. "I sent the sheriff to accuse Layton of the crime, but he dismissed it as ridiculous. According to Layton, he paid my father thirty thousand dollars for the *Belle*, and he insisted Papa had been robbed of his cash roll. But I know better. Yet who could possibly contest the word of the all-powerful Layton Breeze and make it stick when the family name carries so much weight?" Cori laughed bitterly. "The only way Lori and I could strike back at Layton was to defeat him at his own game. And we were beginning to make him feel the pinch until you came along."

Cori muffled a sniff and glared at the shadowed face above hers. "You *are* my enemy. You represent all I've lost. You and your loathsome cousin are enjoying the profits my father's steamer has made." She turned her head away, letting the river of tears bleed down the side of her face. "Go ahead, drag me to the constable's office and have me hanged for banditry. At least I've had the satisfaction of knowing I've hounded Layton for the past eight months . . . even if I can never fully repay your family for the anguish you caused me."

194

"I had nothing to do with the loss of your steamer," Jake muttered.

"And of course you will offer to help me bring your cousin to justice," she scoffed cynically.

"There has been some kind of mistake," Jake declared.

"Indeed there has and I made it," Cori spat at him. "My mistake was getting caught. I knew you wouldn't believe the truth about your cousin. Why do you think I refused to tell you?"

"And you delighted in stringing me along with your confession of love," Jake harshly accused. "Since you wanted to destroy my family for what you *thought* we did, you employed your feminine charms to have your laugh on me as well. Ah, the amusement you have enjoyed at my expense."

"But you will be fully compensated, won't you?" Cori snapped at him. "You'll watch me hang, knowing you were the only man I ever allowed close to me."

"Ah, what sacrifices you have made to have your revenge," Jake snorted derisively. "You bedded your enemy, hoping to gain favors."

Cori was about to admit it was love that compelled her to make those choices. Jake wouldn't believe her now. He had thrown the words back in her face earlier that evening and he was doing it again.

"Go ahead, little witch, ply me with a few more tender loving lies," Jake taunted as he lowered his head, letting his lips hover a scant few inches from hers. "Tell me how you loved me despite your hatred for my family. Tell me you didn't give this delicious body of yours to distract me and save yourself . . ."

The feel of his muscular thigh gliding between her legs didn't provoke the response Cori wanted to feel. She wanted to experience repulsion and disgust, but her traitorous body responded instinctively, just as it always did. Unwanted sensations of pleasure assaulted her while her defenses struggled to reconstruct themselves. Her emotions were in a turmoil and she was vulnerable to this lion of a man, even while he taunted and mocked her.

"Aren't you going to offer me your body again to save your lovely hide, Cori?" he jeered at her. "I'm a man, after all. Isn't sex all you think a man wants from a beautiful woman, no matter how cunning and deceptive she is?"

"I hate you," Cori sputtered in frustration.

"Of course you do, sweet witch," he taunted unmercifully. "But to spare your miserable life you'll swear undying love and surrender to me, won't you?"

His lips swooped down on hers, wanting to punish her for all the torment she'd put him through the past week. But just as before, the need to hurt her was eclipsed by the need to make wild passionate love to her.

Jacob could list a score of reasons why he should drag this minx to jail and let her rot while she awaited trial. He didn't believe her tale of vengeance against Layton. He suspected she had turned her grieving for her father into bitterness against the Breeze family. Vengeance had poisoned her. She wanted restitution, even if Layton wasn't to blame for her father's mysterious death. Cori had decided Layton was guilty and nothing would change her mind.

And yet even knowing Cori was guilty of thievery, knowing she had vowed love when she truly loathed him and all he represented, Jake still couldn't withdraw when her luscious body was lying intimately beneath his. This one woman—this impossible female—affected him the way no one else did. She had lied to him, betrayed him, used him. She had clubbed him over the head and left him unconscious when he tried to rescue her from disaster. He could never trust her. But God help him, he still wanted her desperately, maddeningly.

His hands began to roam over her shapely body of their

own accord, tunneling beneath her skirt to make contact with her silken flesh. A tormented groan rattled in his throat when he felt unappeased desire spearing through him. When Cori arched against him, Jake cursed her a thousand times over for making him want her more than he already did. She had learned to use this delectable body of hers to devastate him. She pretended to be aroused by his touch, skillful actress that she was. She had learned how to destroy a man's thoughts and leave him shuddering with primal instincts.

Although Jake was thinking the worst of her for reacting to his masterful touch, Cori was lost to the sweet hypnotic magic that he instilled in her. If this was to be the last time she lay in Jake's sinewy arms, she would cherish every splendorous moment, commit every wondrous sensation to memory. There was simply no hope for it. This one man had the power to devastate her with his explosive kisses and titillating caresses. He could make her beg for his touch, revel in the pleasure that flooded over her.

Cori closed her eyes and let her foolish heart rule her head for this one moment. She needed his practiced caresses as she needed air to breathe. The taste of his ravishing kisses was the nourishment she required to survive.

Impatiently she tugged at his muddy shirt, longing to feel his flesh beneath her fingertips, aching to instill the same mindless need in him that channeled through her. Wantonly she trailed her hands over his nipples and explored the lean muscles of his belly. Her lips met his, her tongue darting into the soft moist depths to entice and explore.

As her adventurous hands brushed over his hips, Jake struggled to inhale a breath that wasn't thick with the scent of this exasperating witch, but she had already fogged his mind and he was a victim of his own lusty needs. He longed to rip away the hindering garments, to hold her to him until these erotic feelings ebbed.

He nibbled at her satiny flesh like a starved man, wanting to devour every exquisite inch of her. He suckled at the rose-tipped peaks of her breasts, feeling her arch toward him in eager response. His hands fluttered down her ribs, pushing the garments out of his way so he could expose her body to his greedy kisses.

For the moment Jake let himself believe that her muffled moans were provoked by the pleasure he bestowed on her, that she wasn't feigning the hunger of mindless passion. Of all the women he had seduced, he wanted this she-male to be shattered by his embrace, and yet he wondered if she truly was, wondered if she was playing another cruel game with him. It shouldn't have mattered so much to him, but it did. Making her succumb to him wasn't enough. He wanted her love, even though he knew she hated him for what she thought her family had done to her father.

"Jake, please . . ."

The words broke from her throat in a tormented plea. Cori was on fire for him, and even stubborn pride couldn't restrain the monstrous cravings he aroused in her.

"More?" he whispered against her quaking flesh. "How much more must a man give to satisfy a witch like you!"

"I want you . . ." Cori gasped as his knowing fingers teased and aroused her by maddening degrees.

"How much, Cori?" he rasped in question.

A wild uncontrollable shudder rocked her soul and she cried out his name as she writhed beneath him, certain she would die if he didn't appease this insane craving that assaulted her. Wild and breathless, she tilted her face to his, studying his ruggedly handsome face in the moonlight. Oh, how she longed to tell him how she adored him. But he didn't want to hear the words. He only wanted to shame her, to appease his animal lusts. She could have been any other woman at that moment and Jake wouldn't have cared. She swore he would have preferred that she was anyone else, if not for the fact that he was having his own brand of revenge on her.

"At least I have the satisfaction of being the only man you have given yourself to, no matter what your reason," he muttered as he felt his body moving instinctively toward hers.

Cori heard his mumbled utterances but she could make no sense of them. She was so overwhelmed by hungry desire that she could think of nothing except appeasing the gigantic need he evoked from her. Shamelessly she drew him closer, stroking him, guiding him until he was the velvet flame that burned within her. As his muscular body enveloped hers, riveting sensations bombarded her, leaving her burning from inside out.

"For this I keep playing the fool and running back to you," Jake breathed against the sensitive point beneath her ear. "Because you're like a fire in my blood, curse you. Because I can never get enough of you . . ." He drove deeply within her, shattered by the intense pleasure that splintered the core of his being.

The world exploded around them, leaving them quaking in each other arms, spiraling in a whirlwind of ecstasy. It was a wild and breathless union of bodies and souls. The splendorous aftershocks held them suspended in a universe that seemed worlds away from reality.

Cori savored each delicious sensation that converged upon her as she sailed across the boundless sky. She wanted the moment to span forever, to compensate for the torment that awaited her when she returned to harsh reality. She adored the feel of Jacob's swarthy arms around her, cradling her against him as if she truly meant something special to him. But she knew it was only passion that prompted his tenderness. When he came back to his senses he would be hating her all over again.

A chill shot down Jake's spine as the numbing pleasure of passion finally wore off. He was suddenly aware of being cold and wet and ill. Pain still throbbed in his skull and his throat felt as if it had been pricked with thorns. He wondered vaguely how he could have felt so good one moment and so nauseated the next.

A rash of sneezes overtook him as he eased away, but he kept a restraining grasp on his captive. He still expected Cori to break and run the first chance she got. Why shouldn't she? he asked himself sickly. This sable-haired tigress had spent more time running *away from* than *toward* him.

"This isn't the end of it, minx," he growled hoarsely, his throat raw. "You're coming back with me."

Cori blinked in astonishment. "You're not hauling me to the Memphis jail?" she gasped.

Jake shook his raven head. "I intend to prove to you that you're wrong about Layton. And if that damned steamer means so much to you, I'll find a way to ensure you get it back."

Cori's eyes were as wide as silver dollars. "Why would you do that when you know perfectly well that I robbed Layton and his prospective investors?"

"I'm not as generous as you think," he sighed weakly as he traced her heart-shaped lips.

Cori noticed, for the first time, how feverish he was. Startled, she jerked away, but Jake misinterpreted her abrupt move and clamped down on her forearm.

"From now on, vixen, I will handle my cousin, even though you and Lori will continue to assume one identity. If Layton discovers there are two of you, he might not be as generous as me."

"And *why* are you?" she repeated warily.

"Because in return for my silence and my willingness

200

to discover who truly is at fault for your father's death, you are going to go on pretending you love me. And you will continue to share my bed," he told her in his plainspoken manner.

If Cori had been standing up she would have fallen down. For the life of her, she couldn't figure this man out!

"You'll get your precious steamer back and I will get you, for as long as I want you," he restated when she stared blankly at him.

Lord, he didn't feel well at all! His throat was on fire and his head pounded. Determined to return to the *Belle* before he collapsed, Jake staggered to his feet. When he swayed and stumbled backward, Cori clutched at his arm. Again he weaved unsteadily and Cori braced herself against him.

"Jake? Are you feeling all right?" She watched his face turn purple in the moonlight. He definitely *wasn't* all right.

Jake shoved a limp arm into his shirt. "Are you going to respect the terms of my bargain?" he croaked sickly.

"We had better get you to a doctor," she insisted as she shrugged on her damp garments.

"Answer me, damn it!" Jake growled, further irritating his scratchy throat.

"Yes, whatever you say," Cori muttered in order to shut him up and get him into bed. He looked sicker with each passing second.

Hurriedly Cori fastened his gaping shirt and then led him toward the steep creek bank. Twice they almost toppled into the water because Jake was wobbling like a newborn foal.

"You definitely need a doctor," Cori said as she waded across the rivulet.

"Just get me back to the *Belle*," Jake groaned. Every word he uttered was a new experience in pain. His throat

201

was so sore he could barely swallow.

"But you . . ." she tried to protest before Jake stumbled and they both landed with a splat in the creek.

Cori floundered to get Jake back on rubbery legs. What he didn't need in his feverish condition was another chill. But he was soaked from head to toe and she feared he had aggravated his condition.

Although Cori preferred to have a physician examine him, Jake insisted on returning to the steamer before it sailed without them. Difficult though it was, Cori maneuvered through the trees and onto the trodden path. Before she revealed herself to the torchlight, she pasted her mustache and beard in place and shoved her hair beneath her unruly wig.

By the time they reached the gangplank Jake's head was drooping noticeably and he staggered more than he walked. Employing a deep voice, Cori summoned two able-bodied crewmen to haul Jake to his cabin. Leading the way, she scurried up the steps to the texas to prepare Jake's bed.

Once she had disrobed Jake and tucked him beneath the quilts, she zoomed down the deck to fetch Dal. When she whipped open the door she found Lori and Dal doing exactly the same thing they had been doing when she had attempted escape.

"If you can tear yourself away from my sister for an hour or so, I could use some help," Cori snapped at the handsome rake in the double bed. "Jake is ill. Go tell Terrance he'll have to man the wheel and then go fetch some broth from the kitchen."

Having given her orders, Cori left, wondering if Dal had enough willpower or strength left to pry himself from Lori's arms. Ah, what Cori wouldn't give for the luxury of lounging in bed with Jake all through the night, to bask in the pleasure of loving and being loved as Lori was doing . . .

Cori scolded herself for envying her sister's good fortune. Dal obviously loved Lori as deeply as she loved him. Cori, on the other hand, would be lucky indeed if she could convince Jake that she had offered no tender loving lies. Realistically, Cori imagined she had the same chance of convincing Jake that she was sincere as an icicle had in hell.

Well, at least Lori had found happiness after a year of grief and bitterness, Cori consoled herself as she stepped into the texas. It was nice that one of them could enjoy life again. Cori had to be content with the fact that Jake still wanted her physically, even if he did hate her. It would have to be enough, she reminded herself bleakly. She knew she would never be able to earn Jacob's love. In his eyes, she had betrayed him once too often.

The most depressing part of all was that Cori couldn't blame him for his contempt. She hadn't proved herself worthy of his love, if he had any to give away, and she wasn't sure that he did. He had once declared that he wanted children but that he didn't care if he loved the wife who gave them to him. If he hadn't fallen in love before, Cori rather doubted he would at this late date, especially not with her!

"Not a snowball's chance in Hades . . ." she muttered as she leaned over to lay her palm against Jake's feverish forehead.

And there she sat all through the night, keeping a constant vigil while Jake thrashed and groaned, just as Terrance had when he came down with the grippe. The only difference was that Terrance hadn't stood out in a bone-soaking thunderstorm and wallowed in mud holes and creeks while he was ailing. Jake had, the fool. He had risked becoming sick as a dog when he chased after her. He must have been delirious *before* he caught up with her

203

or he wouldn't have come after her at all, she reckoned.

But revenge had a way of overshadowing good sense, Cori reminded herself glumly. She was a shining example of that fact. Hadn't she risked a hanging to repay Layton for murdering her father? And where had it gotten her? It had gotten her into a hopeless bargain with the one man who would never accept her love for what it really was. And that was the hell of it. Cori would be forced to share Jake's passion until he tired of her and sent her on her way. He intended to punish her for the trouble she'd caused him and his family. If she tried to escape he would probably send a posse after her and then cart her off to jail if she didn't observe the terms of his bargain.

Cori breathed a heavy-hearted sigh and shivered beneath her damp clothes. She truly should make her escape while Jake was too delirious to send bounty hunters after her. But then he would think less of her than he already did, and sooner or later he would chase her down. She couldn't run far enough or fast enough to elude this mountain of a man, she realized gloomily. It was time she accepted her fate.

Resigning herself to a dreary destiny, Cori drifted off to sleep beside Jake. Oh, how she wished she could have enjoyed what Lori had found with Dal. But that was wishing for too much and Cori damned well knew it. This, she knew, was as good as it would ever get between her and Jacob Wolf—a one-sided love affair that was entangled by his mistrust and contempt.

Chapter 15

Unaware of what had transpired, Skully went about business as planned. It wasn't unusual for him to go a day or two without making contact with the twins. They had been extremely cautious about being seen with Skully since they began their scheme to bleed Layton and his investors dry. Skully would sneak to their room on occasion to plan a robbery or he would prop himself against the railing to pass on information without glancing in their direction. But the threesome made certain no one on the *Belle* knew there was any connection between them.

Having cast his eyes on the haughty Lord *Dum*phrey, as Skully insisted on calling the foppish Englishman, he picked his victim's pocket with experienced ease. Skully had taught Cori and Lori the art, but he was a master at lifting wallets. The dim-witted Englishman hadn't even noticed his wallet was missing until he was forced to cough up his cash after losing to Skully at the gaming table. Skully derived double pleasure in watching Lord *Dum*phrey throw a tantrum English-style.

And that evening, after Cori performed her songs and dances for the passengers in the saloon, Skully dropped the confiscated wallet in her purse as he brushed past her on the boiler deck.

A muffled groan bubbled in Cori's throat. She had been so busy fretting over Jacob's bout with the grippe that she had completely forgotten about Skully's scheme to bring the English lord down several humiliating notches.

"We have to talk . . . *now*," she whispered as she strolled away. "I'll be in your cabin in five minutes."

As Cori circled the deck, Kyle Benson rounded the corner. Her heart ceased beating when Kyle glanced around, finding no one within earshot. His hand snaked out to yank Cori to his bony frame. If he expected her to be intimidated by the pistols that were draped on his hips, he was disappointed. Cori jerked her arm from his grasp and glowered disdainfully at him.

"How ironic that Layton would appoint the likes of you to guard this steamer," she hissed.

"I've tolerated enough of your haughty airs, bitch," Kyle growled, attempting to recapture her.

As quick as Kyle was, he was way too slow in shackling Cori's wrist. Flesh cracked against flesh, leaving the imprint of her fingertips on his cheek. With a snarl he lunged at her, but Cori was lightning fast. She snatched one of the pistols from his holster and jabbed him in the belly.

"Touch me again and I'll kill you," she vowed.

Since the moment she began her crusade Cori had been forced to tolerate Kyle's unwanted presence. At first he had simply tossed propositions at her and she tactfully rejected them. But Kyle had become increasingly persistent and they had finally clashed head-on in St. Louis. His true nature had come pouring out when he resorted to threatening her position on the steamer if she didn't accept his affections. And since that fateful clash of wills, Kyle's lusty fascination had transformed into spiteful obsession.

Cori wasn't stupid. She knew this womanizer wanted her and she swore she'd die before she succumbed to him.

"Someday I'll feel that silky body of yours beneath mine," Kyle sneered, glaring at the barrel of the pistol that filled the gap between them.

"Hell would sooner freeze over," Cori jeered.

The sound of footsteps heralded the approach of passengers and Cori stepped away, tucking the pistol in her purse. "I'm sure you are as incapable with women as you are at apprehending thieves," she taunted.

The snide remark set Kyle's teeth on edge and his arm automatically drew back to slap her. The moonlight glistened on his snarling face and Cori instinctively ducked away before he struck her.

Flinging Kyle a mutinous glower, Cori darted toward a middle aged couple strolling arm in arm. With a cordial greeting to the passengers, Cori scampered on her way, leaving Kyle fuming from their most recent confrontation.

Cori shoved all thoughts of Kyle aside, squared her shoulders and pushed open Skully's cabin door. She had to inform Skully of the latest developments! She found him lounging in his chair, puffing on his cheroot and smiling in wicked glee.

"I wish you could have seen the look on Lord *Dum*phrey's face when he was forced to pay his gambling debts and found his pocket empty," he snickered.

"That is the very last robbery," Cori announced. "Jacob knows . . ."

The triumphant smile slid off Skully's lips and he bit down on the end of his cigar. "How did he find out?" he croaked.

"He trailed me back to the cabin and stayed long enough to catch Lori," Cori grimly reported.

"Damn . . ." Skully grumbled. "Is he pressing charges?"

Cori shifted uneasily from one foot to the other and glanced the other way. "No, if we promised to turn the money over to him, he said he would keep silent if I would . . ." Her voice trailed off and she focused the wall as if something there had demanded her undivided attention.

"If you would what?" Skully growled, reading the handwriting on the wall. "Pleasure him?" A snort erupted from his curled lips. "That scoundrel! Is he blackmailing you into his bed? That lowdown, miserable rat! He's as bad as that cousin of his!" Skully was on his feet in a single bound. "That rascal will deal directly with me and there will be no . . ."

Cori clutched his arm as he buzzed by, madder than a hornet. "He doesn't know of your involvement and I intend to keep it that way," she informed him hastily. "As for our bargain . . ."

Skully scowled ferociously. "Damn his bargain!"

"It isn't so bad." Her long lashes swept up to peer into his disgusted frown. "He has promised to get the steamer back if I will give up my thievery and . . ."

"And you believe him?" Skully scoffed. "He's using you, Cori. You're smart enough to know that. Why would you possibly agree to such degradation?"

Cori stared at the tip of her slippers, which peeked out from under the ruffles on the hem of her emerald green gown. "Because I think I love him," she murmured.

A muffled groan vibrated in Skully's chest. "Of all the eligible bachelors in this world that have chased you and your sister, you had to go and fall for Jacob Wolf? Good God, girl, this will never . . ."

She flung up a hand to forestall his tirade. "If you'd ever been in love before perhaps you'd understand."

A faraway look passed across his sky-blue eyes as bittersweet memories of days gone by engulfed him. His shoulders slumped and he expelled a heavy sigh. "I understand better than you know, little one." Skully clasped her hand and pressed his lips to her fingertips. "I was in love with a dark-eyed beauty who was every bit as breathtaking as her twin daughters."

Cori blinked bewilderedly. Her mouth fell open but no words passed her lips.

Skully smiled remorsefully as he led Cori to his bed and sank down on the edge beside her. "Ah, how well a gambler's poker face can conceal the truth. Although I try to project a carefree attitude, I bear a few scars of my own." Holding Cori's hand in his own, Skully glanced back through the window of time and sighed. "I loved Lelia and I do believe she loved me too. But I was a restless soul who wanted to view the world and make my living at the gaming tables. Lelia wanted more than a vagabond's life." Pain slipped through his well-disciplined mask. "When I wandered off to find a new challenge in Independence, she accepted my brother's attention and his courtship. I returned six months later to learn that Lelia had consented to marry Michael."

"I'm sorry, Skully. I didn't know," Cori murmured.

"I didn't realize how much Lelia really meant to me until I lost her. I knew Michael could provide for her better than a shiftless gambler." A melancholy smile hovered on his lips as he traced Cori's exquisite features. "I have but to look at you and your sister and I see your mother, just as she was when we first met. I look at you knowing you could have been my little girl instead of Michael's. You represent what I could never have, and if you accept the terms of Wolf's bargain, you'll wind up hurting the same way I did."

Hollow laughter tumbled from his lips. "Ah, yes, for a time, until Wolf tires of his little game of promises and threats, you'll tell yourself it doesn't matter because you love him. But you'll still wind up getting hurt," he predicted bleakly. "As far as I can tell, that's about all

209

love is really good for—hurting people. Your mama wanted more than I could give so she turned to Michael. And I think she even came to love him through the years. But each time I came to visit on my way through from hither to yon, we both felt the old familiar stirrings and suffered the same regrets. And when she died . . ."

His voice cracked and it was a moment before he could compose himself. "I would have been better off not loving her. The pain has never gone away. Michael knew there was still an old flame burning between us and that was *his* pain. When Lelia died trying to bear him the son he wanted, he threw himself into dreams of this steamer and the lovely Mississippi belle he'd married, even when he knew her heart still belonged to another man. And he knew Lelia had tried to be a good wife to him in every conceivable way."

Skully dropped his hand, gathered his feet, and ambled across the cabin. "I think the reason Michael refused to sell the *Belle* was because he thought of it as some sentimental symbol of Lelia. This steamer was his lifeline—a living memory."

"Are you sure Papa knew how you and Mama felt about each other?" Cori queried softly.

Skully nodded affirmatively. "He couldn't help but know. But he loved Lelia and he accepted the bargain of getting half her heart. Michael was too good a man to blame me for continuing to carry a torch for her. He understood what loving her was all about. He never once condemned me for wanting her."

Absently, Skully paused to scoop up his private deck of cards that set on the table. With experienced ease he shuffled them and then miraculously produced the queen of hearts. He twirled the card in his fingers and then presented it to Cori. "She's a dangerous lady, this one," he warned. "She can deal you a royal flush or misery. If you play Wolf's game, you'll need a handful of

210

aces, Cori, more than you'll find in an unmarked deck."

"I'm aware of the odds," she murmured softly.

"So was I, Princess," Skully insisted as he plucked the queen of hearts from Cori's fingertips and slid it into the middle of the deck. "Too late I learned that what I lost to my younger brother was the one thing I should have clung to." He stared pointedly at Cori. "Just make sure you know that when the cards are dealt that even a gambler's luck can't hold out forever. Everybody loses sometime or another."

Cori didn't confess that she saw no other choice in her dealings with Jacob. He wanted her physically, she knew. And because he did, he had bargained with her. But if he discovered Skully was involved in the scheme to bankrupt the Breeze Company he wouldn't go lightly on her uncle. Skully was all the family Cori and Lori had left. She wasn't about to allow Skully to be hurt, especially now that she knew of the triangle in which he and her parents had been involved those long years ago. Skully had paid for his past mistakes; he had consented to teach Cori and Lori the art of picking pockets and dealing cards so they could enjoy their revenge on Layton. Skully had agreed because, way down deep, he was a sentimental softy who saw Cori and Lori as a living memory of the woman he lost and the brother who had been needlessly murdered.

"Lori and I will be disembarking from the steamer in Natchez," Cori announced, shrugging off her pensive musings. "It seems my sister and Dal Blaylock are talking of a wedding."

Skully's jaw swung off its hinges. "Good God, not her too!" he squawked.

"I do believe Dal is sincere. He loves Lori as much as she loves him," Cori assured her uncle.

Skully rolled his eyes ceilingward. "I thought I'd trained the two of you better than to get mixed up with

211

men. Lord, where did I go wrong?"

Cori ambled over to pluck up the cards from the table. With a master's skill, she spread the cards face down on the table and then flipped over the queen of hearts. "At least this fickle lady has allowed Lori to marry the man she loves," she contended.

"And you're going to settle for loving a man you can't marry because you robbed his family every chance you got," Skully muttered. "I think I'd prefer the jail sentence if I were you."

"You chose a prison of your own making." Her sullen gaze locked with his. "You spent half your life in the chains of regret because you didn't marry Mama when you had the chance. I know I can't have forever with Jacob, but I'll have a few precious months with him."

"Don't overplay your hand, Princess," Skully grumbled, shuffling the deck. "And if you need me, all you have to do is send me a message. No matter what, I'll come running back to retrieve you."

Cori pushed up on tiptoe to press a kiss to his cheek. "I love you, Uncle Skully."

He gave her a heartfelt squeeze. "And we both should have stuck to this kind of love. It's a helluva lot safer on the heart. I don't want to see you hurt by that clumsy gorilla."

"He isn't clumsy," Cori defended. Insulting Jake was a privilege she reserved for herself, and she didn't take kindly to Skully's remark.

"That's right, go ahead and defend him," he smirked. "And when he breaks your heart you'll call him every name in the book, just see if you don't."

Cori tilted a proud chin and marched toward the door. "At least I'm walking into this bargain with my eyes wide open."

"Maybe, but I don't think you're playing with a full

212

deck," Skully grumbled. "Wolf holds all the aces. Don't you forget that!"

Cori couldn't forget, and yet she was foolish and vulnerable when it came to Jake. Her only hope was that one day he'd come to feel something more than physical desire for her. Perhaps she could beat the odds and prove to him that she cared for him.

Well, it was worth a try, she encouraged herself. If she convinced Jake that there was far more to their relationship than the deceptive game they'd been playing, she might find the same happiness Lori was enjoying. And if she didn't . . .

After two days of battling a throbbing headache and queasy stomach, Jake managed to dress and struggle up the steps to the pilothouse. While Jake was under the weather, Terrance had begun teaching the young steward, who had aspirations of becoming a pilot, to read the river. Terrance had put Barry Odum behind the wheel when he was sure the channel was clear of debris, and then he dozed on the wooden bench while Barry manned the wheel. Terrance refused to be too far away in case trouble arose, and Barry had taken his every instruction to heart in his eagerness to learn. With a little more experience, Terrance was sure Barry would be worth his salt.

While Terrance was rattling off vital information to Barry, Jake stumbled into the pilothouse, looking like death warmed over.

"Get yourself back to bed," Terrance ordered. "We're managing just fine. Barry shows a great deal of promise."

"I feel fine," Jake insisted.

"Of course you do," Terrance sniffed. "That's why your eyes are sporting dark circles and your face is as

213

white as the sheet you should be lying under. Hell, I've never seen you look better, Jacob," he added sarcastically.

"I can handle the steamer," Jake declared with great conviction.

"But the point is, you don't have to. Barry is a whiz at the wheel. Give the kid a chance."

The clomp of heavy footsteps outside the pilothouse interrupted the conversation. Jake glanced around to see his cousin, looking very much like a waddling penguin in his jacket and breeches. Layton's face was puckered in a scowl that did nothing to compliment his plain features.

"Something wrong, Layton?" Jake questioned hoarsely.

"Wrong?" Layton exploded furiously. "What could possibly be wrong? I was robbed of every cent I had two nights ago and now Lord Humphrey has had his wallet stolen! I swear to God, if I ever catch the thieves that have been victimizing my ship, I'll have the bastards shot and hanged!"

"*Our* ship," Jake corrected him through gritted teeth.

"The *Belle* would have been all mine, if not for this rash of robberies," Layton trumpeted. "And you!" His flashing gray eyes riveted on his cousin. "You came along to take over the *Belle*, the same way you took everything else from me. But when we reach Natchez, I'm going to tell Gram about your domineering attitude. It would suit me just fine if we split the company right down the middle. You can have two steamers and I'll manage my two without your trying to tell me what to do all the damn time and without you firing my employees whenever it meets your whim!"

Layton stamped out, emitting muffled curses, and Jake stared after him. Layton still reminded Jake of a spoiled child who threw tantrums and tattled when he didn't get his way. Layton had grown older but he had never matured. He still clung to his childish ways.

That was about all the thought Jake spared his sulking cousin. Mostly, Jake was entertaining ideas of wringing Cori's lovely neck! Curse that woman! He had vowed to see that her precious steamer was returned to her. But she couldn't wait until Jake had recovered from illness to make necessary arrangements. Hell no, she just plowed ahead with her thieving schemes. If Layton ever found out, he'd make an example of Cori, female or no!

Leaving Terrance to teach Barry the ropes, Jake stormed off. He still felt tired and miserable, and Cori's latest shenanigan wasn't improving his foul disposition. Like a charging rhinoceros, Jake headed toward Cori's cabin. He barged inside without knocking and scowled at the scene that lay before him. He was already annoyed to no end, and seeing Dal enjoying all the pleasures of love with the light of his life turned Jake green with envy.

"Is that all the two of you ever do?" Jake muttered resentfully. What he really wanted to say was "I wish that was all I had to do."

"Next time kindly knock!" Dal demanded as he eased up on an elbow in bed. "Just because you don't happen to have a bed of roses doesn't mean the rest of us must lie on thorns."

"Where the hell's Cori?" Jake questioned grumpily.

Lori peeked up at Jake through a tangle of black velvet lashes. "She's fraternizing with the passengers," she responded, eyeing Jake warily. "What's she done wrong now?"

"Hell's fire, what has she ever done *right?*" Jake exploded before he pivoted on his heels and stamped out.

Jake's eyes blazed over every face he passed while he searched high and lo for Cori. He found her several minutes later, smiling sweetly while she conversed with the very man she'd robbed. Jake snarled under his breath. Ten to one she planned to pluck Lord Humphrey again! Damn it to hell!

"I want to talk to you." Jake's voice boomed like thunder.

Cori flinched when the gravely voice came from so close behind her. What terrible timing on Jake's part! She had been in the process of replacing Lord Humphrey's wallet in his pocket when Jake arrived to interrupt her. Before she could move close enough to the English dandy to stash his wallet in his pocket, Jake yanked on her arm, dragging her along with his quick, impatient strides.

"I'm glad to see you're feeling better." She tried to sound cheerful but she was met with a disgruntled grunt.

"I'm not feeling a damned bit better," he scowled as he hustled her up the steps to his cabin. "And I have you to thank for it . . . as usual!"

Cori had the inescapable feeling Layton had tattled to Jake about the previous night's robbery. Jake was glaring at her as if she were a condemned prisoner. Unless she missed her guess, he intended to accuse her of banditry. Cori refused to incriminate her uncle. Before Jake had time to frisk her, she brushed again him as they rounded the corner of the staircase. The wallet dropped into the pocket of Jake's crumpled jacket.

There. If Jake asked her if she had possession of the missing wallet she could honestly say she didn't. And when he frisked her he would find nothing. Thank the Lord that Skully had taught her all the tricks of the trade. Without her unsavory skills and sleight of hand tricks she would have looked worse in Jake's eyes than she already did. And when this conversation ended, she would simply pick Jake's pocket and be on her way to give Lord Dimwit back his wallet . . .

The door shuddered and groaned as Jake slammed it shut behind him. His hollowed eyes drilled into Cori and his handsome face twisted sardonically as he breathed down her neck.

"You couldn't leave well enough alone, could you?" he said. "We made a bargain and you promised not to victimize anyone else. But the minute I was incapacitated you rushed off to swipe another damned wallet!"

"I kept my part of the bargain," Cori told him truthfully.

Of course, Jake didn't believe her. "Oh really?" he smirked. "How then, do you explain the fact that one of our illustrious passengers was robbed last night? The same one, oddly enough, that you were flirting with a moment ago."

Her chin jutted out and her dark eyes threw hot sparks. "I said I didn't do it," she snapped. The fact that he didn't believe her and would never trust her hurt her as nothing else could.

Jake snatched away her purse and emptied its contents on the table. He found Kyle's pistol, but no wallet. When he came up empty-handed, he yanked her close to search her garments.

A furious gasp erupted from Cori's lips as his hands dived down the front of her gown to ensure there was nothing out of the ordinary in her bodice. When he got his hands on was *not* a roll of cash, and Cori sorely resented the fact that he'd groped at her as if she were a pile of dirty laundry.

"I said I didn't have the money," Cori growled, slapping his hands away.

"Liar," he snapped hoarsely.

Her chin shot up to that defiant angle that he'd come to recognize at a glance. "Do you think I'm the only thief on this ship?"

"Well Lori sure as hell isn't picking pockets!" Jake growled caustically. "She and Dal haven't crawled out of bed long enough for her to swipe anybody's wallet!"

"Why is it that when anything goes wrong you

automatically blame me?" she questioned hotly.

"Because you're as guilty of sin and I damned well know it," Jake bit off testily. "I offered you a solution, but you don't have enough patience to fill a thimble. You think Layton is a hardened criminal and, stubborn as you are, you refuse to let me deal with my cousin in my own time and in my own way."

"*Deal* with him?" Cori scoffed. "I'll be lucky indeed if you slap his chubby little hand and tell him not to commit murder again!"

Jake's hand snaked out to jerk her to him. With his lips curled in anger and frustration, he breathed dragon's fire on her flushed cheeks. "You seem to forget that you are in no position to make demands. One word from me and Layton will have you dragged off to jail—you *and* your sister, who is so hopelessly infatuated with Dal that they've spent more time in bed than on their feet the past few days!"

He'd really done it this time. He'd set fuse to her temper, and he damned well knew it. "I told you I didn't steal the wallet, but you think I'm guilty, no matter what I say. And since you are so quick to accuse me of crime, then perhaps I'll just live up to your expectations from now on," she hissed spitefully.

"You do and you'll wind up staring at the world through the iron bars of a prison cell until the day you hang!" he muttered in threat.

"It couldn't be worse than agreeing to your bargain of keeping me as your whore and letting you cousin run around scott free after he killed my father," she yelled at him as if he were not only sick but deaf as well.

"You'll get your damned ship back, one way or another," he roared.

"The Sahara would sooner be encased in ice!" she thundered.

"Where's that wallet?" Jake flared, glaring into her

rebellious face.

"In your pocket," she gritted out. "If you think you're so damned smart, you figure out a way to get it back to the Englishman. I would have already seen to the task if you hadn't interrupted me."

Jake's pallid features registered shock when he fished into his pockets to find the missing wallet. "You ornery little witch."

Cori was so agitated with him that she didn't care if she did take the rap for snatching the wallet. He hadn't believed her anyway. To hell with him! Rotting in jail couldn't be worse than the torment of loving a man who judged her guilty of every crime committed on the continent, a man who would never trust her or love her back. Skully was right. The queen of hearts was a mean and fickle woman!

"This ship docks in Natchez in three hours," he scowled as she marched stiffly toward the door. "Put on one of your many disguises, mistress of many faces. I should hate for Layton to learn there are two of you. It would grieve me that he would get to enjoy the revenge of making you pay for your crimes before I do."

Cori whirled on him, glaring. "You will have no trouble recognizing me, no matter how I'm disguised," she hurled at him. "I'll be the one who *hates* you!"

"And I'll see that you pay a dozen times over for the trouble you caused me," he flung back.

"And you'll pay as well," she hissed furiously.

"I haven't committed any crimes," he smirked at her poisonous glare.

"You committed the crime of false accusation," she gritted out. "And you're going to pay. Oh, how you're going to pay for it!"

When she stomped out, Jake expelled a string of unprintable curses that hung over the room like a black cloud. In a fit of temper Jake hurled the wallet against the

219

wall and then cussed another blue streak.

He had to devise a story to offer Layton and figure out a way to return the stolen money. Setting his problems with Cori aside, Jake sat down to organize his thoughts. When an idea finally hatched in his mind, he gathered the wallet and stolen money and trotted off to the supply room on the opposite side of the hurricane deck. After summoning Layton, Jake requested that his brooding cousin take inventory of the supply room so they would know what needed to be replaced for the last leg of the journey to New Orleans.

As Jake anticipated, Layton stumbled onto the knapsack of cash, watches, and wallets that had been stashed there. So delighted was Layton that he momentarily forgot how furious and upset he'd been. However, recovering the money put new ideas in his head.

Things didn't turn out as Jake expected. In fact, his brilliant scheme only proved the extent of Layton's greed. Instead of returning the money to its proper owners, Layton decided to keep it, intent on using it to buy the *Mississippi Belle* outright from the family company.

Jake swore under his breath when he saw Layton waddle away, gloating like a fox that had feasted on a brood of plump chickens. That scoundrel! Maybe Cori was right about Layton after all. And if she were, she would never forgive him for refusing to believe her or trust her.

Heaving an exasperated sight, Jake gathered his belongings and ambled toward Cori's cabin. Maybe clearing snags and sawyers on the Missouri River wasn't so difficult after all, Jake mused dispiritedly. At least he knew how to battle the hazards of the river. He did not, however, know how to handle that weasel of a cousin of his without causing family problems. And he sure as hell didn't know how to handle Cori Pierce. Hell's fire, Jake still didn't know what her real name was. It couldn't have been Pierce or Layton would have instantly made the connection from the deed and bill of sale for the ship!

Pensively, Jake glanced toward the railing and the churning river below. There was something to be said for drowning one's troubles, he thought. If he were smart he would throw himself overboard. But that would make Cori immensely happy. For that reason alone, Jake didn't dive in headfirst. He couldn't bear the thought of letting that sassy hellion have the last laugh!

Chapter 16

When Jake held out an arm to the feeble-looking old woman who appeared at Cori's cabin door, she flatly refused his assistance. Jake couldn't help but grin at his companion. Cori's disguise reminded him of his grandmother, with that mop of gray hair, thick spectacles, and the parasol she employed as a cane. His eyes twinkling in amusement, Jake clasped Cori's luggage and followed in her wake.

"I have to make arrangements to hire another pilot before the *Belle* continues on to New Orleans," Jake called after the dowager who waddled in front of him.

"Then be quick about it, sonny," Cori muttered in a nasally voice. "Old as I am, I may not last another hour."

"You'll last," Jake chuckled at the pinch-faced harridan. "You're the one who's driving me to an early grave, Madam Atilla."

Cori was still plenty mad. That billygoat of a man didn't recognize love when it walked up and slapped him in the face and he refused to trust her even after Cori had honored his request to cease her thievery. Most likely, all she would get from this bargain of theirs was a broken heart. Layton would still be running around loose, the steamer would still belong to the Breeze family, and all

222

the money she had in the world had wound up in Jake's possession. Jacob had forced her to become dependent on him for her mere existence. Thunderation, she should have taken Skully's advice and selected the prison sentence instead. As clever as her uncle was, he would have devised a way to free her . . .

Her troubled thoughts trailed off when she glanced up at the sun-splashed hill above the dock. The red-brown bluffs of Natchez rose two hundred feet above the river and were crowned with wild grape vines, magnolias and oaks. Spreading out along the docks was Natchez under the Hill. To Cori's way of thinking, Natchez possessed a split personality. She had often heard it said that everything came big in Natchez—the plantations, estates, alligators, mosquitos, and the bandits along Natchez Trace.

The stately buildings above the river boasted wealth and elegance and the weather-beaten huts beside the Mississippi catered to the rowdy roustabouts and keelboatmen. Only William's Tavern suggested its owner made an attempt at dignity Under the Hill. The stone and timber inn set among a string of raucous gambling dens, gaming halls, bordellos, and dance halls that were filled with habitual brawlers, muggers, and thieves. William's Tavern Inn was the only establishment in which decent folks could take a meal and bed down for the night without fearing they would wake up robbed or dead. According to the reports Cori had heard, William Chandler was well respected Under the hill, thugs didn't prey on the man who never turned another human away because he was down on his luck.

When Jake left Cori standing beside the Breeze Company office to track down a capable pilot, Cori spied Layton waddling off the gangplank. Layton was toting a satchel that he clutched so protectively against him that Cori frowned suspiciously. She watched the rotund little man clamber into a waiting coach and whiz up Silver Street toward Natchez on the Hill.

Cori's gaze swung back to the giant of a man who cut his way through the crowd on the waterfront. Damn that Jacob Wolf! What game was he playing? Unless Cori missed her guess, and she doubted that she had, Jake had forked over the missing money to his crooked cousin. The way Layton cradled the satchel against him it had to contain cash, she knew it with absolute certainty.

Why had Jake given his cousin that money? Only God knew! But if Jacob truly intended to see justice served he had a most peculiar way of going about it. Cori had the sinking feeling that Jake had no intention of investigating Layton's dealings. And sure as hell, Cori was going to lose all the way around.

And while she was losing, she resolved to make Jacob Wolf miserable. Damn him, he held all the cards, but she wasn't giving up her noble crusade! Somehow or another she would see to it that Layton Breeze received his just desserts. She would ruin that slimy little snake of a man. And while she was at it, she was going to make Jacob Wolf sorry he'd tangled with her! He wasn't trying to help her discover the truth. He was doing just what she expected he would do—protect his family. Curse it, if Layton had the money she'd stolen from his investors she would never get the *Belle* back!

When Jake had located a reputable pilot, he strode across the dock to see the stoop-shouldered old woman grinning wickedly at him. Cori was scheming again. He could sense it. Jake didn't have the faintest idea what was running through that firebrand's mind, but he swore she was up to no good.

In grim resignation, Jake escorted his companion into a carriage that took them away from Natchez under the Hill and onto the bluff that overlooked the river. The town spread out in all directions from the ancient plaza that dated back to the days of Spanish plantations and immaculate homes owned by some of the wealthiest planters along the Mississippi. Tree-bordered streets fanned out over the graceful hills and slopes, presenting a most impressive scene of prosperity and elegance.

Jake wondered idly if the mischievous imp who sat beside him didn't belong with the thieves who prowled the settlement Under the Hill. With all Cori's unsavory talents, he couldn't help but speculate on who had trained her in the unseemly arts of picking pockets and holding victims at gunpoint.

There were times when he doubted her story of a murdered father and stolen inheritance. This minx hadn't spent all her life in the lap of luxury, that was for sure. She had too many quirks of personality to be one hundred percent genteel lady. The fact was, Cori Pierce (or whoever she really was) was still a mystery to him. Quite honestly, Jake never knew when to believe her.

"You're awfully quiet, sonny," Cori smirked in observation.

"I'm thinking," he murmured absently.

"I thought I smelled wood burning," she sniped.

Jake leveled her a challenging glare. "There is a cure for that sharp tongue of yours . . ."

Her face brightened. "You're going avoid being sliced by my sharp tongue by dissolving the bargain and letting me go?" she asked hopefully.

"Not hardly," he scowled. "I was thinking of having that viper's tongue of yours bobbed off."

"You are going to be eternally sorry you didn't just let me go my own way," Cori warned with a wry smile that made Jake cringe in trepidation.

"I have no doubt of that." Instinctively, his hand lifted to trace her delicate chin coated with layers of makeup and painted wrinkles. "I already regret that I . . ."

225

She knew what he intended to say, or at least she thought she did. Jake was wishing he'd never laid eyes on her, she reckoned. "Indeed you do," she muttered, concealing the hurt of the words she'd refused to let him utter. "And you are no better than me. You gave the stolen money to your swindling cousin. Perhaps you have no reason to trust me, but I have no reason to trust you either!"

Jake grimaced, knowing it hadn't set well with Cori to discover Layton had possession of the stolen money.

Cori glowered at him. "Now you and your cousin are also accomplices to crimes," she accused. "I bargained for your silence and now you will be forced to bargain for mine. We both wound up entangled in a trap of our own making. And we shall see which one of us emerges with the best end of this dreadful bargain!"

The silence that filled the carriage was thick as a fog. Even though Jake tried to make peace by escorting Cori to the finest restaurant in town, she payed little further attention to him. Jake didn't enjoy his meal. It tasted like sour grapes.

"Where are we off to next?" Cori quizzed him as she touched her napkin to her lips.

Jake reached into his pocket to retrieve his wallet and found nothing. Suppressed rage boiled through his veins when the persnickety little minx smiled devilishly at him.

"Forget your wallet, did you, sonny?" she purred pretentiously. "Do, by all means, allow me to pay for our delicious meal."

To Jake's further outrage, Cori dipped into her purse to fish out *his* wallet and paid the waitress before tossing the woman a generous tip.

It was humiliating enough to have this charading sprite purchase his meal, but seeing her pay for it with the money she had picked from *his* pocket annoyed him

226

beyond words! Damn her, she was purposely trying to infuriate him, and it was definitely working. Jake was livid!

Cori didn't even flinch when Jake glared at her. She pushed out her chin and grabbed her parasol. "It's only the beginning of your torment, my dear Jacob," she snickered wickedly. "It's only the beginning . . ."

Jake knew he was doomed. Cori was out for revenge. She was going to make him regret bargaining with her. Blast it, all he had wanted when he dreamed up this bargain was to enjoy the same pleasure Dal was enjoying with Cori's twin sister. Dal was the lucky one. He had gotten the beguiling beauty who didn't possess her sister's fierce spunk and relentless will. It was apparent that although Cori and Lori were identical in every visible way, one of them was hell on wheels! And guess who had gotten hold of the hellion?

"I have something I want to show you before you meet my grandmother," Jake declared, towing Cori out of the restaurant.

The brisk walk down the street to the courthouse landed them in front of a dreary building. Without a word of explanation, Jake dragged Cori inside and directed her into the ladies toilet room, where he instructed her to shed her disguise.

Clutching her arm, Jake hauled her into the constable's office. After a brief word with the official in charge, Jake tugged Cori past a row of foul-smelling cells filled with the dregs of society.

A chorus of wolfish whistles erupted from the riffraff who were locked behind bars. Apprehension slithered down Cori's spine when dozens of lusty stares raked over her, leaving her with the urge to cover herself as if she were standing there start-bone naked.

"Envision yourself sharing one of these rat holes with its inhabitants," Jake murmured with wicked glee. "This is where the murderers and thieves spend their days before receiving sentence. The penitentiary is worse."

Repulsed though she was, Cori refused to be intimidated by Jake's tactics. "I'm sure the two of us will manage to find our niches in jail when all the scandalous facts are revealed to the constable. I can already see the headlines in the newspaper: 'Prosperous Natchez family convicted of victimizing their passengers on company steamer.'"

"Wealth and influence do have their advantages," Jake drawled as he led Cori back to the main office. "My family, both sides of it, has a great deal of prestige in Natchez. My grandmother is a pillar of society. We shall see, if it comes down to it, which one of us is rotting in that hellhole and which of us isn't."

If Cori had been the type who buckled under adversity she would never have taken on Layton Breeze and his powerful family in the first place. But she was by no means one to wilt under threats. She had every intention of giving as good as she got where Jake was concerned. He could threaten her with prison, and she might even wind up there, distasteful as that thought was, but she would make him regret every moment of every day he spent with her until her time came. Layton Breeze was guilty of murder, no matter what Jake thought, and Cori damned well intended to prove it.

After escorting Cori back to the brougham that waited in front of the restaurant, Jake plunked down beside her on the seat. "When we reach my grandmother's estate, I expect you to behave yourself. She will not be caught in the middle of our feud," Jake insisted.

Cori stared across the cotton fields, admiring the elegance of Natchez. She had no intention of being dictated to. And if Jake thought she wouldn't needle him in front of an audience, he had another think coming . . .

When they arrived at the Breeze plantation home, Cori

was suddenly struck by how wealthy the Breeze family really was. The mansion was a monstrosity. The two-story structure was encircled with galleries, sunken gardens, and flagged passageways that led to latticed summer houses half swallowed with vines. Even the outbuildings and servants' quarters boasted a fresh coat of paint.

"This is Gram's house," Jacob informed her as they strode up the marble steps that led to the hand-carved double doors. "When my parents died in the steamboat accident, I came here to live with Gram. The Wolf plantation is a mile down the road." He indicated the spacious mansion in the distance, one that surpassed this monstrosity in elegance. "It is there that you and I will live . . . for a time . . ." he tacked on.

"But you will have to wait a bit before you tour your new home. I would be remiss if I didn't pay my respects to my grandmother after being away for a year." Jake stared down into Cori's bewitching features, wishing for the companionable moments that were so few and far between in their stormy courtship. Involuntarily his gaze dropped to her heart-shaped lips, longing to feel the honeyed softness of her mouth beneath his. "At least be civil to Gram, Cori. You can give me hell when we get home . . ."

Cori wasn't about to let him sweet-talk her into submission, even though his husky tone very nearly melted her into sentimental mush. And she wasn't going to succumb to these betraying tingles of pleasure that skitted down her spine when he stared at her in ways that made her go hot all over either! She and Jake were conducting civilized warfare and she wasn't going to let herself forget that, no matter what her forbidden feelings were for this impossible man.

Her hand swept gracefully toward the front door. "Lead on, my love," she insisted, her tone as sticky as molasses. "You have kept Gram waiting for a year. She must be as anxious to see you as I am to see Layton punished for his despicable crimes."

"You never let up, do you, vixen?" Jake growled.

"Letting up and giving in are not a part of my nature, my sweet," she purred in a voice that could have drowned a stack of pancakes.

Grimly, Jake opened the door, wondering just how far this ornery spitfire intended to push him. Just wait until he got her home! If she antagonized him in front of Augusta, he was going to ensure that she had hell to pay!

"Jacob!" Augusta rounded the corner of the parlor to see her long lost grandson. "You are a sight for sore eyes. I thought you were never coming back . . ."

Augusta's voice trailed off when she spied the shapely brunette behind Jake's broad frame. Jake had brought a woman home with him? He had never done that before in his whole life. Could it be that he had finally decided to settle down, that her lectures had finally soaked into that hard head of his? Wonders never ceased!

"And who might this lovely vision be?" Augusta quizzed Jake. "Your wife, I hope! I've waited years for you to provide me with a granddaughter-in-law and toddlers, Jacob. I only hope to God they don't turn out to be as offensive as Layton's stepsons. Those boys are holy terrors. The last time they invited themselves over they nearly wrecked the place."

Cori had her heart set on disliking Augusta Breeze, but the dowager was vivacious and personable. The frail-looking old woman who dressed in black and propped herself on her cane had a lively sparkle in her hazel eyes. Then and there, Cori decided that Jake was a chip off the family block—at least off Augusta's corner of it. The dowager didn't mince with words or keep her opinions to herself either. It was little wonder why Jake was so plainspoken. Augusta didn't dillydally around with diplomacy or tact. She said exactly what she thought.

In silence Cori watched Jake embrace his feisty grandmother, who fussed at the sentimental tears that clouded her eyes as she was reunited with her favorite grandson. The touching scene made Cori miss her family and the home they had lost because of Layton's treachery.

When Augusta pivoted expectantly, Jake made the proper introductions. "Cori Pierce, this is Augusta Breeze. And Gram, I would like you to meet Cori."

"And what a pretty young lady you are," Augusta piped up, extending a bony hand. "I didn't think this wayward grandson of mine would be so lucky as to find a fiancée as attractive as you are, ornery rascal that he is." Her eyes twinkled mischievously. "So . . . when's the wedding?"

Jake cleared his throat and darted Cori a wry glance. "The truth is I proposed to Cori and she turned me down flat."

Augusta gaped at her guest in astonishment. "You would turn all this down, just because Jacob has a few inherited flaws? My God, girl, don't you know he can't help it? I've had too much influence on the poor boy, but our family is filthy rich. Surely you can overlook his peccadilloes when he lays the world at your feet."

Cori couldn't contain her giggle. Augusta Breeze was the personification of her name—a veritable whirlwind. She was dynamic and delightful in her own unique way. "Money, so I have been told, is not always the key to happiness," Cori contended.

"Perhaps not," Augusta replied with a lackadaisical shrug. "But it can buy the keys that unlock many a door." She stared impishly at Cori from behind her thick spectacles. "Everybody has a price, my dear Cori. How much will it cost me to get you to marry this unruly swain?"

"Gram, for God's sake!" Jake interjected with an indignant gasp.

Augusta waved him to silence. "Go fetch us some tea and put a jigger of brandy in mine. I want to celebrate your upcoming wedding."

Tugging at Cori's arm, Augusta guided her into the ornately decorated parlor that boasted the finest furnishings to be found on the American or European continent.

With a flick of her arm, Augusta gestured for Cori to sit on the red velvet couch. "So . . . how much will it cost me to dissolve your reservations, my dear? Five thousand? Ten? I'm prepared to be generous, you see. I've waited forever for Jacob to take a wife and I'm getting older by the second. My greatest aspiration nowadays is to see him settle down." She paused to inhale a quick breath. "Twenty thousand dollars delivered on the day of your wedding. Future payments are negotiable. That's my best offer. Take it."

"Gram, I sorely resent being sold like a stallion on the auction block," Jake grunted as he strode back into the room with the tray in hand. "You're being unnecessarily pushy."

"Rubbish!" Augusta sniffed. "I'm conducting business here. The fact that Cori didn't immediately give in indicates that she has backbone. She'll need one if she has to put up with the likes of you, Jacob." Her hazel eyes sparkled with a youthful glimmer. She delighted in teasing her grandson.

"Gram, for pity's sake," Jake blustered.

"Oh, sit down and be quiet," she insisted before turning her sly smile on Cori, who adored watching the spunky dowager give Jake what for. "Now then, do we have a deal?"

Cori returned Augusta's elfin grin. "Do I have to live with him or simply share his name?" she teased.

"He owns a gigantic house. You'll never have to see him if you don't want to. If you find his company dull and boring, make him call on you only by appointment," Augusta suggested flippantly.

Jake sank down beside Cori, who popped up to amble around the room. She wandered over to the fireplace to inspect the silver candelabrum that was obviously worth a fortune all by itself.

"I've always wondered what it would be like to own something as priceless as this," Cori mused aloud, sliding Jake an ornery glance.

Her look said it all and Jake gulped hard. Damn that saucy witch! If she dared to steal his grandmother's most valued possession he'd strangle her!

"And this . . ." Cori plucked up the diamond-studded broach that had been in the Breeze family for almost a century.

Jake adamantly shook his head while Gram glanced toward Cori. Hell's fire, he swore this little minx was casing the place so she could return to swipe everything Augusta held dear. If Cori dared to steal so much as a cracker crumb he'd have her beheaded! She was doing this just to infuriate him.

"Would you like to see the rest of the house while you're contemplating my offer?" Augusta questioned. "It's a veritable museum of relics and heirlooms."

"I'd like that very much," Cori gushed as she discreetly tucked the expensive broach in her purse.

Jake's jaw tensed when he noticed what Cori had done. The instant Augusta hobbled out the door on her cane, Jake was on his feet. In two swift strides he was beside Cori, snatching away her purse to retrieve the broach.

"If you steal one thing, I'll have you in jail beside the rest of the muggers and thieves we met earlier," he threatened as he propelled her into the foyer.

"And if you tattle, I'll tell Augusta that both her

233

grandsons are river pirates. I'll bet she'd be shocked to learn how much stolen money Layton is toting around in his carpetbag," Cori countered.

"This dining hall used to be the site of renowned dinner parties with visiting dignitaries," Augusta was saying when Cori took time to listen. "The past few years I've had little cause to entertain. That's Jacob's fault, of course. If he had found you earlier, my dear Cori, I would have planned many a grand ball to entertain our friends and relatives." She stared unblinkingly at the pert brunette. "Twenty-five thousand and I'll see to all the arrangements for the wedding and reception myself. You won't have to plan a thing. All you'll have to do is show up at the altar on your wedding day and smile once or twice at the reception."

"What magnificent crystal," Cori gushed as she inspected the dinnerware that adorned the table, purposely ignoring Augusta's remarks.

"It's yours," Augusta teased with a playful wink. "All you have to do is marry this big brute and make an old woman deliriously happy."

Jake stared over his grandmother's gray head. His green eyes drilled into Cori's elegant features. "Offer her the floating palace Layton purchased during my absence, Gram," he suggested. "Cori has a penchant for steamships, especially the *Mississippi Belle.*"

"Does she now?" Augusta tapped her cane, apparently considering Jake's suggestion. "Surely you know how proud Layton is of that ship. And it is, after all, the most magnificent vessel ever to sail the Mississippi. Layton is constantly boasting about what a shrewd bargain he made in acquiring it."

Didn't he just! Cori mused bitterly.

"You realize, of course, that if I give my consent to such an agreement that Layton will be furious and would insist on splitting the company in half. And he'd be

234

forever complaining that he got the worst end of the deal. That boy has been straining under the yoke since you left town, constantly trying to prove himself to me. But he can't even handle those two brats of his." Augusta expelled a long sigh. "I shuddered to think of leaving him in charge of the company while you were gone. And if I know Layton as well as I think I do, he'd somehow manage to lose his half of the company in two years."

"But if you truly want to see me married, you may have to make a few concessions. This lovely little lady drives a hard bargain, Gram," Jake declared, watching Cori like a hawk. "It may cost you dearly to get me off your hands. Selling grandsons doesn't come cheap, you know. And buying your grandson a wife is tremendously expensive." His gaze circled back to Augusta. "Your move, Gram. Just how badly do you want me to have a wife with backbone?"

From across the room, Cori stared into those garnet green eyes that were flecked with gold. If she lived to be a hundred and ten she would never figure this man out! He had backed her into one corner after another and now he was doing it again. He had given his cousin the stolen money and yet here he was bargaining with his grandmother for the steamer he knew Cori wanted back. He was even going so far as to enter into a marriage that she knew he didn't really want. He had sworn she would never be more to him that the concubine he toyed with when the mood suited him.

Thunderation, Jacob Wolf was a walking contradiction. What did he really want from her? Was he trying to strike another bargain that he had yet to reveal to her? Was the marriage and the steamer his way of bargaining for Layton's freedom from any charges against him? What, exactly, was the point of all this? Cori wondered.

Augusta drummed her fingers on her cane and peered thoughtfully at Cori. She hobbled around to stare meditatively into Jake's ruggedly handsome features. Her gaze shifted again, watching the play of emotions on one young face and then the other. She hadn't the slightest idea what was going on between these two strong-willed individuals, but Augusta was wise and astute enough to know they were waging some kind of silent war and that she was standing on their private battlefield.

If she consented to Jake's terms, it was bound to cause trouble with Layton. He had always been envious of Jake, always trying to prove himself the better man. Augusta wasn't blind to her children or her grandsons' faults. She had never made excuses for them. What all this really boiled down to was who was competent enough to run the company and who wasn't.

The fact was that Jacob was also in charge of his father's fortune as well. Layton didn't have the extra added income, even though he had married for money and had squandered most of it. The truth was that Jacob had been making the company's critical decisions for years. He simply had the courtesy to let Augusta have the final, but still token, say in the matter. He had allowed her to remain the matriarch out of his respect for her.

Perhaps that was one of the reasons Augusta was so fond of Jacob, even though she harassed him unmercifully for the mere sport of it. Jacob was a man who was confident, ingenious, and was certain enough of his capabilities and masculinity to let Augusta think she still ruled the roost. It was that tactful display of respect that separated men from boys. Jacob was a man. Layton was still a lazy little boy who preferred to take the easy way out as often as possible.

A slow smile worked its way across Augusta's aging features. "The *Mississippi Belle* and the *Natchez Queen* will be Jacob's to command when the company splits in half," Augusta said finally. "Layton can have the *New*

Orleans Spirit and the *St. Louie Lady*. He'll buck and snort but he'll take what he can get unless he wants to be cut out completely."

The old woman sobered as she stared at Jacob. "Of course, Layton will expect monetary compensation, since the *Belle* is by far the most elegant ship in our line. I hope you will be prepared to pay extra for the privilege of taking command of the *Belle*."

A wry grin pursed Jake's lips when a fleeting thought skipped across his mind. He knew exactly where he would find the cash to pay his cousin off. "I'll see to it that Layton receives compensation," he promised.

Augusta glanced at Cori who was still staring ponderously at Jake, wondering what had put the devilish gleam in his eyes. "Now it's *your* move, Cori," Augusta announced to the shapely brunette.

Marry into one of Natchez's elite families, the one, unfortunately, that was responsible for her father's death and the loss of her inheritance? Accept the *Belle* as a wedding gift from her new grandmother-in-law? Now what woman of sound mind and body would turn down a deal like that? A fool who wanted Jacob's love more than she desired the deed to the steamer and a wedding that would salvage her reputation and her pride, that's who! Cori was hounded by crosscurrents of emotions. She would have loved to be Jacob's bride, but she also wanted to see Layton brought to justice. Thus far, that was not part of this tempting bargain.

"Gram and I are waiting, Cori," Jake prompted her. He made no move toward her, no attempt to persuade or discourage her. Jake simply stood on the far side of the room, watching the indecipherable emotions chase each other across Cori's stunning features.

Cori wondered how the blazes she could juggle times with her twin sister and keep their duel identity a secret if she consented to marry Jake. It was bound to cause complications for Dal and Jake. She also wondered how she and Lori could drag a confession of guilt from Layton when Jake obviously planned to let the matter drop. She was also curious to know if Augusta would offer such a bargain to the first female who came along after Cori rejected it. It seemed Augusta was in an all-fired hurry to see Jake married. Ah yes, Augusta would find someone to replace Cori, she reckoned. That thought stung like a wasp!

"Well, my dear?" Augusta chimed in when Cori refused to respond immediately. "I can't imagine what else a bride could possibly want. I practically bent over backward to strike this bargain."

With the most feminine poise imaginable, Cori swept across the room and grasped Augusta's hand. Fool that she was, she was going to follow her heart and let her head catch up with her later. "We have struck a bargain . . . provided you add one more stipulation."

Augusta's gaze narrowed warily. "And what might that be?"

"I would like permission to come visit you when this future husband of mine becomes too domineering and demanding," Cori teased with a playful wink.

"Are you going to grant my grandson his every whim and treat him as if he alone were the master of your fate?" Augusta quizzed her.

"I will consider myself his equal. I will expect nothing less than his respect and demand nothing more." Her chin tilted to a stubborn angle and Augusta very nearly giggled with glee. "And that, Augusta, is *my* best offer."

"Done," Augusta declared with finality.

Now here was the kind of woman Jake needed. Cori wasn't the shy retiring type, thank the Lord. She was Jake's match. Unfortunately, Augusta wasn't quite certain what was going on between them. Something sure as hell was, and Augusta's curiosity was eating her alive.

Jake had been very deliberate about asking for the *Belle* and Cori had been very cautious about accepting the bargain. It made Augusta wonder . . .

Jake swaggered toward Cori. A wry smile quirked his lips. With a flair for gallantry, he lifted her hand to press a kiss to her wrist. "And now, my dear Cori, since that is settled and out of the way, would you grant Gram and me a few moments of privacy to discuss business details. Feel free to tour the house." His voice dropped to a whisper of warning. "But for heaven's sake, don't steal anything."

Cori did, of course, just to be contrary. But it was just a small insignificant trinket—Augusta's heirloom broach that was studded with diamonds! That would really get Jake's goat, she reckoned, and that was exactly why she swiped it.

Chapter 17

Cori's eyes bulged from their sockets when the brougham rolled to a halt in front of Wolfhaven. She couldn't fathom herself living on such a grand estate, temporarily or otherwise. The place was a veritable palace! The rolling acreages were lined with towering oaks and magnolias, and the shadowed reaches were filled with the warble of hundreds of birds. The majestic mansion set on a sloping hill. A series of terraces gradually dropped to the immaculately tended, low-lying gardens. Azaleas, roses, and wisteria, with their pale lavender blossoms, added an enchanting splash of color to the red brick home. In the distance a dairy, plantation office, school, and servants' quarters dotted the plush green countryside.

"Disappointed?" Jake questioned, watching Cori peer at her surroundings.

"It's lovely!" Cori gasped, astounded.

"It also runs quite efficiently whether I'm here or not," Jake chuckled as he assisted Cori from the coach. "The secret is to surround oneself with capable individuals who make their vagabond employer looked as if he is competent and organized."

Cori paused on the brick steps and turned squarely to

240

face Jacob. He was beginning to regain his color after his bout with the grippe. Impulsively, she reached up, longing to trace the smile lines that bracketed his sensuous mouth, wanting to enjoy the sweet companionable silence they had shared on rare occasions.

Remembering herself, Cori dropped her hand by her side and glanced away. "Why are you being so nice to me, Jacob?" she asked suddenly. "And why did you allow Augusta to plan a wedding you swore you didn't want, not with me leastways, not after you learned I had been victimizing your passengers?"

Before Jake could respond to the questions, the door flew open and a dozen servants rushed out to greet the master of Wolfhaven. Cori found herself pushed to the perimeter of the circle that closed around Jake. It was clearly evident that Jacob had exceptional rapport with the slaves and servants who kept his plantation operating at top-notch efficiency. And he cared for them. It was in his easy smile, the twinkle in his eyes, his teasing words.

Cori was stirred and yet saddened as she watched the reunion. There had always been a certain amount of hostility between her and Jake. Obstacles stood between them like mountains. Cori looked at this giant of a man in his natural habitat and she saw all that her family had lost because of Layton's treachery. She also saw a man she couldn't even begin to understand, and yet she was still infatuated with him. It was torment pure and simple . . .

Her contradicting thoughts trailed off when Jacob introduced her as his fiancée. She was suddenly swarmed by well-wishers who assured her she was getting herself a most worthy husband.

When the servants scattered to gather the luggage and prepare the rooms, Jake guided Cori into the vestibule. Each time she paused to brush her hand over some expensive trinket Jake promptly reminded her that she had no need to steal what would soon be lawfully hers.

241

"You still haven't answered my question," Cori prompted as he escorted her up the spiral staircase.

"What question was that?" Jacob asked nonchalantly, and then gestured to the right. "This will be your bedchamber until the wedding."

Cori gasped at the sprawling room decorated in shades of blue. Even her own room in her father's townhouse didn't compare to this. Cori felt as if she had stepped into someone else's dream.

"You haven't figured it out yet, have you?" Jake murmured as he watched her wander around the room in a daze, absorbing the luxuries he had generously bestowed on her.

Cori halted in mid step and wheeled to face Jake's quiet, watchful smile. "I haven't begun to figure *you* out," she amended. "Why are you doing this?"

One thick brow lifted and he grinned again. "Don't you think you deserve my generosity, little imp?"

"I cheated. I lied. I deceived," Cori reminded him. "I want to see your cousin locked behind bars and hanged for his crimes." Dark eyes fastened on the towering figure of a man who filled the spacious room to overflowing. "And you keep contradicting yourself all over the place. I truly don't know what to make of you or your baffling bargains."

Jake ambled across the room to retrieve the purse Cori had set aside. Her chin went up when he opened her purse to fish out the costly brooch she had spitefully snatched from the mantle in Augusta's parlor.

"Take it, my dear. It's yours to keep," he murmured as he pinned it on her gown.

Cori gaped at him. Of all the things she had expected him to say when he discovered what she'd done that wasn't even on the list! "Why?" she croaked. "You know I stole it just to be contrary and yet you . . ."

He pressed his forefinger to her lips to shush her.

242

"Sometimes, it is best to defeat one's enemy with kindness rather than force. I have threatened you, intimidated you and offered you a dozen challenges. But nothing else has worked. I simply switched tactics."

As if that explained everything, Jake pivoted on his heels and swaggered out the door. For a full moment Cori stared after him, toying with the diamond-studded broach that had been in the Breeze family for generations.

Cori was so baffled and confused she wanted to scream at the top of her lungs. She glanced around her and saw the luxuries she had been deprived of the past year.

"Kill me with kindness?" She shook her head bemusedly and sighed. Well, the tactic was definitely working. Jake was taking the wind out of her sails. When Jake refused to argue with her she was at a loss as how to deal with him.

Muttering, Cori removed the broach and tossed it onto the bed. It took all the fun out of stealing when Jake refused to burst into a fit of temper.

In frustration, Cori stamped off to locate Jake. She found him in the elegant chamber next door, shucking his jacket.

"What do you want from me?" she demanded to know that very second.

Jake graced her with a grin that would melt a woman's heart if she wasn't guarding it closely. Cori wasn't, and the smile devastated her. "I would very much like for you to ride around the plantation with me this afternoon. You do ride, don't you?" He chuckled as he swaggered toward her. "Of course you do. There is nothing you can't do and do exceedingly well, whether it is singing and dancing or picking pockets." He offered her his arm. "Shall we go?"

"Thunderation! Will you answer me!" Cori blurted out as he aimed her toward the steps.

He didn't answer her; he kept right on walking. "Would you prefer a gentle mare or a spirited gelding?" he queried.

"A spirited gelding," she grumbled as they swept out the front door. "Maybe the animal will unhorse me and trample me. Then, while I'm lying on my deathbed, maimed and mutilated, you'll finally answer me."

"Gram is already planning a ball to celebrate our upcoming wedding," Jake remarked conversationally. "I haven't quite figured out how we'll handle all the arrangements with Dal and your twin." He frowned in thought. "Layton is going to be fit to be tied when he learns that I am to get control of the *Belle*. And if he discovers there are two of you before we solve the mystery surrounding the purchase of the steamer, he could very well cause us trouble."

"Damn it, Jake!" Cori exploded halfway between the mansion and the red brick stables. "Why are you doing all this? Why not tell Augusta all the sordid details? Why not expose me for what I am and let Layton have a field day? Augusta will simply wave her arms and magically dismiss the problem by finding you another bride. Why are you bothering with me when you could have any woman in Natchez as your wife?"

Her tirade didn't earn her the explanation she so desperately wanted. She may as well have been raving at a stone wall for all the good it did her.

"This mount should suit you perfectly," he announced, motioning toward a buckskin gelding, who tossed his proud head much the same way Cori did.

Cori finally threw up her hands and admitted defeat. All she had gained for her efforts was a headache, a headache by the name of Jacob Wolf.

"The buckskin suits me fine," she said deflatedly. "I'm sure the two of us will get along superbly."

While the stable attendants scurried about, saddling

the buckskin and a long-legged strawberry roan thoroughbred for their master, Cori listened to Jake boast about the lineage of the steeds that lined the stable. Although he had been upriver for the past year, Jake seemed to be a racing enthusiast, just as Dal Blaylock was. Jake spoke of attending the races at Pharsalia, the renowned track that was located along St. Catherine's Creek.

Cori also learned that Jacob's parents and the Blaylocks were instrumental in making Pharsalia the widely acclaimed race track it had become. The stable of horses at Wolfhaven had been well-bred and meticulously trained for racing. They had won their fair share of honors because Jake had seen to it that he had experienced jockeys and trainers to tend his prized livestock while he was away.

After Jake had lifted Cori into the saddle and mounted the roan stallion, he led her across the plush meadows. For a few moments Cori allowed herself to enjoy the simple pleasure of racing across the scenic surroundings. It had been a long time since she turned her face to the wind and thundered off at breakneck speed.

Jake paused to converse with the overseer and the field hands, and Cori nudged the buckskin into a gallop and flew across the pasture, letting the breeze caress her face. It was an exhilarating ride that reminded her of days gone by, days when she hadn't had a care in the world. She had spent almost a year hell-bent on revenge, and she hadn't had time for the simple pleasures of life.

Cori knew her sister was probably experiencing the same feelings while she toured Dal's plantation. The only difference was that Lori was secure in her love for Dal. It made Cori want more than the constant conflicts she and Jake experienced. But as long as Layton was running around loose, Cori could never truly be content. She had made a vow to see her father's murderer punished and she refused to break that promise, no matter what personal sacrifices had to be made.

A melancholy smile pursed Jake's lips as he watched Cori canter across the meadow as if she were sitting atop a winged steed. She had discarded propriety and straddled the gelding instead of trotting off in a ladylike manner.

Jake wasn't surprised to learn the little minx could ride like the wind. She was, after all, the most ingenious, versatile and multi-talented female he had ever met. With Cori's fierce will and determination, she would be successful at whatever she decided to do, whether it was ride, sing, or indulge in thievery. You name it and Cori could do it, even if it was for the mere challenge of it.

There had been countless times when Jake had contemplated throwing up his hands and bidding that feisty vixen good riddance. And yet he could never quite let her go, not without sacrificing a part of himself. He didn't just want any woman for his wife, he realized. Females *weren't* all the same, and he had paid dearly for that blundering declaration. Even Cori's twin sister—the one woman on earth who had beauty comparable to Cori's—wasn't as willful and persistent as Cori was. No, it was this one woman Jake wanted, even though he knew for certain it was going to cause conflict in his family before her crusade was over.

"Was there something else you wanted, Jacob?" the overseer asked when Jake continued to stare off into the distance. "Is there something else I can do for you?"

Jake chuckled enigmatically as he stepped into the stirrup. "No, my friend. What needs done, I'm going to have to do all by myself."

Grappling with that thought, Jake chased after the dream he'd been having since he spied the dark-haired spitfire on the docks of St. Louis, battling Kyle Benson with her parasol.

*   *   *

246

Cori tethered her mount in a clump of trees and ambled down to the stream that meandered through Jake's property. She was so immersed in thought that she didn't hear him approach. Preoccupied, Cori walked along the bank, plucking wildflowers as she went. Her mind teemed with unanswered questions, with wanton longings she had been forced to smother in her never-ending struggle against the invincible Jacob Wolf.

"That isn't a flower. It's a weed. I wouldn't pick it if I were you. It's poisonous," Jake cautioned.

Cori jerked back, startled by Jacob's voice. Her foot caught on the driftwood that lined the boggy creek. The bouquet of wild flowers went flying as Cori flapped her arms like a windmill to maintain her balance. Nothing helped. With a splash, she kerplopped in the stream, much the same way she had in Memphis when she tried to make her escape.

Instead of charging over to rescue the soggy beauty, Jake moseyed down the steep slope to gather the strewn flowers. With a mischievous grin he stretched out his arm to offer her the bouquet.

"For you, a mere token of Mother Nature's handi-work, which, I'm sorry to say, cannot compare to your exceptional beauty," he declared gallantly.

Cori pulled a face at him. "Stop trying to be so nice and get me the hell out of here!" she spluttered, floundering in her dripping petticoats and gown. "You're beginning to sound like the chivalrous Dal Blaylock, always quick with his adoring flattery."

Jake still made no move to assist her to her feet, even when the gooey mud tugged on her like quicksand. He squatted down on his haunches, two steps away from where she lay sprawled on her back, blocking the current like a human damn.

"You are opposed to flattery then?" he queried. His eyes flooded over her heaving bosom and the clinging garments that accentuated her curvaceous figure.

247

"The last thing I need right now is flattery. I know perfectly well that I look like a wet mop lying here!" Cori spumed. "What I need most is a helping hand. This mud is like mortar. I may be stuck here for the rest of my life."

Try as she may, she couldn't pry herself loose from the silted creek bed. Each time she tried to brace up on an arm, it sank deeper into the murk.

"Flattery got Dal what he wanted," Jake pointed out. "I thought perhaps my plainspokeness offended you."

"Your lack of consideration offends me more!" Cori all but shouted at him.

A puzzled frown knitted her muddy brow when she took time to contemplate what Jake had said. "What is it you think Dal wanted?" she questioned, assessing the indecipherable smile that quirked his full lips.

"Lori's love," Jake said simply. "When it came right down to it, beneath his wounded pride and his confusion, Lori was all Dal really wanted. I think perhaps I'm beginning to feel the same way."

Cori misinterpreted his meaning. There had been times on board the steamer when Jake had wound up in Lori's company when it was impossible for the twins to make the switch. It seemed that Jake preferred Lori's milder manner and her generous heart to Cori's somewhat feisty behavior and contrary nature. It also appeared Jake had decided to settle for Lori's lookalike, even if he had wanted the gentler of the two sisters. The realization stung Cori like a scorpion. Jake's generosity and his new tactic of kindness were his attempts to tame the sister he had gotten stuck with because of Augusta's fervent desire to see her favorite grandson married . . . and quickly.

Cori knew she had faults. Her temper was legendary. Her stubborn pride constantly got her into trouble. Her fiery disposition always came out, even when Skully warned her to disguise her emotions behind a calm demeanor . . .

"Do you understand what I'm saying, Cori?" Jake murmured, watching the emotions that shimmered in her obsidian eyes.

Her chin went up a notch. "Perfectly," she snapped. "You would prefer to have Lori, but you got stuck with me. Now you're trying to handle me the way Dal handles Lori, showering me with flattery and generosity, hoping I'll respond in like manner." She glared at him. "Forget it. I'm not my sister. This ploy of yours is never going to work. The marriage is off!"

"Hell's fire," Jake exploded as he vaulted to his feet. Curse that woman. No matter what he said or did, he couldn't get through to this tenacious sprite. "If kindness won't work, then tell me what will?"

"What do you care?" Cori asked with childish vindictiveness. "You won't have any trouble finding yourself another fiancée. I'll go my way and you can go yours. What more do you want?"

"What I *don't* want is to play out a charade for the rest of my life. I don't want you to leave, damnit. And I don't want to hear you say you love me when I know it's a lie. I don't want you to use that tender torment to make me stay put while you go trouncing off on another of your wild escapades, either!" Jake threw up his hands and then let them drop limply by his sides. "What I want is exactly what Dal's got!"

His bluntness and his poor choice of wording crushed Cori's feminine pride. "Then why don't you trot off and get down on bended knee. Maybe Lori will consent to leave Dal and marry you instead," she hissed at him. "Augusta will never know the difference."

"You little idiot, that's . . ."

"I am not an idiot! You are!" Cori flared indignantly.

"Aw, the hell with it. Maybe I am at that," Jake scowled as he reached down to yank Cori out of the mud. Unfortunately, the bog held her fast. Jake found himself flung off balance, emotionally as well as physically.

Shock registered in Cori's eyes when Jake's huge body eclipsed the sun and he teetered like a felled redwood. Hurriedly, she inhaled a breath, knowing she would be buried in the mud when his heavy weight plunged down on top of her.

Cori read the situation correctly. With a squawk, Jake fell on top of her, squashing her deeper into the gooey mud. When Jake tried to brace himself on an arm, the silted creek sucked at his hand. Knowing Cori was due for a breath of air, Jake reared back far enough to clutch her by the hair of her head and drag her face from the murk.

They floundered like two hogs in a wallow. Jake tried to squirm sideways, but all he wound up doing was jabbing Cori with his knees and elbows. Bubbles burst to the surface, alerting Jake that Cori was in desperate need of another breath.

When he lifted her face, he barked an order at her. "Try to grab hold of my waist."

Gritting her teeth, Cori attempted to lift herself from the bog and latch onto Jake's belt. Worming and squirming, they both finally managed to ease onto their bellies and crawl toward the opposite bank like salamanders.

With a grunt and a groan, Jake shoved his left arm through the slime, setting his sights on the protruding tree roots that were anchored on the bank. With his left hand secured, Jake dragged himself, with Cori clinging to his hips, toward the trunk of the tree.

"Hell's fire," he growled as he tugged on his buried right arm until it very nearly came loose at the socket. "It's a wonder we haven't lost a herd of cattle in this swamp. We're going to have to get this creekbed cleaned out. This mud must be at least five feet deep!"

Cori said nothing. She was merely thankful to be alive. A few moments earlier she wasn't sure she would last the day. To be sure, she relished any excuse to clutch at Jake.

250

The feel of his muscular body meshed to hers was oddly satisfying, even if he did wish she was like her twin sister.

It was absolutely ridiculous, Cori knew. But the overwhelming feelings she felt for the muscled giant rose like a flood tide inside her. This was hardly the time or the place for confessions Jake didn't want to hear, but the words poured from her muddy lips, just the same.

"I love you . . ." she murmured.

Jake heard her voice behind him, at the base of his spine to be specific. "You picked a helluva time to tell me that," he grumbled as he willed his right hand to rise from the deep bed of mud. With a growl, he mustered every ounce of strength and tried to yank his arm from the quagmire. Unfortunately, the fierce jerk caused his elbow to slam against Cori's shoulder.

Her discomforted groan followed his frustrated growl.

"If we were going to be buried alive in this swamp, I just wanted you to know," Cori mumbled into the back of his shirt, one that was now a dingy shade of brownish green.

With a heave, Jake yanked his right arm loose and grabbed the protruding tree roots. Hand over hand, he pulled them up the steep bank until there was a carpet of grass beneath them instead of sticky slime. Gasping for breath, he rolled to his back and pulled the muddy nymph atop him.

Jake stared into Cori's smudged face from beneath his mud-caked lashes. His expression was so intense that it made her flinch. "We survived the bog. If you want to retract what you just said, now's the time."

Cori gave her head a shake, flinging slime hither and yon. Twice before she had confessed her love. It hadn't been the time or the place to make Jake believe. But now, judging by the somber expression on his craggy features, he was willing to listen. Indeed, he looked as if he wanted to believe her. Was she actually mistaken? Was it truly

251

her that he wanted, faults and all?

"I can't take it back," Cori whispered as she traced his commanding features, leaving a trail of mud around his eyes and mouth. "It isn't a tender lie, Jake. It's the tender truth . . . I do love you and I'm afraid I always will, whether you want to hear that or not . . ."

When her lips slanted over his, Jake didn't mind the mud one little bit. Throughout the day he had encouraged himself by thinking Cori would have rejected all of Augusta's offers if she was fiercely opposed to marrying him. Of course, he had taken into account that this crusading sprite was so obsessed with reclaiming her precious steamboat that she would even marry him as a last resort. But the fact that she had become outraged when he mentioned Lori left him wondering if she really did care for him in her own unconventional way.

Breathing that hope, Jake let his hungry desire for this muddy minx carry him over the edge. When he kissed Cori back, he held nothing in reserve. His arms slid around her, rediscovering the luscious feel of her supple body against his. He gave himself up to the primal needs that only this feisty hellion could appease.

Amid the mud, a flame of passion burst anew, one that burned with the heat of a thousand suns. Jake welcomed the feel of Cori's hands exploring his body. She tugged impatiently at the garments that separated them, anxious to make contact with his flesh. Her explosive kisses fanned the already blazing fire that swept through him. Her bold caresses sent sparks spiraling in his bloodstream, and he groaned with the torment of having her so close and yet so agonizingly far away.

Cori had discarded all feminine reserve when she set her hands and lips upon Jake's powerful body. Nothing mattered except convincing him that she wanted to enjoy the same bond of love that Dal and Lori had discovered. Cori longed to express the emotions that blossomed in

252

the core of her being, to share the pleasure he aroused in her. She yearned to earn his love and cherish it as if it were twenty-four karat gold.

Achingly tender caresses glided over Jake's flesh, leaving him moaning in desire. Cori had become a proficient seductress, adding another impressive credit to her extensive list of talents. But this one . . . ah, this one was the one Jacob loved the most. Cori could spin a web of sweet hypnotic magic around him, entrancing him with butterfly kisses and bone-melting caresses. Her hands and lips were everywhere at once—arousing, exciting, instilling needs that mushroomed into monstrous carvings long before she satisfied them. This seductive little witch made him half-crazy with wanting, aroused cravings that screamed for satisfaction.

Jacob wasn't even sure he could survive the maelstrom of sensations that bombarded him. His heart was hammering so furiously against his ribs that it beat the air out of his lungs. Breathing became impossible and his body throbbed with spasms of rapture.

"Cori . . ." he choked out when her hands and lips migrated over his belly and hips, leaving him blazing on a white-hot flame.

"I want to show you all the ways I love you," she whispered against his rough flesh.

"Don't do that!" Jacob gasped when another wave of fire undulated through his nerves and muscles.

Cori smiled secretively to herself, wondering if perhaps his "no" wasn't in fact a "yes." He really didn't seem to mind all that much what she was doing to him, inventing techniques to arouse and pleasure him.

Caressing him excited her. She marveled at the power she suddenly seemed to hold over this mountain of a man. He had given into her, allowing her to have her way with him, permitting her to discover each ultrasensitive point on his magnificent body.

When her kisses and caresses trailed lower, Jake knew positively, absolutely, that he was going to die. It would be sweet satisfying death that left him uncaring if he ever viewed another sunrise. Pleasure this incredible demanded supreme sacrifices . . .

A shuddering groan floated from his lips as Cori stroked him, kissed him, drove him over the edge into oblivion. The sensations that converged on him were so intense and compelling that he swore he couldn't bear another moment of her tantalizing fondling. He wanted her madly.

"Come here, damn you," Jake growled, out of his mind with ravenous hunger. Without waiting to determine if she was going to obey him or not, he snaked out an arm to drag her sweet mouth back to his and then he devoured her as if she were a long-awaited feast.

His gentleness evaporated as he rolled sideways, pinning Cori beneath him. Her tangled lashes swept up to peer into his taut features, marveling at the wild need that glistened in those big green eyes. Jake was in the throes of a passion so fervent and demanding that it startled her. He had stared down at her before, in the heat of passion, but never quite like this! My goodness, what had she done to him?

"Brazen wench," he breathed hoarsely. "You'll pay dearly for making me so crazy with wanting you."

The impish grin that captured her bewitching features melted Jake into liquid fire. Her arms glided around his neck to draw him ever closer. "So much talk, my lusty dragon," she taunted him. "I showed you my love, now show me yours . . . if you have any to give . . ."

If? If? Hell's fire, his love for her was bursting out all over! *Making* love to this delectable pixie wasn't even going to be enough to satisfy him. *Being* in love with her forever and ever was all that would appease him when he'd wanted her since the moment he laid eyes on her.

"Lord, woman," he groaned, trying to restrain his raging passions. "Don't you know how much I love you? Couldn't you see it every time you looked into my eyes?"

His body uncoiled upon hers, aching to become a living breathing part of her. As he lifted her to him, Cori was assaulted by shudders of mounting pleasure. Her body cried out to his, begging him to send her skyrocketing past the moon and stars. A surrendering sigh escaped her lips as he took complete possession, satisfying each burning craving that consumed her.

"Look at me," Jake demanded breathlessly. "I want you to see what you do to me. I want you to know that having you isn't nearly enough. Only loving you—heart, body, and soul—will ever come close to satisfying these indescribable needs you arouse in me . . ."

His voice trailed off when Cori arched shamelessly toward his driving thrusts, setting the frantic cadence of love that was as ancient and instinctive as life itself. It wasn't a time for talking. It was a time for feeling and believing in the emotions that swirled between them. As he drove deeply into her, Cori kissed him with all the bottled up love that rippled inside her. All their verbal battles and her stiff-necked stubbornness had only been another way of conveying her love for him. Even when she swore she hated him, she was communicating the frustrated love that boiled just beneath the surface. Only this one man could provoke her to anger that was always tempered with forbidden love. Only this one man could make every emotion intensify and explode like a colorful kaleidoscope.

It was a splendorous coming together, like a devastating hurricane that tossed the waves out on the sea and scattered the stars to kingdom come. Cori held on to Jake as if he were her lifeline in a turbulent storm. Uncontrollable shudders ricocheted through her body as he made love to her, filling her with unrivaled ecstasy.

His mouth plundered hers, his tongue probing with each demanding thrust of his body. He trapped her cry of pleasure in his throat and whispered a promise that, very soon, he would satisfy each ardent need they had aroused in each other.

And when they found sweet release, Cori dug her nails into his back and hung on for dear life. Remarkable sensations swamped and buffeted her. The crescendo of passion swelled like a tidal wave. The pleasure that unfurled inside her defied description. Her composure came completely unwound and Cori swore her body would burst beneath the wild, intense emotion that swelled inside her.

Tears of rapture flowed down her cheeks as Jake shuddered convulsively above her. For what seemed eternity, Cori lay in the grip of a passion so fierce and devastating that she doubted she would ever find her way back to reality.

Hearing Jake's confession of love held her suspended in a dreamlike trance. Leaving his arms was unthinkable. Now Cori knew why Dal and Lori had such a difficult time prying themselves out of bed. Mutual love, especially this fresh and new and so long in coming, boggled the mind. It made a person want to cling tightly to it and squeeze out every deliciously wondrous feeling, to savor it as long as it would last.

The rumble of laughter that reverberated in Jake's chest provoked Cori to glance up into his rugged features. She couldn't fathom what he found so amusing. She was still so numb with passion that thinking was difficult and moving as impossible as it had been while she was stuck in the swamp.

"What's so funny?" she queried, her voice thick with the aftereffects of their lovemaking.

"We're a pathetic looking pair," Jake snickered as he dropped a quick kiss to her lips. "You'd have thought we would have enough restraint to take time to wash off the grime before we . . ."

Cori pressed a muddy finger to his even muddier lips. She grinned into his blackened face, one that boasted white circles around his eyes and lips. Even the cleft in his chin was full of mud. "Some things just can't wait," she teased impishly.

"Apparently not," Jake agreed with a rakish leer. "But next time I get completely carried away, I plan to be . . ."

Her hand glided provocatively down his backbone, sending those familiar sparks leaping from his body to hers and back again. Her caress wandered lower, exploring his muscled hips and the hard columns of his thighs.

"Mmm . . . you were saying . . . ?" Cori whispered as she stirred seductively beneath him.

This bewitching nymph had Jake contradicting himself for the past two weeks. And damn if she didn't have him doing it again! When he was with her his willpower was nonexistent. She broke every rule he'd ever made about women. And when she teased him with her luscious body, Jake couldn't care less that they were draped on the creek bank, half covered with mud.

Jake let his actions do his talking for him. And this time he created innovative ways to express his love. There had been a time not so long ago when Jake doubted he would ever discover the meaning of love. He had never experienced anything remotely close to what he felt for this ebony-eyed sprite. Thirty-one years of hard living hadn't prepared him for the entangled emotions that now took hold of his heart.

Through all the complications and conflicts, the compelling need to win Cori's love constantly tugged at him. He knew she would never be completely content until she knew the truth behind her father's death. But together, he promised himself, they would untangle the

257

mystery. He would try not to tie this wild dove down; rather, he would let her spread her wings and soar. She could have all the freedom she wanted in this marriage as long as she always came back to him.

For Jake, there hadn't been a time since he met Cori that he'd wanted anyone else. He hadn't craved the reckless adventure that left him wandering like a tumbleweed. Cori satisfied that unexplained restlessness within him. She made him long for no more than she could give.

As they set sail on the most intimate of voyages into ecstasy, Jake abandoned all thought. For that space in time he wanted to revel in a love he had doubted he would ever enjoy with this woman.

It was much later before the fire of passion cooled and Jake showed any concern at all for their soiled clothes. But even when he led Cori down stream to bathe, cleansing himself wasn't foremost in his mind. One thing led to another and suddenly the coals of desire were leaping with flames again while they stood in midstream. Jake quickly realized there wasn't enough water in this creek to douse the fire that this sultry brunette ignited in him.

Even the sun hid its head long before Jake gave any thought whatsoever to retrieving the horses and returning to the house for a fresh set of clothes. And even then, he and Cori didn't stay in them long enough to justify putting them on.

It turned out to be a long, pleasurable night of compensation for all those tormenting times when Jake wanted Cori in his arms and found himself in bed alone . . .

Chapter 18

"Give up the *Belle*?" Layton raged when Augusta told him of her plan. "I most certainly will not!"

Jacob sat calmly behind the desk in his grandmother's study, watching his cousin throw his typical childish tantrum. The veins in Layton's face popped as he thrashed around the room on his stubby legs, emitting spasms of muffled curses.

"I purchased that luxury steamer all by myself. *I* . . ." He paused to tap himself on his inflated chest to emphasize his point. "*I* alone handled all the business transactions and hired the crew. It will be a cold day in hell before I turn that ship over to Jacob," he trumpeted.

"What's all the fuss?" Augusta sniffed distastefully. "Jake has offered you a generous sum in compensation. More than what's fair, if you ask me."

"More than fair?" Layton mimicked caustically. "I have never in my life had a fair shake. You always catered to Jacob while I was forced to come second. Well, he is *not* perfect, Gram!"

"We have something in common, then, don't we, cuz?" Jake mocked dryly.

"Did you hear that, Gram?" Layton's bottom lip jutted out in an exaggerated pout and he pointed an accusing finger at Jake. "He's always insulting me!"

Never mind that Layton had started it, thought Jake with an amused grin. It still amazed him that Layton, at age thirty-three, still resorted to childish behavior and arguments.

"You have mentioned several times the past six months that you wanted to split the company and take control of your half," Augusta reminded him crisply. "You're getting your way, Layton. All four of our steamers are luxurious and seaworthy."

"Is that so?" he questioned disrespectfully. "Then why does Jacob want the *Belle*? Why not the *St. Louie Lady*?"

"Because he wants to give it to his fiancée as a wedding gift," Augusta responded sharply.

"Fiancée?" Layton blinked like a disturbed owl. "What fiancée?"

"Cori Pierce," Jake informed his thunderstruck cousin. "I proposed and she said yes. She worked on that steamer. Let's just say I developed a sentimental attachment to it since that was where I met her. She harbors the same sentiments."

"Rubbish!" Layton snorted derisively.

Jacob had allowed his cousin to rant and rave long enough. "Take the offer, Layton. You won't get a better one. I want the deed to the *Belle* and you'll have your monetary compensation. With all the money I'm paying you, it won't take you long to make a down payment on a new vessel, if you so choose. By the time you enlist the support of a few investors, you can design a steamer that far exceeds the *Belle*."

"With all the robberies that have plagued our line?" Layton scoffed. "We were lucky to show a profit last year . . ." He slammed his mouth shut like a drawer when he realized his objection was a slur on his ability to manage the company in Jake's absence.

A wry smile quirked Jake's lips. "Then I should think

260

the jinx of the *Belle* would be something you would eagerly abandon. We wouldn't want anything to destroy your unblemished record of competency, now would we?"

"There he goes again," Layton pouted.

"Oh, for heaven sake," Augusta muttered in annoyance. "You're the one who said your profits were nothing to boast about. Just fetch the deed to the *Belle* and let's consult the attorney about dividing the company. I'm getting too old for these family squabbles. You take your inheritance and do as you see fit and Jacob will do the same."

Layton glared at his grandmother, who glared right back at him.

"Bring the deed to the courthouse Monday morning at ten o'clock," Jacob ordered in a businesslike tone. "All the necessary papers will be drawn up and you'll have your cash compensation."

Layton turned his fuming glower on his cousin. "We shall see whose company controls the Mississippi, mine or yours. Gram is going to wish she had put me in charge years ago. I'll be making money hand over fist!"

When Layton stamped into the hall, Augusta and Jake followed in his wake. As luck would have it, Dal Blaylock and Lori rumbled down the road in the carriage while the threesome stood on the veranda.

Layton turned a froglike grin on his cousin. "*Your* fiancée, you say?" he snickered in taunt. "It seems your best friend has other ideas, just as he did on the steamer."

Jake disguised his irritation. He was definitely going to have to make some sort of arrangements with Dal and Lori. If he and Dal were seen courting the twins at the same social functions, it might start Layton to thinking. God forbid that should happen! Mental exercise would overtax Layton's childish mind.

"I won't hold my breath waiting to see you married to

261

that fickle beauty," Layton ridiculed. He fixed his gaze on Augusta who seemed terribly disgruntled to see Jake's fiancée cuddled up next to Dal. "Are you sure your precious Jacob can handle his own company, Gram? Why, he can't even keep tabs on his betrothed!"

After Layton strutted off, gloating every step of the way, Augusta peered over at Jake. "What the devil is going on here?"

"Nothing is going on," Jake said with perfect assurance. "Dal is quite fond of Cori. They became the best of friends on the steamer."

"They were setting a mite close together, don't you think?" Augusta remarked. "I'm perfectly aware that Cori is high-spirited and independent, but . . ."

"You're the one who assured her she didn't have to behave like my devoted slave," Jake reminded his grandmother with a teasing wink. "If I'm not upset to see my fiancée with my best friend, I can't fathom why you should be."

"I suggest you have a little chat with Cori," Augusta advised. "I should hate to see her and Dal become quite such good friends. It will only start rumors and cause trouble. Layton will have a field day!"

Jake was beginning to understand the difficulties Cori and Lori had faced when they assumed a single identity on board the *Belle*. There had been a few ticklish situations then and there were bound to be more now, especially since the twins weren't sharing the same room. They couldn't brief each other on what had transpired while one was in and the other was out. And until Jake knew of Layton's specific involvement in the acquisition of the *Belle* and Cori's father's death, he couldn't risk exposing the fact that there were twins running around. There was no telling how Layton would use the information.

Blackmail? Threats of prison sentences? Bargains to

take full control of the company? Jake wouldn't put anything past Layton. After all, the weasel had absconded with the stolen money and hadn't made a peep about finding it.

A sly smile hovered on Jake's lips as he swaggered down the steps. Very soon, Layton would regret swiping the money without returning it to its proper owners . . .

"Do you suppose if I offered Cori a bribe she would curtail her outings with Dal?" Augusta called after her grandson.

Jake chuckled as he pivoted toward the gray-haired woman who was perched on the porch. "She loves me, Gram. I'm certain of that. Don't fret. Cori can gallivant all over town with Dal if she pleases. But I have her heart. Dal only has the pleasure of her company."

Augusta wasn't so sure about that and she proceeded to tell Jake so. But he shrugged her off in that nonchalant way of his. Jake might not have been concerned, but Augusta was plenty worried. More than anything, she wanted to see Jake married to a woman who could make him happy, one who would remain true. Augusta had thought Cori was Jake's equal. Now she wasn't so certain. After all, it had taken an expensive steamboat to swing the bargain! It made Augusta wonder if Cori's love didn't come with too expensive of a price tag!

As had become his nightly habit, Jake had crept along the balcony into Cori's room. For appearance sake, he refused to enter her chamber through the hall, in case servants were prowling about. But Jake had no intention of restraining himself until after the wedding. It was difficult to keep his hands off that gorgeous minx in public and absolutely impossible in private.

The welcoming smile on Cori's heart-shaped lips brought Jake toward the bed like a victim of a trance. She

263

looked utterly tempting lying there, her silky body clad only in a sheet. Jake heaved a longing sigh and shucked his robe to join her.

As his muscular body slid beneath the sheet beside her, Cori shivered in erotic anticipation. She had become a wanton woman with positively no shame, she decided. The mere sight of this magnificent man left her aching in places she hadn't known she had until he taught her the meaning of passion.

"I thought you'd never get here," Cori whispered as she inched closer to nibble at his sensuous lips.

"Shameless wench," Jake teased playfully. "What would the servants think if they knew?"

"They'd wonder how I managed to resist your magnetic charm as long as I did," she purred seductively, her hand wandering over his ribs and belly.

Jake grabbed her wayward hand and held it in his own. "We've got to talk." He honestly thought he deserved a medal for making that declaration when his body demanded something far more stimulating than conversation.

Cori did a double take. "We did that in the dining room. Unless I've been misinformed, a man doesn't join a lady in bed for idle conversation." Her lips hovered enticingly over his, testing Jake's willpower to its very limits.

"I'm serious, Cori." He swore his voice had rusted and his body had burned into charred ashes when she teased him with a kiss. "There's something I want you to do for me."

He was serious, she realized. Cori blinked bemusedly. "What is so all-fired important?"

Ignoring the warm tingles that lying beside her evoked, Jake raised himself on an elbow to stare into her inquisitive features. "I want you to steal the money from Layton that you stole from his investors on the steamer," he requested out of the blue.

Cori gaped at him as if he were addle-witted. "For more than two weeks you have scolded me for utilizing my unsavory talents of fleecing passengers and picking pockets. And all of a sudden, you want me to resume my thievery. Why?"

A wry grin quirked Jake's lips as he smoothed away her befuddled frown. "After stamping and snorting, Layton agreed to deed the *Belle* over to me, providing he acquired cash compensation. It seems only fitting that we should pay him with the money he carted out of the storeroom."

Cori snickered at the irony of Jake's suggestion. "You're a devil, Jacob Wolf."

"Ain't I though?" he drawled unrepentantly. "Layton certainly can't rush to the constable's office to report a theft when he was guilty of stealing the stolen money. It serves that weasel right."

The thought of doublecrossing Layton had devilish appeal. "Just when do you propose that I relieve Layton of his ill-gotten gains?"

"The night of our engagement party," Jake declared, and then eyed Cori speculatively. "That is, if you consent to switching places with Lori while you're tending to the task."

Cori peered dubiously at him. "And what, exactly, are you and Lori going to be doing while I'm doing my nocturnal prowling?" she wanted to know.

"Jealous?" he teased with a roguish grin.

"Immensely," Cori insisted. "I wonder if I can trust you to remember that my identical twin is not me."

Jake leaned over to drop a quick kiss to her pouting lips. "If I do forget, you can refresh my memory the moment we get home . . ."

The intimate promise in his kiss stoked the fire that his nearness always aroused in her. But it did nothing to squelch Cori's apprehension. Cori and Lori had found themselves in uncomfortable situations that were too numerous to mention while they played their charade aboard the *Belle*. Unforeseen problems always cropped up to test and entrap the twins.

Although this scheme sounded simple enough, Cori had reservations. Loving Jake was still so new to her that she couldn't help but wonder how easily this fragile bond could be broken. It wasn't that she didn't trust Jake or Lori, exactly. But the painful truth was that Jake would be staring at her twin and he just might forget *who* was *who* when it was impossible to tell them apart! And chances were, Dal wasn't going to take kindly to the idea either.

"It will only be for an hour or two," Jake assured her when she frowned warily. "What can possibly happen in such a short span of time?"

"You might be surprised," Cori grumbled.

Jake stared her squarely in the eye. "I am allowing you another chance to retaliate against Layton. Do you want to take your revenge on him or don't you?"

Phrased as such, Cori couldn't decline the offer. Layton Breeze was an arrogant little worm who deserved every disaster that came his way. Knowing how greedy he was, Cori suspected he had been making all sorts of plans for that stolen money. Layton had crowed at the injustice of having his prospective investors robbed. But the minute he got his greedy little hands on the cash he had hoarded it.

Cori nodded agreeably. "I'll do it, but you're going to have to take me to visit Layton's home. I'll have to learn my way around the house."

"Tomorrow afternoon," Jake told her. "I already invited us over to introduce you to Sylvia."

Cori leveled Jake a glance. The last hint of mischief dwindled in her dark eyes. "If you're thinking this scheme will satisfy my need for revenge against Layton, you're wrong," she told him somberly. "He is guilty of killing my father. I want him punished for that."

"And I assured you that I would handle Layton in my own time and my own way," Jake grumbled when they landed on this controversial issue that always caused friction between them. "First I have to obtain the deed before I can question his means of purchasing the ship. If I infuriate him he might back out of the deal."

"And in the meantime that scoundrel is fluttering around, free as a bird," Cori muttered, her voice registering her resentment.

"I don't happen to believe Layton is capable of murder. Theft? Yes," he qualified. "Murder? No."

"And I happen to think you're letting family ties influence your thinking," Cori shot back.

"If Layton is guilty, he'll be punished," Jake promised her, his tone sharper than he intended.

"Won't he just!" Cori smirked. "Your idea of punishing a relative is scolding him and sending him on his way."

It had happened again, just as it always did. This touchy subject landed them squarely in the middle of an argument.

"I said he would be properly punished," Jake growled, grasping futilely at the reins of his runaway temper. "and you had damned well better not take matters into your own hands again."

Her chin jutted out rebelliously. "And if I do, will you wag your finger in my face and order me to behave myself from this day forward?" she asked in a sarcastic tone.

"No," he contested through gritted teeth. "I'll strangle you for disobeying me."

"So that's the way of it, is it?" Cori muttered. "I get strangled for trying to see justice served while your dear cousin gets away with murder!"

"He did not kill your father!" Jake muffled his roaring

voice before he roused the servants.

"He most certainly did, and I intend to prove it, with or without your help," Cori hissed, trying to keep her voice down.

"If you dare to . . ."

When Jake resorted to brandishing his fist in her defiant face, Cori's arm shot toward the balcony door. "You may take your leave now," she interrupted his threat. "I have nothing more to say to you."

"Fine," Jake bounded to his feet and snatched up his discarded robe. With angry jerks, he tied the sash around his waist. "I can see that your stubborn nature is seeping out again, but I warn you, if you take it upon yourself to confront Layton, you will get yourself into more trouble than you already did. Layton would like nothing better than to have a weapon to use against me. And he'd use it. You can bet your life on it!"

"All the more reason to entrap him," Cori grumbled resentfully. "You are being generous and forgiving because he's family. But he would stab you in the back the first chance he got. You're a fool to give him the benefit of the doubt and the slightest of considerations!"

Jacob was vividly aware that, even though he and Cori were wonderfully happy in each other's arms, they were worlds apart when it came to determining how to handle Layton. They never could avoid an argument on this sensitive subject. He was headstrong and she was infuriatingly stubborn! Theirs would never be a dull, uneventful marriage. Lord, it would be anything but!

"Good night, Cori," Jake snapped as he stomped off. "Pleasant nightmares."

"I hope you sleep like a rock," she retorted.

For dramatic effect, Cori flounced in bed, jerked the sheet over her bare shoulders and buried her head under the pillow as if the sight of him annoyed her.

"Impossible woman," Jake muttered on his way out.

"Horrible man." Her muffled rejoinder nipped at his heels.

"If you're wrong about Layton, I will expect you to get down on your knees in humble apology," he said over his shoulder as he veered around the corner.

"I'm right, and you're walking around with blinders on!"

"You're dead wrong."

"Go to hell, Jacob!" Cori snatched up the pillow and hurled at the raven head that had poked inside the partially opened door.

"Where, my dear Cori, do you think I've been for the past half hour? As near as I can tell, I've been arguing with the devil's advocate," Jake said snidely.

Cori was so frustrated that she yanked up the figurine from the night stand and flung it at him. Jake caught the missile before it slammed into his skull. With a thump, he thrust it down on the end table beside the door. But in his anger, he set the fragile statue down a bit too forcefully. It shattered in his clenched fist.

"That's going to cost you," he growled at her.

"*You* broke it," she sassed with a goading smile that made her ebony eyes sparkle in the lanternlight. "But if it was of sentimental value, I'll be only to happy to *steal* enough money to replace it for you."

Jake allowed her to have the last word because he was so furious with the way the evening had evolved that he didn't dare reopen his mouth. In his present mood he would have called that ornery spitfire every name in the book and they would be right back in the middle of another argument that would drive another wedge between them.

With a wordless scowl, Jake turned around and stamped off.

"The big baboon," Cori muttered, punching the other pillow that had cradled Jake's head before they wound up in a shouting match. "Spare that murdering swine, will he? No, he most certainly will not!"

Cori was too angry to sleep. Like a mountain goat, she leaped out of bed, rummaged through her belongings and snatched up her breeches, cape and shirt. It was time to make a few arrangements of her own, despite Jacob's threats.

Chewing on that determined thought, Cori eased onto the terrace and tiptoed through the shadows. Quietly, she crawled over the rail and climbed down the lattice that was choked with ivy. With the silence of a stalking cat, she made her way to the stables to retrieve a mount.

Dictate to me, will he? No, he will not, Cori mused belligerently. Just because she loved Jake didn't mean she was going to obey him like a humble servant. One day soon, Layton Breeze was going to own up to his vile crime. Cori had vowed a year ago to ensure that he did. Until she had accomplished her crusade, she could never find peace. For consolation, Cori assured herself that Jacob would be as relentless as she was if the boot was on the other foot. And if he couldn't understand the tormenting emotions that plagued her then maybe they didn't need to be married at all!

Ah, what a frustrating emotion love was, thought Cori as she trotted her steed toward Dal Blaylock's plantation. One moment she swore she loved Jake so much she would burst a seam. And the next instant she wanted to shake him until his pearly white teeth fell out! Now was that deep abiding love or insanity? Cori asked herself as she rode off into the night. Then she wondered if love and insanity might be one and the same. If they weren't, they could have fooled her!

Chapter 19

Cori muttered in irritation as she tiptoed along the gallery that encircled Dal Blaylock's home. For the past fifteen minutes she had been window peeking, trying to determine which room her sister inhabited. but it was difficult to tell with only the silver of moon to illuminate the darkened chambers. When Cori stubbed her toe on the stone planter that set against the outer wall, she feared her wail of pain would rouse the entire household. Inwardly groaning and limping, Cori shuffled around to press her nose against the glass door and search out her sister.

Finally Cori spied what she hoped was her sister's form on the bed. But she realized the error of her ways when she crept into the room and discovered Dal's blond head protruding from the quilts. He was in bed alone? My, that was a surprise! The way he and Lori had carried on in the cabin of the steamer one would have thought they had become inseparable. Trouble in paradise, Cori predicted. Another shining example that true love didn't always run smooth. Didn't she know it!

Reversing direction, Cori left the room and crept to the next door on the south wing of the home. She breathed a sigh of relief when she stepped inside and saw Lori's long hair flooding over the white pillowcase.

Quietly, Cori eased down to tap her sister on the shoulder. When Lori gasped in fright, Cori clamped her hand over her sister's mouth—one that was wide open, prepared to cry for assistance.

"It's just me," Cori whispered as she tugged the wide-brimmed hat from her head with her free hand. "I have to talk to you."

Lori nodded in recognition and pushed up against the headboard. An amused grin rippled across her lips as she surveyed her sister. "I assume Jacob gave you permission to do your nocturnal prowling," she smirked.

"I don't have to ask permission," Cori declared, tilting a proud chin. "Anyway, we aren't speaking at present."

Lori flung a sour glance at the wall that separated her from Dal. "Then it must be something in the drinking water that causes men in Natchez to be muleheaded."

"You had a lover's spat," Cori snickered. "I never would have thought it, the way the two of you usually hang all over each other."

"*Used* to hang all over each other, you mean," Lori corrected grumpily. "Dal insisted that I tell him why we were robbing Layton's would-be investors. When I finally told him he assured me that we had no business doing private detective work and that Layton wasn't guilty. Harmless as a fly was the way Dal put it!"

Cori gaped at her sister. The longer Lori talked the angrier she became. From the sound of things, Lori and Dal had wound up in the same sort of shouting match that had put Cori and Jake at odds.

"Then he had the nerve to *demand*, demand mind you, that I drop the matter entirely and put the past behind me," Lori went on to say in a resentful tone. "He even had the audacity to warn me not to become as stubborn and contrary as you are." Dark eyes flashed in the moonlight. "And that was when I told him that when he criticized my sister he was insulting me. And if he thinks

272

for one minute that I'm going to let Layton off the hook then he doesn't know me as well as he thinks he does! And if he wants a docile wife he had damned well better start courting someone else!"

"Sh . . . sh." Cori pressed her forefinger to her sister's lips. "Keep your voice down or Dal will be storming in here."

"I haven't forgotten why we took the job on the steamboat," Lori whispered. "And until this matter with Layton Breeze is settled to my satisfaction, things will never be right between us. Dal wants to ignore the problem, as if that will make it go away. I want the questions answered and the murder solved."

"That's why I'm here."

"I thought as much," Lori eased onto her side and stared intently at her sister. "What are we going to do about Layton Breeze?"

Cori proceeded to inform Lori about the money Jake had planted in the supply room and Layton had subsequently stolen. The news had Lori muttering under her breath. Then Cori revealed Jake's scheme to retrieve the cash and offer it back to the weasel when the deed to the *Belle* was presented. Finally she unfolded her own plan to harass Layton until he was so rattled that he confessed to the murder.

Sporting a devilish smile, Lori gave her sister a congratulatory pat on the shoulder. "You always did have a flair for intrigue, dear sister. By the time we finish with Layton he's going to think he's losing his mind . . . at least what little he had to begin with," she added glibly.

Cori frowned as a worrisome thought flashed through her mind. "Do you think you can keep Dal from discovering that you're coming and going in the middle of the night? If he does, you know he'll throw a ring-tailed fit."

"Let him," Lori said stubbornly. "He may as well learn

273

he can't order me around. I draw the line at submissive obedience. I agreed to marry the man, but I said nothing about wearing a leash around my neck!"

Cori bit back an amused grin as she rose from the edge of the bed. Although Lori possessed a gentler nature, she did have her feisty moments. Probably because she had spent too many years with Cori. The stubbornness had apparently rubbed off. And when Lori was provoked, that Shelton pride won out. Sure as the world, Dal was going to have to apologize unless he wanted to remain crosswise of his future bride. Lori didn't look and sound as if she intended to budge an inch. Good for her!

After detailing their plans, Cori crept back to the terrace to shinny down the colonnade. She was in a cheerful mood when she trotted her mount back to Wolfhaven, mentally organizing the first phase of their scheme to drive Layton into a confession.

Her reentry into Wolfhaven was going superbly until she swung a leg over the balcony railing. A looming shadow fell over her. Cori instinctively jerked back and lost her grasp on the railing. Frantically, she hooked the toe of her boot around the railing before she plunged into the shrubs below. While she hung upside down, a steely hand clamped around her ankle. Jake yanked her up none too gently, flipped her end over end, and set her to her feet.

"Attending a witch's convention this evening, I suppose," he growled sarcastically.

With all the dignity she could muster, Cori rearranged her twisted garments and squared her shoulders. "How'd you guess?" she sassed at the terrorist in the blue velvet robe.

"I saw your invitation on the night stand," he smirked as he propelled her toward her room. "Don't tell me. Let me guess. You were unanimously elected to preside over the evil sister's unholy society." One dark brow lifted to a sardonic angle. "Is anyone I know going to be burned at the stake in human sacrifice?"

His snide sarcasm was not well received. "How strange that you should ask. We voted to sacrifice a muleheaded male. You won hands down."

"Now why doesn't that surprise me?" he muttered caustically.

"I can't imagine why it should," she countered just as sarcastically, jerking her arm from his bone-crushing grasp. "You're the world's most muleheaded male. Nobody I know even runs a close second."

"Enough of this, Cori," Jake snapped brusquely. "Where have you been?"

"I thought we just established that," she flashed.

Muttering a string of epithets to her name, Jake yanked off her cape and hurled it against the wall. "If you were prowling around Layton's house, searching for clues, I swear I'll . . ."

"You needn't swear. I wasn't," she told him truthfully.

"Then where were you?" he demanded, thrusting his scowling face into hers.

"Enjoying a midnight ride." It was a partial truth, the closest thing to fact that Jake was going to drag out of her.

"You expect me to believe you were doing nothing more harmless than trotting around in the dark?" he hooted.

Cori's chin came up to meet his challenging glare. "That's my story and I'm sticking with it."

Jake lost his temper. He had been stewing and pacing for two hours, ever since he had returned to Cori's room to find her gone. He had imagined all sorts of terrible things that might have happened to her. Twice he had considered hunting her down, but he had waited, knowing it would have offended her independent nature to have him following after her as if she were a helpless

275

child. She was already put out with him, and that would have made the situation infinitely worse. But he was also agitated at her for leaving in the first place and then refusing to divulge where her midnight caper had taken her.

Cori found herself hoisted off the floor by the collar of her shirt. She hung in midair, forced to meet Jake's ominous scowl.

"Are you reverting to woman-beating?" she taunted him. "Go ahead then, blacken both my eyes if you're so inclined. But I'm not discussing the subject further, no matter what you do to me."

Jake dropped her like a hot potato. The back of her knees slammed against the edge of the bed and Cori plopped backward. Jake was there, looming over her, and oh, how this muscular giant could loom. Cori kept telling herself he wouldn't actually strike her, but he certainly looked as if he was visualizing where he would land a punishing blow . . . or three.

"You leave Layton to me," Jake snarled. "I'll find out what you want to know when the time is ripe. And until then, you leave well enough alone!"

Thank goodness he was too agitated to think of demanding her promise of doing nothing. If he had, the conversation would have lasted the remainder of the night. But to Cori's relief, Jake pushed himself upright and stalked out.

Grumbling under her breath, Cori pulled off her clothes and shrugged on her nightgown. Men! They were so cocksure of themselves. Apparently Lori had also discovered that universal flaw in the male of the species. Even though Lori swore the sun rose and set on her beloved Dal Blaylock, she was beginning to realize he did have one or two foibles. Until today, Lori had been walking around with her head in the clouds. Thank God she'd come back to earth!

Muttering a quick curse to all men in general and Jacob Wolf in particular, Cori closed her eyes and willed sleep to overtake her. It was long in coming. She was tempted to tiptoe into Jake's room and make amends. but intractable pride won out. Cori was fully aware that she still loved that stubborn, headstrong, billygoat of a man. But at the moment she didn't like him very much. And she wasn't going to like him a damned bit better in the morning either if he insisted on using those infuriating strong-arm tactics on her.

Cori didn't know what she expected Sylvia Breeze to look like, but she was unprepared for the stout, big-boned woman who stood four inches taller than Layton.

The reception Cori and Jake received from the Breezes was lukewarm at best. Layton slung disgruntled glances at Jake, and Sylvia kept looking Cori over for flaws. Layton's new stepsons were exactly as Augusta had described them—holy terrors. The brats were loud, disrespectful nuisances who charged through the house, slamming into walls and swinging fists at each other.

For the most part, Layton and Sylvia ignored the boys. Cori itched to grab hold of them and bang their heads together. In her opinion, the whole passel deserved each other.

When Sylvia finally offered to take Cori on a tour of their home and boasted about the expensive furnishings she had purchased abroad, Cori breathed a thankful sigh. Her purpose of casing the home was two-fold. She fully intended to steal the cash Layton had stolen and also to familiarize herself with the mansion so she and Lori could torment Layton into a confession.

The plantation home was a perfect setting for discreet comings and goings. The portico that graced the back of the house was surrounded with lattice that would serve as a ladder to the upper gallery. The second-story balcony offered entrance to the bedchambers as well as the spacious upstairs sitting room. The thick clump of oaks that encircled the house provided refuge for sneaking up and creeping off in the dark. The possibilities for terrorizing Layton were endless!

While Cori and Sylvia were wandering through the house and around the gardens, Jake dropped into the chair in Layton's study and started firing questions like bullets.

"I saw Kyle Benson at the docks this morning with that overgrown bully who works for you," Jake announced. "Why isn't Benson on the *Belle*, guarding the passengers who are on their way to New Orleans?"

"Because he has decided to take to the land and pursue other business interests," Layton replied defensively. "He plans to become my part-time body guard."

Jake scoffed at his cousin. "I should think that wooden-headed Bruce Dobson would be guard enough for you."

"Natchez under the Hill is a rough place," Layton reminded Jake. "A man needs protection down there with all the brawls and thievery going on."

A speculative smile hovered on Jake's lips. "Or perhaps the truth of the matter is that you are using Benson as a hired henchman to discourage passengers from purchasing tickets on other steamboat lines. I wonder if that is a common practice of yours."

Layton's face turned a remarkable shade of purple. "How dare you accuse me of skullduggery!"

"Are you denying it?" Jake interrogated.

"I never once told Bruce or Kyle to muscle passengers into taking our line instead of the competition!" he fiercely protested.

"But I imagine you suggested such things," Jake smirked.

Layton slammed his fist onto the desk. "I don't have to sit here and listen to your accusations."

"Would you prefer to stand up?" Jake mocked.

"Just what, exactly, is it you're accusing me of?" Layton muttered sourly.

"Undermining our competition with unscrupulous methods, for starters," Jake declared. "And second, after studying the company ledgers, I think Kyle Benson was grossly overpaid and I want to know why. What sort of deal did you make with that scoundrel in my absence?"

"I made no deals," Layton contested hotly.

"You couldn't prove it by me," Jake snorted in a disdainful tone. "The man acts as if he owns an interest in the company."

"Whether he does or doesn't will be no concern of yours at the first of next week when we dissolve the company and go our own way," Layton parried.

"Did Benson help you acquire the *Mississippi Belle* or was it Bruce Dobson who convinced the previous owner to sell out at rock-bottom price?" Jake fired back.

It was glaringly apparent to Layton that Jacob had gone over the ledgers with a fine-toothed comb, looking for incriminating evidence. Jake would dearly love to turn Augusta against him and cut him completely out of the Breeze inheritance, Layton thought huffily. And if he hadn't married Sylvia three years earlier, he would be limping along, forced to remain under Augusta's control—Augusta, who was only the figurehead who acted under Jake's advice. They were ganging up against him, that's what they were doing! And it was all Jake's fault!

"I handled the transaction all by myself," Layton spouted. "The former owner was a poor manager and he found himself losing money faster than he could make it. I offered him a price and he took it. That was all there was to it."

279

"Then how do you explain the death of the former owner immediately after the business transaction?"

Jake knew he was prematurely pressing Layton for answers. But after his row with Cori, he felt he needed to delve into the matter before she took the law into her own hands again and got herself in more trouble. And Cori would, Jake predicted. That hellion attracted trouble as easily as she attracted men.

"How'd you find out about Michael Shelton's death?" Layton croaked.

Michael Shelton . . . Jake digested the information, learning at long last what Cori's last name really was.

Jake realized Layton's shocked reaction had aroused his own suspicion. It certainly wasn't proof, but it did leave a man to wonder to what extent Layton had been involved. Jake still couldn't agree with Cori that Layton was involved in murder. But he did admit to himself that he had been wrong before.

"I have my sources," Jake answered, distracted by his own thoughts.

"I had nothing to do with it," Layton defended indignantly. "The man was carrying a sizable bankroll. The wharf in St. Louis is every bit as dangerous as Natchez under the Hill. A man without a bodyguard who carries large sums of money is asking for trouble. Obviously, Michael Shelton was robbed and murdered."

"Were Bruce Dobson and Kyle Benson with you at the time you made the transaction?" Jake questioned, his astute gaze drilling into his cousin.

"Yes, as a matter of fact, and they were also on board the *Belle*, celebrating with me when the murder supposedly occurred," Layton declared.

"How convenient," Jake snorted. "Three alibis for three likely suspects."

Layton's fist hit the desk again. His face turned the color of cooked liver. "You'd love to pin a crime on me, wouldn't you? Then all the Breeze fortune would be yours and I would be conveniently out of your way. Well, it isn't going to happen because I'm innocent and so are my men . . ."

The conversation died a quick death when Layton's stepsons rudely barged into the office, clenched in a bear hug. They crashed to the floor, snarling and growling at each other.

Although Layton chose to ignore them, Jake did not. Like a shot, he darted across the room to grab the squabbling brats by the nape of their shirts. After dragging the twosome onto the stoop, he gave them both a good shaking.

The two boys, who had never had a hand laid on them, gaped at the thunderous scowl on Jake's lips.

"If you're going to fight, you'll do it outside . . . and never again in my presence," Jake snapped at them. "And the next time you pay Augusta a visit, you had better behave like angels. If I hear reports that the two of you tried to demolish her home, you'll answer to me." Jake jerked them up off the porch, leaving their feet dangling in midair. "Do we understand each other, boys?"

Two ruffled heads nodded in quick affirmation.

"Good! I should hate for demons of the dark to hound you for your evil ways. And if they don't, I most certainly will!"

Jake set the boys to their feet, but he didn't release them. He stuck his face in theirs and admonished them once more for good measure. When he was finished, two meek youngsters slinked down the steps and headed for the stable.

When Jacob spun around, Cori and Sylvia were standing in the foyer. An amused grin pursed Cori's lips, but an outraged frown puckered Sylvia's features. Before she could open her mouth, Jake stalked forward, looming

281

ominously over her.

"Did you have something you wanted to say to me, Sylvia?"

His rumbling tone warned her to keep her mouth shut. Clutching Cori's arm, Jake herded her out the door and down the steps.

"I admire your gumption," Cori complimented as Jake swung her into the carriage.

"Perhaps I should have employed the same tactic on you to keep you in line," Jake grunted, casting her the evil eye.

"You did," she reminded him flippantly. "It just didn't happen to work worth a damn in my case."

"I'd give my inheritance to know what would," Jake muttered as he hopped up beside her. "I hate it when we fight."

Cori was almost tempted to end the war they had been waging. Almost. She knew full well that if she gave in to Jake that he would expect her to sit idly by while he conducted his own investigation of her father's death. Since he couldn't be totally objective where his cousin was concerned, Cori couldn't give in to him. Never mind that she couldn't be totally objective where her father was concerned. In her mind, that was altogether different. And until the murder was solved, she and Jake were going to be at odds. That, unfortunately, was a fact of life.

"If you are going to be churlish today, I'll not bother trying to carry on a civil conversation with you," Cori announced, looking down her nose at him.

"And if you're going to continue being stubborn, I could care less," Jake grumbled as he popped the reins over the horse's rump. "Layton proclaims he's innocent."

"And you'd believe him, even if he said the sun rose in the west," Cori grumbled bitterly.

282

The conversation was officially over. Neither Cori nor Jake uttered another word all the way back to Wolfhaven. When they reached the plantation and Cori had stepped down from the carriage, Jake headed toward the company office on the wharf. He was a frustrated man groping for any excuse to distract himself. Jake had enjoyed the foretaste of heaven with Cori before their bubble burst. Cori had been loving and playful until they had clashed on that sensitive subject of Layton Breeze. And suddenly they were right back where they started—at odds.

Wanting Cori every hour of the day and night was playing havoc with Jake's disposition. Hell's fire, he felt as if he were tripping along an emotional tightrope. He could have selected any woman he wanted for a wife. But no, he had fallen in love with a woman who was out to convict his cousin of a crime Jake wasn't positively certain Layton had committed. But Cori *was* certain, and that put them, and kept them, on a constant collision course with conflict.

With a wide yawn, Layton plopped down on his bed. As had become his habit, he lifted the corner of the mattress to ensure his pouch of cash was still where he'd stashed it. He had considered placing the money in the safe in his office, but since Sylvia had access to it, he didn't want her to find it and start posing questions and demanding her share. The woman was as frivolous as he was and she believed she owned half of everything he had. But this was his money, not hers and Layton had no intention of sharing it.

Assured that his nest egg was where it was supposed to be, Layton stuffed his stubby legs under the quilt. A startled squawk erupted from his lips when his toes collided with a slimy object. When the unidentified obstacle leaped onto his leg, Layton shrieked like a stuck pig. He quickly untangled himself from his night gown and quilts and stared.

"*Rivet . . .*"

Layton glowered at the lump in his bed. With a muttered curse, he flipped back the quilt to find a frog staring up at him.

"Damn those ornery little brats," he scowled.

Layton snatched up the frog, stamped to the terrace and heaved it through the air.

And that's when he saw, or at least *thought* he saw, a shapeless incandescent figure floating through the shadows of the night. Layton swallowed and backed toward his bedroom. Safe behind the protective glass door, he squinted into the darkness, searching for the eerie specter that had startled him.

"Layton Breeze . . ." The haunting voice sounded as it came from somewhere within his own house, even though the weird vision drifted in and out of the crisscrossed shadows in the gardens below. "I have come back for you . . ."

Layton very nearly leaped out of his skin when a low, oddly familiar voice rattled with mocking laughter.

And then the apparition and the disembodied voice evaporated into nothingness. With an apprehensive shudder, Layton scurried back to bed. As he reached over to snuff his lantern, he jerked back as if he'd been stung. There, lying beside the lantern, was a corncob pipe that resembled the one Michael Shelton had smoked during their confrontations in St. Louis.

Layton's face blanched and he swallowed with a strangled gulp. "It can't be . . ." he muttered as his shaky fingers folded around the pipe from which a swirl of smoke rose upward, filling the room with the faint hint of tobacco.

Frightened and confused, Layton rushed toward the door to send the pipe sailing in the same arc the frog had

284

taken. But hurling the object through space seemed to invite the goading laughter that came from only God knew where!

Glancing in every direction at once, Layton scampered back to bed and clutched the sheet protectively under his chin. Wide-eyed, he listened for other sounds to alert him to a ghostly presence in his room. But not a single unfamiliar noise reached his ears. The wraith that had come to haunt him had apparently retreated back to the other side of eternity.

Layton's teeth chattered and his eyes darted back and forth expectantly. It was several hours before he could relax enough to close his eyes and drift off to sleep. And during those unnerving hours, he swore he heard a distant wailing in the wind. Something out there was haunting him!

"There are no such things as ghosts," Layton assured himself, his voice two octaves higher than normal. And even though he had uttered the statement aloud, he couldn't quite convince himself. He had heard enough spooky tales of witches and wraiths on the docks of the river to leave him speculating if such unexplainable happenings were links to the spiritual world. As much as Layton wanted to deny it, he had the inescapable feeling that a disembodied spirit was roaming around his plantation, waiting to collect its debt . . .

Chapter 20

Augusta Breeze's estate was a hubbub of activity on Saturday evening. Guests had come from miles around to help the dowager celebrate her grandson's engagement. Augusta had hired musicians to entertain her throng of guests. Food and beverages were in huge supply. For three days the servants had been bustling about, obeying Augusta's demands to have the plantation in splendid shape for her party.

With a satisfied smile, Augusta smoothed her black lace gown into place and glanced around her. All her distinguished friends were awaiting the arrival of the guests of honor—Jacob Wolf and his fiancée. Augusta had two reasons for wanting the party to be a success. First of all, she was anxious to introduce Cori into Natchez society. And second, she wanted to dispel the rumors that Layton had started—the rumors suggesting that Cori had been seen in Dal Blaylock's company too many times the past few days for a wedding with Jake to take place.

Since Layton had come to tattle to her the previous day, after he'd seen Cori riding around town with Dal, Augusta had been in a stew. Even though Jake assured her there was nothing going on between Cori and Dal,

Augusta didn't appreciate the attention her grand-daughter-to-be was heaping on the handsome blond rake. Tonight she would ensure every guest in attendance knew where Cori's affection lay. Seeing Jake cuckolded would demolish Augusta. She had raised Jake from a young lad and she had waited an eternity to see him take a faithful wife.

A disgruntled frown puckered Augusta's wrinkled features when Jake arrived with his bewitching fiancée—accompanied by none other than Dal Blaylock. Curses, couldn't that man back off for at least one night? This was Jake's engagement party, after all!

"Augusta, how delightful to see you again," Cori gushed as she approached the dowager.

The reception Cori received was cordial, but hardly what one could call enthusiastic. Cori knew why Augusta's nose was out of joint. Layton had also stopped by to inform Jake that he had seen his betrothed gallivanting around town with Dal. And although things weren't quite right between Cori and Jake, she didn't want to hurt Augusta. The dowager was a spirited old woman who had nothing to do with Cori's woes.

Without ado, Augusta clutched Cori's arm and hustled her into a vacant corner of the vestibule. "I don't like what I've been hearing," Augusta said without pre-amble. "Your friendship with Dal has become the subject of too much gossip and I don't want to see my grandson hurt."

Cori stared the dowager squarely in the eye. "Although Jacob and I have had a bit of a disagreement, I want you to know that I care deeply for him."

"More than Dal?" Augusta questioned point-blank.

"I love Jacob," Cori assured her with genuine emotion. "And no matter what happens, or what you might *think* is happening, Jacob is the only man I have ever loved."

A wary frown knitted Augusta's brows. "You're making this sound terribly intriguing, my child. I don't suppose you want to explain yourself."

Cori patted the hand that was gripped on the intricately carved cane. "One day perhaps, but not tonight."

Augusta heaved an exasperated sigh. "Oh, very well, play your mysterious little games. I, myself, have little use for them. I've always believed in handling problems in a straightforward manner."

"There are times when that tactic falls short of the mark," Cori murmured cryptically.

With her usual vim and vigor, Augusta grabbed Cori's elbow and steered her back to the receiving line. "You must make your debut in Natchez society. And as for your mysterious insinuations, you might find that blunt is best. For seventy-four years I've been calling a spade a spade. Just beware that you don't grab a shovel and dig youself into a hole you can't crawl out of. I want to see Jacob happily married, and I think you are the one who can keep him content if you cease this association with Dal Blaylock!"

Cori bit back a grin as Augusta towed her toward her string of friends. She truly liked this feisty dowager. Even if Cori couldn't be honest with Augusta without inviting all sorts of problems, she admired the dowager's individuality and spunk. What a shame it was that Augusta had wound up with that weasel Layton Breeze as a grandson!

For fifteen minutes, Cori was shoved at one stranger and then another, voicing several rounds of polite how-do-you-dos. The entire time that she was gracing the guests with disarming smiles, Jake was beside her, lavishing her with compliments. It was uncomfortable having Jake offer flattery when he had flung nothing but insults at her for two days. They were still observing civilized warfare and neither of them had attempted to call a truce. Cori was firm in her convictions and Jake stood unyielding in his. In his estimation, she had falsely accused Layton, and on her part, Cori proclaimed she was right about the scoundrel. Only time would determine who was right.

"And of course, you remember Layton and Sylvia," Augusta commented, dragging Cori from her pensive musings.

How could Cori forget Layton? She and Lori had crept to his house twice to pay him midnight visits. She wanted to ask Layton if he'd been sleeping well with frogs and mice planted in his bed and floating specters whizzing around the gardens, but she didn't need to bother. Layton's nocturnal visitors and his sleepless nights were beginning to take their toll. His gray eyes boasted dark circles and a permanent frown of frustration creased his plump features.

"Aren't you feeling well?" Jake questioned, scrutinizing his sour-looking cousin.

"I'm fine, thank you," Layton bit off. "And I'll be even better when we complete our business transactions on Monday. The less I have to do with the *Mississippi Belle* the better."

Cori swallowed her mischievous grin. Obviously, Layton's conscience (what meager amount of one he possessed, that is) was beginning to hound him.

"What do you suppose prompted Layton to say that?" Jake mused aloud, staring accusingly at Cori.

"I'm sure I don't have the slightest idea," she replied, looking so innocent that Jake expected to see a halo form around her dark head and feathery wings to flutter from the straps of her stunning gold gown.

"I'll just bet you don't," he grunted as he escorted her into the ballroom. "What have you been up to now?"

Cori pirouetted in front of him and blessed him with a

289

dazzling smile that made her eyes sparkle like obsidian. "Why, nothing except showing my betrothed how much I adore him," she purred with sticky sweet sarcasm.

For the benefit of the curious eyes that had fallen on them, Jake forced a smile, even if it was as brittle as eggshells. "If you don't be nice to me, my beloved little witch, I'll sic my grandmother on you."

"For your information, my darling, the reason Augusta pulled me aside was to threaten me. She insisted that I relinquish my fascination with Dal and devote all my time to you."

His green eyes slid momentarily to Augusta, who was watching them like a hawk. Jake lifted his hand to caress Cori's flawless cheek and restrained himself from clamping his lean fingers around her alabaster throat. "What prank have you been playing on Layton that I don't know about, minx?" he demanded to know.

Cori folded her hand over his fingertips and dug in her nails, causing Jake to grimace behind his false smile. "Why, nothing except stealing back the money tonight, just as *you* asked me to do, my sweet," she murmured in a sugary tone.

When Jake came within a hairbreadth of growling at her in reprisal, Cori patted the taut muscle in his jaw. "Careful, my love," she cooed at him. "Someone might notice the venom in your eyes. We wouldn't want these curious guests to think we were having a lover's spat instead of whispering sweet nothings to each other."

A wide grin split his craggy features, disguising the irritation he was experiencing. "Just wait until I get you home, sweetheart. You're going to tell me what I want to know."

"Over my dead body, honey lamb," Cori countered with a false smile that failed to disguise the defiant sparkle in her eyes.

"That, my precious, can easily be arranged," Jake

drawled as he bowed over her hand, which he was squeezing tightly.

Cori bit back a yelp of pain and waited for Jake to unloose her throbbing hand. Reaching up on tiptoe, Cori pretended to place an adoring kiss to his lips. She felt Jake flinch when she bit him.

"I must beg a moment's privacy," she murmured with wicked delight. "Excuse me while I powder my nose. I will be counting the seconds until I return to you."

Like hell she would be, Jake fumed as Cori whirled around to make her regal exit from the ballroom. That little witch couldn't wait to exchange places with Lori, who waited in the upstairs guest room. Cori was anxious to trot off on her mission. Jake almost regretted asking Cori to swipe the money Layton had stolen. He knew damned well she delighted in her daring escapades. The fact that he had invited her to revert to her old antics left him scowling at his own stupidity.

"Where's she off to now?" Augusta demanded to know as she squeezed through the crowd to reach Jake.

The dowager's gaze circled the room to ensure that Dal didn't fall into step behind Cori. When Dal pivoted to leave, Augusta whizzed toward him.

"You stay where you are, young man," she ordered as she hooked the curved end of her cane around Dal's arm and yanked him backward. When Jake strode up behind her, Augusta glared at him. "Curse it, Jacob, will you kindly tell this friend of yours that you are the one who is marrying Cori! He keeps forgetting it."

Jake frowned at his grandmother. "I think you owe Dal an apology for your insinuation."

"I owe him nothing of the kind," Augusta sniffed as she riveted her penetrating hazel eyes on the handsome blond. "I have always been fond of you. Your grandmother and I are the best of friends. But I warn you to keep your distance from my future granddaughter-in-

291

law. People are prone to talk and I don't want you to give them food for gossip."

Dal met Augusta's stern glare and frowned thoughtfully. The atmosphere at the Blaylock plantation wasn't one smidgen better than it was at Wolfhaven. Dal had muttered sourly when Jake told him about Layton stealing the money from the supply room and the request to steal the cash back. Dal and Lori had also been at odds, and Dal sorely resented involving her in Jake's scheme. The fact that Lori was about to exchange places with Cori rubbed Dal the wrong way. He didn't want Lori on Jake's arm for fear she would employ the opportunity to annoy him more than she already had ─ .

"Well?" Augusta persisted when Dal didn't promise to keep his distance from Cori.

"I will try to remember whose fiancée is whose," Dal replied with a stiff bow.

Although the comment carried a double meaning, Augusta had no way of knowing what Dal really meant. Jake certainly did. Dal had already expressed his reservations with the tactic of switching places and sending Cori to prowl around Layton's home.

"Now that you've read Dal the riot act, Gram, let's enjoy ourselves, shall we?" Jake suggested, steering the dowager on her way.

"Just remember, I'll be keeping a watchful eye on you, young man," she called over her shoulder to Dal.

When Augusta was out of earshot, Dal rounded on Jake. "Let's not forget whose fiancée you will be spending the evening with," he scowled. "Lori is already put out with me and I . . ."

"Over what?" Jake queried curiously.

"She told me why she and Cori have been hounding Layton," Dal grumbled. "I told her to leave well enough alone and she told me to mind my own business."

"That sounds exactly like the conversation I had with

292

Cori," Jake grunted disgustedly.

"Things haven't been the same since," Dal sighed in frustration.

"Personally, I think those two hellions leaped to the wrong conclusion about Layton," Jake declared. "That is not to say that I'm not suspicious of my cousin, but he does have an alibi and witnesses."

"I think the twins are wrong, but nothing I said would convince Lori. I swear she and Cori not only look exactly alike, but what's infinitely worse, they also think alike."

"And I think they have been going behind our backs to harass Layton," Jake speculated.

Dal's mouth fell open. "Good Lord, now what?" he hooted in dismay.

"I'm not sure, but I'll wager neither of them are spending their nights sleeping. I think it might be a good idea if we . . ."

"Ah, there you are, my love," Lori gushed as she sailed into the ballroom in Cori's stunning gold gown. "I'm sorry I took so long. I was detained by a woman who insisted on quizzing me about our marriage." Ignoring Dal completely, Lori looped her arm around Jake's waist. "It leaves me to wonder if that pretty blond who goes by the name of Jennifer Hanley was one of your admirers. She certainly seemed to know a lot about you."

When Lori batted her chocolate brown eyes at Jake and inched closer, Dal scowled under his breath. "Don't overplay your role," he warned her.

Lori displayed an angelic smile that was in direct contrast to her biting words. "Go soak your head in the fish pond, Mr. Blaylock. I was told that Augusta thinks you're being a mite too friendly with me. Why don't you trot off and stop making a nuisance of yourself."

When Lori tugged Jake onto the dance floor and went all too willingly into his arms, Dal aimed himself toward the study, where Augusta had lined up her stock of liquor. This evening was going to test his temper, he just knew it! Lori was spoiling for a fight and she was purposely antagonizing him. The ornery little witch!

"Cori briefed me on everything that has happened since she walked in," Lori whispered against Jake's neck. "Is there anything else I need to know that transpired while we were upstairs?"

"Indeed there is," Jake chuckled, watching Dal stomp out of the ballroom. "Your fiancée is very peeved with you."

Lori tossed her head in a gesture of indifference and dark ringlets rippled around her enchanting face. "That makes us even. I'm not pleased with his tyrannical behavior. He can fry in his own grease for all I care."

"You're every bit as mischievous as your sister," Jake grumbled into her rebellious features.

The remark provoked Lori to grin impishly. "We are two peas in a pod, Jacob, and don't forget that. When you're talking to me, you are also talking to my sister. If you don't want her to hear what you have to say, kindly don't convey it to me because I am her eyes and ears."

"Good. Then kindly tell your sister that the two of you are liable to get yourselves into a tangled mess if you persist in hounding Layton." Green eyes bore into Lori's fading smile.

"I don't have the slightest idea what you're talking about," she parried, tilting her belligerent chin in the same gesture Cori employed.

"That's what *she* said," Jake snorted as he swung Lori around the dance floor. "I didn't believe her either . . ."

After Cori had ascended the stairs and disappeared into one of the bedrooms, she had peeled off her gold silk gown and fastened Lori into it. Once the switch was made, Cori donned her breeches and shirt. Cori made her discreet exit from Augusta's mansion via the balcony. Employing the mount Lori had left for her beside the vine-covered pavilion, Cori headed toward Layton's plantation. She anticipated no difficulty in recovering the money. She had been hiding under the bed the first night Layton had been visited by the specter. While Lori flitted around in a white sheet in the garden, Cori had whispered eerie threats to Layton. She had seen him tug at the corner of the mattress and she knew exactly what he had stashed there.

When Cori reached Layton's home, she utilized the lattice to climb onto the gallery. Quick as a wink, she scurried into Layton's bedroom and then cursed her forgetfulness when she rammed into the night stand that set directly beside the bed. The lantern wobbled precariously and Cori outthrust a hand to catch it before it crashed to the floor. Unfortunately, in her haste, her fingertips collided with the glass of water Layton kept beside his bed. The glass hit the floor with a splash and a thud. Muttering at her clumsiness, Cori snatched up the glass and returned to its normal resting place.

"What's that?" came a voice from the next room.

"Spooks!" replied the second wobbly voice.

"Thunderation," Cori grumbled as she lifted the mattress to retrieve the canvas pouch. She knew Layton's stepson's had heard the racket. Suddenly a wry smile pursed her lips. She well remembered the day Jake had told those two misbehaving youngsters that demons of the dark would descend on them if they didn't change their wicked ways. So why not let Layton's stepsons think the house was haunted by avenging ghosts? With those two little rascals' active imaginations, they would swear the home was under siege by ghastly apparitions. When Layton returned home, he would be bombarded with fantastic tales to corroborate his belief that wraiths had been floating on the lawn.

Cori wailed like a banshee and then scooped up the money before backing toward the door.

"They're coming to get us!" the oldest boy howled.

A bloodcurdling scream clamored down the hall, rousing servants who had been placed in charge of the children while their mother attended the ball.

When the boys leaped out of bed and stampeded down the hall, Cori swung a leg over the railing and quickly descended the lattice. Her prank might have worked doubly well, she mused as she scurried toward her steed. She might just have scared some sense into Layton's stepsons and scared the wits out of Layton himself. He would return to find his nest egg gone and he would hear the tales of demon specters. That should frighten the living daylights out of Layton.

Chomping on that mischievous thought, Cori galloped back to Wolfhaven to deposit the money under her mattress. With her task accomplished, she trotted back to Augusta's estate to resume her place at Jake's side . . .

The vision of green eyes flecked with gold rose above her. Cori scolded herself when betraying tingles skittered down her spine. Even though she and Jake had very little to say to each other of late, she missed the intimacies and companionable silence they once shared. She had been tempted to go to him, to put their differences aside, just for the night. But each time she faced temptation, stubborn pride saved her in the nick of time. Cori feared words of love would tumble from her lips and Jake would employ her affection for him as a weapon. He would make her promise to let him handle Layton. But Cori couldn't abandon this crusade, not when Jacob was skeptical of his cousin's guilt.

Cori heaved a frustrated sigh. She simply had to keep a tight grip on her desires and her wayward heart until the

296

dilemma was resolved to her satisfaction. Her relationship with Jake would just have to suffer. If he could refrain from tiptoeing into *her* bedroom then she could deny herself the pleasure of stealing silently into his. He could have apologized for his domineering attitude just as easily as she could have apologized for her stubbornness, after all. And if he wasn't budging an inch, then neither was she!

Resolved to that opinion, Cori bounded from the saddle and sneaked toward Augusta's house. After scaling the colonnade, she scampered across the gallery and slipped into the room to wait for Lori.

"You're blind, Jacob Wolf," Cori declared to the handsome image that floated above her. "Layton is guilty, and because you fail to realize that, we are crossways of each other. Not only that, but Lori and Dal are barely speaking these days because Dal sided with you. *Men!* You defend each other, even when evidence suggests there is a murderer in your midst."

There was no question in Cori's mind that Layton Breeze was responsible for her father's death. It was as obvious as the nose on her face. Why couldn't Jake see that? Because Layton was his cousin and Jake refused to believe the worst, that's why. But Cori and Lori would eventually wear Layton down, and he would be ready to unburden his conscience. He would admit to his guilt and then perhaps she and Jake could get on with their lives. . . .

Cori groaned miserably, wondering if Layton would always be an insurmountable obstacle between them. Would Jake ever forget that Cori was responsible for seeing his cousin brought to justice? Thunderation, Cori had known from the onset of this rocky courtship that she was treading on dangerous ground.

Why did Jacob Wolf have to be the man Cori fell in love with? Her greatest aspirations were to see her father's murderer punished and earn Jake's love. But the dismal truth was that she couldn't have it both ways. One heart's desire was in direct conflict with the other. She could love Jake and forsake her crusade or pursue her purpose and forsake Jake. But no matter what, there would be bitter feelings on one side or the other.

"Thunderation!" Cori pummeled the pillow on the bed where she sat. Life had never been a bowl of cherries, but Lord, lately it had been nothing but the pits!

Augusta waved the orchestra into silence. "A toast!" she trumpeted.

On cue, a string of servants filed into the ballroom, carting trays of champagne. When each guest had a glass, Augusta shuffled onto the dance floor to single out her grandson and his fiancée (or so Augusta assumed, unaware that Cori's twin was present.)

Jake held his breath. He didn't know what his grandmother was planning, but it appeared she intended to make the most of opportunity. Dal, green with envy, had stolen Lori from Jake's arms three times in the past hour and a half. Augusta had cringed each time. Now it seemed Augusta wanted to establish Jake's rights to the bewitching brunette—even when it was actually the *wrong* bewitching brunette. Augusta's heart was in the right place, but she wasn't doing the relationship between Dal and Lori one whit of good.

"To a long and happy marriage!" Augusta announced, raising her glass in toast. "Begin it with a kiss to prove your lasting affection for each other."

Lori stared up at Jake, whose gaze shot across the room to lock with Dal's (decidedly jealous) glare.

When Jake hesitated, Augusta gouged her reluctant grandson in the ribs. "Well, kiss her, for heaven's sake. It's your right, you know. You'll be married in a few weeks."

Despite Dal's wordless scowl, Jake bent to place a hasty peck to Lori's lips.

"If that's the best you can do, it's no wonder you haven't found yourself a fiancée before now," Augusta muttered disgustedly. "When I said kiss her, I meant *kiss* her. Birds *peck*, Jacob; people *kiss!*"

Ignoring the warning signals that flashed in Dal's golden eyes, Jake hooked his arm around Lori's waist and bent her over backward. This time he really kissed her a good one, permitting himself to pretend it was Cori who was in his arms. The fact that Cori hadn't come within ten feet of him in four days left Jake with quite a lot of pent-up passion. It came pouring out while he portrayed his role as the smitten groom-to-be. And to ensure that Augusta didn't force him into another uncomfortable situation during the course of the evening, Jake made certain the kiss lasted overly long. That delighted Augusta, but it nearly killed Dal who had been drinking far too much for his own good.

While the crowd hooted, hollered and applauded, Dal wheeled around and stomped upstairs. Somewhere on the second floor, Cori Lee awaited her sister's return. Of course, Lori Ann was having the time of her life kissing Jake while Dal watched. But by damned, turn about was fair play, Dal thought drunkenly. He could pretend he was kissing Lori. Jake certainly didn't seem to have any trouble forgetting whose betrothed *he* was kissing!

The third door Dal opened earned him a startled gasp from its occupant.

"What the blazes are you doing up here?" Cori hissed as she clutched her palpitating bosom.

Dal had given her a start when he came bursting in. If he had been somebody else, Cori would have had a great deal of explaining to do.

"I came for this . . ." Dal slurred out as he made a beeline for the bed on which Cori was sitting.

Before she realized what he was about, Dal encircled

her in his arms and plopped on top of her, mashing her into the bedspread. When his lips slanted over hers, Cori could taste the brandy he had consumed. She wasn't sure if Dal knew which twin he was kissing, but he didn't seem to care all that much. He simply kissed the breath out of her until the door creaked open and a thunderous growl wafted across the room.

"What the hell's going on?" Jake snapped, striding over to yank his drunken friend off Cori.

"That's what I want to know," Dal countered, wobbling unsteadily on his feet. "And don't tell me you didn't enjoy kissing Lori blind in front of a ballroom full of guests!"

Cori's gaze bounced back and forth between Jake and her flush-faced sister, whose lips were swollen from a ravishing kiss. From the look of things Jake was guilty as charged. My, my, all sorts of guilt seemed to run in his family, the two-timing rat!

"It was Gram's idea," Jake muttered in explanation when Cori glared accusingly at him. "Every time this drunken imbecile broke in to dance with Lori, Gram had a fit. Then she demanded that I stake my claim on my fiancée for all to see. A respectful peck wouldn't suit Gram. She wanted to see steam rising from the kiss!"

"It looked more like a forest fire to me," Dal scowled disdainfully.

"So naturally you made an ass of yourself by coming up here to attack Cori," Lori bit off, glowering daggers at Dal. "Well, could you tell the difference between one pair of identical lips and the other?" Voicing her own bitter thoughts put Lori in huff. Her dark eyes flashed at Dal. "That's all it is, isn't it, Dal? Pure physical attraction. The moment we disagreed you forgot all about your confessions of love. Well, maybe I don't want to marry a man who could march upstairs and attack my sister just to satisfy his sexual appetite!"

Hell's fire, thought Jake. Lori and Cori were chips off the same block. When Lori got fired up she was every bit as sassy as her sister.

"I didn't see you resisting the passionate kiss Jake planted on you," Dal slurred out in annoyance. "Maybe the truth is that the new wore off and you've decided one man isn't enough to satisfy you."

Lori gasped when he slapped her with the insult. "Of all the dirty, rotten . . . oh!"

Cori didn't know what to think. She wasn't on hand to witness the controversial kiss that had put Dal in a snit so she couldn't sit in judgment. But of one thing she was certain, she wasn't all that crazy about the kiss that went on between Jake and Lori, either. As much as she hated to admit it, the jealous green monster was hounding her as much as it was Dal.

"And just what point were *you* trying to prove?" Cori hurled at Jake. "That one twin is as good as the other?"

"This has gone far enough . . ." Jake's voice trailed off as he heard the thump of Augusta's cane in the hall.

In the bat of an eyelash, Cori latched onto Dal's arm and shoved him into the closet ahead of her. Wheeling, she eased the door shut, leaving a crack through which she could peek.

Desperate for an excuse not to have to explain why he and Lori were upstairs, Jake tugged the shapely brunette into his arms and kissed her again, just as his grandmother opened the door.

Inside the closet, Dal slid his arm around Cori's waist and nibbled at her neck. She gouged him in silent reprisal, but drunk as Dal was, he continued his amorous assault.

"Will you *please* try to remember which twin I am," Cori hissed, jabbing him with an elbow when his hands began to wander once again.

"I remember," Dal slurred against her ear. "I think

301

Jake and I wound up with the wrong woman."

"You're drunk," Cori muttered in irritation. "And tomorrow, when you're sober, you'll regret letting your numb tongue outdistance your soggy brain."

While Cori was in the closet, trying to ensure that Dal kept his hands to himself, Augusta was grinning in smug satisfaction. She waited until Jake finished kissing the breath out of his fiancée before she chortled in delight.

"I'm glad to see I started something with that toast in the ballroom. It's about time, you know, Jacob. If you want privacy to continue what you're doing, you're welcome to it!" Another pleased smile erased years from her aging face. "I'll keep your guests entertained while the two of you practice up on your kissing."

The instant Augusta left, Jake released Lori. The tactic of getting rid of his snoopy grandmother had worked superbly. But Jake knew he'd have hell to pay to the couple in the closet. Of course, he was right.

When the coast was clear, Cori flew out of the closet like a wild bird released from captivity. Her abrupt movement left Dal wobbling on rubbery legs. He tripped over the pair of boots in the closet and fell flat on his face.

"Get up, you idiot," Cori snapped as she grabbed his arm and hoisted him to his feet. Her gaze swung to Jake and she punished him with a glare. "Since you and Lori are playing your charade so splendidly, you don't need Dal and me. I'm going home."

"Hell's fire," Jake muttered. "I only did what had to be done."

"Didn't you just!" Cori smirked as she led Dal toward the gallery. "And from now on I intend to follow that same policy."

"And what is that supposed to mean?" Jake scowled at her departing back, one that was as rigid as a flagpole.

"Figure it out for yourself," she retorted over her shoulder.

Swearing under his breath, Jake clamped onto Lori's hand and led her into the hall. "That sister of yours infuriates me to no end."

"That friend of yours is positively impossible," Lori grumbled bitterly. "If I never see Dal again, that will be all too soon."

Determined to play out their roles as the happy couple, Jake and Lori descended the steps to mingle with the guests.

Meanwhile, Cori had her work cut out for her. Easing the intoxicated Dal Blaylock over the railing was no easy task. Too much whiskey had impeded his coordination. He slid down the pillar and landed with a thud in the shrubs.

"That sister of yours is a horrible woman," Dal mumbled as Cori pulled him to his feet.

"I know, no conscience, no morals. She's a disgrace to the family name," Cori patronized Dal in order to keep him moving.

"I thought she honestly loved me," he slurred. "But we had one tiny argument and poof . . ." He attempted to snap his fingers to demonstrate how quickly their relationship had crumbled. His fingers refused to function properly. His arm dropped limply by his side. "Now she rarely acknowledges my presence."

"I'm sure it's all her fault," Cori humored him.

With tremendous effort, Cori heaved Dal into the saddle and climbed up behind him. While he called Lori every disrespectful name in the book, Cori guided their mount through the trees toward Dal's plantation. Once she had deposited him on his doorstep she headed toward Wolfhaven.

Alone at last! Cori sighed and grappled with the disturbing memory of watching Jake kiss her sister. She knew Jake's intent was to shoo his grandmother on her way. But it cut her to the quick to watch him envelop Lori

303

in his sinewy arms. The frustrating emotion the scene evoked assured Cori that she still loved him, but she was hounded by the grim realization that she could never marry him. Her feud with Layton would spoil whatever happiness they might find together.

It simply wasn't going to work. Cori had ignored the bleak truth in her eagerness to love and be loved. But when common sense and logic finally took control of her foolish heart, she knew that bitterness on both sides would poison the fragile blossom of love between them. Layton would always be a thorn that aggravated their relationship—today, tomorrow and forevermore.

Accepting the gloomy realization, Cori galloped toward Wolfhaven. This was the end of her stormy affair with Jake. She couldn't risk letting their conflict spoil another of her precious memories. Their love simply wasn't meant to be. And when dawn came, Cori intended to pack her bags and travel into Natchez to find a room and a job to support herself. And then . . .

Cori expelled a deflated sigh. She didn't know what then. She would have to cross that bridge when she came to it. All she knew was that leaving Jake would be worse than tearing off an arm, even if it was the logical, sensible thing to do.

Chapter 21

Without bothering to knock, Jake barged into Cori's room. He had endured the last two hours of the party, smiling until he swore his face would crack. And while he danced the night away with Lori in his arms, he mentally rehearsed what he intended to say to Cori when he had the chance. It couldn't wait until morning!

"You could have done the polite thing and knocked," she scolded him.

"We have to talk and it won't wait," Jake declared as he strode across the room to plunk down on the edge of the bed as if he belonged there.

Cori turned her back. "There is nothing left to say. It's over between us and you know that as well as I do. It won't work. I've tried to ignore the problems but that doesn't make them go away. They only swell out of proportion when I'm not staring at them."

Growling, Jake jerked Cori upright and clasped his hands on her forearms. "You're letting your obsession with Layton destroy what's between us. Having your revenge for what you *think* happened to your father is more important to you than I am, isn't it?" When she didn't respond immediately, Jake gave her a rough shake, spilling the tangled sable tresses over her shoulder.

"Isn't it?"

"No," Cori protested, clamping her teeth together to prevent yelling in his face.

"The hell it isn't!" Jake blared at her.

"You're hurting me," she yelped when his lean fingers clamped tightly around her arms.

"And you're hurting both of us," Jake muttered acrimoniously.

"Would you allow *your* father's murder to remain unsolved?" she hurled at him, fighting back the tears that threatened to cloud her eyes. "Would you turn your back on that obligation and brush it aside for your own personal pleasures? As long as Layton is prancing around, gloating over his ability to escape his crimes without punishment, I can't put my father's memory to rest!"

"And I'm telling you Layton didn't do it!" Jake bit off.

"I knew my father," Cori snapped. "He didn't sell the *Belle* of his own free will. It was his sentimental memorial to my mother. He was forced, threatened, and murdered!"

"Murdered for the money he carried on him," Jake reasoned. "If Layton didn't pay him, how do you explain the money withdrawn from the Breeze Company's account? And why would Layton have been catering to prospective investors if he didn't need cash to reimburse company funds?"

"How should I know what devious scheme hatched in Layton's criminal mind?" Cori railed. "All I know is what is in my heart . . ."

"You don't have one," Jake snorted derisively. "If you did, you wouldn't so quick to end this relationship because of your thirst for misdirected revenge!"

"I love you! Curse your soul!" Cori hissed into his frustrated frown. "But I'll never be able to marry you because of Layton."

306

"Because your obsession for revenge is more important to you than I am . . ."

Jake couldn't bare the thought he'd put to tongue. It was killing him, bit by excruciating bit. In exasperation, Jake grabbed Cori to him, longing to kiss away her arguments, aching to end the celibacy caused by their constant conflicts.

His mouth came down hard on hers, taking possession, stripping the vengeful thoughts from her mind. By damned, if she planned to leave him, she would carry his burning memory with her. He would make her regret leaving him, made her reevaluate what she stood to lose. And damnation, if she didn't come back to him after she had time to sort out her emotions he'd never forgive her!

Cori didn't even try to battle the onrush of emotions that swamped her when Jake's muscular body surged familiarly against hers. She knew this would be their last night together and she yearned to create a memory that would last her a lifetime.

"You're a fool," Jake breathed against her parted lips. "You're taking something rare and special and spoiling it, all in the name of revenge." His hands swept impatiently over her nightgown, tugging it out of his way to make contact with her silken flesh. "You may one day have your revenge, sweet witch, but you won't have this magic between us . . ."

His caresses teased and tormented her, forcing her to weigh the options of his love against her obsessive crusade. Cori felt herself melting into the mattress, becoming a slave to the passion they created at first touch. His greedy kisses sought to smother all argument, to make her realize what she was throwing away in the name of justice. But Cori knew full well the price she had to pay. There was no greater sacrifice than forsaking her love for Jacob. But her father's memory haunted her and it always would . . .

307

"Cori . . . I need you . . ." Jacob murmured against her quaking flesh. She not only heard his hushed words, she felt them vibrating against her pliant skin.

Tears boiled down her cheeks as his hands and lips slid over her body, sensitizing every trembling inch. Oh, how she wished Jacob could understand how she felt, what a tug of war her emotions were undergoing! But no matter what, she vowed to prove that he was vitally important to her, even if loving him could never be enough to hold them together.

A muffled groan tripped from Jake's lips as he rediscovered the pleasure of kissing and caressing her. Little by little, the conflicts between them faded into oblivion, leaving him completely vulnerable to the flame of passion that spread through every nerve and muscle. Nothing seemed to matter except this moment. The burning needs that had lain dormant for days on end erupted like a bubbling volcano. Jake was a man caught up in the grips of unquenchable needs—needs so fierce and urgent that they blinded him to all else.

Like a starved creature he devoured Cori's lips, stole her breath and then gave it back the instant before she swore she had sacrificed her life to revel in the sweet swirling storm of passion. His skillful hands flooded over her like clouds hovering over the earth. She could feel herself being swept into the currents of a windstorm, buffeted by wondrous sensations that assaulted her from every direction at once. Splendor washed over her submissive body as his tongue flicked at the crests of her breasts, leaving her moaning in indescribable pleasure.

Over and over again, his caresses flooded and receded, preying on every conceivable emotion. A tiny gasp bubbled from her throat when his sensuous lips drifted from the throbbing tips of her breasts to spread a draft of tantalizing kisses over her belly.

When he pressed his lips to her stomach, he felt her

308

instant reaction. His tongue traced her ribs and wandered over the indentation of her waist. His lips drifted down her thigh as he shifted above her, letting his caresses blaze a titillating path across her trembling flesh, shattering her self-control. His fingertips teased and aroused her until she was so on fire for him that his name burst from her lips in a breathless plea.

But still Jake refused to ease the aching needs that bombarded her. He transformed the needs into maddening cravings. His hands and lips were everywhere at once, offering promises of intimacies to come. He taunted her with his body and denied her what she wanted most.

Shock waves shook the core of her being as he taught her things she had never known about passion. He left her arching shamelessly toward his hands and lips, writhing with the pulsating spasms of rapture that assaulted her body. And just when Cori swore she would split apart at the seams, another wild tremor riveted her. Pleasure streamed through her again and again, as if the maelstrom of ineffable sensations would never go away. The hot sweet ache that he ignited in her shattered her very soul.

Gasping for breath, Cori clutched at him, reduced to begging for him to take total possession. Jake crouched above her, willing himself to control the ardent needs that raged inside him. He peered down into her shadowed features, reading the hungry desire that matched his own. He longed to drag a promise from those sweet tempting lips, but he was in the throes of such churning passion that thoughts refused to translate into words.

No other woman could infuriate and torment him so. And yet no other woman could satisfy him in all the incredible ways this feisty nymph could. He looked down at her satin body and he ached all over. He stared into those melting eyes and he forgot all except the mindless cravings that riveted him. He could feel the hot sparks that leaped from her body to his and he longed to be a part of her, to take her with him to ecstasy.

Of all the thoughts that tangled in his mind, one shred of truth became painfully clear. No matter what happened, he was going to love this woman all the days of his life. Perhaps they couldn't enjoy a future together, but no one would ever replace this doe-eyed sprite in his heart. She had come to mean all things to him and it was killing him to know she would leave him the first chance she got—all for the sake of mistaken revenge!

"Damn you," Jake growled hoarsely. He could feel his body moving instinctively toward hers, even as he cursed her. He could feel the overwhelming craving compelling him to her. There was so much he had wanted to say, but words failed him. His body demanded to communicate his love and his tormenting frustration.

Cori's hand folded around him, caressing him as she guided him to her. He could curse her if he wished. She was long past caring. All she wanted was to feel his muscular body molded intimately to hers, to express this love she felt for him.

When the dam of self-restraint burst, his body slid down upon hers and he clutched her to him. A tidal wave of primal desire toppled upon him. He drove into her with savage urgency, seeking ultimate depths of intimacy, wondering if even this hot sweet magic would sustain him when she went away and left him in agony.

Sensations avalanched upon them as their bodies moved in perfect rhythm, satisfying the needs that boggled their minds. Cori felt herself tumbling in a mindless swirl, absorbed by the breathless splendor that transcended time. She was held suspended in ecstasy that seemed to span forever. The powerful currents of passion carried her away, sending her plunging into the very depths of dark desire. Cori held nothing back when they made wild sweet love for the very last time. The raw emotion that engulfed her was so fierce and wild that nothing could contain it.

When Jake shuddered above her, another spasm of rapture riddled her body. Cori couldn't contain the cry of pleasure that tumbled from her lips. Like a wild thing she clenched her nails into Jake's back and gave herself up—heart, body and soul—to the climactic onrush of splendor that cascaded over her.

It took a long time to navigate her way back through the dark sensual fog that clouded her mind. But when Cori finally opened her eyes, Jake's ruggedly handsome face loomed over hers, haunting her. She knew she would see his face in her dreams in the endless years to come. Even when they were miles apart, he would be there with her, reminding her of this love they could never fully enjoy.

That disturbing thought filled her with desperation. If tonight was all they had left, Cori swore to spread this forbidden love of hers all over him. She longed to return the pleasure he had bestowed on her—kiss for tantalizing kiss, caress for devastating caress.

Unwilling to let go of the moment, Cori twisted above him to map his broad chest. Her forefinger circled his nipples and trailed down the thick matting of hair to his lean belly. Her kisses followed in the wake of her adventurous hands, rekindling flames that Jake swore had burned themselves out moments before.

Cori had proven herself to be an imaginative lover before, but nothing compared to the way she touched him now. Her gentle hands and butterfly kisses aroused him by titillating degrees. Pleasure uncoiled inside him like a flower petal unfurling to seek the precious warmth of the sun. He could feel himself arching toward her seeking mouth and exploring hands.

Wanting no more than she could give and giving all she

wanted from him, his body became hers to command. Jake surrendered without a fight to the power of love that tugged at him.

A hoarse moan trickled from his lips as her tantalizing caresses glided to and fro, offering the intense pleasures that awaited him. Her lips whispered over his hair-roughened flesh, leaving him trembling with a need that rose from nowhere to consume him. When her lips feathered over his abdomen, Jake forgot how to breathe. He waited, knowing she would shatter his self-control with her skillful fondling. In a few more moments he would no longer care if he burned alive, so long as this wild-hearted firebrand made love to him.

Cori couldn't drag her hands and lips away from Jake's masculine body. It was as if she were addicted to the taste and feel of him, as if touching him was her very reason for her existence. She was bold and yet tender in her sensual assault. She stroked him and teased him until he groaned in sweet agony. She caressed him and aroused him until he whispered her name and begged her to come to him.

She reveled in the power she held over him. When she straddled his hips, the glowing flames in his eyes assured her that he was ablaze with need, a need she alone had created within him. Her body unfolded over his, caressing him with the tips of her breasts, her lips, her hips.

Jake couldn't endure another second of the torment-ing pleasure that throbbed in his loins. His hands clenched her waist, setting her exactly where he wanted her. With a maddening groan he arched upward, aching to become the burning flame within her.

Another storm of passion burst between them. Each thrust was like lightning sizzling in a darkened sky. Their hearts pounded like thunder as passion seared them together—body to body and soul to soul. Desire, like a fierce, sweeping gale drove them together and left them clinging to each other in wild abandon. Torrents of rapture drenched them as they moved as one, driven by primitive needs that defied logic and threatened sanity.

When Jake felt the wild convulsions of passion overcome him he clutched Cori to him, seeing the blackened universe explode into a multitude of fiery colors. Shudders rocked his soul and still he clung to her, afraid to let go, afraid he would die. He wanted her to be in the circle of his arms when he did. It was the most welcome kind of death that life could offer—the sacrifice born of passion and bounded by love.

Ever so slowly the numbing pleasure ebbed, leaving Jake drifting back to reality like a butterfly soaring on drafts of wind. In that moment of sublime fulfillment came a tremor of despair. He had loved this feisty nymph for all he was worth and yet it still wasn't enough. She was going away . . .

With a dispairing sigh, Jake combed his fingers through the long silky tendrils that formed a waterfall over her shoulder. Impulsively, he pressed a kiss to her flushed cheek. "Where will you go, Cori?" he murmured in question.

"To a hotel or inn," she whispered against the column of his throat.

"There are several of them in Natchez. Which one?" he prodded.

"It's better that you don't know. We shouldn't see each other again. Besides, Augusta will keep you busy searching for my replacement." The thought stung like a wasp.

"How will you . . . ?"

Cori pressed her index finger to his lips to shush him. "Just let me sleep in your arms tonight. Tomorrow will take care of itself."

Jake wanted to rave in frustration, but he knew it

would do no good whatsoever. Cori had made up her mind to go, and once that decision was etched in the stone foundations of her brain, nothing would deter her. Jake didn't like it one damned bit. He hated it, in fact. But proving Cori wrong about Layton would be all that would bring her back to him. Finding her father's real killer was all that would bring her the kind of peace that would allow her to get on with the rest of her life.

For the time being, Jake chose to dwell on the sweet dreams they had created in the still of the night rather than speculate on his future—one that would be dreary without Cori in it. With a sigh, he closed his eyes and his mind to all except the lingering sensations that loving her aroused in him.

Cori was right, thought Jake. There was only to-night. He didn't really want to contemplate tomorrow either . . .

In the dark hour before dawn, Cori eased from Jake's side and tiptoed across the room to collect her belongings. She dressed in a simple cotton gown, then slipped her hand under the corner of the mattress to retrieve the money she had stolen from Layton. Removing the exact amount Jake intended to pay his cousin in compensation for the *Belle*, Cori gathered the rest of the cash and stuffed it in her satchel.

Her gaze dropped to Jake's powerfully-built figure; his craggy features were soft in repose. Jacob lay on his back with the sheet draped across his hips. The dark hair that capped his head lay recklessly across his forehead. The arm that had held her protectively to him all through the night was flung across the empty space she had occupied.

Cori was tempted to press a farewell kiss to his lips, but she didn't dare rouse him. Saying good-bye was more than she could bear. Carefully, she leaned over to drop

314

the roll of cash on the pillow and then retreated into the shadows. With a backward glance that expressed her heartfelt regret, Cori stepped onto the terrace. She made her way quietly down the lattice to retrieve the mount that she had tethered in the trees the previous night.

When the sun peeked over the horizon and bathed the bedroom with streamers of crimson and gold, Jacob's thick lashes fluttered up to find Cori had taken everything with her except her sweet tormenting memory. Jake muttered a curse as he slammed his fist into the pillow. The roll of cash tumbled onto the sheet and Jake swore again.

From heaven to hell in the course of the night, he thought bitterly. Fighting the treacherous Missouri River and renegade Indians had never been as painful as losing that dark-eyed, dark-haired firebrand. She had left a hole as wide and deep as the Mississippi in his heart. He missed that sassy little sprite and she hadn't even been gone more than a few hours. If he felt this miserable already, he shuddered to think what the rest of his life was going to be like without Cori in it.

"Hell's fire and damnation!" Jake growled at the room at large.

Chapter 22

Augusta knew something was amiss the instant she opened her front door to find Jake standing sullenly before her. He looked as if he had lost his best friend and didn't have the slightest idea where to begin searching for a new one.

"What's happened?" Augusta demanded to know.

Jake forced the semblance of a smile. "Nothing, Gram. I only came by to escort you into town for our meeting with Layton and the attorney. Are you ready to go?"

Warily, Augusta hobbled out the door and down the steps. Although Jake tried to project a cheerful image and chatted idly about the weather and anything else that sprang to mind, Augusta wasn't fooled one bit.

"It's Cori, isn't it?" Augusta speculated. "Are you going to tell me or must I pry it out of you?"

Jake expelled a heavy sigh. "The wedding is off. We decided it simply wasn't going to work out between us."

"Why not?" Augusta exploded in exasperation. "You're rich, handsome, and well-bred. I can't imagine what fault she could find with you, nor you with her except that she's a mite too friendly with Dal Blaylock. And don't tell me he's the better man, for he most certainly is not!"

"You're partial, Gram." Jake managed a chuckle, hollow though it was.

"And with good reason," she declared with absolute certainty. "I know a decent man when I see one. You are going to take me to see that girl the minute we complete our business transactions. I have a few things to say to Cori!"

"I don't even know where she is and I couldn't care less," Jake declared. He had practiced telling himself that for the past two days, but he didn't sound convincing, even to himself. When he tried it out on Augusta, she didn't buy it either.

"Of course, you don't," she scoffed sarcastically. "You look happier than you've looked in all your life."

"I don't care and I *am* happy," Jake insisted.

Augusta clamped her false teeth together and held her tongue. Blast it, she had been riding high since the party, thinking Jake's life was falling neatly into place. And all the while it had been falling apart! Well, she was not going to let that mere whisp of a woman dash her hopes and dreams for Jacob. Augusta had taken Jake in at a tender age and raised him when his parents died. She had watched him go off in search of rainbows and adventure in his attempt to fill the emptiness in his life. But the only thing that had brought him back home and kept him content was that high-spirited Cori Pierce.

Confound it, Jake honestly cared about her and Cori cared about him. She had assured Augusta of that. But this mysterious business of which Cori had spoken at the party had torn her and Jake apart. Augusta would have given most anything to know the secret Cori harbored.

Well, no matter what, it was apparent to Augusta that Cori and Jake belonged together. Damn the obstacles between them! Augusta vowed to talk some sense into Cori the first chance she got! This wedding wasn't off, Augusta mused as she drummed her fingers on her cane,

317

it was only temporarily postponed. She promised to see to it that Jake wound up with the woman he wanted!

The moment he walked into the company office on the wharf, Jake knew Layton was feeling almost as miserable as he was, even if it was for altogether different reasons. Layton obviously knew his little nest egg of cash had disappeared. That probably rankled Layton to no end, greedy rascal that he was, and partially explained Layton's testy disposition. But Jake had the inescapable feeling there was something else bothering his cousin. He not only looked distraught, he seemed unduly rattled. Jake couldn't help but wonder what else Cori had done to the man besides swipe the stolen money. Aware of her obsessive need for revenge, Jake knew she had definitely done something! If any woman could rattle a man, Cori Pierce Shelton could do it. Jake was living proof of that!

"Let's get this over with, shall we?" Layton muttered impatiently.

In jerky motions, he extracted the deed to the *Belle* from his vest pocket and handed it to the attorney. Within a few minutes the lawyer had explained the bill of sale he'd drawn up and gestured for both men to sign the necessary legal papers. The next order of business was to divide the holdings of the Breeze Company, which took only a few more minutes of shuffling and signing deeds and documents.

And that was that. The Breeze Company was no longer in existence. Jake was in control of his two steamers and Layton owned the two vessels Augusta had designated as his. After Jake offered Layton the cash compensation, Layton buzzed out the door and sped off in his carriage.

While Augusta and Jake stood on the wharf, watching Layton depart with fiend-ridden haste, Dal and Lori arrived at the docks. The sight of the comely brunette in

Dal's carriage put Augusta in a temper. Before Jake could latch onto his feisty grandmother, she marched forward, halting the coach by placing herself directly in its path.

"I want to talk to you, young lady," Augusta demanded tartly.

Lori's gaze flew to Jake before returning to the stiff-lipped dowager.

"I think perhaps . . ." Lori began tactfully, only to be cut off by Augusta's impatient snort.

"I mean to see you now!" She rapped her cane on the wooden planks and glared at the woman whom she presumed to be Jake's ex-fiancée.

Reluctantly, Lori stepped down. Waving to one of the rent coaches on the wharf, Augusta gestured for Lori to climb in beside her.

"I'll get right to the point." When didn't Augusta Breeze get right to the point? "I want you to marry my grandson and cease this . . . whatever it is you're doing with Dal," she finished with a distasteful sniff. "My grandson is quite fond of you and you insisted you were fond of him. So what's the problem?"

Lori was at a complete loss as how to handle Augusta. She had received a note from Cori indicating she had moved to King's Tavern and that she would meet her at Pharsalia race track on Wednesday. But that was all Lori knew. Obviously Cori had broken her engagement with Jake and Augusta was fit to be tied.

"Well . . . it's a matter of . . ." Lori floundered, unsure of what to say without drawing suspicion. "A . . . a . . . you see, Augusta, Jake and I . . . a . . . have decided . . ."

"That you'd be better off without each other?" Augusta speculated, since the bewitching brunette was stumbling over her tongue. "Rubbish! He is everything a woman could possibly want. And believe you me, there are oodles of females hereabout who'd rob, cheat, and

319

steal to get Jake as a husband."

Funny that Augusta should mention robbing, cheating and stealing, Lori mused uneasily.

Augusta leaned forward to stare at Lori who sat on the opposite seat. "If you need money, you'll have it. How much?" she demanded in her customary plainspoken manner. "When we had this conversation the first time we met, I spoke in jest about bribing you into wedlock. Now I'm dead serious. Name your price."

Lori blinked in astonishment. "You *are* serious!" she realized and said so.

"Of course I am," Augusta bit off. "I want Jacob married and he wants you. I'm here to see that he gets what he wants for the first time in his life."

"Very well, I'll speak with him, if you insist," Lori replied for lack of anything else to say.

"Good!" Augusta thumped her cane on the ceiling and poked her gray head through the window to instruct the groom to reverse direction. "Now you march yourself up to Jake and resolve your differences," she commanded, giving Lori a forceful nudge the instant the brougham rolled to a halt. "And when he comes around to see me, things had better be patched up between you two." She punished Lori with a stern glare. "Do I make myself understood?"

"Perfectly," Lori murmured, biting back a grin.

Augusta Breeze was a fiery old woman, but it was comical to watch her defend her favorite grandson, as if Jacob Wolf needed defending. Lori was quite certain that Jacob allowed Augusta to get away with such nonsense simply because she enjoyed doing battle. It kept her youthful and made her feel needed.

When Augusta whizzed off in her rented carriage, Lori pivoted to face Jacob who stood alone in front of the ticket office. Dal had strolled along the dock to await the steamer from New Orleans. Adam Castleberry, his friend and racing rival, was due to arrive within the hour.

A wry smile pursed Jake's lips as Lori approached him. Damn, it was difficult not to look at this stunning beauty without seeing Cori, difficult not to remember the pain of losing someone who was precious and dear to him.

"I'm sorry Gram raked you over the coals," Jake apologized. "She lives for those little confrontations. Thank you for humoring her."

When Jake saw his grandmother crane her neck out the carriage window, he clasped his hand around Lori's elbow and escorted her through the milling crowd. "Dal tells me the two of you are back on speaking terms."

A faint blush stained Lori's cheeks at the thought of how friendly they were these days. When she had returned home from the party, Dal was sprawled on the front steps, sleeping off his bout with brandy. When she roused him he had apologized all over the place for behaving ike an ass. One thing had led to another and it had been the wee hours of the morning before they finally fell asleep in each other's arms. And every night since they had repeated that romantic performance.

"Our wedding is on again," Lori informed Jake, still blushing profusely. "We agreed to avoid arguments about . . ." She glanced uneasily at her muscular companion, suddenly aware of the difficulty he and Cori had found in their courtship—Layton Breeze to be specific. That weasel of a man was a sensitive topic for both of them. "Anyway . . . I just refrain from telling Dal what he doesn't want to hear and he refrains from barking orders about . . . certain delicate subjects."

Jake knew full well what Lori was trying not to say. Layton was the number one cause of trouble in his relationship with Cori and a sore spot between Lori and Dal. And because of Layton, Cori was gone.

"You and your sister had better watch your step," Jake advised, pausing to peer intently into those warm brown eyes. "You are treading on thin ice."

When Jake saw Lori's chin tilt to that stubborn angle he had viewed so often in the past, he expelled a heavy sigh. "Whatever the two of you have been doing to torment Layton might backfire, just as it did on the *Belle*. And next time you two get caught, you may face serious repercussions."

Lori shifted uncomfortably and stared into the distance, watching the Natchez-bound steamer ease toward the dock. "What are you going to do about Augusta?" she questioned, purposely switching the topic of conversation.

Jake shrugged enigmatically. "I'll handle Gram. Her bark is much worse than the actual bite."

"And what about Cori?" Lori questioned point-blank.

Now it was Jake's turn to stare into space. "I'll do nothing."

Lori studied his craggy features for a long pensive moment. "My sister is staying at King's Tavern, room seven," she murmured. "I thought you might like to know, even if she did swear me to secrecy." When his gaze swung back to her, Lori smiled impishly. "I didn't tell you that, of course. And if you tell Cori I did, I will vehemently deny it."

When Lori ambled off to rejoin Dal and his associate who had disembarked from the steamer, Jake stared after her. He wasn't going to make contact with Cori. It was officially over, he reminded himself. He would find another woman to court, just to pacify Augusta for a time. And then he would return to the river where he should have stayed in the first place. Cori wasn't ever coming back and some men simply weren't meant to settle down. Obviously, Jacob was one of them.

Mentally kicking himself for dwelling on that frustrating sprite who had abandoned him, Jake ambled over to renew his acquaintance with Adam Castleberry, his racing rival from New Orleans who had long been Jake's friend as well as Dal's.

Jacob had become passive and blasé since Cori had walked out of his life. It was time he put on a smile and closed the door on yesterday. He didn't need Cori Pierce Shelton to make his world complete, Jake encouraged himself. He had gotten along just fine without her before he met her and he would manage just dandy without her now. She had been like a severe case of the grippe. He'd had her and now he would get over her. He would find himself another woman to preoccupy him. Why, in a week or two he wouldn't even remember the sound of her voice, the way she smiled, the magical ways she touched him . . .

A ferocious scowl twisted Jake's face, detracting from his good looks. He was going about this forgetting business all wrong! Remembering what he wasn't going to think about left wrinkles in his soul and an ache in his loins.

"Women," Jake muttered cynically and then plastered on a smile when Adam Castleberry strode over to pump his hand. Jake immersed himself in conversation and tried not to spare Lori more than a fleeting glance. She reminded him far too much of the intractable, headstrong beauty he was trying so hard to forget.

Layton nearly jumped out of his clothes when a shadowed figure loomed in front of him in the darkness. He had returned late that evening, dreading another visit from the haunting specter that had hounded him for more than a week. He had seen floating spirits and heard taunting voices so much lately that it was difficult to distinguish his nightmares from reality. His room was a constant fog of tobacco smoke that matched the aroma of Michael Shelton's pipe. And on top of all else, his stepsons reported seeing ghosts and hearing strange noises the night his pouch of stolen money had disappeared.

These days Layton was afraid of his own shadow! When Kyle Benson stepped into the light that sprayed from the window of the mansion, Layton didn't know whether to slump in relief or flinch in apprehension.

"What the hell's going on?" Kyle snapped at Layton, who looked as frightened as a gun-shy rabbit.

Layton grimaced. He knew Kyle would find out about the business transaction sooner or later. Layton had hoped it would be later.

"I was forced to deed the *Belle* over to Jake," he grumbled, eyeing Kyle uneasily.

"And just where does that leave me?" Kyle snorted in question. "We made a deal, Layton. You aren't upholding your end of it."

Even the darkness didn't conceal the threatening glare Kyle flung at Layton.

"We can make other arrangements," Layton squeaked when Kyle took a step closer to loom over him. "Your interest in the *Belle* will be transferred to one of the other steamers. Nothing has changed . . ."

Kyle grabbed Layton by the front of the shirt and thrust his face forward to breathe down the man's chubby little neck. "Don't forget that I know enough to have you locked away for the rest of your days," he growled ominously. "It's time I made some plans of my own."

"What kind of plans?" Layton chirped.

"I need cold hard cash . . . plenty of it, and you're going to get it for me. I've decided to open my own business and you are going to give me the down payment."

"How much?" Layton asked.

A frosty smile glazed Kyle's lips. "I should think fifty

thousand dollars should be enough to buy my silence for your unscrupulous dealings."

"Fifty thou . . ." Layton gasped for breath. "We just split the company. I don't have that kind of cash laying around."

"Get it," Kyle demanded, jerking Layton closer. "And if I don't have the cash by the end of the week, I'll tell the constable everything I know about your business dealings with Michael Shelton. I'm sure the law and all of Natchez will be shocked to learn that one of the pillars of society employed dastardly tactics to acquire one of his ships."

Kyle flung Layton away roughly, leaving him staggering to maintain his balance. "Thursday night I'll be back to collect the money, and if you don't have it . . ."

Kyle let the threat hang in the air, allowing Layton to draw his own grim conclusions as to what would happen if he didn't come up with the cash. Unfortunately, Layton had been harassed into a frenzied state, thanks to visitations from haunting wraiths.

Before his addled mind could contemplate the consequences of issuing his own threat, his tongue flung out the words, "You might find yourself faced with troubles of your own, Benson," he sneered. "My man Dobson will make mincemeat of you if you dare to . . ."

A sinister chuckle filled the muggy air. "Your man Dobson now works for me. How ironic it would be if your own henchman used your strong-arm tactics on you instead of your business rivals."

Layton's jowls sagged when he realized how precarious his situation had become.

Another mocking snicker hovered over Layton. "Dobson will side with me, of course, when we testify against you in your shady dealings with Shelton. Either way, Layton, you're a dead man if you don't come up with the money." With a taunting bow, Kyle swaggered into

325

the shadows. "Until Thursday . . ."

Layton stared after the retreating silhouette and tried to still the frantic palpitations of his heart. Visions of terror flashed through his mind. He had waded in over his head when he bargained with that devil! He had been a fool to manipulate Michael Shelton and force him out of the shipping business. Not only had the spirit of a dead man come back to haunt him, but Benson was calling in the blackmail debt. And now Benson had convinced Dobson to side with him, to speak out against his former employer and destroy Layton.

Desperately, Layton scurried into the house to count the cash in his safe. A tormented groan bubbled from his lips when he found himself lacking the cash to save his reputation and his life. Curse it, if only he had the money that had been stolen from under his mattress he would have enough to buy Benson's silence! Even with the cash compensation Jake had given him that morning he couldn't come within shouting distance of fifty thousand dollars.

Steaming and stewing, Layton paced the office, considering his options. Somehow he had to come up with some quick money. There were several options, but time was a serious factor. Finally an idea sprang to mind, and Layton vowed to pursue the only avenue open to him. With any luck at all, he would have the money he needed by this time tomorrow. Mulling over that encouraging thought, Layton trudged up the stairs to his room. His breath caught in his throat when the faint aroma of tobacco clogged his nostrils. He glanced around the darkened room apprehensively, seeing the glowing ashes in the pipe that he'd hurled off the balcony the week before.

"Damn you, Shelton, leave me be!" Layton hissed.

Low laughter echoed across the terrace and evaporated into silence. And to further frustrate Layton, an unidentified glow of light shot across the garden. In abject frustration, Layton stamped away from the balcony door, plunked down on his bed, and covered his head with a pillow. All of a sudden the world was closing in on him. Now his days were as haunted as his nights. Kyle Benson had threatened him and Michael Shelton's ghost had returned to seek revenge. No matter which way Layton turned he saw torment. He was so frightened and frustrated he couldn't think straight . . .

Muffling a snicker, Cori eased over the terrace railing and climbed down the lattice to unfasten the rope that was tied to the covered lantern she had utilized for special effects. She had been soloing the past two nights while her sister remained at Dal's plantation, entertaining the house guest from New Orleans.

Playing these pranks on Layton had become Cori's preoccupation. Each time thoughts of Jacob Wolf rose to haunt her, she dreamed up new ways to antagonize Layton. However, the tactic wasn't totally effective. There were too many moments when garnet green eyes, rimmed with black lashes, materialized above her, reminding her of what she had sacrificed to see Layton Breeze pay his due.

Earlier that day Cori had spied Jacob ambling down the street with a pert blond on his arm. A pert blond hanging all over him was nearer the mark. The sight struck a painful emotional blow that Cori was still nursing. It seemed Jake had gotten over her much quicker than she had gotten over him, which as of yet wasn't one whit! He had replaced her and cast her memory aside as if she meant nothing to him at all.

Cori had told herself countless times that leaving Jake was for the best, but her foolish heart refused to listen to reason. She sought distractions every hour of the day, but nothing helped.

Cori had refused to spend the stolen money she had obtained from Layton. In fact, she had every intention of getting rid of it forever. She had considered tossing it out the window of her room, but she reckoned that would invite too many questions that she didn't want to answer. But now she had a plan. By this time tomorrow, the money would no longer be in her possession and her past escapades as a river robber would be no more than a memory.

To support herself, Cori had garbed herself in a red wig, padded clothes, and thick glasses and had taken a job as a waitress in William's Tavern. William Chandler, kind-hearted man that he was, felt sorry for the homely wench who begged for a job.

Cori was barely surviving on her earnings as a waitress, and the displeasing appearance of her disguise wasn't winning generous tips from customers. But she vowed to endure as best she could until she had put the finishing touches on her scheme to drag a confession from Layton. She had planned that fateful night, right down to the last insignificant detail. Soon Layton would confess his sins and this long crusade would be over.

Harboring that thought Cori swung into the saddle and trotted off into the darkness. She felt an eerie presence trailing behind her, a memory that refused to die. It seemed Layton had his tormenting wraith and Cori had hers—a mountain of a man who had found another woman to take her place while she was pining for a love that lived only in memories.

Jake ambled aimlessly down the street after escorting Jennifer Hanley home from the theater. The shapely blond widow had invited him inside, but he had mumbled an excuse and left her on the front step. Jake had been all set to accept the provocative offer until a pair of obsidian eyes, embedded in a beguiling face, leaped out at him.

To block out the haunting vision, Jake had plied Jennifer with a steamy kiss. Nothing. Not even one damned little tingle of excitement spurted through him. He may as well have kissed a lamppost for all the reaction he had experienced.

Nothing about the embrace had seemed right. Her lips held an eagerness that Jake couldn't reciprocate. And when he peered into her pale blue eyes they deepened to dark brown just like . . .

"Hell's fire," Jake kicked at the rock beneath his feet, stuffed his hands in his pockets, and stamped down the street.

Jennifer had undoubtedly thought him mad when he rejected her invitation to spend the night and scurried down her front steps. He had thought the tactic of forgetting one woman by distracting himself with another would cure what ailed him. But it didn't . . .

Jake halted in front of King's Tavern. The sturdy, unadorned establishment set on the slope of a hill just outside Natchez. The lower bricked floor led to a second level constructed of timber and surrounded by a narrow railed gallery. Above was the third level, perched like the pilothouse on a steamboat. The tavern had been in existence since the Spanish regime. The dons had granted the land and building to "Richardo King," a Long Island Yankee who had enjoyed a wealth of income in the durable property that served travelers, gamblers as well as distinguished gentleman.

Jake had frequented the tavern in years past. It was a rustic establishment in which a man could find food, drink, and lively conversation. Every inch of the barroom had been put to good use and liquor flowed freely around the gaming tables that lined the main room. Thick beams, steadied with wooden pegs, supported the old structure. Small windows and doors bore evidence of the building's age. On the upper floor, away from the raucous tavern, ladies of quality could enter the private guest rooms without risking the rougher elements below.

Jake ambled toward the narrow side door that had been cut into the brick wall to give entrance into the smoke-filled taproom. Jake decided he could use a drink, anything to help him forget why his footsteps had brought him in this direction in the first place. Fool that he was, he had strolled away from his carriage to walk off his frustrations. And when he wound up in front of King's Tavern he reminded himself that he wanted no more association with the impossible female in room number seven.

Well, he hadn't seen her and he didn't plan to, Jake mused as he plopped into a chair with a tankard of ale in hand. He had only come by to have a drink and listen to the chatter of politicians and boasts of racing enthusiasts who had congregated, planning to place their bets at the track the following day.

Preoccupation, that's what Jake had wanted at King's Tavern, nothing more and nothing less. The doe-eyed firebrand who occupied room number seven didn't mean a thing to him. Nothing at all. After a few more drinks, he wouldn't even remember her name.

Famous last words . . .

Chapter 23

Exhausted, Cori tossed her cape aside, uncaring that she had missed her target. The garment fluttered off the edge of the bed and drifted noiselessly to the floor of her rented room.

Groping, she located the tinderbox and lit the lantern. A shocked gasp erupted from her lips when the light revealed the man who sat in the corner on his wooden throne. Jacob lounged negligently in the chair, clasping a tankard of ale in his hand. A blank look floated in his glazed eyes.

"You're drunk," she muttered as she assessed the way his eyelids drooped and his hat sat cockeyed on his ruffled raven head.

"And you're gorgeous," Jake slurred out. His blood-shot eyes flooded over the trim-fitting black breeches and shirt that did more to accentuate her appetizing figure than to disguise it.

"How'd you know I was here?" Cori demanded to know.

His broad shoulder lifted in a characteristic shrug. "I knew you had to be somewhere," he chortled drunkenly.

Cori bolstered her sagging defenses and plastered on a frown. Jake looked and sounded ridiculous, but she wasn't going to giggle at him because she was put out with him. "I cannot imagine what you cared where I was. I thought you would be out on the town with your latest lover."

Another enigmatic shrug caused his shirt to ripple sensuously over his massive shoulders.

Cori rolled her eyes heavenward, summoning divine patience. She was tired and weary of battling Jake's tormenting memory. He was the last person she'd expected to see tonight. And ironically, he was the only person she really wanted to see. Thunderation! She couldn't keep herself on an even keel because what she wanted directly contrasted with what she knew she could never have.

"Where have you been so late, Cori?"

The slurred question brought her head up and she stared curiously at Jake. This looked exactly like the Jacob Wolf she had come to know and love. But he seemed different somehow. Gone was the panache, the vital spirit he had once possessed. The last time Cori saw Jake drunk was on the steamer when he lit into her and cursed her soundly because he thought she was going to marry Dal Blaylock. But now he just sat there like a slug, staring up at her with glazed eyes, droopy eyelids, and a turned-down mouth.

"I had an errand to run," she answered belatedly.

"Ah yes, the capering comedienne who prowls about, searching out unsuspecting victims." One thick brow arched and then slid lazily downward as he brought the mug to his lips. "Is that how you're supporting yourself these days? Robbing from the rich? I'm sure you had a prosperous evening, accomplished thief that you are."

Cori gnashed her teeth. "What do you want?"

The mug moved slowly from his lips. His bloodshot eyes were still fixed on her. Setting the mug aside, Jake staggered to his feet. When he weaved toward her, Cori retreated, step for step, until she had backed herself into the corner.

Wide brown eyes peered into his handsome face as his fingertips fumbled over the buttons of her shirt. Her heart slammed against her chest when his hand tunneled inside the garment to caress the tips of her breasts. And suddenly both hands were upon her, evoking sensations that nothing could control.

A tiny moan tumbled from Cori's lips when his warm breath whispered over the sensitive point beneath her ear. She cursed herself a hundred times over as her body melted into a puddle of liquid desire. This was not the way to forget how vulnerable she was to the man who tormented her dreams. But Lord, denying him meant denying herself. It seemed an eternity since she had felt his masterful caresses gliding over her skin. It had been forever since she'd felt those sensuous lips taking skillful possession.

"I came here because I needed you . . ." Jake murmured before his mouth slanted over hers, drinking deeply of a kiss that was far more potent than wine. "I want what I can find nowhere else . . ."

With that hoarse admission, gentleness vanished. Jake became a creature of instinct, a captive of forbidden memories. Urgently, he tugged at the garments that concealed Cori's silken flesh. He greeted every exposed inch of her with hot, demanding kisses. His hands wandered on their own accord, rediscovering the soft texture of her skin, each luscious curve and swell.

Neither Cori nor Jake had enough patience to retire to the bed. Emotions exploded and hungry lips sought each other out. Restless hands memorized muscled planes and gentle swells. Passion reared its unruly head and demanded fulfillment. Flames burst and sizzled as Cori and Jake gave themselves up to the needs they had long denied themselves. The carpet became their pallet and the flickering lantern light revealed the raging desire that shimmered when their gazes locked.

"God, I've missed you," Jake breathed against her tempting lips.

He couldn't seem to get enough of her—quickly enough—to satisfy the monstrous needs that gnawed at him. In his impatient yearning to reacquaint himself with every delicious inch of her, his lips roved over her belly, sketching lazy circles that left her arching helplessly toward his teasing hands and lips. Lower still his caresses wandered, exciting and arousing. His amorous fondling became much bolder and more compelling, entreating her to surrender in wild abandon.

Cori gasped for breath as his lips trailed lower, sensitizing every inch of her quivering flesh, instilling a hunger that only this one man could appease. Her wanton body cried out to his, accepting his intimate kisses and caresses, begging for more until she was writhing against him in impatient urgency.

Shudders of wild delight riveted her body and Cori twisted away, unable to endure another moment of sweet torment. Her hands and lips moved restlessly over his hair-matted flesh. She committed every touch and every sensation to memory. His muffled groan of pleasure encouraged her to bring him to heights of ecstasy so he could join her there, so he would fully understand the wondrous sensations he had evoked in her.

Over and over again, her kisses and caresses mapped his steel-honed body, transforming muscles into the consistency of jelly. She left Jake burning inside and out with a gigantic need that screamed for release. His nerves had spun into tangled twine and his overworked heart threatened to beat him to death when Cori did such incredible things with her hands and lips.

And then Jake found himself enduring the wildest torment imaginable. Seductively, Cori glided above him, brushing her silky body over his, hovering so close and yet so maddeningly far away that Jake swore he would go insane with wanting. He could feel the rose-tipped crests of her breasts teasing his chest, feel her satiny thighs skimming over his hips. Her petal-soft lips courted his with unspoken promises, while the provocative language of her body conveyed erotic fantasies. A longing sigh escaped his lips when her moist breath whispered over his eyelids and cheeks. The intense pleasure they had denied each other for what Jake swore had been an eternity swelled inside him until he was certain he'd burst.

He could endure no more. He wanted Cori so badly that his body was on a hot, tormenting burn. He needed her to the point that he was prepared to sacrifice life itself if only he could feel her delicious body molded to his.

Obsessed with that thought, Jake rolled sideways, pulling Cori beneath him. His hooded gaze dropped to the hauntingly lovely face below, seeing the unbridled passion that shimmered in the depths of those obsidian eyes.

"God help me, Jacob," Cori whispered raggedly. "I don't think I'll ever be able to stop loving you . . ." Her trembling hands uplifted to cup his face, guiding his full lips to hers as she arched her hips toward him. ". . . I'll never stop loving you . . ."

As his mouth plundered hers with savage urgency, his body surged forward, answering her need with his own hungry impatience. Only when they were one beating, breathing essence did he feel like a whole man instead of an empty shell who went mechanically through the paces of living. Since Cori had taken the sunshine from his days he had walked under a black cloud. She had stolen his will to live, his vitality. The two of them had become tortured soulmates in perdition, constantly compelled to each other and yet restrained by obstacles that sought to keep

335

them apart . . .

A muted groan tripped from Jake's lips as his body drove into Cori's soft pliant flesh, setting the wild cadence of passion. He clutched her to him, wanting this moment of sublime rapture to last forever, knowing it would come to an end and he would be hurtled back into bleak reality. Jacob clung to every soul-shattering sensation that pelted him like driving rain. He savored the unparalleled pleasure that loving this high-spirited hellion evoked. He felt the hot brand of her body meeting his and gave himself up to the indescribable sensations that splashed over and through him . . .

And then the dark dimension of passion collapsed upon him like a waterfall. He was spinning in a mindless whirl. He was completely out of control and numbed with a pleasure beyond bearing. When Cori was in his arms, lovemaking was always a wild splendor that long lingered in his dreams. She was his addiction.

When, at last, he collapsed against her, his body spent and his energy drained, Cori combed her fingers through his wavy raven hair. "What a fine pair we are," she whispered against his throat, feeling his pulse matching her heart's accelerated pace. "Midnight lovers sharing impossible secrets . . ."

"At least we have that." Jake tangled his fingers in the silken tresses, pushing the thick mane of sable hair out of his way to tease that ultrasensitive spot beneath her ear. "At least we'll have that until I find myself a wife and get Gram off my back . . ."

Cori flinched at his slurred words. She couldn't bear the vision of Jennifer Hanley and Jake nestled together in their marriage bed. It was too vivid. But Cori forced herself to imagine Jake married to the comely widow, to cosider the pressure Augusta was probably putting on Jake after the broken engagement.

Jake braced himself on his elbow and stared down into

the face that haunted all his dreams. "It doesn't even bother you, does it?" he scowled at her. "You know I'm going to marry someone, but you won't let it be you. You swear you love me, but you really don't love me enough to put aside our differences, do you, Cori?"

"We've been through this time and time again," she sighed disheartenedly, unable to meet his bloodshot gaze. "I'm leaving Natchez at the end of the week. My . . ." Cori caught herself before she revealed her uncle's name. "It's difficult for Lori and Dal while I'm flitting around town, even if I employ disguises. For Lori's sake, I have to go."

"Always the martyr," Jake mocked cruelly. "Hasn't it occurred to you that I'm going to spend the rest of my life looking at your twin and wanting you? That I can't be faithful to the future wife Gram wants so desperately for me to have? Doesn't it matter that I'll see your face each time I stare at my wife, that I'll be making love to you while she's in my bed?"

Jake was painting a picture that was even more painful than the one Cori had already visualized. "Thunderation, do you have to be so blunt and descriptive?" she grumbled resentfully.

"Thunderation, do you have to be so damned stubborn?" Jake snapped, unable to contain his frustration. He curled his finger under her chin, forcing her to meet his probing stare. "And what will you do, sweet witch, if you find yourself carrying my child, the child *I* want to coddle and spoil?"

Cori blanched. She had tried to avoid thinking about that the past week. Another conflicting complication to compound her difficulties, she mused dispiritedly. As much as she would love to have Jake's child, she would find herself without a husband. That would force her to live a lie, insisting that her husband had perished somehow or another. And how would she care and support this child of theirs . . . ? Cori forced herself to stop contemplating the possibility and set it aside as another of the bridges to be crossed when the time came.

"I want our child," Jake told her point-blank. "I'll have the wealth and the means to provide for him and you won't. You have sacrificed my happiness and yours to satisfy your obsessive revenge. Our child, if we have begotten one, will be mine."

Cori couldn't believe they were having this conversation. "For goodness sakes, I'm not even sure we . . ."

"But if our lovemaking produces a child, no one will raise him except me," Jake insisted. "If I can't have both of you, at least I'll have him."

With a fierce shove, Cori pushed him away and darted toward the bed to snatch up the sheet. "I think you'd better leave. I have to be up and about quite early for my job."

"Thieves work the early shift?" Jake smirked as he clutched his breeches and shoved a muscled leg into them. "I thought you kept graveyard hours."

A slender arm shot toward the door. "Get out. We always wind up in arguments and we are not having another one tonight!"

"I'll be back," he promised as he shrugged on his shirt.

"I won't be here."

"I'll come looking for you, just as I will if you attempt to keep my child from me!"

"You're impossible!" she spewed in frustration.

Suddenly Cori was glaring at the old Jacob Wolf—the forceful, domineering, dictating rake. Oh, how he'd love to see her carrying his baby, all plump and round and waddling like a duck. And here he'd come, after she'd borne the pain and worry of wondering if the baby would be strong and healthy. Jake would be anxious to strip the precious life from her arms. Well, he wouldn't get his hands on her child, *if* she ever had one! She deserved

338

something in return for all the sacrifices she'd been forced to make in the name of justice and family obligation!

When the door slammed shut behind him, Jake broke into a wickedly mischievous smile. Let that feisty minx chew on the possibility of giving up her child and see how she liked it. Let her consider the possibility of him marrying another woman at Gram's insistence and see if that upset her.

Okay, so he had resorted to threatening her future, of assuring her that he would never truly be out of her life. Jacob was a desperate man who was grasping at straws, anything to shock some sense into that strong-willed termagant. He was going to pester her every single day, every single night until she relented and married him. He'd tell her everything she didn't want to hear, just to rattle her. He'd make her face the prospect of life without him. He would come at her from every direction until she realized both of them were going to be miserable without each other.

The truth of the matter was, Jake knew he wasn't going to be able to marry anybody else. Courting Jennifer Hanley for the past few days had taught him as much. Jennifer couldn't hold a candle to that dark-eyed hellion.

Earlier, when his footsteps had brought him to King's Tavern, that had been the final blow for Jake. He knew he couldn't outrun Cori's memory, not now, not ever. Cori was tormenting Layton and Jake fully intended to give her a taste of her own medicine until she gave up and gave in. No more mister nice guy, Jake promised himself. No more sitting back and letting the world buzz by. He wasn't going to forcefully drag that stubborn she-male to the altar, but he would ensure that she came running! When he was through with that minx she would be begging *him* to marry *her* for a change!

Determined of purpose, Jake clomped down the steps

to the registration desk. "I need to know the name of the woman who rented room number seven," he demanded.

The clerk peered owlishly at Jacob. What in heaven's name would this wealthy aristocrat want with that wild-haired wench who was closeted in room seven? Lord, she was a pathetic sight!

"You can't mean Tilly Trahern," the clerk croaked. "Red hair, ax-handle hips, and . . ." He cupped his hands to visually describe her huge sagging bosom. "The waitress at William's Tavern?"

Jake struggled to prevent snickering at the shocked expression on the clerk's face. No wonder Jake hadn't recognized Cori in crowds. She had garbed herself in another disguise. Lord, the woman was lousy with them. Every day found her with a new face and a new personality. He wondered if her penchant for masquerades was her way of rebelling against the fact that the Lord had placed her on earth with an identical twin. Obviously Cori was unconsciously seeking her own unique identity with her many disguises.

"Yes, that's the one. Tilly Trahern, you say?" Jake questioned, shrugging off his pensive thoughts.

"Tilly's her name," the clerk repeated and then shook his head. "What in the world would a man want with her?"

"You'd be surprised," Jake mumbled before he ambled back to the street and disappeared into the night.

An annoyed frown puckered Cori's brow when she spied Jacob escorting the chattery Jennifer Hanley into the pub for their midday meal. She didn't have the foggiest idea how he'd found out she was working at William's Tavern in disguise, but here he was to aggravate her again.

The instant Jake had seated his companion, he

340

motioned for the pudgy, wide-hipped waitress to approach. It was next to impossible for Jake to contain the gurgle of laughter that bubbled in his chest when he met those big brown eyes behind those thick wire-rimmed glasses. No wonder Cori couldn't navigate her way around the tables without bumping into something. She could barely see where she was going. He knew why the clerk at King's Tavern appeared so astounded when Jake sought information about Tilly Trahern, alias Cori Pierce Shelton. She looked positively revolting in her copper wig, padded garments, and pasty makeup. Who would ever have guessed there was a gorgeous figure beneath that ridiculous getup?

"Tilly, my dear, bring us your finest wine," Jake requested as he clasped Jennifer's hand and brought it to his lips.

Cori gnashed her teeth. That ornery rascal was purposely antagonizing her and flaunting his escort, just to get Cori's goat. Damnation, his technique was working a little too well. Cori was already seeing various shades of red through her thick spectacles.

"Whatever you wish, Mr. Wolf," Cori drawled in a nasally voice that was reminiscent of a caterwauling cat.

As she waddled off, Jake eased back in his chair to study the menu that hung above the bar. The tavern was the most respectable establishment Under the Hill, but there were still some rather rough-looking characters milling about. Yet none of them were paying Tilly much mind. Even men of indiscriminate tastes were taking a wide berth around her!

"Jacob, how good to see you again," William Chandler declared as he emerged from his private rooms that were attached to the back of his tavern.

Jake glanced up to see the elderly gentleman moving slowly forward, a greeting smile etched in his wrinkled features. Rising, Jake clasped William's hand and

341

returned the welcoming grin.

"You have been out of circulation for quite a long time," William chuckled. "I heard you were up the Missouri. Glad you're back. I'm sure Augusta is relieved." A cryptic smile surfaced on his lips and then vanished quickly. "How is your grandmother getting along, Jacob? Well, I hope."

"She's as feisty as ever," Jake informed the old man.

Although Jake considered the comment harmless conversation, William flinched. For the life of him, Jake couldn't fathom why William suddenly looked pained.

"She wasn't always so willful and headstrong," he murmured. "I knew her in her younger days, when she allowed her family to make her decisions for her." Quickly, William masked the emotion that had engulfed him and he forced a smile. "Give my regards to Augusta."

Gesturing for Jake to reseat himself, William ambled over to confer with the cook and then returned to his private quarters.

Jake had no time to mull over William's baffling remark. The clumsy Tilly Trahern had returned with the wine, to which she had spitefully added a jigger of whiskey to Jake's glass. She sat one glass in front of Jennifer and leaned in front of Jake, purposely gouging her elbow into his jaw.

"S'cuse me," she drawled. "Hope I didn't bruise you up none." She pinched his cheek a mite too hard. "Wouldn't wanna mar such a handsome mug as this."

Jake scooped up his fork and frowned over it. "I would prefer clean silverware, if you don't mind." He stabbed the fork into her hand and grinned at her grimace. "Fetch me some other eating utensils, preferably the kind that have seen dishwater since the last customer used them."

Before the pathetic-looking waitress returned to the table, Jake detected the glint of mischief in her eyes. He knew she intended to reciprocate, but he didn't know how until it was too late.

Cori started to set the shiny silverware beside Jake's wine glass, but the utensils clanked against the side of the table and toppled into his lap. Quick as a wink, her hand shot downward. After inflicting a stab wound to his crotch, Cori slammed the silverware onto the table and watched Jake grimace in pain.

"Sorry 'bout that, lovey. Hope I didn't hurt you . . . much."

When Tilly strutted away, swinging her padded hips, Jennifer frowned bemusedly. "Do you suppose William actually pays that walking disaster to work here?"

"Good help is difficult to find," Jake croaked uncomfortably.

Jennifer stared after the plump waitress and shuddered repulsively. "Obviously so! William is too tender-hearted. He should fire that chit."

For the next hour, Cori and Jake waged their private war. She fumbled around the table serving the meal. She listened in wicked amusement when Jake choked on the spiked wine she had prepared for him. She spilled food and beverages in his lap and apologized in insincere tones. Jake countered by tripping her once and con-stantly demanding better service—whether it be spicing the bland food, refilling his glass—anything to monopo-lize Cori's time while he fawned over his companion, just for spite.

When the twosome finally departed from the tavern, Cori's shoulder's slumped in relief. She didn't know what game Jake was playing with her, but she was tired of it already. In some ways that infuriating man reminded her so much of herself that it was scary. He had scolded her for needling Layton but Jake was trying to turn her into a human pincushion with his ornery pranks. He'd be back, Cori was sure of that. But thankfully, she would be off duty in less than an hour. If Jake intended to return for his evening meal, he would be disappointed to learn Tilly had come and gone.

Well, at least she could enjoy the afternoon, Cori consoled herself. She was on her way to the race track to *lose* the money she had stolen from Layton. If she had known how desperate the man was for cash, she would have been delighted. But Cori didn't know what a frantic state Layton was in. He had more trouble than he knew what to do with.

A disgruntled groan erupted from Cori's lips when she spied none other than Jacob and Jennifer striding toward her. Cori had been standing beside Lori, Dal, and Adam Castleberry, waiting to place their bets at Pharsalia race track. But lo and behold, here came Jacob.

Cori's accusing gaze swung to Lori, who had the good sense to glance the other way. Ten to one, Jake had dredged information from Lori. Suddenly Jake was turning up everywhere!

After Lori introduced Cori as her visiting brother from St. Louis, Cori shied away from the group. Although she was garbed in fashionable men's clothes and had donned a thick mustache and wide-brimmed hat, she didn't dare risk having Jennifer make more of the family resemblance than she already had. Even though brains didn't seem to be Jennifer's largest commodity, she wasn't totally stupid. Cori decided to drift away from the group to place her losing bet on the first race.

Intent on her purpose, Cori wandered over to the starting line to scrutinize the thoroughbreds that pranced beneath their jockeys. Dal and Adam had been boasting about their prize stock, so Cori knew better than to wager on their horses if she wanted to lose the stolen money.

According to Dal, Jake had entered some of his stock in

344

the races and Cori wasn't about to bet on them either. She was looking for a loser, a steed that would come in dead last. Once she'd been parted from the stolen money she could return to King's Tavern and catch a nap before she began her midnight prowling around Layton's house.

A steady drizzle of rain dripped from the cloudy sky and Cori unconsciously pulled her collar around her neck to ward off the chill. So intent was she, as she surveyed the horses, that she didn't hear Jake approach.

"Are you trying to double your ill-gotten gains, *Corbin?* Do tell me, *Corbin,* how can you afford such elegant garments on the meager wages you earn as a waitress?" he snickered in question.

"Why don't you go away and leave me alone?" Cori muttered sourly. "Go fawn over Jennifer. She thrives on your flattery."

"Because *I* thrive on *your* rejection," Jake chuckled, undaunted by her insulting remark.

Presenting her back, Cori continued to assess the string of horses. A thick-chested, stump-legged gray mare caught her eye. She measured the unlikely looking nag and decided the animal didn't stand a chance against the well-bred racers that tossed their proud heads and skitted sideways in anticipation of the run. Here was Cori's loser. All she had to do was bet the ten thousand dollars she had stashed in her pocket on the gray mare and the stolen money would be gone forever. A less likely candidate for victory had Cori ever seen!

When she wheeled toward the betting tables, Jake snagged her arm. "What the hell are you really up to, minx?" he wanted to know.

Cori stared at the arm that held her fast before tipping her head back to glare into Jake's ruggedly handsome face. "I'm going to lose the money I stole from the *Belle,* the money you asked me to steal back from Layton."

Jake's dark brows jackknifed. "Are you mad?"

345

"Apparently. I let myself get mixed up with you when I knew better, didn't I?" Cori jerked her arm loose from his grasp. "Now, if you will excuse me, Mr. Wolf. I have a ten thousand dollar bet to place."

Jake stared after the crazed brunette who was masquerading as Lori's brother. Try as he may, he simply couldn't figure this woman out! Why was she throwing the money away while she was living a hand-to-mouth existence? No one knew she had the cash. She could have been living quite comfortably instead of parading around William's Tavern, serving meals. Could it be that her conscience was nagging her? Did she feel uncomfortable spending stolen money? Who would have guessed it? Certainly not Jake. With all Cori's varied escapades and shenanigans, he had begun to think she was a habitual thief who derived pleasure in banditry. It seemed the only wicked glee she enjoyed was harassing Layton every chance she got. Obviously, the only reason she stole the money in the first place was because Layton wanted it.

When the crowd swarmed toward the track in anticipation of the first race, Jake elbowed his way toward Cori. He was curious to see which horse she had selected as a likely loser. At the crack of the pistol, the horses plunged over the starting line and thundered around the park, splattering mud everywhere. From the outset, Dal and Adam's prize steeds were running neck and neck. But the slick track played havoc with the long-legged creatures, who were known for their speed, not their sure-footedness. The wild-eyed animals slammed into each other as they rounded the curve and attempted to stretch out on the straightaway.

Jake could tell nothing from Cori's reaction. Although Adam and Dal were cheering their horses and jockeys on, Cori displayed no emotion until the gray mare edged up beside the floundering racers that had claimed the inside railing.

Then Cori began to look concerned.

"Which horse did you bet on?" Jake wanted to know as the horses thundered toward the finish line.

"A sure loser . . . or so I thought . . . Damn." Cori slammed her fist against the rail as the gray mare inched out the two thoroughbreds by a nostril.

Jake couldn't help himself. He burst out laughing at the disgusted expression that puckered Cori's stage mustache. Never had a prospective bettor looked so dismayed over winning against tremendous odds.

"You should have asked for advice, Corbin, m'boy," Jake said between snickers. "Never *ever* bet against a gray on a rainy day." He slapped the young dandy on the back. "Shall we go collect your winnings? You must have won a bundle."

Although Cori would have preferred to be left alone to sulk, Jake propelled her through the crowd to receive her winnings. Horrified, she watched the rotund man slap thirty thousand dollars into her hand.

Even more determined than before, Cori stamped through the mud to assess the horses that were brought forward for the next heat.

"Don't bet on the chestnut," Jake advised. "He's mine. If he wins, places or shows, you'll increase your winnings again."

Cori glowered at her antagonist. He was amusing himself at her expense. This scheme had sounded so perfect when she dreamed it up. But this stolen money kept sticking to her like glue. She couldn't seem to get rid of it!

When her circling gaze landed on the black mare that looked as if it should have been hitched to a milk wagon, a satisfied smile crossed her lips. "Now there's a loser if I ever saw one," she announced with great conviction.

Jake tended to agree. The steed looked as it were standing on its last leg. It would be a wonder if the

347

creature even finished the race. Its head sagged notice-ably as the jockey nudged it into the line. "If you have your heart set on losing money that pathetic animal seems a sure bet."

With Jake trailing behind her, Cori returned to the betting table to make her wager. That done, she aimed herself toward the track.

And damn if it didn't happen again! The black mare never did lift its head. But it ran hell for leather, passing Jake's long-legged chestnut as if it were standing still! The sure-footed black mare stretched into her stride at the sound of the pistol and never broke it until she blazed over the finish line. It wasn't even a close race. Cori knew she's won the moment the mare grabbed the bit in her teeth and shot off like a cannonball.

"Well, I'll be damned . . ." Jake couldn't believe his eyes. "I guess you should never bet on a dark horse on a muddy track either."

Cori chose to bypass the third and fourth races, hoping to break her winning streak. She had only one chance to get the enormous pile of cash off her hands. The fifth race was her salvation.

With Jake still following at her heels, Cori strode back to study the field of horses. Twice before she had bet on two unlikely candidates and they had won. This time, she selected a pure-blooded thoroughbred that was so flighty it wouldn't stand still. The rain had begun to pour down from the sky, turning the track into a sloppy mud hole. Cori wasn't about to bet on a stocky, sure-footed steed that was built close to the ground this time!

Although her pick was a dappled gray, it possessed a feisty temperament. Cori suspected that splattering through mud would distract the steed and that the jockey would have his hands full simply keeping the creature in the middle of the track.

Jake refrained from voicing his opinion. He merely watched on as Cori plunked down every cent she'd won and then headed for the railing. There was a smug expression on her face as she stared at the starting line, knowing the third time would be the charm. But her satisfied smile sagged on the corners of her mouth when several of the horses bolted forward and collided with one another the instant after the pistol discharged. To her amazement, the dappled gray squirted from the pack. As Cori predicted, the flying mud startled the horse. But instead of leaping sideways, the gray gelding shot off in a dead run. The field of horses that thundered behind the gray and the splatter of mud beneath him kept him whizzing around the track as if he were attempting to outrun danger. And the damned horse didn't even slow down when it flew across the finish line. The jockey had one helluva a time bringing him to a halt after he'd run a race and a half!

A peal of laughter rang through the soggy air and Cori pivoted to glare into Jake's sparkling green eyes.

"I told you never to be on a gray on a . . ."

"Oh, hush," Cori snapped in annoyance. "I hate it when you gloat. You do it too cussed well." In a fit of temper, Cori flung her winning ticket at him. "*You* go collect the money. I want nothing more to do with it!"

When she squeezed through the crowd and stomped off, Jake, still chuckling, headed toward the betting booth. Jake didn't notice his cousin standing sullenly in the distance until he wheeled around with money in hand.

Layton stared enviously at the roll of cash that Jake had collected as it it were the key to his salvation. Swallowing his pride, he cut through the departing crowd like a fish swimming upstream.

"Jacob, I need a favor," Layton began, watching with envy as his cousin stashed the lump of cash in his vest pocket. "I need to borrow some money."

Jake eyed Layton with consternation. Layton looked desperate. He couldn't help but wonder if Cori had something to do with Layton's need for cash. There was no telling what that minx had done in her attempt to push Layton to the limits of his sanity. Whatever it was, it was working. Layton looked haggard and harried and frantic.

"How much money?" Jake question curiously.

Layton swallowed hard. He had lost every cent Jake had paid him in compensation for the *Belle* in his attempt to win enough cash at the race track to meet Kyle's demands. "Fifty thousand."

"Fifty thou . . ." Jake hooted. Hell's fire, Cori had put a steep price on Layton's life. That ornery little scamp! Jake would have given most anything to know what she had said and done to Layton. "Good Lord, cuz, I just paid you twenty-five thousand dollars Monday."

A pensive frown knitted Jake's brow as he watched the rain dribble down Layton's hatless head like perspiration. Jake turned several options over in his mind, wondering how he could put an end to whatever harassment Cori was causing Layton, wondering how he would worm the truth out of his chubby cousin.

"Well?" Layton prodded impatiently. "Are you going to loan me the money or not?"

"I'll have to think it over," Jake murmured, distracted by the thoughts of Cori that clogged his mind.

"I need an answer," Layton insisted with a frustrated scowl.

"You'll have your answer this evening," Jake promised as he shouldered his way past his cousin.

Mulling over his conversation with Layton, Jake returned to Jennifer. She promptly scolded him for ignoring her for the majority of the afternoon while he watched Cori's latest caper at Pharsalia race track. Jake politely voiced his apology and led Jennifer away, but he didn't spare the comely blonde another thought. His mind was on Cori and on Layton's mysterious desire for money.

Chapter 24

Chilled to the bone, Cori shivered her way through the garden that surrounded King's Tavern. Discreetly she made her way to her room in the cloak of darkness. Tonight, Lori had joined Cori in her latest attempt to drive Layton mad with haunting ghosts and floating objects. And Layton was definitely showing signs of instability!

In Cori's estimation, he was like a ripe pecan—ready to crack. Layton had howled like a banshee when the taunting voices echoed around his room. He had sent statues and pictures crashing against walls while he muttered curses to the wraiths that tormented him.

Cori had no way of knowing about Kyle's blackmail and death threats, which put Layton in an even greater frenzy. But she felt Layton was ripe for the picking. She and Lori had made their final plans for Layton.

Very soon, Cori told herself. Michael Shelton's murder would soon be solved and she could get on with the rest of her life . . .

The door, which she distinctly remembered locking before she left, swung open without the use of the key. Cori craned her neck around the corner to peer cautiously into her room. The lantern had been lit and

Jacob occupied the chair which set in the corner.

"How did you get in here?" Cori grumbled as she doffed her damp cape.

An amused smile pursed Jake's lips before he leisurely sipped his brew. "You're not the only one who can pick locks."

Cori eyed him speculatively. "What do you want this time? I thought you and Jennifer would be painting the town red."

"It's after midnight," Jake reminded the bedraggled imp. "Most decent folks can do all that needs to be done before the witching hour. Gram always told me that anything I might think of doing after midnight probably didn't need doing. It's a shame you don't follow that policy."

Cori was tired, cold, and irritable. In order to keep her job and prowl the night to haunt Layton she had been forced to forego sleep. Watching the sly smiles that kept spreading across Jake's full lips wasn't helping her disposition. He was a constant reminder of what she couldn't have, the temptation she was constantly forced to ignore, a love that refused to die.

"If you came to make some profound point, make it and leave me in peace. I'm in no mood for a lecture. It's been a long, exhausting day," Cori muttered as she stepped behind the dressing screen to peel off her soggy breeches and shirt.

Jake watched her head bob up and down behind the screen while she disrobed. He allowed himself to fantasize about the curvaceous figure that was concealed from him. After being deprived of the tantalizing vision, Jake sighed and took a sip of his ale.

"I thought you might be curious to know what I did with the money you won at Pharsalia today," he baited her.

"Not particularly, no," she countered.

His shoulder lifted nonchalantly. "That's a shame because Layton was extremely interested in the cash I collected for you at the betting table."

Cori took the bait this time, just as Jake predicted she would. She emerged from behind the screen, clutching her robe around her. Her gaze locked with those sparkling green eyes that had long been haunting her dreams.

"What did you do with the winnings?"

While Cori was studying him with open curiosity, Jake surveyed her expression. But he was unable to tell if Cori knew why Layton was desperate for money. Chances were she did, he speculated. But Cori was a master at disguising her emotions and masking her bewitching face in all sorts of disguises. Jake still wasn't sure how much she knew or what she was up to.

Leaning back in the chair, Jake casually stretched his long legs out in front of him. Letting the suspense and her inquisitiveness build, he took another sip of his ale before responding. "My dear cousin asked for a fifty-thousand-dollar loan and, being family and all, I gave it to him." Jake knew the information would put her in a full-blown snit. He was right, of course.

"You *what!*" Cori exploded in frustration.

"You heard me," Jake smirked, watching her pace and curse under her breath. "You didn't want the money so I gave part of it to Layton. The rest I kept to return to your unfortunate victims on the *Belle.*"

"How could you!" Cori railed as she stamped over in front of him to chew him up one side and down the other. "You know how I feel about that murdering ogre! You purposely gave Layton the money I won just to infuriate me, didn't you?"

"You said you didn't want your winnings," Jake parried in a more reasonable tone than Cori had employed. "You told me I could have it so I did with it what I wanted."

"I'll never forgive you for that, damn you," Cori hissed bitterly.

So she had found some way to threaten Layton and demand money from him, Jake surmised. Had she concealed her identity in one of her many disguises and blackmailed him? Had she purposely asked for more cash than she assumed Layton could acquire, just to force his hand? Hell's fire, what was going on?

"I want to know what you are up to and I want to know now!" Jake scowled into her animated features.

Her chin shot up, just as it always did when he made harsh demands to which she had no intention of complying. "What I'm doing is nobody's business but my own," she bit off.

His breath came out in a growl. "Damn it, woman, if you keep needling Layton, you're going to get yourself in so much trouble you'll never get out!"

"That's my problem," she hurled defensively. "All you have to do is court prissy Jennifer and marry her to satisfy Augusta. And judging by the way Jennifer hangs all over you like creeping ivy, I doubt she'll reject your proposal." The very thought bent Cori out of shape. "Indeed, I doubt Jennifer Hanley has said no to any proposition you've made to her!"

"Leave Jen out of this," Jake muttered. "I want . . ."

"*Jen* is it?" Cori interrupted with a caustic smirk. "So the two of you are on intimate terms, are you?" The jealous green monster sank in its teeth, giving Cori a nasty bite. "You've probably been in her bed already tonight, but being the lusty rake you are, you came here to repeat last night's performance with me!"

"What do you care where I've been?" he snapped. "You're more the rake than I ever thought to be. I wanted a wife, but you . . ." He stuck his face into hers. "You only wanted my body. You even offered to become

354

my mistress because you didn't want my name. Now you tell me, minx, who is using whom?"

Cori hated it when he twisted the truth to suit his arguments. He knew perfectly well why she couldn't marry him then or now. And he knew damned well she loved him, despite the insurmountable obstacles that stood between them. And still he tangled the facts to his advantage and utilized them as weapons against her.

With a furious curse, Cori wheeled away. "I don't want to see you ever again. In two days I'll be gone and you can marry empty-headed Jennifer and make Augusta's lifelong dream come true. I'll *steal* something nice for your wedding gift . . ."

Jake whipped her around so quickly that her last word was ripped from her lips. "Hell's fire, you do it ever blessed time!" Jake scowled resentfully. "I came here with every intention of carrying on a civil, reasonable conversation with you, but you drag me into arguments on subjects I never even considered discussing!"

His voice boomed around the room and ricocheted off the walls like an exploding cannon. "And curse it, Cori, you know the reason why I'm here, the reason I keep rolling back to you like a damned yo-yo."

"What you want from me is the same thing you can get from Jennifer." She wrapped the spiteful words around her tongue and hurled them at him.

"That's where you're wrong, my feisty little witch," Jake growled as he scooped her up in his arms and tossed her on the bed.

With an impatient jerk, Jake popped the buttons off his shirt and cast the garment aside as he approached the wild-haired vixen who was sprawled on the bed. Cori yelped indignantly as Jake came at her like a cavalry answering the order to charge. As she rolled sideways to make her escape, Jake hooked his arm around her waist, dragging her thrashing body beneath his.

Cori knew the moment he touched her that she was fighting a lost cause. Despite the fact that he could overpower her with his superior strength if he'd wanted to, her own body betrayed her. The feel of his masculine contours meshing against hers was enough to replace her anger with the simmering passion Jake so easily aroused in her.

Her tangled lashes fluttered up to see the roguish grin that suddenly surfaced on his sensuous lips. In spite of everything, Cori couldn't contain her own impish smile. They both knew their biting words and harsh accusations counted for nothing when they were lying in each other's arms. This was where they had wanted to be, even if differences of opinion caused them to shout at each other.

Languidly, Cori reached up to run her forefinger down the cleft of his chin and then traced the smile lines that bracketed his kissable mouth. He reciprocated by brushing his knuckles over her delicate cheek bones and then kissed the tip of her dainty nose.

"You aren't ever going to tell me what you're planning to do with Layton, are you?" he whispered in question.

"No," Cori assured him as she looped her arms over his broad shoulders to toy with the crisp black hair that capped his head.

Her lips parted in invitation and suddenly Jake didn't give a flying fig if Layton locked horns with this fiercely determined firebrand. At the moment, Cori was in his arms, smiling up at him in that special way of hers that melted his heart and left it dripping all over his ribs.

Like a bee courting nectar, his lips hovered over hers, drinking in the sweet intoxicating taste that befuddled his mind. His tongue probed into the soft recesses and Cori answered with a welcoming sigh. While he kissed her with all the bottled-up emotion that bubbled inside him, his hands glided beneath her robe, peeling away the garment that concealed what he longed to gaze upon and caress.

His stroking hands sensitized and aroused. He worshiped each silken plane and contour, conveying his need to love and to be loved as only Cori knew how. She responded eagerly, returning each heart-stopping kiss, each bone-melting caress. So often in the past, their passion for each other had swept them up like a raging river, carrying them along with passion's wild current. But tonight they cherished each other like a forbidden treasure. Each moment, each touch was so very precious and dear.

Cori's lashes swept down to block out all except the warm tingling pleasures Jake offered. She was his to do with what he would, and he did the most incredible things to her pliant body with his brazen caresses and achingly tender kisses. His sleek muscular body glided down hers, spreading a path of living fire over her flesh. Cori craved the intimacy of his touch, reveled in the giddy sensations that spilled through her. She arched upward as his tongue flicked at the taut buds of her breasts. She begged for the feel of his fingertips kneading and stroking her skin.

Like a rolling surf, his body unfolded upon hers. He took her lips under his before he recoiled to whisper love words over the swells of her breasts and the trim indentation of her waist. A gasp broke from her throat when his moist lips skimmed her thighs and his skillful hands drifted enticingly over her belly.

Another breathless moan tumbled from her lips as he drew her to her knees and crouched before her. While his lips hovered over hers, his hands glided down her hips, nudging her thighs apart, teasing her until she ached with hot, sweet torment. He moved again, lifting her above him so he could suckle at the throbbing tips of her breasts. Cori groaned, overwhelmed by such ardent needs that she swore she'd die long before he satisfied this burning need that left her on fire for him. Urgently, she tried to guide him to her, to end the hungry agony that his hands and lips aroused.

"Not yet, my wild sweet love . . ." he murmured seductively. "Not yet . . . There is so much more I want to teach you about the ways a man can pleasure a woman. Like this, for instance . . ."

His fingertips slid over her hips and swirled over her knee. Ever so slowly, his hands moved, blazing a path for his lips to follow. The enormous ache he created with his intimate explorations didn't go away. It burned Cori alive.

"And this . . ." Jake murmured against her thigh, sending tremors of delight undulating through her.

When he shifted her quivering body above his, Cori's brain malfunctioned. Her body was a mass of uncontrollable shudders. Sensations so wild and devastating that she wondered if she could bear them, burst from the very core of her being. Pleasure streamed out in all directions at once. Shock waves rippled through every fiber as the maddening need expanded, triggered by the skillful seduction of his kisses and caresses.

Wild with wonder and urgent passion Cori reached for him, wanting him so badly, needing all of him as she needed air to breathe. And this time he didn't refuse her broken pleas to make the tormenting ache go away. His muscled body unfurled upon hers. His hand glided up her arms, holding them above her head as he nudged his knee between her thighs and lifted her to him. He took possession and then slowly withdrew, watching the expression of desire claim her exquisite features.

There were so many things about this wild-hearted woman over which Jake had absolutely no control. She was like a misdirected whirlwind that came and went from his life. She was charming, versatile and resilient.

She possessed exceptional talent and she was teeming with undaunted spirit. She bore incredible depths of character and she was the most multidimensional female Jake had encountered in all his thirty-one years. This dark-eyed daredevil matched him in all arenas . . . except one . . .

When it came to passion Jake was still the master whose titillating instruction could make this sassy sprite a slave to her own desires. He could make her beg for him, as if he alone were the nourishment she needed to survive, as if she wasn't whole and alive until they were of one mind, body, and soul.

Jake savored the power he held over this shapely beauty. He adored the hunger that glistened in her obsidian eyes when she stared beseechingly up at him. Her heart-shaped lips were swollen from his ravishing kisses. Her curvaceous body was his possession, and he knew things about her that she never knew about herself until he taught her those intimate secrets . . .

"Jake . . ." Her voice wavered with the multitude of tormenting sensations. "Please . . ." Cori bit her lip when he teased her with that magnificent body of his, promising fulfillment but withholding the ultimate pleasure that she knew waited in his arms. "I need you . . . I want you so badly that I . . ."

His mouth twisted over hers, stripping the last ounce of breath from her lungs. He wondered then if he hadn't just lost this tender battle of domination. When she pleaded with him to take her to the heights of ecstasy he felt his willpower crumbling like a sand castle eroding in the wind.

He had wanted to demand that she stay with him forever, wanted to force the words from her lips before he appeased both their ravenous needs. But as always, his self-control buckled as if it never even existed when she peered up at him with such incredible needs. And when she whispered to him in that sultry, pleading voice he found himself succumbing to her whim. It was disastrous to be so lost in this woman, to care about her to the point of absolute distraction. But when Jake had finally fallen in love it had completely consumed him.

With a tormented groan he buried himself within her, meeting her writhing body with hard driving thrusts. He clutched her to him, afraid he would squeeze her in two and yet helpless to loose his tight grasp on her. His savage needs took command of his mind and body, leaving him to respond to the torrent of passion that channeled through every nerve and muscle.

Jake felt himself reaching upward to capture that one wild ineffable sensation that always lured him when sharing this fiery splendor with Cori. Only when they were flesh to flesh and heart to heart could he cast off the hindering garments of the soul and soar into that magical dimension of time. And when they reached that pinnacle of ecstasy, that elusive sensation that compelled him was suddenly within his grasp. The world spit asunder and sparks flashed in the dark universe like a pitcher of stars cascading onto the black velvet sky.

His body strained against her soft flesh, seeking ultimate depths of intimacy. Convulsive shudders of passion racked his body. Numbing pleasure gripped him, demanding all his energy and strength.

Cori couldn't seem to let go either. She knew their minutes together were numbered. There would be no more nights of ecstasy. Her plans for Layton would destroy Jacob's family and his love for her. The mental anguish of loving him and knowing she was about to hurt him cut through her like a double-edged sword. She had waited a year to bring her father's murderer to justice, but her feelings for Jacob would be the price she had to pay for revenge and justice.

"Stay the night," Cori murmured, swamped by the

crosscurrents of emotions that hounded her. Oh, why did she have to chose between her obligations to her father's memory and her love for Jacob, knowing how much she was about to lose? "Just once before I have to go, I want to hold you all through the night and pretend there's no tomorrow . . ."

As if he could have climbed out of bed and left this gorgeous imp who had stolen his heart, thought Jake. He never had any intention of leaving her tonight, even if she had demanded that he go.

Jake frowned down into her enchanting features. There was something in the way Cori murmured her request that worried him. She had made tomorrow sound like doomsday. Well, he would fret over tomorrow when it got here, he decided drowsily. Tonight . . . ah, tonight he would be sleeping in this angel's arms.

When he felt this mystical sorceress's hands gliding familiarly across his hair-matted flesh Jake realized he was nowhere near as sleepy as he thought he was. Cori stoked the fires of passion into a raging blaze and suddenly Jake didn't care if he slept a wink. . . . And he didn't either . . .

Since the moment Jake had returned home at dawn he had been preoccupied. His thoughts were on Cori, just as they had been so much of late. Jake had been the recipient of a scalding kiss delivered by the pathetic-looking Tilly Trahern, who scurried off to work at William's Tavern, leaving him to make his way back to Wolfhaven. There had been something about that parting kiss that disturbed Jake greatly. Even in her ridiculous disguise, Jake had detected an unexplainable sadness in Cori's dark eyes. She hadn't said good-bye to him, but he could almost hear the hushed words in her remorseful expression. Her gaze had lingered on him before she closed the door behind her, as if she were committing his image to memory before she left him.

Something was about to happen. Jake could feel it in his bones. But the maddening part was he didn't have the foggiest idea *what*.

Desperate to puzzle out what Layton wanted with the money he'd asked for, Jake's pensive gaze poured over the company ledgers. Frantically, he searched for some clue to Layton's dealings. Layton should have had enough ready cash to meet the demand. Although Jake had told Cori otherwise in an attempt to infuriate her and draw her out, he had, in actuality, refused to give Layton the money he'd wanted.

The truth was Jake had searched out the owners of the black and gray mares that had won at the track. Since he would have more free time on his hands than he'd had before, Jake intended to build a blood line of racers to compete at Pharsalia. He had purchased the horses Cori had bet on to breed to his thoroughbred stallion. The colts would be a living memorial of that day at the track when Cori couldn't lose a bet to save her soul. It had been a silly whim to make the purchases, but he thought it fitting to buy the horses with money Cori hadn't been able to lose, and so he had paid for the steeds with her cash winnings.

That evening, when Jake stopped by to inform Layton that there would be no cash forthcoming, his cousin had been beside himself. But Layton wouldn't disclose why he needed the money immediately. Jake didn't know what the hell was going on, but he had the unshakable feeling Cori was about to embroil herself in an another madcap caper that might produce serious repercussions. How and what had she told Layton to leave him so frantic and desperate? Did Layton know Cori was Michael Shelton's daughter—one of two lookalikes who were out to destroy him for what they thought he had done?

With a frustrated sigh, Jake restlessly combed his fingers through his hair and turned the page of the ledger. The excessive fees Kyle Benson had collected as captain of the *Belle* disturbed Jake. Layton had never explained the exorbitant wages to Jake's satisfaction. And even when Jake fired the sour-faced, hot-tempered Benson from his duties, Layton had taken him on as a security guard. Why?

There was something fishy here, but Jake wasn't sure how the two men were involved. He knew Benson had feasted his eyes on a new business endeavor in Natchez, but that was all Jake knew. Benson seemed to be a man of diverse interests, just as Jacob was. The only difference was that Benson appeared the type who looked for easy ways to acquire wealth—a leech who preyed on any advantageous situation that came his way. Kyle's attempt to coerce Cori into his bed while he was the captain of the *Belle* lent testimony to the scoundrel's policy of playing to his advantages every chance he got.

A ponderous frown knitted Jake's brow. He wondered if Benson knew about Layton's dealings with Michael Shelton, even if Benson hadn't been hired by the company until after the *Belle* was acquired. Or did Benson's association with Layton stem from the man's obsessive lust for Cori? Jake knew for a fact that Kyle dreamed of getting her into his bed . . .

The repugnant thought provoked Jake to scowl sourly. Muttering, he flipped the page and began tallying the amount of money Layton had paid Benson . . .

A clatter in the hall dragged Jake from his calculations. He glanced up when he heard the tap of a cane in the tiled foyer. And sure enough, Augusta Breeze blew in. As always, she was garbed in black, contrasting her silver hair and gold-rimmed spectacles.

"I demand to know what the hell is going on." As was her custom, Augusta dispensed with courteous greetings and plunged headfirst into conversation. "One of the local gossips dropped by yesterday evening to announce she had seen Jennifer Hanley on your arm and in your carriage quite a lot the past few days. It has also come to my attention, *via* the grapevine, that you escorted Jennifer to Pharsalia yesterday and that you were chumming around with Cori and Dal."

Augusta stamped forward, her aging features puckered in a frustrated frown. "I thought you and Cori had things squared away. Now I'm told that it is Dal who is marrying Miss Pierce and word of your future engagement to Jennifer is spreading, by Jennifer herself no doubt. Now which is it, Jacob? And when, if ever, am I going to have any of your babies to fuss over before I go to my grave? All this pussyfooting around on your part is taking years off my life. And curse it, I don't have many to spare!"

"Perhaps if you wouldn't meddle quite so much, Gram, you wouldn't be so upset with the way my life is going," Jacob teased with a playful wink.

Augusta was in no mood to be taunted. "Your life is going around in circles, you young fool! For ten years you have floated up and down the river like driftwood without an anchor. When I finally get you home where you belong to accept the position to which you were born, I find you hopping back and forth between women, seemingly unable to land a wife. You can't seem to keep a firm grasp on the one you want so you cast your roving eyes on a widow who doesn't have enough brains to fill a thimble."

"Jennifer is bright enough to fulfill the position of wife," Jake felt compelled to say in Jen's behalf. True, she wasn't as quick-witted or as intelligent as Cori, but then who the hell was, besides Augusta?

"Poppycock!" Augusta sniffed in contradiction. "You met your match in Cori and you let her slip through your

364

fingers. Now your best friend has caught her. I'm beginning to think I have given you more credit than you deserve and not nearly enough guidance in the area of courtship. For goodness sake, Jacob, don't you know how to charm a woman, or have you channeled all your time and energy into simply bedding the ones of easy virtue?"

"Gram . . ." The tone of Jake's voice warned his outspoken grandmother to guard her tongue. His love life was off limits to discussion. No doubt the gossips had had a field day bending Augusta's ears in years past, tattling of his promiscuity. But if his grandmother dared to ask about his private relationship with Cori . . .

"Well?" Augusta snapped, undaunted by the warning glance Jake flashed at her. "Aren't you man enough to satisfy that rambunctious young woman? Heaven knows I had to prod you into kissing her. With your reputation with women I would have thought . . ."

"We are not having this discussion," Jacob declared, his tone anticipating no argument, but he got one just the same.

"Oh yes we are!" Augusta assured him tartly. "Lord forgive me for this distasteful suggestion, but if you have to compromise her vir . . ."

"The Lord won't forgive you," Jake cut in before Augusta completed the outrageous remark that stampeded to the tip of her tongue.

"Damnation, Jacob!" Augusta pounded her cane on the carpet. "I want to see you married to a woman who can match you stride for stride. I spent my life wed to a man who was everything I wasn't, a man my family selected for me without caring if I loved, if he loved in return. The man I wanted when I came of age wasn't good enough for my family and I was forced to sacrifice what I wanted to meet their demands . . ." Her voice cracked noticeably and Augusta struggled to regain her composure.

"I want more than that for you. Just look at Layton. He married for money and position and he has paid for it by sneaking around on Sylvia. I know perfectly well how you feel about Cori. I can see it every time you glance in her direction. The two of you belong together, even if you won't admit it. And if Dal was as good a friend as you think he is he wouldn't keep butting into your love life to steal Cori away."

It would be so much easier to set Augusta straight and explain this escapade with Cori from beginning to end. But Jake couldn't do it. Augusta saw only the rippling waters on the surface. She knew nothing of the powerful crosscurrents in the depths. She was too influenced by what she wanted for Jacob to give a whit about the conflicts and complications.

Jake frowned when a hint of tears misted Augusta's hazel eyes. Something else was bothering her. He wasn't sure what it was, but her wobbling voice indicated her churning emotions.

"You need a drink," Jake diagnosed.

"I needed a granddaughter-in-law and babies!" Augusta spouted.

Calmly, Jake unfolded himself from the chair, strode around his grandmother, and stepped into the vestibule. After calling to the servant to deliver coffee to the office, he turned to confront Augusta's stabbing glare.

"First you're going to have the coffee and calm down," Jake insisted. He guided her toward a chair. "Sit down and tell me what is really bothering you."

Defeatedly, Augusta plunked into the chair. "Curse it, Jacob, all I wanted was to . . ."

Jacob squatted down on his haunches and smiled comfortingly into Augusta's wrinkled face. Gently he took her clenched fist in his and gave it a pat. "There are many things Cori and I have to resolve. Sometimes leaping in with both feet, attempting to solve problems,

366

and making permanent arrangements doesn't suit the situation. I tried the direct approach with Cori in the beginning, but things aren't always as simple as they appear. There are instances when I believe time and patience are required. It isn't my way particularly and I know it isn't yours, but I've had to adjust and so must you."

Augusta studied Jake's ruggedly handsome features for a long deliberate moment before a faint smile traced her lips. "Something's going on here that you refuse to tell me about, isn't it? That's why you're as vague in explanation as Cori is."

"Yes," Jake answered honestly. "There are many things going on."

"And it has something to do with Cori's previous life, I suppose," she speculated.

"In a way, yes." His face became a carefully guarded stare that revealed none of his emotions.

"I was afraid of that." Her shoulders slumped.

When the housekeeper entered the study with a tray of coffee and biscuits, Augusta accepted the refreshments and dropped the matter for several minutes, at least long enough to pass on the other information the town gossips had conveyed to her. Augusta spoke of a political scandal, the fire that had demolished one of the steamers downriver. She finished with the report of a murder Under the Hill. Her voice cracked again, just as it had earlier, arousing Jake's curiosity.

Unsolved murders and bloody banditry were painfully common occurrences along Silver Street and along Natchez Trace. Through the years, skeletons washed to the surface of shallow graves and unsuspecting travelers stumbled onto corpses on the edges of dried bogs. They speculated on who and what was the cause of death and then they went about their business without getting involved. Cheats, thieves, and brawlers found a haven along the wharf. From time to time the authorities tried to restore law and order Under the Hill, but it was and always would be the rough part of town.

But for some reason, unbeknownst to Jake, Augusta seemed unduly upset by the most recent murder. She hadn't named names, but she was obviously disturbed by the latest injustice.

"Who was it, Gram?" Jake queried quietly, scrutinizing her pained features.

Augusta fiddled with her coffee cup and stared pensively at its contents. "I suppose it's because of him that I came in here ranting and raving," she admitted sorrowfully.

Another muddled frown knitted Jake's brow. It had been a long time since he'd seen his grandmother in such a deflated mood. She had endured many tragedies in her seventy-four years, but she was visibly distraught by the mysterious incident.

"William Chandler has been killed," Augusta blurted out tearfully.

A stunned gasp erupted from Jake's throat. He had seen William the previous day, cajoling his customers in the tavern where the pathetic-looking Tilly Trahern worked.

Augusta dabbed at the tears that swam in her eyes. "William was a man with a good heart who overcame a great deal to make his niche in life. In a brawling community, William commanded respect and usually got it. Oh, he wasn't one of society's dandies who was born with a silver spoon in his mouth. But he tried to make something of himself and bring some dignity to the shabby life from which he had been born and raised."

It was true that William Chandler owned one of the most respectable tavern houses Under the Hill. It was the only one, in fact, where steamboat travelers dared to stay the night without fearing for their lives. William had been like a historic landmark Under the Hill, a man who had been there forever and had never married, so far as Jake knew. William had been a warm, generous man who offered compassion to those who were down on their luck.

Even though Augusta had never been prone to tears, Jake noticed another spring had erupted from her eyes.

Muttering at her lack of self-control, Augusta retrieved a second handkerchief from her purse and blotted her face. "They found Will's body lying face down in the mud last night. He'd been shot in the back and his pockets had been picked clean . . ."

Her voice broke completely and it was two full minutes before she could compose herself well enough to continue. Her clouded gaze focused on Jacob and her trembling hands folded around his. "William was the man I wanted to marry those long years ago, even though my dignified family forbid it. I was very young then, and I was told it was disrespectful to disobey the wishes of my father. But I never forgave myself for submitting and I have regretted it for almost sixty years. But plantation owners weren't supposed to mix with the likes of William's family."

Jacob floundered for something suitable to say, but no words formed on his lips. He had never known of Augusta's secret love.

"Maybe that's what I really came to say to you this morning," Augusta murmured, muffling another sniff. Her bony hand squeezed into Jake's. "Do you understand what I'm trying to tell you? I don't care what is in Cori's past or who she is to the rest of this world. None of that matters if she is the woman you love. Do you want to live out your life like me, forgoing my own happiness? Your grandfather was a good man, but we never loved each other. I wasn't allowed the chance to spend my life with the man who meant the most to me. And if you let Cori go, you'll regret it all the rest of your days."

Tears poured from Augusta's eyes like a flooding river. "In every crisis in my life, William was there for me, standing just beyond the crowd, offering silent support and compassion. And now he's gone and I . . ." A huge sob erupted from her heaving chest. "And I want to send him to his reward with the dignity and respect he deserved . . ."

"I will see to the necessary arrangements," Jacob promised her softly.

At long last he understood why Augusta had been so adamant about seeing him married to a woman he loved. He had been surprised when she scoffed at the possibility of having Jennifer become his wife. Augusta wanted Jacob to enjoy what she had been deprived of. And now she was grieving the brutal murder of the man who had loved her from a distance and had remained true to her, even if her family had given her to a man of wealth and position . . .

"And this time, I won't be standing on the perimeter of the crowd the way William did," Augusta choked out, dragging Jake from his silent reverie. "Since the day I was forced to marry, I've been rebelling against myself and everyone else. It was my way of battling my frustrated emotions, I suppose. But this time I intend to come forward and declare my affection for William and to grieve his passing openly. I want his murder investigated and I won't rest until his assailant has paid for his cruel crime!"

Watching Augusta reduced to grieving tears and vengeful vows struck a raw nerve. Jake had witnessed a similar scene before, and he was beginning to understand Cori's fierce need for justice, no matter what the cost.

Assisting Augusta to her feet, Jacob accompanied her back to her estate. He left her with the solemn promise to tend the arrangements and demand an investigation of the death of William Chandler. Jake was forced to set aside his concerns for Cori and her mysterious dealings with Layton for the time being. Seeing his grandmother so distressed about William's death spurred Jake into immediate action. William Chandler was going out in style, he swore to himself.

Wearing a grim frown, Jake swung into the saddle and headed for Natchez under the Hill. For Augusta's sake, Jake wouldn't let this murder go unsolved, no matter how long it took to find William's killer. Augusta, like Cori, couldn't rest until she had the satisfaction of knowing the guilty party had paid for taking the life of a man whose loved ones grieved his passing.

For the first time, Jake fully understood the tormenting inner drive that motivated Cori. And as soon as he took care of the business at hand, he was going to apologize to Cori for not being compassionate and sensitive to the pain she had endured since her father's death.

Jake felt like a heel for forcing Cori to make a choice between him and her crusade. He should have channeled his energy into helping her instead of discouraging her. Well, he was going to change his ways, he vowed sincerely. He would drag information out of Layton if he had to beat it out of his chubby cousin! And if Layton was at fault, as Cori believed, he would pay in full for his dastardly crime, family or no!

Chapter 25

It had not been a good day. Cori had reported for work in her disguise to be informed that the kind, generous proprietor of William's Tavern had been brutally murdered and robbed. The distressing news brought back tormenting memories of that day a year earlier when her father had been killed. So many needless killings. Such a waste of fruitful lives . . .

Cori squeezed her eyes shut and forced back the tears and agonizing thoughts. When she had left for work that morning, she had bid Jacob a silent farewell, knowing she would never see him again after she completed her crusade. And then she had arrived at the tavern to learn of William's death. The elderly, tender-hearted gentleman had never turned a customer away because he didn't have the coins to pay for his room and board, not even the homely Tilly Trahern, who needed work.

Muttering at the frustrating events that sought to depress her, Cori shrugged on her dark trousers and shirt. With her hair tucked under the unruly black wig and her beard and mustache pasted into place, Cori headed toward the door. Well, tonight at least one murder was going to be solved, she promised herself fiercely. Tonight she and Lori were going to frighten

Layton Breeze into a long-awaited confession. Jacob would have to contend with Layton's guilt, just as she had to cope with her father's senseless murder.

Quietly, Cori eased the door shut behind her and climbed up the steps that led to the street. Lori, dressed in like manner and armed to the teeth, waited with the horses she had sneaked from Dal's stables. Hell-bent on their purpose, the twins trotted off into the night, intent on frightening Layton into admitting to his guilt.

In grim silence, the twosome dismounted in the thick skirting of trees that surrounded Layton's mansion. They had expected to have to bind and gag Layton and haul him from his chamber. But to their surprise, they spied the stocky man scurrying away from the back entrance of the house in fiend-ridden haste.

Layton, unbeknownst to the twins, was high-tailing it out of town before Kyle Benson showed up to demand the blackmail money that had been impossible to raise on such short notice. Layton had planned to lay low and then sneak onto the *Belle*, which was due back in Natchez the following day.

Layton's luck, it seemed, was running out. As he scampered toward the mount he had tethered in the trees, two shapeless figures leaped from the shadows to capture him. A strangled gulp gurgled in his throat when a gloved hand thrust a pistol into his spine and another silver barrel appeared from the folds of the other assailant's cape to stab at his protruding belly.

He had assumed, quite naturally, that Kyle had hired two local thugs to retrieve him. Frantically, his gaze darted around him, expecting to see Kyle emerge from the darkness. But Kyle didn't appear.

Too frightened to speak, Layton stood frozen to the spot while one of his captors stuffed a gag in his mouth and tied his hands behind his back. After he had been ordered to mount his steed, a difficult task with his hands clasped behind him, to be sure, the twosome led him away.

Layton's mind teemed with options of escaping from disaster. He would beg for mercy, beg for more time to raise the cash. He would promise Kyle anything! Part ownership in his two steamers, the profits from the ships, whatever it took to buy Benson off . . .

A muddled frown knitted Layton's brow when his captors, employing the thickly vined avenues outside Natchez, led him toward the wharf. Below the bluff he could hear the music of tinny pianos, the roaring laughter of drunken riverboatmen, and the giggle of harlots who sought to entertain the customers in the bordellos.

Layton swallowed with a gulp when his captors dragged him from the saddle and shoved him through the tangled underbrush that led to the water's edge. There a rowboat awaited them.

Where the hell were these hooligans taking him? Midstream to be stabbed and dumped into the Mississippi, never to be seen or heard from again? The terrifying thought had Layton yelping beneath his gag. In earnest, he attempted to make his break and dash through the bushes.

Grumbling at Layton's frantic attempt to escape, Cori flipped the pistol over in her hand and clubbed Layton on the head with the butt. With a dull groan Layton pitched forward, his body draped half in, half out of the sloop.

"Lord, he's heavy," Lori muttered as she and Cori attempted to shove the limp body into the skiff.

"Two hundred pounds of flabby greed," Cori grumbled as she hooked her elbows under Layton's arms and dragged him backward. Her foot caught on the oar and she landed with a plop and a moan. Worming about, Cori tugged the hem of her cape from beneath Layton's lifeless form and pried the oar loose.

374

Cori and Lori paddled away from the shore, steering the vessel across the silvery water toward the horseshoe bend. Tucked back in what had once been the channel of this changing river was a bayou that was snarled with trees and vines and swamp. Half-hidden from view was a ghost ship that had run aground five years earlier. The steamer's captain had taken a wrong turn and the ship had been so heavily snagged in the sand and so extensively damaged that the owner had abandoned it. The ship had never been dislodged from the clutches of the river, and it made a perfect hiding place to stash their captive.

"You could have selected a better place to interrogate the lout," Lori gulped as she peered up at the vince-covered steamer in the moonlight.

Abandoned steamers along the river were common sights, but this one . . . Lori shivered apprehensively. It looked haunted as it sat half sunk and completely snagged in the tangle of vines and reeds. Tree limbs, like bony hands and fingers, hovered over the dilapidated steamer. Vines clung to the weather-beaten railings, making the boat look like a shabby cottage setting admist a jungle.

"I couldn't risk having someone recognize the illustrious Layton Breeze if we hauled him to my room, now could I?" Cori questioned in defense. "At least here we'll have some privacy."

"Us and the specters who haunts these decks," Lori muttered uneasily. "How do you suppose this ship got snagged in the first place?"

Straining against the oar, Cori steered toward the bow of the rotting ship. "According to what I learned while working at William's Tavern . . ."

Cori grimaced, remembering the tale William himself had told her when she noticed the smokestacks of the ship peeking above the clump of trees. William . . . Dear William was gone . . . Cori forced that agonizing thought to the back of her mind.

"According to reports," she began again. "The steamer's owner put an inexperienced pilot at the helm. The man had a tendency to tip the bottle. When the ship cruised upriver from New Orleans they confronted a storm. The pilot didn't recognize the warning signs of the changing channel and he veered too far west. The flooding current sent him skidding sideways into the sand. The snags ripped open the bow. Some of the passengers managed to climb into the rowboats."

"And the ones who didn't?" Lori hated to ask, but she had to know.

"Panic set in," Cori reported bleakly. "Several passengers were killed when they dived into the river in hopes of swimming to the rowboats."

"And you brought us here?" Lori croaked. "No wonder this ship looks haunted. It is!"

"You've been portraying the wraith too long," Cori taunted her sister. "You've been scaring the living daylights out of Layton. Now you're starting the see things yourself . . ."

Layton's pained moan bought quick death to their conversation. As their plump captive stirred and thrashed like a gigantic overturned beetle, Cori and Lori propped him upright in the skiff. Once they had secured the sloop, the twins strained to haul Layton onto the main deck. Propelling him along between them, they moved up the stairway, testing each rotting step before they placed weight upon it.

All the while, Layton was babbling beneath his gag, wondering what fiendish torments awaited him. To his horror, he was shoved into a chair that Lori had retrieved from the saloon. The chair had been meticulously placed backward at the top of the staircase and Layton was tied to his precarious throne. Terrified, Layton peered down at the back legs of the chair, realizing that if he wiggled and wormed he would topple down the flight of steps to his death. He was trapped, subjected to the fear of a nasty fall, certain his minutes were numbered!

Cori and Lori had been so preoccupied while they rowed across the river that they hadn't noticed the skiff that lurked in the distance. Enshrouded in the shadows of the cliff, Kyle Benson had peered down at the two figures who had spirited Layton away. Kyle had gone to the Breeze estate to collect his blackmail money, only to see the two mysterious figures apprehend Layton before Kyle could get his hands on the rotund little weasel.

Clinging to the shadows and trees, Kyle had silently followed the threesome through the vine-covered avenues to the wharf. After the darkly clad assailants had dumped Layton in the skiff, Kyle procured his own boat and followed them around the bend. When the coast was clear, he pursued them, wondering who else was holding something over Layton's head. Kyle was itching to find out! It could work to his advantage, and Kyle was a man who seized every opportunity to improve his station in life.

The instant Cori tugged the gag away, Layton swiveled his head around to stare down the steps again. He was stung by the grim realization that if he rocked the rickety chair he was as good as dead.

"What do you want with me?" Layton chirped. "I tried . . . to gather . . . the money . . ."

When Cori pulled the wide-brimmed hat and beard away, Layton gasped in stunned disbelief. "What the devil are you . . . ?"

Before he could grapple with that shocking realization, Lori removed her disguise. Layton very nearly swallowed

377

his tongue. He was seeing double; he swore the blow to his head had impaired his vision. Two identical faces peered mutinously down at him. Layton's complexion turned a ghastly shade of white.

"You!" Layton yelped when he finally gained control of his vocal apparatus. It suddenly dawned on him that he had confronted the thieves who had plagued the *Belle*. The dark garments matched the descriptions he had been given by the victims. The witnesses had never been able to agree on the size of the bandits, only their garb. Layton surmised these two female thieves had employed padding and stack-heeled boots to make themselves appear tall, thin, heavy and short, thereby confusing the descriptions offered by their victims.

And all the while these two entertainers were aboard the *Belle*, they had been targeting wealthy gentleman to assault. While the enchanting Cori Pierce sang and danced in the saloon, her look-alike was preying on passengers.

"I don't have your money. It . . ." Layton choked out, certain these female bandits had kidnapped him in an effort to regain possession of the stolen cash he had swiped from the supply room.

Cori cocked the trigger of her pistol and glared murderously at Layton. "We don't want the money. We want to know exactly what happened to Michael Shelton the night you forced him to sign the bill of sale that granted you legal right to the *Belle*."

"You . . ." Layton's vocabulary had become quite limited all of a sudden. Between the gasping *yous* and the open-ended declarations, he wasn't making a whole lot of sense. Cori intended to remedy that. Layton would sing like a bird to save his stubby little neck.

"Michael Shelton was our father," Cori announced in a bitter hiss. "We know perfectly well that he had no desire to sell the *Belle*, even though you hired riffraff to undermine his profits by warning would-be passengers away."

Layton didn't deny it. He merely cursed under his breath.

"You forged our father's signature to that document and then you killed him and dumped his body in the alley behind his office, didn't you?" Lori gritted out through clenched teeth. When Layton refused to answer, Lori cocked the trigger of her pistol and aimed it at his heaving chest. "Didn't you?"

Layton gasped at both silver-barreled pistols and the murderous faces behind them. "Yes, I forged his name," he croaked in confession. "But I didn't kill him. I gave him the cash and sent him on his way!"

"Liar!" Cori growled as she stepped forward to press her booted foot against the leg of the chair. One quick kick against the leg of the chair that set on the stair and Layton would plunge to his death. He knew that as well as she did.

"I swear to God I didn't!" Layton blared frantically. He could feel the chair scooting backward. Another half inch and the back legs would drop off the edge of the step, sending him tumbling pell-mell.

"No more lies, Layton," Lori sneered, looming over him in her flowing black cape.

"Michael refused to sign," Layton gulped. "And I did forge his name, but I paid him thirty thousand dollars for the *Belle*. He left the ship and I never saw him again. He knew he'd been beaten by his competition. He couldn't show profit because the passengers thought the *Belle* was a death trap. He took the money I offered and admitted defeat, even if he did refuse to sign the document. It was only a display of defiance on his part."

Cori couldn't bear another lie. With a growl she slapped his pudgy face as she'd wanted to do so often on the steamer when Layton tried to coax her into his cabin to grant him sexual favors.

"The truth, Layton," Cori spat at him. "Only the truth is going to save you from a disastrous fall."

"I swear it!" Layton hooted in panic, watching Cori kick at the leg of his chair. "I threatened Michael's life if he dared to bring charges against me. But I didn't have to follow through with the threat. I told you, Michael knew he'd been beaten. I had no need to ensure his silence after he wound up dead. And I had nothing to do with that!"

Lori peered indecisively at Cori. For a year they had believed, beyond the shadow of a doubt, that Layton had killed their father. Could it be true that Michael Shelton had fallen victim to a robbery after he departed from his late-night confrontation with Layton?

Limply, Cori's arm dropped by her side. Her tormented gaze locked with Lori's, wondering if Jacob had been right about his cousin all along, that she had been too vindictive to be logical.

"Now what are we going to do?" Lori muttered in question.

"We'll fetch the constable," Cori declared. "Layton is going to confess his unscrupulous dealings to the proper authorities. He is still guilty of forcing Papa to sell and forging the document. He paid hoodlums to undermine his competition. For that, at least, he is going to serve his sentence."

"And what if he denies it when the constable confronts him? The Breezes are a powerful family in Natchez, you know," Lori argued.

"We witnessed his confession. That should count for something," Cori countered, glaring at Layton. "And he certainly can't accuse us of thievery when he was the one who stole the money from the *Belle* and kept it for himself. It's our word against his. And we haven't come this far, haven't gone to such extremes, just to let Layton slither off like the devious snake he is."

"What are you going to do with me?" Layton demanded when the twins put their heads together to quickly discuss their plans. "You can't leave me here like this!"

Cori pivoted, smiling wickedly into his pasty face. "Ah, but we can, Layton," she taunted. "If you worm and squirm to free yourself while we're gone, you'll plummet down the steps. This way we'll be assured that you will be here when we return. And we will return. On that you can depend . . ."

A muted curse sprang from Jake's lips as he waited impatiently for Cori to answer the knock on her door. Where the hell was that woman?

Jacob had spent most of the day, interrogatng everyone on Silver Street about William Chandler's mysterious death. Unfortunately, the code of the streets Under the Hill was never to meddle in business that wasn't of personal concern. Those whom Jacob had quizzed expressed their grief in losing William. However, asking and answering questions Under the Hill was considered dangerous folly. The inhabitants of the unseemly village on the wharf were wary of winding up in the same condition William had. Nobody volunteered information to aid Jacob. That frustrated him to no end. His last hope was Cori.

Muttering, Jake retrieved a key from his pocket, the one he had employed to gain entrance the previous night. After the door swung open, Jake scanned the abandoned room. A quick search assured Jake that wherever Cori was, she was spiriting around in her breeches and cape.

"Hell's fire," Jake scowled, walking back out of the room.

The fragments of an unsettling vision hounded Jake as he took the steps two at a time to retrieve his steed. As

381

grim as that particular scene was, he kept seeing flashbacks of William Chandler's body lying in state in the parlor of his house. Another far-distant memory nagged Jake as he trotted toward Dal's plantation in hopes of dragging information from Lori about Cori's whereabouts.

The bloody gash that marred William's face kept flashing in Jake's mind like a warning signal. Somewhere, in the forgotten corners of his brain, another similar scene tugged at his thoughts. It wasn't so much that he remembered seeing that gash on someone's cheek. It was more like he remembered thinking . . .

"Thunderation." Jake flung away the infuriating puzzle that taunted him. He was anxious to confront Cori and to ensure she was safe when intuition kept whispering that she wasn't.

But even as Jake thundered toward the Blaylock plantation, the vision of William Chandler's face kept leaping up at him, assuring him that he had the piece of a puzzle in his fingertips but that he couldn't quite put it in its proper place.

After a frantic ride, Jake leaped from his steed in a single bound. In long swift strides, he hurried up the walkway and pounded on Dal's door. In less than a minute, the butler appeared to greet Jake with a welcoming smile.

"Where's Dal?" Jake questioned, dispensing with formalities.

"He and Mr. Castleberry are in the parlor, engrossed in a game of piquet." The butler frowned at the grim expression on Jake's face. "Is something amiss?"

"Plenty, I fear," Jake mumbled before sailing toward the parlor.

The footsteps that heralded Jake's approach caused Dal to glance from his hand of cards. "Pull up a chair, Jake," he invited. "Join us. Maybe you can halt Adam's winning streak. He's bleeding my purse dry."

"Where is your fiancée?" Jake blurted out of the blue.

"In her room."

Dal frowned. Lori had damned well better be in her room, he thought. That was where she said she was going. Dal gulped apprehensively, realizing Lori had declared she was *going* upstairs but she had said nothing about *staying* there. In her case, a man was a fool to presume too much.

"Damn . . ." Dal scowled, leaping to his feet.

To Adam Castleberry's amazement, Dal tossed his cards aside and took off like a shot. "What's happened?"

"That's what I'd like to know," Dal muttered as he followed in Jake's wake.

"If she's not here and Cori isn't where she's supposed to be . . ." Jacob left the remark dangling in the air as he opened the door to Lori's room. "Hell's fire . . ."

"Who's *she?*" Adam questioned, confused. "I thought *she* and *Cori* were one and the same . . ."

"So does everybody else," Jake muttered.

When Jacob started yanking open the chest of drawers and flinging unmentionables hither and yon, Adam gaped at him. And when Dal joined Jake in his frantic search, Adam threw up his arms in frustration.

"What the sweet loving hell are you two doing? You have no right to rifle through the young lady's belongings!"

"Damn it all," Jake growled when he found no trace of Lori's black cape, breeches, and shirt. If Cori and Lori were both garbed like thieves and neither of them could be found, that spelled serious trouble.

A muted scowl tumbled from Dal's lips. "I should have known something was coming," he mused aloud. "She had been fidgeting and stealing glances at the clock all evening . . . Good Lord, you don't think they . . ."

"What the blazes is going on and who the devil is

they?" Adam erupted in exasperation.

Without responding, Jake whizzed out the door and practically ran down the hall.

"If Lori . . . I mean Cori . . . comes back while we're gone, tie her down," Dal demanded hurriedly.

Adam blinked like a disturbed owl. "Do what? *Lori who?*" he peeped.

"You heard me, Adam," Dal threw over his shoulder, anxious to keep step with Jake. "Don't let her leave again, not under any circumstances. Hold her at gunpoint if you must, but don't let that woman out of this house!"

And then Dal was gone, leaving Adam staring after both men in astounded disbelief. Grumbling at their mysteriousness, Adam clomped downstairs to pour himself a much-needed drink. He had always considered Dal and Jacob to be sensible men and courteous sporting rivals at the race track. But tonight they were both behaving peculiarly. The pert brunette's unexplainable disappearance and the frantic search of her room had Adam miffed. He had planned to catch a steamer to New Orleans the following morning. But Adam vowed then and there that he wasn't leaving Natchez until Dal and Jacob explained this strange incident to his satisfaction. Something was going on, and his friends were excluding him!

"Hold her at gunpoint?" Adam mimicked sarcastically. "What kind of crazy talk is that?"

While Lori and Cori were circling the deck of the half-sunken steamer in the bayou to return to their skiff, Kyle Benson was slinking out of his hiding place on the hurricane deck. He had secured his sloop at the opposite end of the steamer, climbed the paddlewheel and eavesdropped on the startling conversation that was in progress.

Kyle had very nearly swallowed his teeth when he realized there were two Cori Pierce Sheltons lurking about and that they were responsible for the banditry aboard the *Belle*. In mute amazement, Kyle had listened to the twins voice their threats before leaving Layton tied to the chair that set precariously at the top of the stairs.

Emerging from the room of a nearby cabin, Kyle approached Layton who was afraid to squirm for fear of plunging to his death.

"Lord, am I glad to see you," Layton breathed in relief.

A sinister smile curled Kyle's lips. "Really? I don't know why you should be. I was very chagrined to hear you were unable to gather the money."

"I'll find a way to get the cash if you'll only untie me," Layton babbled as he stared over his shoulder at the flight of steps. "We've got to stop those troublemakers before they summon the sheriff. My life and my reputation are at stake."

Kyle swaggered forward, but he made no move to loose the ropes that held Layton fast. "I'm not sure I can trust you to gather the money I requested."

"I will, just as soon as we dispose of those two termagants," Layton promised. "Untie me, damn you. They'll be long gone before we can catch them."

"*We?*" Sardonic laughter bubbled in Kyle's throat. "I will handle those cunning twins," he corrected. "You have outlived your usefulness to me."

His voice echoed around the deck of the ghost ship like the death knoll. Stark terror filled Layton's eyes when he realized Kyle's intentions. "No!"

With a vicious growl, Kyle backhanded Layton. The fierce blow caused Layton's head to snap back against the chair. The chair reared up on its hind legs and then toppled downward, end over end. Layton's head crashed against the steps and a bloodcurdling scream gurgled in his throat. The clatter of the chair, which held Layton's mangled body, crashed to the bottom of the staircase.

And then there was silence.

A devious smile hovered on Kyle's lips as he ambled down the stairs, past the limp body of Layton Breeze . . .

"Did you hear something?" Cori murmured, glancing back in the direction they'd come. Both women dragged the oars from the water and listened to the muffled sounds that wafted their way toward them.

"Most likely it's Layton calling us back," Lori speculated as she plopped her oar back in the river and strained against it.

"We may never find out who really killed Papa," Cori mused aloud, rowing methodically toward shore. "But I'm going back to St. Louis to open an investigation. I'm still not certain whether we should believe Layton."

Lori was pensively silent. Her desire to finally wed Dal and call an end to the search for their father's murder warred with the obligation to accompany Cori. Lori had been disappointed when Layton hadn't openly confessed to murder. Either the man was an exceptionally accomplished liar or he was telling the truth. Lori honestly believed Layton wasn't involved in murder, only in the destruction of Michael's dream to own the finest steamer on the Mississippi.

"Like Natchez, St. Louis is also plagued with one too many unsolved murders," Lori murmured defeatedly. "The wharf too easily lends itself to victims and thieves who come and go without a trace. I'm not sure we'll ever learn the truth."

"I've got to try," Cori choked out. "When Layton is taken into custody, Jacob and his grandmother will be

386

humiliated by the scandal. I will be a painful reminder to Jacob. You can marry Dal, but I have to walk out of Jake's life. It's best for both of us."

Lori fell silent again, understanding the frustration with which Cori was forced to cope. Cori had gone undercover and she had broken her engagement with Jacob so that Lori could find happiness. Lori had teased Cori about marrying Jacob for her own private revenge of sorts, but the fact was Cori had fallen hopelessly in love with that brawny giant.

And Cori was right, just as she had been in the beginning of this stormy affair with Jacob. Her feelings for that raven-haired rake had brought her own private brand of torment. Cori was the reason Layton would be rotting in jail, and Jacob could never forget that his cousin had been publicly humiliated and sentenced because of her relentless search for the truth.

"Skully will arrive tomorrow," Cori murmured as she stared at the lights on the wharf. "He'll help me with the investigation in St. Louis. But you will have to step forward to tell what you know about Layton. And when he swears there are two of us, I intend for there to be only one of us around. Let the constable think Layton's crimes have snapped his mind."

Lori nodded in compliance.

In grim silence, they rowed back to the tangled brush where they had left their horses. After securing the skiff, they mounted their steeds to return to King's Tavern to change into respectable attire. They had no intention of summoning the constable while they were garbed in black. It was Lori who volunteered to summon the authorities while Cori followed at a safe distance behind her.

Knowing they had failed to solve the mystery of Michael's death, the twins slipped into the inn to change their clothes. Somewhere on the continent was a murderer who had yet to answer for his despicable crimes. Cori refused to halt her search for answers. Her crusade was all she had left. She had forsaken Jacob's love to bring her father's memory eternal peace. If she didn't concentrate on her noble purpose she would drive herself mad. Already she was missing those laughing green eyes and that rakish smile on the face of the man who would steal softly into her dreams every night of her life . . .

Chapter 26

A frustrated growl erupted from Jake's lips after his conversation with Sylvia Breeze. Sylvia didn't have the faintest idea where Layton was. He had said nothing to his wife before he disappeared out the back door. Sylvia hadn't even known Layton was gone until Jake arrived, requesting to speak with him. A quick search of the house turned up the same thing Jake's other searches had revealed this evening—nothing. That spelled even more trouble!

Jake was so exasperated he wanted to yank his hair out by the roots. Dal was faring no better. He was swearing a blue streak.

"I told Lori to stop this dangerous game." Dal grumbled. "But would she listen to me? Hell no, she just kept right on doing whatever it was she's been doing behind my back!"

"You may as well have lectured a brick wall," Jake grunted disdainfully. "I tried the same tactic, but to no avail. Those daredevil she-males refuse to listen to reason and they'll probably pay dearly for whatever they've done to Layton this time."

"Where the devil do you suppose they took him?" Dal questioned the darkness at large.

"Only God knows," Jake sighed as he reined his steed toward the lights of Natchez. "And I doubt the Lord is all that crazy about their latest escapade either. Curse those little fools! I swear they are not only sharing the same face and figure, but also the same brain. Their intelligence is only half what it should be."

"I second that," Dal chimed in. "The Shelton twins have appointed themselves private investigators without legal license. Their hearts may be in the right place, but when they dare to take the law into their own hands, they're asking for trouble. I'm afraid they're going to learn that what goes around comes around like a confounded boomerang! They could both wind up. . . ."

"Keep your bleak thoughts to yourself," Jake interrupted. "I prefer not to hear you voice what I'm already thinking."

Dal gulped hard when he realized he had only depressed himself with his grim predictions. He could smell trouble brewing. So could Jacob. It was in the wind. . . .

While Cori and Lori were rowing back in the direction they'd come, Kyle Benson circled the bayou and returned to the east shore, letting the flow of the river aid in his progress. Although he had been a few minutes behind the twins, his knowledge of the river and the surrounding area allowed him to come ashore shortly after Cori and Lori arrived. Trailing them at an inconspicuous distance, Kyle followed the twins to King's Tavern and lurked outside, waiting for them to reappear.

Just as he anticipated, Cori and Lori blundered outside, caught totally unaware.

"Good evening, ladies." Kyle's low voice shook with goading laughter as he grabbed the nearest twin and stuffed his pistol into her neck.

Wasn't Cori the lucky one? She wound up chained in Kyle's arms with a pistol barrel gouging her in the throat.

Lori's knees very nearly folded up like an accordion when she recognized the sinister smile and gruff voice that belonged to Kyle Benson.

"As if it wasn't enough that you deceitful little bitches robbed the passengers on the *Belle*, you have added another crime to your extensive list," Kyle growled in mocking disdain. "I followed you when you took Layton Breeze captive."

Cori and Lori gulped simultaneously.

"I even rowed out to that abandoned steamer to discover what evil designs you had on Layton this time."

In unison, Cori and Lori swallowed hard.

"Imagine my horror when I crept across the decks and heard the clatter on the steps of that abandoned ship. Now you have murdered Layton and you'll answer for his death," Kyle sneered at them.

Two pair of brown eyes registered shock. Neither Cori nor Lori had expected Layton to strain against the ropes and topple from his precarious perch at the top of the steps. They had only left him there to ensure he stayed put until they returned with the constable. Thunderation!

A satanic smile hovered on Kyle's lips. These little spitfires were convinced they were responsible for Layton's death, just as he hoped they would be. They would never know that Kyle had caused Layton to plunge to his doom. And that was definitely to Kyle's advantage. In fact, the thought had struck him the instant he spied Layton tied to the chair at the top of the stairs. Things were working out splendidly, so splendidly in fact that he almost snickered in wicked glee when the twins gaped at him in horror.

"For a price, I will hold my tongue and allow Layton's

death to become another of Natchez's unexplained mysteries."

Cori's mind was whirling like a runaway top. Maybe the rest of the world wouldn't be able to puzzle out who had killed Layton, but Jacob and Dal would know. Jacob would never forgive her for that! She hadn't been correct in all her assumptions about Layton's involvement in Michael's death. Jacob had tried to tell her so, but she wouldn't listen, fool that she was. Jake had told her a dozen times not to hound Layton, that he would handle his cousin. Hadn't he told her she'd get herself neck-deep in hot water?

"Let my sister go and we'll find a way to . . ." Lori bartered, only to be cut off by Kyle's derisive snort.

"You'll do exactly what I tell you, bitch, or your sister will be floating down river on her way to the Gulf!"

Lori shrank away from the gloomy threat and the bone-chilling voice that conveyed it. Cori, however, could only swallow with a constricted gulp.

"You go find Jacob Wolf and tell him I'll need one hundred thousand dollars to forget what I know about the two of you. I'll give him until dark tomorrow to bring the cash to the wharf. The *Belle* will be sailing upriver tomorrow night and I intend to be on it, cruising off to a new life, far away from Natchez."

His grip on Cori tightened around her throat to emphasize the gravity of his threat. "And if I'm not allowed the cash and free passage on the *Belle*, you will no longer have a look-alike running around on this planet. You won't see each other again until you're both roasting in hell for your crimes!"

Lori struggled to breath while her palpitating heart threatened to leap from her chest. She and Cori had clashed numerous times with Kyle on board the *Belle*. Lori hated to venture a guess as to how Kyle would while away the hours until the ransom money was delivered . . . *if* it was delivered . . . Lord, Lori didn't know if Jake had that kind of money lying around. He was wealthy, it was true. But one hundred thousand dollars? Sweet mercy, even Dal and Jake put together might not be able to raise such a huge sum of money on such short notice!

"Get moving," Kyle snarled at Lori. "You had damned well better be on the dock tomorrow night with the cash."

"How will I find you?" Lori squeaked, casting apprehensive glances at her sister who was being dragged into the clump of trees that skirted King's Tavern.

"*I'll* find *you*, bitch," Kyle hissed from the shadows. "And if you have the money, I'll tell you where you can find your sister. And if not . . ." He let his threat hang in the muggy air, allowing Lori to form her own gloomy conclusions.

On a choked sob, Lori dashed up the steps and flew toward her steed. So frantic was she that she couldn't stuff her foot in the stirrup. With a muffled curse, Lori clasped the stirrup with her trembling hands and tried again. Once astride her mount, she galloped off in haste. Her sister's life hung in the balance and Lori rode hell-for-leather, thundering down St. Catherine's Street toward Wolfhaven, refusing to let her steed slow his swift pace even when he showed signs of laboring under the strenuous demands made on him.

"Hell's fire," Jake muttered after searching the wharf twice. He could find neither hide nor hair of Cori, Lori, or Layton. He had seen his grandmother in the crowd of mourners who had come to pay their respects to the old man Under the Hill. Augusta sat beside the coffin, enshrouded in her black gown and veil, keeping vigil while the string of mourners filed in and out of the dimly lit tavern. But there was no sign of the threesome who had mysteriously disappeared.

"Now what?" Dal sighed dispiritedly. "We've searched high and lo. I think we should return to my plantation and wait until Lori shows up."

"Let's try King's Tavern again," Jake suggested. "Maybe Cori finally returned to her room."

It was a long shot, to be sure, but Jake was desperate. Troubled thoughts hounded him all the way up Silver Street. He was worried sick about Cori and her ongoing feud with Layton. And to compound his frustrations, he kept thinking there was something he should have remembered when he peered down into William Chandler's pallid features. Something was wrong. Something from the past was linked to the present, but he couldn't quite put his finger on what it was . . .

Jake cast his tangled thoughts aside and dismounted. Swiftly he took the steps and burst into Cori's room. A roar of frustration exploded from his lips when he spied two sets of capes, shirts, and breeches lying recklessly across the bed. Those two witches had changed forms again and he had missed them coming and going!

Hell's fire and damnation, was that a good or bad omen? He hoped it meant that whatever shenanigan they'd pulled with Layton was over and done and they had whizzed home. Surely Lori, at least, was on her way back to Dal's plantation. She had to know Dal would check on her before he retired for the night after playing piquet with Adam Castleberry.

"Now can we go back to my plantation?" Dal questioned as he watched Jake hurl the dark garments against the wall and swear fluently.

Without responding, Jake spun on his heels and stalked out, cursing Cori every step of the way. He was going to strangle that minx when he got his hands on her.

Jake expelled another round of unprintable curses. Cori had led him on a merry chase. He was so concerned about her that he could barely think straight. Sometimes he wondered if she was worth all the torment she put him through.

And he thought he had craved adventure all his life. Ha! Battling the treacherous Missouri was mere child's play compared to the frustrating romp Cori Pierce Shelton had led him on since the day he met her. That dark-eyed daredevil was adventure personified. Nothing slowed that hellion down. Nothing deterred her from her purpose. She was a female cyclone if ever there was one, and even Augusta Breeze was a small-sized whirlwind in comparison!

As if she were pursued by the hounds of Hell, Lori had thundered toward Wolfhaven. There she was given the distressing news that the master of the house had left several hours earlier, destination unknown. Wheeling her steed around, Lori had hightailed it to Augusta's estate, only to find that neither Augusta nor Jake were to be found. Riding like a bat out of hell, Lori had raced back to Dal's plantation. Frantic, she bounded from the saddle and flew up the steps.

Adam Castleberry vaulted to his feet the instant he heard the front door bang against the wall. He veered around the corner, only to have Lori fire a question at him instead of the other way around.

"Where's Dal?" she demanded breathlessly.

"He's out looking for you," Adam informed her, surveying the wild tangle of sable hair and the pinched expression that claimed her bewitching features.

When Lori pivoted to dart out the door, Adam latched onto her arm and towed her backward. "Dal and Jake told me to keep you here if you got back before they did."

Frantic, Lori wormed for freedom. "I have to go! It's a matter of life and death!"

"I have orders to ensure you stay put," Adam insisted. "And while we're waiting Dal and Jake's return, you can tell me what the devil is going . . . Argh! Come back here!" he bellowed when Lori kicked him in the shin and shot toward the door.

Although Adam was very much the gentleman, he was forced to utilize drastic extremes to ensure the rambunctious brunette stayed put. Discarding propriety, Adam tackled Lori, knocking her to the floor with a thud. To his disbelief, the wildcat came up fighting.

Adam had scoffed when Dal suggested tying this female down or holding her at gunpoint. But it seemed Dal knew his fiancée quite well. It would indeed require a pistol and rope to make this minx stay put!

Muttering in frustration, Adam clamped his arm around the struggling misfit and literally dragged her into the parlor. Desperate and breathing heavily from the tussle, he snatched the tassled cords off the drapes and bound her wrists behind her. While Lori protested loudly, he shoved her into a chair and tied her up with the drapes like a mummy. If this firebrand had any thoughts of leaving, she was damned well going to take the chair and drapes with her!

"Adam, you're making a horrible mistake," Lori wailed. "I've got to get help and I . . ."

"You *need* help," Adam declared with great conviction. "Your mind has snapped. Lord, woman, you're nothing like I thought you were!"

When Lori erupted like a geyser, Adam crammed his handkerchief in her mouth to shut her up. He was appalled at himself for having to treat this lovely lady so abominably, but she had refused to cooperate.

Once Adam had done as he had been instructed, he scurried into the study to pour himself a stiff drink. He had come to Natchez to race his prize steeds and renew his acquaintances with Dal and Jake. He had wound up binding and gagging Dal's fiancée while his friends darted off on their mysterious mission.

Adam shook his head in dismay and sloshed another drink in his glass. Dal had declared life was never dull in Natchez, but this . . . ? This was ridiculous!

While Adam was begging for divine forgiveness for treating a lady so shamelessly, Lori was thinking frantically. She kept envisioning Kyle Benson doing unspeakable things to Cori, things he could have been doing to Lori if luck hadn't been on her side. Lori shivered in revulsion, wondering if there was even a remote possibility that Cori could escape from imminent disaster. Lori didn't think so, and that bloodcurdling thought had her suffering all the torments of the damned.

"Hold still, damn you," Kyle hissed as he attempted to haul Cori from the saddle of her steed. Although he had tied her to her horse, Cori kicked and bit and squirmed when he tried to put her to the ground.

And fight Cori most certainly did, with every ounce of strength she could muster. She knew exactly what Kyle would do to her the first chance he got, the same thing he'd wanted to do to her every time he laid his hands on her. Cori vowed she'd die before she let this ogre touch her intimately!

With a bust of fury, Cori kicked Kyle in the groin and sprinted away as he doubled over. Frantic to escape, she plunged through the underbrush that cloaked the bluff that rose from behind the dilapidated shacks of Natchez under the Hill. Behind her, she could hear Kyle's sizzling curses and his scuffling in the jungle of weeds and vines that choked the steep incline.

Breathlessly, Cori clawed her way up the slope, praying she could remain a step ahead of the growling beast behind her. Kyle was furious, she knew. She could tell by the vicious snarls and wild thrashing behind her.

When his hand clamped around her ankle, Cori grabbed an overhanging branch and kicked like a bucking bronco. Her heel caught Kyle in the chin, forcing another murderous growl from his curled lips. With her heart thumping, Cori scrambled up the hill, cursing the hindering gown that impeded her progress.

Again, Kyle grabbed at her, clutching the hem of her gown in his fist, and again Cori anchored herself to a tree limb and hauled herself upward. The rending of cloth was followed by Kyle's explosive curse. Cori didn't spare the time to glance over her shoulder when she heard Kyle topple backward into the bushes, clinging to the torn portion of her skirt.

Swearing vehemently, Kyle hurled the fabric away and scraped himself off the ground. He lunged up the steep slope in hot pursuit, vowing not to let this minx elude him.

Cori breathed a hasty sigh of relief as she dragged herself onto the precipice and coiled her legs beneath her. Hiking up the front of her gown, she bolted through the underbrush, feeling the cuts stinging her cheeks in the cool evening breeze.

Before she had sprinted twenty yards, Kyle hurled himself at her. His arms locked around her knees, flinging her forward into the grass. Cori managed to brace her arms before her face smashed into the ground, but she couldn't leap to her feet before Kyle fell upon her.

Cori muttered curses into the grass when her assailant jabbed her with his knees and elbows in attempt to restrain her. Fight as she might, she couldn't hurl Kyle's heavy body sideways and worm away. A shriek burst from her lips when Kyle clutched her shoulder and shoved her back to the ground, forcing her peer up into his malicious snarl.

"You little bitch," he huffed and puffed. "Before I'm through with you, I'll hear you beg for mercy!"

Like hell he would! Cori vowed to defy this ruthless bastard to the death, just see if she didn't! When his scowling face dipped toward hers, intent on plundering her lips. Cori spat at him like an angry cat.

"Damn you!" Kyle sneered, instinctively lifting his arm to backhand her.

Cori jerked her right arm loose in the nick of time to ward off the blow to her face. Kyle's oversized ring sliced her arm, causing her to yelp in pain. When he tried to grasp her hand, Cori raised her knee, jabbing him in the spine and knocking him off balance. As Kyle toppled forward Cori uplifted her free hand, catching him in the jaw. Quick as a striking snake, she clutched at one of the pistols he had tucked in his belt and suddenly the battle for control of the weapon was on.

The silver barrel gleamed in the moonlight as it swerved one way and then another, pointing first at Kyle and then at Cori. While they wrestled for possession of the weapon, Cori raised her knee again, knocking Kyle sideways. With every ounce of energy she had Cori clutched the weapon and squeezed the trigger before Kyle could knock it away.

The barking pistol echoed in the night, resounding above the groans and growls of the two bodies that were entangled on the ground. Kyle howled like a wounded coyote as a searing pain shot down his right arm. Furiously, he struck out with his left arm, landing a solid blow to Cori's cheek. Like a wilted flower, Cori collapsed in the grass and the pistol dropped from her fingertips.

Muttering a string of profanity, Kyle sank back on his haunches and clutched at the bloody wound on his right shoulder. After he caught his breath, he ripped the fabric from Cori's petticoat to make an improvised tourniquet for his arm.

Once Kyle had tended his wound, he scooped Cori's limp body over his good shoulder and sidestepped through the tangled vines to retrieve his horse. Leaving her steed where it stood, Kyle flung her body over the saddle and swung up behind her. His first order of business was to find a place to tie this troublesome bitch and then seek out a physician to tend his injury.

Kyle felt nauseated and weak. The shot at such close range left powder burns, jagged edges of skin, and agonizing pulsations up and down his arm. Gasping for breath, Kyle headed toward the back of William's Tavern, where he'd rented a room. Employing the outside stairway, Kyle trudged up the steps with Cori draped over his shoulder. Wobbling unsteadily, he leaned a hip against the wall and fumbled for his key. Finally he staggered into his room and dumped his lifeless baggage on the bed.

Damn, how he hungered to plunder this feisty wench's body, to punish her for denying him the enjoyment of her feminine charms all these months. But the throbbing pain in his shoulder prevented him from raping this bitch here and now.

Scowling at the difficulty he'd encountered with Cori, Kyle tugged at the sheet and employed it as a rope. When he had bound Cori's ankles and wrists to the bed posts, he stumbled back out the door. He had to reach a physician and quickly. He was growing dizzier and more nauseated by the second. If he passed out he knew he'd lose so much blood that he'd never wake up.

With tremendous effort, Kyle dragged himself back into the saddle and nudged his steed up Silver Street to locate a doctor. And with each pulsating throb of his arm, he soundly cursed the vixen who'd shot him.

She'd pay dearly for this, Kyle promised himself

stormily. He had never intended for that she-cat to survive this ordeal in the first place, but now he would make doubly certain her last few hours of life were like hell itself. When he mustered the energy he would humiliate by subjecting her to his sexual demands, over and over until she was sobbing and pleading with him to kill her.

A sinister smile hovered on Kyle's ashen lips as he rode up the hill to Natchez. He could endure this pain in his arm, knowing he would soon teach that feisty bitch the meaning of mortification and humble submission! And he was going to relish every moment of it!

Chapter 27

Weary to the bone, Jake stepped from the stirrup and trudged up the steps beside Dal. Before they reached the stoop, Adam flung open the door.

"Thank God you're back! I'll never forgive either of you for what you made me do to her!" he raved at them.

His emphasis on *her* sent Dal and Jake clattering through the vestibule. Both men came to a halt when they spied Lori; there she sat, tied to her chair in the parlor drapes.

"That was the only way I could restrain her from leaving," Adam hurriedly defended. "And I had to tackle her before she dashed back out the door! Won't somebody around here tell me what's going on?"

Nobody bothered to explain. Jake tugged the gag away and glowered into the flushed face and desperate eyes. "Are you Lori?"

She nodded affirmatively.

"Where's your sister?"

"Lori?" Adam croaked, peering bemusedly at the curvaceous brunette. "Her sister? Good Lord, don't tell me there's two of them!"

Nobody told him anything again and that frustrated Adam to no end.

The exasperation and fear that had been bottled up behind Lori's gag came flooding out in a rush. "We kidnapped Layton and we . . ." Tears boiled down her cheeks. "And we accidentally killed him."

When all three men gasped, Lori plowed on, determined to give an explanation. "We left him in a chair on the stair on the boat that's half afloat in the bayou. He fell . . ." Another flood of tears streamed down her face. "Then Kyle Benson leaped at us out of nowhere and grabbed hold of Cori . . ."

"So there are *two* of them," Adam muttered. "And I suppose there really wasn't a Corbin Pierce either. Why didn't you tell me what was going on?"

Dal waved Adam to silence, waiting for Lori to continue her grim tale.

"Kyle said he knew we'd killed Layton, knew about the robberies on the *Belle* . . ." Lori sucked in a shuddering breath. "He said if Jacob didn't raise one hundred thousand dollars and bring it to the wharf tomorrow night that he'd kill Cori."

Jacob looked as if someone had punched him in the midsection. It wasn't the thought of gathering that kind of money overnight that worried Jake. Since he hadn't given Layton the winnings from the track he had a hefty amount of cash in hand to add to what he already had tucked in his safe. What tormented him was knowing what Kyle would do to that spitfire while he was biding his time.

Hell's fire! Hadn't he told that daring she-cat that she'd get herself into serious trouble? Hadn't he warned her to leave Layton alone? Had she listened? Hell no.

Lori's shoulders shook as the tears tumbled from her dark eyes. The instant Dal freed her hands, they flew to her face, catching the flood of sobs. "I can't bear the thought of what Kyle will do to her," Lori wailed hysterically. "If we don't find her before tomorrow night it will be too late . . . if it isn't already . . ."

Jake grabbed Lori by the shoulders and lifted her out of her chair, giving her a fierce shake. "Did Benson give you any clue as to where he might be staying?"

"Layton might have known the answer to that but now he's dead . . ." Lori muttered with a muffled sniff.

"Are you sure?" Jake prodded.

Lori gulped over her sobs. "Kyle followed us to the old steamer in the bayou. He said Layton was dead when he arrived."

Jake released Lori so quickly that Dal had to catch her before she collapsed. Like a shot, Jake whizzed across the room and into the foyer.

"Where are you going?" Dal called after him.

"To see if Layton might still be alive. Maybe Kyle was only bluffing them into believing his story," Jake threw over his shoulder.

Clutching Lori's arm, Dal tugged her along at his swift pace. Not to be left behind, Adam scampered behind them, curiosity eating him alive.

As if hounded by demons, Jake thundered down the lane, taking a shortcut through the steep-sided trails that cut through the hillside. Yanking his steed to a halt, he bounded to the dock, glancing in all directions at once.

"We left our skiff over there," Lori announced, gesturing toward the clump of vine-choked trees.

Jake dashed off in the direction she had indicated and plunked down in the sloop. Manning the oars, Dal and Jake rowed across the river while Adam wrapped a comforting arm around Lori.

"Now will somebody tell me what the sweet loving hell is going on?" Adam pleaded.

"I'm not sure you want to know," Jake grumbled sourly.

"I most certainly do!" Adam insisted.

"Tell him," Dal demanded of Lori.

"I'd rather not," she muttered.

"Tell him!" Jake scowled.

Frantically, Lori attempted to organize her thoughts. She didn't see why it was so all-fired important that Adam Castleberry of New Orleans knew the whole sordid story. He'd probably blab it all over Natchez and New Orleans and make matters worse than they already were.

When Lori hesitated, Adam heaved an impatient sigh. "Although my hobby is horses, my business is law, young lady. And from the sound of things, you're going to need an attorney before you're through. Now do you wish to be represented by a reputable lawyer or a ne'er-do-well who can do nothing but come to sympathize with you while you're rotting in jail?"

Phrased as such, Lori felt she had no alternative but to blurt out the entire episode that had begun the previous year. Although Adam gasped and muttered at irregular intervals, Lori was determined to present an uninterrupted narrative while they rowed toward the ghost ship.

Once Jake had secured the skiff, he scurried along the slanted deck to find Layton's body tied to the chair at the bottom of the stairs. Instantly, his fingertips glided around Layton's neck, searching for a pulse. There was none.

"Damn," he growled as he unfolded himself and stood over the broken remains of his cousin. "It's too late . . ."

His voice trailed off when the shaft of moonlight that sprayed across the deck illuminated the right side of Layton's face. The slash on his chalky cheek caused a fleeting thought to dart across his Jake's mind.

Frowning, Jake squatted down to tilt Layton's face sideways. Pensively, he studied the bloody gash—one that looked exactly like the one on the right side of William Chandler's face. . . .

Like a bolt of lightning, the confusing pieces of the

puzzle dropped into place. Jake cursed violently. Now he remembered what Cori had told him when he had interrogated her about her father's death. She had claimed Michael Shelton had been shot in the back, his pockets had been picked clean and he had an unexplained gash on his right cheek—just like William Chandler and Layton . . .

With vivid clarity, the vision that had sparked the nagging memory unfolded in Jake's tortured mind. It wasn't that he had *seen* someone strike a blow that left a mark like the ones on Layton and William's faces. But he remembered *thinking* what would happen to Cori if the monstrous ring on Kyle Benson's right hand struck her. He could visualize Kyle attempting to backhand Cori that day on the wharf in St. Louis. That same thought had stung him on the *Belle*, when Cori had provoked Kyle's temper. If Kyle had struck Cori, she too would have borne that nasty gash.

Jake swore under his breath. It was Kyle Benson who had struck Michael Shelton and then shot him in the back when he spun away from the painful blow to the cheek. It was Kyle Benson who had employed the same tactic on the defenseless William Chandler. It was also Kyle, not the Shelton twins, who had caused Layton's fatal fall. And it was Kyle who had captured Cori . . .

Jake shook off the dreadful thought. With a furious snarl, he darted back to the skiff. Frantic desperation tormented him every step of the way. He had faced danger in the past without batting an eyelash. He had never walked away from trouble and he had never let it walk away from him. But knowing Kyle was capable of murder and that he had already killed three times terrified Jake beyond words.

Cori's hours were numbered. Hell's fire, her *minutes* were numbered! Jake grimly corrected himself. That bleak thought horrified him as nothing else ever had. If he didn't find Cori . . . and quickly . . . there would be no need to collect the ransom. She wouldn't live long enough to be exchanged for the cash. Kyle would dispose of her, send Jake on a wild-goose chase, and board the steamer for parts unknown . . .

The clatter of footsteps behind him caused Jake to wheel about. When his tortured gaze focused on Lori, his heart twisted in his chest. If he lost Cori, he would never be able to stare at her lovely twin without enduring the pains of hell.

"Do you have even a clue where Kyle might have gone?" he questioned as he set Lori in the skiff. "Anything? What did Kyle say to you?"

Grimly, Lori shook her head and slumped defeatedly. "He only said to meet him on the wharf tomorrow. He said I wouldn't have to find him because he would find me. I didn't see which way he went . . ." Her voice cracked and gulping sobs burst from her throat, making it impossible for her to speak at all.

Gnashing his teeth, Jake scooped up the oar and paddled across the river. His tormented gaze lifted skyward and he prayed as he'd never prayed in all his life. Somehow he knew the world would always be as black as it was at this moment if he didn't manage to rescue Cori before Kyle . . .

Jake quelled that gloomy thought before it took root. He couldn't bring himself to think about life after Cori. Fear, the likes he'd never known, plagued his mind. Odd, he thought as he strained against the oar, hearing nothing but the lapping of water against the sloop. He'd never really known what it meant to be frightened before. He'd battled the Mexicans in Texas, Indians and treacherous rivers, but he'd never felt as frightened or helpless as he did now. Frightened for Cori . . .

Sparkling brown eyes rose above him, haunting him. Amid the twinkling diamonds that studded the black velvet sky he could see that impish smile of hers, that thick sable mane of hair. Cori . . . She was delighting passengers with her siren's voice. She was scampering across the decks of the *Belle*, garbed in black. He could see so many faces in that elfin smile. The canopy of stars overhead suddenly became the forget-me-nots of memory—the symbol of a love that struggled to survive when all the odds were stacked against it.

"We'll find her," Dal consoled his disheartened friend.

Hollow solace, thought Jake. Comforting words weren't going to lead him to Cori. What he needed right now was a miracle.

With a pained groan Cori returned to consciousness to find herself strapped spread-eagle on an unfamiliar bed in a dark unfamiliar room. Her head throbbed from the blow to the jaw and the gash on her forearm stung like fire. She expected Kyle to pounce on her any second, but to her amazement, she found that she was alone.

Coveting that thought, Cori strained against the improvised rope of sheets that held her flat on her back. She knew full well that if there was any saving to be done, she was going to have to do it herself.

Frantically, Cori wormed her wrists and ankles, trying to loosen the knots. But even though she didn't meet with success, she never ceased her struggles to free herself. Over and over again she strained and relaxed, hoping the sheets would stretch enough for her to slide her hands free. Only one hand, she prayed silently. Was that asking so much? Just one small chance for escape? She wasn't asking for an earth-shaking miracle, only a sporting chance!

Cori guessed she was indeed asking too much because no matter how hard she tried, she got no closer to freedom than she was when she started. Half collapsing, she racked her brain for solutions and rejuvenated her energy. Her gaze shifted to the commode that set directly beside the headboard of the cramped room. Then her eyes swung to the night stand that was wedged up against the other side of the bed.

When an idea hatched in her mind, Cori began to buck and rear, as if she had been besieged by convulsions. If she could jostle the table and commode and cause the water to spill or the lantern to tumble she might be able to grasp some sort of makeshift weapon.

She knew she was clutching at straws, but that was far better than lying there, awaiting impending doom, she reckoned. There was no way in hell that she was leaving this world, quietly submitting to her dismal fate. She would still be struggling to survive when she breathed her last breath!

Determined of purpose, Cori shook the bed that shook the table and commode. The pitcher and lantern wobbled, but that was about the extent of it.

"Thunderation," Cori muttered when she paused to regather her strength. Hope rose inside her when she realized the two objects that might very well be her salvation had walked a few inches toward the edge of the night stand and commode.

Gritting her teeth, Cori began flouncing and jerking and praying for all she was worth. Ever so slowly, the pitcher and lantern rocked and teetered, making a gradual migration toward the edge.

After what seemed forever, the objects were standing on the edge, nowhere within her grasp but close enough to fall on the bed . . . she hoped! Calling upon her failing strength and sheer will, Cori shook the bed and rattled the lantern and pitcher.

To her relief, the lantern tumbled down by her left hand, but it didn't break, nor did it start a fire, since Kyle hadn't taken time to light it before he left. It simply lay there beside her.

Again Cori flopped like a fish out of water, jarring the pitcher until it tipped forward, splashing water all over her right arm. With a quiet thud the object rolled across the mattress to rest against the back of her hand.

Blast it, nothing would break! She needed a jagged edge of porcelain or glass to saw at the sheets and all she got was wet and frustrated.

"Thunderation," Cori growled as she contorted her hands and body every which way to grasp one or the other object. What did a woman have to do to free herself and escape with her life?

More than this, Cori decided, refusing to admit defeat. Her wild gaze flew to the door, wondering how much time she had left. She hoped Kyle had passed out somewhere in the street. But Cori didn't allow herself to cling very long to that thought. Kyle Benson would be back, she assured herself glumly. The wicked, after all, had the devil's luck.

And knowing the nefarious Kyle Benson was as rotten as they came prompted Cori to keep worming and squirming to grasp the lantern globe or the pitcher. All the while she struggled, she could see Jake's ruggedly handsome face hovering above her. She had resigned herself to the depressing fact that she would never see Jake again, but she had expected to live with the precious memories until the end of her days. Kyle Benson wasn't going to deprive her of years of treasured memories, Cori vowed determinedly. She was going to survive . . . somehow . . . or another . . . maybe . . . ?

Before the heavily laden skiff had even reached the shore, Jake bolted to his feet and leaped to the dock. In the distance he could hear the tinkling of a piano and the

410

drunken shouts of keelboatmen. His anxious gaze swung about, and he wished he could tear off in all directions at once to locate Cori.

The whinny of a riderless horse caught Lori's attention as Dal set her onto the wharf. She squinted in the shadows, searching for any clue that might lead her to her sister.

A squeal of relief burst from Lori's lips when the gelding Cori had been riding pranced uneasily beside the other horses that were tethered in front of one of the bordellos Under the Hill.

"That's Cori's horse," Lori declared as she dashed forward.

All three men darted after her to search the area for the missing rider. Jake snatched up the lantern that hung outside the bordello and shot off through the underbrush that clung to the steep slope. Holding the lantern above his head, he surveyed the bushes. when he found the spot where the brush had been trampled, he led the way up the slope . . . until he spied the ripped fabric that was draped over a bush.

"It's Cori's," Lori gasped as she plucked up the cloth and hugged it to her. "Oh God, what has that beast done to her!"

Jake would have preferred not to speculate on that dismal thought. With a muttered curse, he forged his way through the tangled vines until he reached the peak of the bluff where Cori and Kyle had had their scuffle two hours earlier.

"Damnation," Jake growled when he spied the gleaming barrel of the pistol that lay in the grass. Grimly, he knelt down to lift the weapon. Dried blood caked the tip of the weapon and Jake died a thousand deaths, afraid he knew exactly whose blood had been spilled.

Jake lowered the lantern to inspect the clump of grass and the bare ground that capped the bluff. His heart stopped stock-still in his chest when he saw the puddles of blood that stained the chalky soil.

Jake half collapsed. For a full minute he wrestled with the dreadful implications, envisioning Cori wounded . . . or dead . . .

Jake's eyes rose to meet Dal's frozen expression. Never in his life had Dal seen such an unsettling look on Jake's face. The utter hopelessness and fear that wavered in those garnet green eyes, the tautness in the lines that bracketed his mouth sent a chill down Dal's spine. But just as suddenly, the incredible strength of character that was so much a part of Jacob Wolf took command of his mind and body.

Like an agile panther, Jake bounded to his feet and charged back down the hill. Murderous rage spurted through Jake's veins. Dal was eternally thankful that the killing fury that glistened in Jake's eyes wasn't directed toward him!

Never in Jacob's life had he wanted to tear anyone to pieces the way he envisioned mangling and mutilating Kyle Benson. That miserable bastard had obviously shot Cori for resisting his lusty advances. Jake could see it all now like a horrible nightmare. He could almost hear Cori screaming bloody murder as Kyle tore at her clothes to climb upon her, to violate and degrade the feisty spitfire as he had longed to do since their tussle in St. Louis . . .

Jake shuddered at the thought and expelled violent curses.

Below, on Silver Street, the thunder of hooves penetrated Jake's agonized mind. As he thrashed through the underbrush, he heard the hoofbeats pause momentarily. Suddenly there were two horses cantering along the avenue instead of one. As Jake burst through the clump of vine-choked trees that rimmed the bluff, he saw the shadowed silhouette trotting away, leading the steed that Lori indicated had belonged to her sister.

412

Another furious growl erupted from Jake's lips as the rider disappeared into the darkness. Without bothering to retrieve his own mount, Jake charged toward the bordello to steal the closest horse. In a single bound he was in the saddle. He wheeled the steed around and thundered off after the demon who had murdered the only woman he would ever love.

"He's gone mad," Lori wailed as she watched the towering figure of a man race along the wharf like Satan himself lunging up from the jaws of hell.

Although Dal and Adam tended to agree with her, they didn't waste time talking. They simply raced toward the wharf to fetch their horses and trail after Jake before he killed somebody. They hadn't arrived in time to see Cori's horse being towed away. And from where they stood Jacob Wolf did appear to be crazed with grief and revenge.

They weren't far from wrong. Jake was a mass of vindictive fury seeking release. But now he had a target upon which to vent his rage. And if the unidentified rider who had confiscated Cori's horse had merely stolen the steed for the price to be obtained, he had still earned himself a one-way ticket to hell. Jacob Wolf intended to send him there. And if by some stroke of luck the man happened to be Kyle Benson . . .

Jake's teeth clenched as he galloped down the street. If it was Kyle Benson whom he was trailing, Jake vowed to show that son of a bitch no mercy!

Once again, Jake was reminded of the deeply imbedded vengeance that had motivated Cori to find her father's killer. He fully understood why she could not be deterred from her crusade. The urge was so great that Jake swore he would never give up his pursuit of Kyle Benson. The man could escape to the ends of the earth, but Jake would follow him, living for the moment when he could unleash this cold-blooded fury that pumped through his veins. All

413

of a sudden, nothing seemed quite as important as killing the man who had murdered the love of his life. He only wished Cori had lived to discover who had murdered her father. At least she could have gone to her grave, knowing the truth. Then perhaps she could have rested in peace . . .

The gruesome thought caused a knot of agony to coil in Jake's belly. After seeing the pistol and pool of blood, Jake had lost all hope of finding Cori alive. Now he wanted revenge, violent unmerciful revenge, the kind that would satisfy this horribly empty ache in the cavity that had once been his heart.

"God damn that Kyle Benson," Jake seethed maliciously. "Damn that bastard's soul to hell!"

Racked with pain, Kyle Benson had ridden up the bluff to the home of a reputable physician to tend his wound. It had taken well over an hour for the doctor to cleanse and stitch Kyle back together. All the while the physician labored over his task Kyle gritted his teeth and promised to repay that daring bitch for the pain she'd caused him.

It was that spiteful thought that kept Kyle in the saddle, that prevented him from following the doctor's orders to tuck himself in bed to rest and recuperate. Kyle intended to tuck himself in bed all right—after he raped that sassy hellion. And when he recovered part of his strength, he would assault her again before he shot her, just as she had shot him!

Never had he wanted to prove his supremacy over a woman as much as now. She and her twin had hoodwinked him and Layton. They had eluded his amorous advances. But not this time. For all those nights when he had envisioned mounting that luscious beauty, tonight his fantasies would collide with reality. Tonight, before the loss of blood and pain drained his strength, he would have that delicious body under his, enjoying all her delectable charms.

Clinging to that vulgar thought, Kyle reined toward William's Tavern, one that was now deathly quiet. Kyle hadn't dared to leave Cori's mount wandering on the wharf for fear that it might be recognized. Now he tethered both horses in the clump of trees behind the tavern.

A sardonic smile pursed Kyle's lips as he swung from the saddle. His eyes lifted to the dark window on the second story and he chuckled satanically. "Very soon, sassy bitch, you will die with the taste of my kisses on your lips, with the feel of my caresses and the imprint of my body on yours. Mine will be the last face you see before you plunge into hell!"

Delighted with that vindictive prospect, Kyle propelled himself up the steps. His mind teemed with visions of ripping away Cori's soiled garments and burying himself within her, of hearing her beg for the mercy he would refuse to grant her. He was going to enjoy this!

Ah, he was going to relish dominating that hellcat once and for all . . .

Chapter 28

While Jake had been thrashing around in the underbrush, forced to accept his worse fears as grim reality, and Kyle was riding toward the tavern, Cori had been floundering to gain freedom. She had wiggled and twisted, trying to grasp either the lantern globe or the handle of the pitcher. It had taken some doing, but she had finally managed to maneuver the pitcher so that she could curl her fingers around the handle. The sheet that had been dampened when the pitcher fell allowed just enough slack to enable her to move her arm a fraction, just enough to swing the pitcher against the commode.

After repeated blows, ones that were limited by the restraining rope that bound her hand, Cori broke the pitcher, leaving a jagged edge. Gritting her teeth, she had turned the sharp object back on her wrists to saw at the makeshift rope. Her fingers and arm cramped as she contorted her hand to cut the damp cloth. Twice she nicked herself with the sharp edge, but she kept cutting at the fabric and straining to make it rip apart. And finally . . . finally . . . the sheet sagged and Cori knew she was on her way to escape.

Summoning her strength, she sawed at the ripped sheet until her right arm was free. Twisting onto her

416

side, she reached up to loose her left wrist. That done, she sat upright to untie her ankles. That was when she heard the steady clomp of footsteps on the stairs, a rhythmic death knell that clanged only for her . . .

Panicky, Cori clutched at her ankles to free herself while she darted apprehensive glances at the door. Knowing Kyle would be upon her any minute, Cori clawed at the knotted sheet. When she had escaped, she rolled from the bed, taking the broken pitcher and lantern with her.

With breasts heaving, she positioned herself behind the door, prepared to pounce on her captor before he realized what hit him. With her heart pounding in her ears, Cori lifted her makeshift weapons and listened to the approaching footsteps on the balcony that surrounded the upstairs rooms.

The creak of the door caused adrenalin to flood through her bloodstream like a rushing river. As the moonlight sprayed across the floor, Cori crouched, prepared to strike.

A mutinous growl rolled off Kyle's lips when the shaft of light revealed the empty bed. But he had no time to mutter a long string of curses because the half-opened portal flew at him, slamming into his wounded right shoulder. It was then that he saw the tigress's face among the shadows and felt the searing pain of the dagger-like edge of the pitcher against his skull.

Instinctively, Kyle recoiled and swung wildly with his left arm. He caught Cori in the chin, causing her to bite her tongue. The sharp blow sent her stumbling backward and Kyle took advantage of her imbalance. He launched himself at Cori, knocking her to the floor, forcing her breath out in a whoosh. But Cori came up fighting. The lantern she held in her left hand collided with Kyle's forehead, sending dribbles of whale oil trickling into his eyes.

A murderous growl boiled from his throat as the oil burned his eyes. Blindly, he struck out to subdue the vicious wildcat. He sank down on her shoulders to prevent her from leveling another punishing blow with her improvised weapons.

A muffled hiss burst from her lips when Kyle plastered himself against her, roughly nudging his knee between her thighs. His position and her hampering gown prevented her from uplifting her leg to knock him sideways. Her infuriated gasp echoed around the room when Kyle groped at the front of her gown, ripping it down the middle, leaving nothing but her torn chemise as protection.

The feel of his hands on her breasts was repulsive, and Cori fought for all she was worth to free her arms and shove him away. Thunderation, after all she'd done to escape, was it still going to come to this? Cori rejected the abominable thought of enduring his degrading mauling. She would provoke him to murdering fury long before he got around to raping her, she promised herself.

"I've waited forever for this moment, little bitch," Kyle snarled as he lowered his head, intent on plundering her mouth. "Now you will succumb to me." Diabolical laughter bubbled from his throat. "Mine is the kiss of death . . ." Roughly, his hands swam over her, plying her with revolting gropes and pinches.

It certainly tasted like it! Cori almost gagged when he ravished her, when his tongue lanced into her mouth to assure her of what awaited her when he shoved up her skirts. Cori bucked and squirmed when Kyle reared back with his left hand to clamp hold of the gown and jerk it up to her hips. With his bent legs pinning her shoulders to the floor, it was virtually impossible to prevent him from baring her thighs to his abusive caresses. But Cori swore she would die before she gave up her attempt to prevent being violated by this devil!

An enraged growl erupted from her lips as Kyle shifted above her once again. He slid both her arms over her head, pinning them with his left hand. Cori was certain she could battle this maniac who had his right arm in a sling, but Kyle's fury gave him twice the normal strength. Even her own rage couldn't match this madman's powers.

When Kyle doubled over to employ his injured arm to unfasten his breeches, Cori tensed in dreadful anticipation. As he slid down her body she turned her head and bit savagely into the arm that shackled both her wrists.

"Curse your soul!" Kyle snarled as he braced his arm far enough away to prevent being subjected to another painful bite. "You're going to get just what you deserve at long last . . ."

He wasn't even planning to let her die with dignity, she thought bitterly. He planned to force her to endure the worst possible degradation a man could impose on a woman.

In frustration, Cori felt her head ram into the wall. She had gone as far as she could go. Outraged at what was about to happen, no matter how hard she tried to prevent it, her lashes swept up to lock gazes with Kyle. Hatred flashed in her dark eyes.

To Kyle's disappointment, there was no fear in those big brown eyes, only venomous loathing. Not once had Cori begged for mercy or bartered to survive. She knew her fate and yet she had fought tooth and nail without admitting defeat. But she faced utter desolation now and she damned well knew it.

"Bastard," Cori spat as Kyle arched his back and strained toward her, sporting that infuriating smile of male conquest.

"Bitch," he chortled sardonically. "And that's how I'll take you, like a bitch in heat, again and again and again. . . ."

The furious growl that rolled across the room like rumbling thunder reminded Kyle of a rabid wolf. Kyle's description was very close to the mark. The man who shot toward the shadowed corner was reminiscent of a bloodthirsty beast. There was a snarl on Jake's curled lips and fire in his eyes.

Jake had located the two steeds that had been tethered in the trees. He had stalked up the steps, hearing the hisses and curses. The relief in knowing Cori was still alive was so short-lived that Jake didn't have time to enjoy it. The thud of bodies falling to the floor and the spiteful growls spurred him into immediate action.

Seeing Cori sprawled in the corner with Kyle atop her drove Jake over the edge. His emotions were already in a turmoil. He couldn't bare the thought of Kyle's hands upon her, couldn't bare the agony of watching that bastard attempt to take her so brutally.

When Jake charged at him, Kyle released Cori's hands to clutch at the pistol that was tucked in the pocket of his jacket. There was no time to retrieve the weapon, only time to grasp it in his fingers and pull the trigger.

Jake was so consumed by killing rage that he barely felt the pain that shot across his left arm. It didn't stop him. In fact, it didn't even slow him down. Before Kyle could fire a second shot, Jake had hurled himself at Kyle, knocking him to the floor.

Gasping for breath, Cori rolled to her knees to watch Jake beat Kyle to a bloody pulp. Against such a worthy opponent Kyle was at a definite disadvantage, especially with his wounded arm. And although the sleeve of Jake's jacket was stained with his own blood, he didn't even wince when he swung at Kyle with one steely fist and then the other.

Sheer rage sustained Jake. He was like a wounded grizzly, drawing his opponent's blood with every fierce blow he landed. Kyle fought back, but the jabs he

420

inflicted didn't seem to faze Jacob. He kept hammering away at Kyle's already bloodied face. When Kyle slumped backward, unable to answer the repeated blows, Jake clenched his fist in the collar of Kyle's shirt, forcing his head up.

"Tell her who killed her father and William Chandler and Layton," Jake demanded in a gritted growl.

"I did," Kyle croaked over his swollen lips.

"And you stole the money from Michael Shelton after you murdered him, didn't you?" Jake snarled.

Kyle tried to inhale a breath and moisten his puffy lips, but he couldn't do it quickly enough to satisfying the raging giant who demanded answers.

"Tell her, damn you," Jake snapped, giving Kyle a hard shake.

"I followed Shelton from his office," Kyle admitted. "I took the money without telling Layton. Then I blackmailed Layton into giving me part interest in the *Belle* to buy my silence in his dealings with Shelton."

"And Chandler," Jacob hissed poisonously. "Why did you kill him?"

"To take control of his tavern when he refused to sell it to me," Kyle answered breathlessly.

Kyle cringed when Cori launched herself at him to satisfy her own vengeance. Her doubled fist slammed against his broken jaw, forcing an agonized groan from his lips.

"And this one's for the hell you've put me through," Jake growled as he reared back with his right arm and threw all two hundred thirty pounds into the punch.

With a dull thud, Kyle collapsed on the floor. Heaving a long sigh, Jake pushed up to his feet. His arms lifted, welcoming Cori into his embrace. She came to him like a pigeon returning to roost. All the frustrated emotion that churned inside Cori bubbled forth like a geyser and she sobbed hysterically against Jacob's shirt. She had never

421

been a crier, but if ever there was a time to let her emotions flood out, this was it.

Cori felt as if a great burden had been lifted from her shoulders. After almost a year of dedicated effort she had found her father's killer, but it had not come quickly enough to prevent two other murders and her own narrow escape from death. Cori had come within an inch of dying, without ever learning the truth.

"Sh . . . sh . . . It's over now," Jake murmured as he brushed the wild tangle of ebony hair from her face. Tenderly he tilted her chin upward. His lips feathered over her trembling mouth, offering the compassion she needed, that *he* needed after fearing the worst about Cori.

"How did you figure out it was Kyle?" Cori questioned through the muffled sobs. "All this time I thought . . ."

His hand slid down her bloodied forearm, gesturing to the gash that Kyle's ring had left. "It was the mark of Benson's ring that finally gave him away," he told her quietly. "It was you who offered the clue, but I couldn't put it all together, even when I saw the slash on William's cheek. It was only after I saw the same mark on Layton's face that it dawned on me what had caused the unexplainable slash."

When Cori frowned up at him, Jake smoothed away her muddled expression. "Kyle followed you to the ship and knocked Layton down the steps. He used you and Lori, just as he has used everyone else to gain advantages."

Shiny tears trickled down Cori's bruised cheeks. "But it was my fault Layton was left in that vulnerable position. I hadn't planned for him to wind up dead on the steamer . . . I'm sorry, Jacob. I never meant to . . ."

His lips slanted over hers, silencing her apology. Jake longed to caress away Kyle's brutal kisses and degrading touch, to replace them with his tender, loving embrace. He was completely oblivious to the throbbing pain in his left arm. All he could think of was how close he'd come to losing this daring spitfire.

With a shuddering groan, Jake encircled Cori in his arms and hugged her to him, cherishing every wondrous moment of knowing she had survived her terrifying ordeal . . .

The clatter of footsteps on the stairs interrupted what had every indication of becoming a long passionate kiss. Grumbling, Jake wheeled to place himself in front of Cori like a shield, preventing the intruders from seeing her shredded gown.

The instant Lori saw her sister's disheveled head behind Jake's broad shoulder, she whizzed over to fling her arms around Cori. "Thank God! We thought . . ." Her voice wobbled and then cracked completely.

Dal assessed the unconscious body of Kyle Benson. "It looks as if you have the situation well in hand. That miserable bastard deserves worse than being beat to a pulp."

"And he'll get worse," Jake declared. "He killed Michael Shelton, William Chandler, and Layton."

Dal and Adam blinked in astonishment.

"How did you . . . ?" Dal croaked and then winced when Jake reached over to hurriedly yank off his jacket and lay it over Cori's shoulders.

"I'll explain on the way to Gram's," Jake assured him. He gestured toward Kyle. "Adam, since you're the criminal lawyer around here, I'd appreciate it if you would haul our prisoner to the constable's office and draw up the necessary charges."

Adam nodded agreeably.

"Why on earth do we have to rouse Augusta?" Dal chirped, bug-eyed. "It's four o'clock in the morning, you know."

"I doubt that Gram has been able to sleep." A rueful smile hovered on Jake's lips, remembering the vigil

Augusta had kept in the candle-lit tavern below this very room. "She'll rest much better knowing William's murderer has been brought to justice. And she needs to hear the news about Layton."

Dal frowned. He didn't have the faintest notion what Augusta's connection with William Chandler had been, but he decided it best not to argue with Jake's decisions. Jake had believed Cori to be dead and had been half out of his mind with fury and frustration. And to top off a perfectly hellacious night, Jake had been shot in the arm. As of yet, the shock hadn't worn off, Dal diagnosed, studying the bloody sleeve of Jake's jacket. But when it did, Jake would probably be in a helluva lot of pain. He had been so concerned about Cori that he hadn't given a thought to his injury . . .

Lori's shocked cry echoed around the room. She had turned in time to see that Kyle had regained consciousness and was inching toward his discarded pistol. All eyes flew to Lori, who charged at Kyle. In the bat of an eyelash, Cori, too, leaped into action. Both women lunged at Kyle, who was cursing fluently, determined to enjoy his own deadly brand of vengeance before being carted off to jail.

Jake's heart leaped to his throat as he rushed forward, certain Kyle would manage to turn his weapon on one of the twins to satisfy his rage. But both Jake and Dal, who reacted simultaneously to the threat of disaster, were a half second too late. While the twins and Kyle wrestled for control of the pistol, the weapon exploded, shattering the tense silence.

Cori and Lori, both sprawled atop Kyle, remained frozen to their spots and stared wide-eyed at each other. Their gazes dropped to the man beneath them, who had prematurely pulled the trigger and wound up shooting himself in the chest.

Fearing the worst, Jake and Dal hoisted Cori and Lori

to their feet to check for fatal wounds. To their relief, it was Kyle who was shot. He died as he had lived, in pain and violence. The killings were finally over, and Jake thought it fitting that Kyle had served himself his own just desserts.

With Kyle's body draped over his horse, the congregation trotted up Silver Street. Jake explained what he had deduced and offered Adam the background information needed to present the facts and charges against Kyle Benson to the constable.

While Adam headed toward the constable's office, Jake turned the procession toward his grandmother's estate. In the meantime, he formulated the best way to convey all his revelations to Augusta. He would use the direct approach, Jake decided. That was Gram's way, after all—straightforward and to the point . . .

His gaze drifted to Cori's shadowed face and his shoulders slumped in relief. God, he'd had the living daylights scared out of him when he thought Cori had perished. Even now, despite the pain that had begun to throb in his left arm, Jake was vividly aware of how close he'd come to losing this spirited hellion.

All the while he had been making his frantic search, Jake had prayed nonstop. He had been so desperate that he had even promised himself he would make no demands on Cori to remain in Natchez with him if the good Lord would just see His way clear to let her live. Jake's prayer had been answered and he dared not ask for more. He wasn't going to insist that Cori stay with him if she wanted to go. There had been a time not so long ago that he had been willing to say and do anything to keep this wild-hearted firebrand with him. But he loved her, so much that he put her happiness and her needs above his own desires.

The Shelton twins had endured a year of torment. They had lost their father, their home, and their inheritance. They had taken it upon themselves to see justice served. They had been through quite enough, and Jake couldn't force Cori to take another step in his direction if she felt the urge to retreat. He knew the twins blamed themselves for Layton's death, and even now, even after the ordeal was over, Layton was still an insurmountable obstacle between Jake and Cori. Cori couldn't forgive herself for what had happened and she didn't expect Jake to forgive her either.

While Jake was peering at Cori, she was quietly assessing the lion of a man who sat next to her. Guilt still hounded Cori. She had blamed Layton for something he hadn't done; she had left him vulnerable to a nefarious villain; and she had defied Jake when he demanded that she let him investigate Layton's involvement in Michael Shelton's death.

Cori dreaded informing Augusta of the loss of her grandson, dreaded allowing the feisty dowager to know the twins had deceived her. And as much as Cori adored Jacob, she had serious reservations about trying to make a future together. She had brought disaster to his family and she wondered if any of them would ever truly forget . . . if she could bury her own feelings of regret and guilt. No doubt those emotions would hang over her head like a black cloud until the end of her days.

Although Cori could now lay her father's memory to rest, her life was still in a tangle. As far as she could see, she would do Natchez and Jacob Wolf a great favor by sailing uprvier when Skully arrived. Lori could wed Dal and enjoy her new life, but Cori needed to close the door on the past and begin again—somewhere besides Natchez. She would walk out of Jake's life and bring him no more trouble. That was all she had been to Jacob from the very beginning. He deserved more than that.

Resigning herself to that fact, Cori stared at the dark silhouette of Augusta's mansion on the hill. Only a faint flicker of light shined in the parlor of the home. Yes, Augusta would hear the bitter truth of Cori's involvement with Layton Breeze, as well as the deception of twins portraying a single identity. Augusta would realize Cori Pierce Shelton was not the woman Jacob needed in his life. And when the smoke cleared, Augusta would badger Jake into settling down with a docile wife who wouldn't lead him on quite so many maddening chases.

But oh, it was going to break Cori's heart when she did the noble thing and left Natchez. When she left, she would leave her heart behind, knowing she would never be able to love again, not with Jake's memory haunting her days and tormenting her nights. This was the price she paid to see justice served, Cori reminded herself dispiritedly. She had achieved her year-long goal and she had to be content with it. She had no right whatsoever to ask for anything more.

Chapter 29

The quiet rap at the door put a muddled frown on Augusta's face. Hoisting herself from her chair in the parlor, she hobbled into the foyer. The instant she opened the portal to see Jake's bloody jacket, a terrified gasp flew from her lips.

"My Lord, what's happened?" she croaked in question.

"A great many things, all of which you need to know," Jake said grimly.

"And you can tell me all about it while we tend your arm," she insisted, latching onto his good arm to herd him inside.

Although Jake had decided to employ the direct approach with his grandmother, he intended for her to face one startling revelation at a time. First he would let her recover from the shock of seeing him wounded, then he would proceed from there.

With a shout, Augusta roused several servants and sent them scurrying to fetch salve, hot water, and bandages. While the suddenly wide-awake servants bustled around him, Jake eased back in his chair and permitted the passel of women to fuss over him.

Damn, he was tired, and he had only begun to realize it.

He had been swinging on an emotional pendulum for countless hours. The tension had finally caught up with him and he felt drained of emotion and strength.

Augusta pressed the healing ointment on the wound and breathed a relieved sigh, knowing her grandson had only sustained a superficial injury. Thank God the wound looked worse than it actually was. Two more inches and the buckshot could have damaged the bone, ligaments, and tendons in his arm.

"How the devil did this happen?" Augusta demanded to know.

"I got shot," Jake replied with his characteristic shrug, as if that explained everything.

"Damnation, I can see that!" Augusta sniffed. "But who the blazes shot you and for what reason?"

Green eyes fastened on his grandmother's concerned face. "I was trying to save Cori from a very perilous encounter with William Chandler's murderer," he told her frankly. "The man is dead and one of the best lawyers in the country is ensuring that he is credited with the crimes he committed. Adam Castleberry is handling everything."

Relief washed over Augusta's wrinkled features. "Thank you, Jacob. You know how much that means to me." Hastily, she shooed the servants on their way. When they were alone, her brows formed a single line over her probing hazel eyes and she stared at Jake for a long ponderous moment. "And what happened to Cori? Is she . . . ?"

The bleak expression on Jake's face indicated there was much more to be told. The frown on Augusta's puckered features testified to her concern about Cori's welfare, even if the flighty chit had difficulty chosing between Jacob and Dal Blaylock. In Augusta's mind, there had never been any choice to make. Being hopelessly partial, she was certain Jake was the better man for Cori.

"Cori survived," Jacob informed his grandmother. "But although she managed to shoot her assailant, she is a mite bruised and battered." He glanced toward the hall. "Dal, bring in our guests." His gaze swung back to Augusta. "Brace yourself, Gram. I'm afraid Cori's appearance is going to be somewhat of a shock to you."

Augusta steadied herself. She expected to see a woman who had been beaten and perhaps sexually assaulted. But what she didn't expect was to be seeing double! The instant Cori and Lori stepped into the light, Augusta clutched her heart before it popped out of her chest.

"Good Lord!" Augusta hooted.

The lovely young women were the spitting image of each other. The only difference was that one of the twins showed definite signs of battle. Her cheeks were swollen and she clutched Dal's jacket about her, assuring Augusta that her clothes had suffered irreparable damage during the confrontation. Augusta couldn't help but wonder what emotional wounds the fetching beauty had also endured. Augusta hated to dwell on the unsettling thought.

"Gram, I want you to meet Lori Pierce Shelton, whom you have actually met several times the past two weeks and didn't know it. She is engaged to Dal," Jake explained, gauging his grandmother's shocked reaction.

So far so good, thought Jake. Augusta was holding up exceptionally well. She was a tough old bird who had endured a great many tragedies and disappointments in her life.

"And this is Cori." He gestured to the bewitching brunette in Dal's jacket. "She has also endured one helluva night."

"What has been going on around here?" Augusta demanded, staring at one identical face and then the other.

"It's a long story," Dal inserted with a feeble smile.

"Isn't it always?" Augusta smirked. "And the whole lot of you presumed that just because I was old and decrepit that I should be allowed to wallow in ignorance." Her eyes glazed at her grandson. "Thank you very much, Jacob. I ought to have you whipped for keeping me in the dark!"

"It wasn't his fault," Cori piped up as she moved courageously forward to meet Augusta's disdainful glare. "It was mine. I got my sister and myself into this mess and . . ."

"I am as much to blame as Cori," Lori insisted. "We were trying to track down our father's murderer and . . ."

"We had to employ rather devious tactics to succeed in bringing the killer to justice," Cori finished.

Augusta blinked. Her gaze bounced from one twin to the other. If she hadn't seen their mouths moving, she would have sworn only one of them was voicing the colloquy.

"The truth is we had to stoop to thievery in hopes of retrieving our lost inheritance," Lori went on to say.

"And that's when Jacob and Dal became involved," Cori reluctantly added. "We hadn't intended for them to, but . . ."

"Things got a mite tangled up." Lori sighed heavily. "And you know how one lie demands another."

Augusta nodded grimly.

"For our own safety, we had to continue to portray one identity so the man we were after wouldn't realize he'd been robbed on board the *Belle*."

"Layton?" Augusta groaned, realizing what the twins were trying *not* to say to upset her. "Layton killed your father and shot Jacob?" Her hands cupped her gaping mouth and her wide-eyed gaze flew to her grandson. "Oh my God . . ."

"No," Jacob quickly corrected as Augusta leaped to the wrong conclusion. "But Layton connived to swindle the Sheltons out of the *Belle* and he was partially responsible for Michael's death. Because of his tactics, he opened avenues for a far more dastardly crime to be committed by a ruthless scoundrel whose avarice even exceeded Layton's."

Augusta slouched in her chair, digesting the bleak facts. "Layton will be scandalized and he'll have to be punished for his part in this atrocity."

Jake leaned forward to grasp his grandmother's bony hand. Holding it securely in his own, his somber gaze locked with hers. "I'm afraid Layton had already paid in full for his crimes." Jake inhaled a deep breath and plunged on. "Gram, the man who killed Michael Shelton and William Chandler and very nearly succeeded in disposing of Cori only an hour ago, also killed Layton this evening."

Hazel eyes flew wide open and then fluttered shut. A dismayed groan tumbled from Augusta's lips. For several moments she sat there, grappling with the shocking news she'd received. The past twenty-four hours her world had been turned upside down again, as it had too many times in the past.

Compassionately, Cori knelt before the dowager who trembled beneath the weight of her burden. "I'm so sorry, Augusta. I feel responsible for bringing this misfortune down upon you. When Lori and I began our crusade for truth and justice, we didn't consider the innocent people who might get hurt along the way. We only wanted our father's murderer punished."

Augusta's lashes swept up, blinking the tears away so she could study Cori's bruised but lovely face.

"For Lori's sake, I hope you will keep silent about our escapades on board the *Belle.* She cares deeply for Dal and I want her to be happy. And as for me . . ." Cori swallowed hard. "I promise from this day forward, I will bring you and your family no further pain and anguish. I have already notified my uncle and he will arrive tomorrow to take me away from here. As far as Natchez society knows, there was and will be only one Miss Pierce—the one who will marry Dal."

Cori sighed heavily and forced herself to meet Augusta's gaze. "I fear I have done far more damage than I set out to do when I vowed to avenge my father's death. I'm deeply sorry that you had to suffer for it."

Gracefully, Cori rose to her feet and graced Augusta with a faint smile. "Despite what you're probably thinking, I greatly admire you. I only hope that I possess your spunk and vitality in the years to come."

Cori dropped her head, unable to decipher the emotion in Augusta's misty gaze. "After I say my final farewell to Jacob, Dal, and Lori, I will be on my way. Again, I am truly sorry for the turmoil I've caused you."

When Cori turned and walked away, Augusta's cloudy gaze shifted to Jake. His eyes followed Cori's every step, sketching her figure as if he were committing it to memory.

Augusta stared at the four young people and made her decision. After uncovering her own long-ago-but-never-forgotten memories of William Chandler, Augusta realized that she should have rebelled against her family's snobbish ways. She would have lived a much happier life if she could have spent it with William. The fact that he had died alone tormented her. Life was too short for crucial mistakes that could bring years of forbidden longings and shattered dreams. And, by damned, Cori Shelton was not going to make a mistake like the one Augusta had regretted for fifty-five years!

"Jacob, don't you have something to say?" Augusta questioned, her gaze bearing down on her only living heir.

Jacob massaged his aching arm. "Indeed I do. It has been a long night."

"For heaven sake, that's not what I meant!" Augusta snorted explosively.

A melancholy smile tripped across Jake's lips and he turned to meet Augusta's disdainful glare. "Sometimes, Gram, we aren't allowed to enjoy our heart's desires. You yourself are living testimony to that. Sometimes, I suppose, we simply have to accept what we cannot change."

"Since when did you become so adaptive?" Augusta smirked, annoyed with Jake's attitude. "You tamed the Missouri and yet you . . ."

Jake towered over his grandmother, blocking out the other three people who hovered by the door. "Let it be, Gram. Sometimes it seems love means letting go. You know that better than any of us."

"And sometimes it means defying the odds and holding on," Augusta countered quietly. "I never thought I'd have to say this, Jacob Wolf, your being my own flesh and blood and all. But you are every kind of fool if you let Cori go. Letting her cling to what she believes to be noble justice and personal sacrifice is a bunch of rubbish. The two of you belong together."

Jake sadly shook his head in contradiction. "I have threatened her and pleaded with her a dozen times before. I prayed that she would survive the night when the odds were heaped heavily against her. I won't ask for more. Cori is very much her own woman and she has to do what she believes is best. And for once, I have to accept that, no matter how much it hurts to see her go."

"You're both so damned noble it makes me sick," Augusta snorted with her customary candor.

Jake couldn't bite back his amused smile. His grandmother never changed. Despite the tragedies that had befallen her, she had incredible resilience and a tongue like a cobra's.

"Good night, Gram."

When he pivoted away, Augusta braced her arm on the

434

chair and peered around her mountain of a grandson to stare at Cori. "You had better be at Wolfhaven in the morning," she demanded. "At least allow me to properly send you off to your new life . . . after I have a chance to compose myself and come to grips with these incidents."

Cori's brown eyes lifted to Jacob. She would like nothing better than to spend one last night in his arms. Augusta was offering her the perfect excuse to stay the night at Wolfhaven.

"I will wait there, until you come to bid me farewell," she promised. "If Jacob consents to it."

"Of course he consents," Augusta answered for her grandson. "He's turned into a mushy vegetable, if you ask me!" Before Jacob could protest, Augusta flapped her hands, shooing the foursome on their way. "Now off with all of you. I need my sleep."

When Augusta was alone in the parlor, she fished into her pocket to retrieve the timepiece she had confiscated from William Chandler's personal effects. It was a keepsake he had kept with him for more than fifty years. Although the watch no longer kept precise time . . .

A rueful smile pursed Augusta's lips as she brushed her hand over the tarnished timepiece. Ironic that the watch allowed time to stand still, she thought to herself. She had given the timepiece to William decades ago and he had carried it with him always. He had told her that time had ceased to exist when her family refused to allow him to take Augusta as his wife. But until the day he died the timepiece remained in his vest pocket near his heart. And on occasion he would open the timepiece to stare down at the portrait of his forbidden love and wish for things that were not to be.

"I know you'd approve of what I intend to do, William," Augusta murmured as she closed the case of the timepiece and clutched it in her trembling hand. "Only you and I fully understand . . ."

Determinedly, Augusta hoisted herself from her chair

435

and grabbed her cane. Even though only the chickens were usually up and around at this ungodly hour, Augusta hobbled to the stable to fetch her groom and a carriage.

Jake had claimed Cori Pierce Shelton was her own women, but so was Augusta Breeze! She also had a mission in life—to do what needed to be done. There was no time to tarry.

"We're not going to let them make the same mistake we did," Augusta announced to heaven above. "I honored my family's wishes and you loved me enough to think you were doing the best for me by graciously bowing out. We were just like Jake and Cori are now—a honor-bound pair of fools. And by God, they will have what we were never allowed to share!"

"Pardon?" The elderly groom swiveled his gray head around to glance at the dowager who sat in the carriage.

"Nothing, Godfrey," she replied, gesturing for him to watch the road instead of her. "Just drive and let me talk to myself without interruption."

Godfrey's lips twitched as he twisted around on his perch and stared at the silhouette of Natchez as the sun peeked over the horizon to bathe the world in silver dew drops and shafts of gold. "Yes, madam, as you wish."

"As I wish," Augusta repeated with a determined nod. "Indeed! *Exactly* as I wish!"

Godfrey didn't have the foggiest notion what the old crone was babbling about. But he supposed he would find out, all in good time. It was a fierce gale that took Augusta Breeze on her early morning outing. And rarely did anything keep this grand old woman from her purpose. Godfrey had served the household long enough to know that. Whatever Augusta Breeze was about this morning, neither high water nor hell would stop her. There was a determined glint in her eyes. Yes, before the day was out, Augusta would have her way . . .

Chapter 30

Uncertainly, Cori wavered in the hall, wondering whether to be so bold as to invite Jake into her room. Even though it was only five o'clock, Jacob had roused the servants to prepare a bath for Cori. But after escorting her to her room, he merely ambled toward his own chamber.

Cori felt awkward and unsure of herself. She wasn't certain how Jacob was taking Layton's death or her announcement of leaving Natchez. The way he was behaving, one would have thought he didn't really care, only that he was relieved the ordeal was finally over. To be sure, his wound was paining him. No doubt, Jake wanted nothing more than a few hours sleep and some peace and quiet—something he'd never had while Cori was underfoot.

Sighing heavily, Cori veered into her room after Jake stepped into his. After the servants had carried buckets of water to her tub and filed out, she peeled off her grimy garments, which still reeked with Kyle Benson's disgusting scent. Cori shuddered, thinking how close she had come to rape and death. Oh, how she longed to cuddle in Jacob's arms, to replace Kyle's bruising kissing and demeaning gropes with Jake's masterful caresses.

But it was not to be, Cori told herself gloomily. Already, Jake had probably collapsed on his bed, alseep the instant his head hit the pillow.

Glumly, Cori sank down into the bubbles and washed away the nightmare and the revolting scents that clung to her skin. The warm water eased her strained muscles and frustration. With a sigh, Cori closed her eyes and eased back against the edge of the tub, letting her forbidden dreams replace cruel reality. . . .

The splash of water caused Cori's eyes to fly wide open. To her amazement, Jake stood before her, naked as the day he was born. One foot was in her tub, the other was on the floor.

"May I join you?" he murmured, his gaze sketching the diamond droplets that sparkled on her honey-colored skin.

"I thought you'd never ask," Cori whispered.

Only the white bandage around his upper arm detracted from this utterly masculine specimen—but not a lot. Jacob Wolf was the most striking man Cori had ever seen, naked or otherwise. Longingly she reached up to grasp his hand, encouraging him to sink down, even if the tub wasn't quite big enough for the both of them. If cramped spaces meant hugging Jake closer, Cori wasn't complaining. Just once more before his forbidden memory became a closed chapter in her life, she wanted to be as close as two people could get.

Jake spoke not a word as he plucked up the soap and lathered his hands. With deliberate concentration, he reached out to wash away the smudges on Cori's bruised cheeks, replacing the lingering pain with tender pleasure. Gently he urged her back against the tub to cleanse every luscious inch of her.

Cori gulped when his skillful hands wandered over her flesh, triggering sensations that had nothing whatsoever to do with bathing. The fires Jake ignited with his stimulating caresses left her speculating at what moment her bubble bath would transform into a cloud of steam.

"If you don't stop what you're doing," Cori breathed raggedly, "you'll have to keep doing it all the rest of the day . . ."

A roguish grin hovered on the corners of his mouth as his hands and eyes drifted over her delectable curves and swells. "That, my wild sweet love, is the whole idea," he murmured provocatively. "You didn't really think the reason I sneaked in here was to bathe, did you?"

"Oh, Jacob, I wish . . ."

He pressed his index finger to her lips to shush her. "Hush, don't talk now. I didn't come to elicit promises, only to offer one . . ."

His hand flowed over her delicate jaw and then down to swirl over the taut peaks of her breasts. "I promise you all the pleasure I know how to give, promise to create a memory that will burn in your mind, now and forevermore. You may leave me, my love, but I swear you will never ever forget me . . ."

His bold caresses slid down her belly and he felt Cori quiver beneath his arousing explorations. His very position allowed him unlimited privileges with her body. To accommodate two bodies in the cramped tub, Cori had been forced to spraddle him. Jake took full advantage of that fact. His hand glided down her parted thighs, teasing her with seductive caresses.

As his hands tantalized and excited, his lips whispered over her petal-soft lips. "If I am to enjoy nothing else from this stormy affair of ours, at least I'll become the smile on your lips when no one else is around, become the memory that will never stop following you wherever you go."

He bent his raven head to trace a path of scalding kisses from that sensitive point beneath her ear to the tip of her full breasts. Cori felt herself melting into a puddle of liquid desire when he assaulted her with sweet tormenting kisses and soul-shattering caresses.

Not too many hours ago Cori had come terrifying close to discovering the difference between sexual assault and lovemaking, between being abused and being cherished. Kyle Benson's face suddenly flashed above her and Cori clutched desperately at Jake.

He could feel her body tremble as she wrapped herself around him and clung to him as if she never meant to let go. Jake didn't have to be clairvoyant to know what emotion had engulfed her. The recent nightmare had produced invisible scars, and Jake cursed Kyle Benson a thousand times over for striking fear in this vivacious beauty. He vowed to erase the horrible memory from her mind and leave the taste of his kisses on her lips.

Nuzzling against her neck, Jake scooped her into his arms and dripped his way across the floor to the bed. Gently, he laid her there, seeing the crosscurrent of emotions in her melting brown eyes. She wanted him, he knew. She always had, despite their differences. They had set sparks afly in each other since their first tentative kiss. But Kyle Benson had left scars that Jake knew he must heal.

Never once had Jake offered sex for his own selfish purposes. To Cori he had offered only the instructions in lovemaking, the giving and sharing of ineffable splendor. They had enjoyed the rapture that a man and woman could only experience when conditions were right. And conditions had always been right to ignite the fiery passion between them, a passion so fierce and wild that it defied the limitations of physical pleasure. What they had always shared, even in the beginning, went far beyond raw desire.

And now, this one last time before this dark-eyed elf took the sunshine from his life, he would shower her with the deeply imbedded affection he felt for her.

"I'm going to show you all the ways I love you, Cori," Jake rasped as he stretched out beside her. His hands mapped the luscious terrain of her body in one long worshiping caress. "And if there comes a time when you think we both have paid dearly enough for letting each other go, I want you to come back to me."

His lips brushed the rose-tipped crests. His tongue flicked at the taut buds, causing Cori to moan and tremble in sensual delight.

"I'll be here, treasuring the memories we made together, yearning to create a lifetime of new ones. You're my one and only love. Nothing matters more to me than you," he breathed against her quaking skin. "Always remember that I love you . . ."

His heart-warming words brought tears to her eyes and a gasp to her lips. His skillful kisses and caresses conveyed his affection, leaving her burning with desire.

Suddenly, Kyle's hideous scowl faded from memory and Jake's craggy features replaced them. Love without any stipulations shimmered in his green eyes. When Cori met his loving gaze she wondered how on earth she would ever live without this man. It would kill her to say good-bye and walk away, and yet she couldn't bear to stay, knowing she had destroyed a member of his family and brought torment to Augusta. They would both look upon her and they would remember what she had done to Layton . . .

The tormenting thought drowned in the sea of Jacob's kisses and caresses. His hands and lips were everywhere at once, tearing all other concerns from her mind. For this one magical moment that burned away time, the past and future didn't matter. She and Jake were two star-crossed lovers reaching out to each other. Cori gave her heart and body to him in wild abandon, cherishing the wondrous sensation that spilled over her.

Anxious to return the ineffable pleasure, Cori

answered each caress. She expressed her love for this raven-haired giant who had come to mean all things to her . . .

The thump of a cane in the hall caused Jake to jerk away and grope for the quilts to conceal them. As the thump grew louder, he considered making a mad dash for the terrace door. Then he thought better of it. He would probably wind up embarrassing himself and his grandmother more than he would if he stayed where he was. If she saw him dashing, start-bone naked, across the room in his present state of arousal . . . Jake gnashed his teeth.

"Hell's fire. What's she doing here already? She said she'd come this morning, but I never dreamed she meant before breakfast!"

Cori clamped the quilt under her bruised chin and stared apprehensively at the door. When the knob twisted she swallowed with a gulp. Thunderation! Augusta Breeze had a miserable sense of timing!

As the door swung open, Augusta marched forth with the aid of her cane. She didn't seem the least bit surprised to see two heads protruding from the quilts.

"It appears the two of you have recovered nicely from your injuries," she observed with an impish smile. "Jacob's wound doesn't seem to be bothering him all that much. In fact, from the look of things it isn't bothering him at all."

"Gram, I'd appreciate it if you would . . ." Jake tried to say, but Augusta cut him off with a flick of her wrist.

"When a man is caught with his breeches down, in a . . . er . . . a . . . respectable young woman's boudoir, he must face the consequences," Augusta announced with great conviction. "The family's reputation has suffered quite enough already. And to prevent any further scandal . . ."

Augusta pivoted to motion for her companions to enter the room. Cori's eyes bulged from their sockets when a red-faced clergyman moved meekly forward, followed by Haskell (Skully) Shelton. Cori sorely wished the mattress would split wide open so she could fall through it. She had never been so embarrassed in all her born days!

"We are performing a marriage ceremony here and now," Augusta trumpeted. "On my way to summon this man of the cloth, I happened upon this nice gentleman who inquired as to Cori's whereabouts. It seems the steamer from New Orleans made better time than expected and he came to fetch his niece. After explaining the circumstances to him, Mr. Shelton volunteered to give the bride away and stand as witness to this marriage."

"Uncle? Shelton?" Jacob hooted, gaping at the gambler he'd met on the *Belle.*

"Uncle Skully?" Cori croaked, flush-faced.

"And I suppose he was also in on . . ." Jacob's voice transformed into an annoyed mutter when he realized Skully had teemed up with the twins to victimize the passengers on the *Belle.*

Pasting on a cheerful smile, Skully sauntered over to pump Jake's hand. "It's a pleasure to see you again this fine morning. When Augusta told me of her wedding plans I had no intention of missing this grand occasion." His disapproving frown was directed to Cori. "But it seems my niece couldn't wait for the honeymoon. And I must agree with Augusta. For all those concerned, a hasty marriage is the only solution."

"Now get on with it, Brother Wagner," Augusta insisted impatiently. "Time's a-wasting."

Brother Wagner hooked his index finger in his white collar and blushed uncomfortably. "Dearly beloved, we are gathered . . ."

"Give us the condensed version," Augusta interrupted with another dismissive flip of her wrist. "Just get to the *I dos.*"

That seemed to suit the pastor just fine. He was

anxious to perform the unconventional ceremony and be on his way.

When Jacob hesitated with his "I do" and glanced apprehensively at Cori, who had blushed crimson red, Augusta muttered and hobbled toward the bed. Hurriedly, she tugged the ring from her right hand and shoved it onto Cori's finger.

"He does and she does and that's that!" Augusta announced triumphantly. "What's done is done. Now the two of you will simply have to settle any differences between you and accept the way of things." This she directed toward Jacob, who had announced earlier that he was prepared to accept what he couldn't change.

After shuffling Skully and Brother Wagner into the hall, Augusta eased the door shut and stared solemnly at the bride and groom. "What is past is past and shall remain so, Cori. I hold no grudge or place blame where it does not belong. It seems to me that you have put my feelings and what you *think* Jacob is feeling far above your own future happiness."

A soulful smile hovered on Augusta's lips. "A long, long time ago, there was another young woman who put aside her own happiness to enter the marriage engineered by her father. She had to forsake the man she loved and wed another whose station in life matched her own. And although she remained faithful to her husband all his days, she never forgot what she had sacrificed. You and my grandson aren't going to allow history to repeat itself."

Augusta gestured toward the small gold band with its small diamond chip. "That was the ring William Chandler gave me so long ago as a symbol of his eternal love." She blinked back the sentimental tears that misted her hazel eyes. "I cherished that ring all these years, Cori. And William and I want you to wear it. We want you to have what we never had—a chance to love. I know

444

how you feel about my grandson and how he feels about you. The two of you are a perfect match and you won't be happy unless you're together."

Her eyelid dropped into a wink and she broke into a smile. "Believe me, in the years to come, you both will thank me for showing up here with a wedding party." She wagged a bony finger at them. "Now be happy . . ."

Augusta drew herself up and whipped open the door. "I'm off to Dal's plantation to perform another ceremony," she declared with a mischievous snicker. "No doubt, I'll find Lori and Dal in the same compromising situation. Dal's grandmother will probably have a fit when she discovers I rushed them into a wedding and stole her thunder. But what the hell," she added with a reckless shrug. "I'm playing Cupid this morning and I'm thoroughly enjoying it!"

The dowager's hazel eyes twinkled devilishly as she peered at the newlyweds. "Once I have Lori and Dal squared away, I intend to give the town gossips an interesting tidbit of information to pass along the grapevine. I will ensure that everyone knows that Cori's twin sister arrived from St. Louis the previous week, unbeknownst to the local chatterboxes who think they know all and see all. I will make it known that Lori met Dal Blaylock and fell in love with him at first sight. There will have been two Miss Pierces circulating around Natchez and that will explain why they were often seen with both Jake and Dal." Augusta smiled in self-satisfaction. "And that will be the end of the ugly rumors that one man was trying to beat the other one's time with the same women. And that is that!" she added as she dusted off her hands and smoothed her black skirt into place.

Like a fairy godmother magically waving her arms to right every wrong she encountered, Augusta marched off to resume the second phase of her mission. In disbelief,

445

Cori stared after the human hurricane who had blown in and out of the bedchamber. When Cori heard Jake's amused chortle she glanced sideways. A grin as wide as the Mississippi stretched across his ruggedly handsome face. Tenderly, he reached over to close Cori's gaping mouth.

"Well, Mrs. Wolf, if you have any complaints about the way things turned out, voice them now." His ruffled raven head moved steadily toward hers. "And when you're quite finished, I'm going to take up exactly where I left off . . ."

Cori searched those fathomless green eyes for a long, pensive moment. "Honestly and truly, Jacob, can you forgive me for what I've done to your family? Can you forgive me for all the trouble I've caused you?"

Jacob smiled an utterly rakish smile. "You're my kind of trouble, sweet witch," he assured her as his wandering hand tunneled beneath the quilt to make contact with her silken flesh. "As Gram said, past is past. Our life together has just begun and I need no one but you to make me happy . . ."

As his lips slanted over hers, staring fires that would soon blaze completely out of control, Cori surrendered heart, body, and soul. The words Augusta had spoken whispered through her mind, making Cori realize how close she had come to making a critical mistake that she would have regretted for the rest of her life, a mistake like the one Augusta had made a half-century before. Augusta was wise in the ways of the world, and Cori relied upon the dowager's vast experiences in living. It must be true that if a man and woman truly loved each other, there was no mountain too high or river too deep to keep them separated. No matter what obstacles Cori and Jake encountered, they always seemed to wind up in each other's arms, expressing their love. As Skully always said, it was in the cards. The queen of hearts could be a

446

fickle woman, but when she was in the right hands, she was a treasure to keep.

Cori had found her treasure in this lion of a man who was strong enough to be gentle. Jacob was a man with a generous, loving heart. He had accepted her for what she was without trying to change her. How could she leave him when he had become her reason for being, when walking away would have torn out her very soul? She couldn't have. And thanks to Augusta Breeze, Cori was nestled in the arms of happiness, needing no more than Jacob could give.

"I love you with all my heart," Cori whispered with genuine emotion.

"I know," Jacob murmured. "From tender lies to tender truths . . . It's been a long and rocky road, my love. But it proves we can face all sorts of difficulties as long as we're together."

Cori blessed him with an elfin grin that made her dark eyes sparkle like ebony. "Get to the point, Jacob," she teased him. "I find that your grandmother's penchant for directness has begun to appeal to me. Do you want to make love or do you want to talk about it?"

Jake returned her mischievous smile as he hooked his good arm around her, settling her exactly beneath him. He let his body do the talking when he came to her, communicating all the love and passion that churned inside him.

"Mmm . . . you are very direct and to the point, Mr. Wolf," Cori murmured breathlessly.

"Pay attention, Mrs. Wolf," Jake growled seductively. "There are quite a few things I have yet to teach you about the ways of love."

"What could you have possibly forgotten to show me? I thought you had already taught me all there was to know . . ."

Her voice trailed off as Jacob showed her a thing or two

447

that she never dreamed there was to know about passion when it was embroidered with all-consuming love. Jake was so thorough and deliberate in his instruction that they had to skip breakfast.

And due to his extensive and exhausting lessons of love they missed lunch. They were noticeably late for supper, too . . .